A World
of
Expectations

A World
of
Expectations

By

Gayle Lynn Messick

*Dedicated to
my three Brothers
and their families*

Thomas, Gary, and Robert

A World of Expectations

Book II –Confrontation

By

Gayle Lynn Messick

Chapter One

Mr. Fitzwilliam Darcy glanced out the window while traveling to London, the scenery barely registering on his consciousness. He had nestled into the seat cushion, recalling his breakfast encounter with Blake.

He had expected to find him with an I-have-won-the-horse-and-the-lady smirk. Instead, Darcy entered an empty dining room, ignored his curiosity, and proceeded with his breakfast ritual—he placed only one pastry on his plate beside his eggs and ham. The cook had not prepared his favored spicy-pork mishmash. He bit into the sweet treat. Rawlings was correct—these were the best pastries. He called the footman over and requested several treats be prepared for the journey back to London and asked if the lemon filled ones sprinkled with a sugary substance—Rawlings' favorites—were available. They would make an excellent surprise for his friend. The servant hurried to the kitchen.

"Darcy." Blake said in barely a whisper when he strode through the door. He headed for the buffet, where he placed a few nibbles of ham and eggs on his plate. He did not include any pastry.

"Good morning." Darcy responded. He did not miss the unusual slouch in Blake's shoulders or his downturned lips.

"I understand you are departing today?" Blake asked.

"After breakfast. I have a need to return to London." Darcy studied his friend who had slumped into his chair and instead of eating, held his forehead. His elbows were on the table. He had never witnessed such a decorum breach from Blake before.

"I no longer have a need to remain here." Blake sighed. "I look forward to returning to town as well." He pushed the food around the plate without the fork ever finding his mouth. "Rain is coming."

"Oh?" Darcy peeked out the window at the shining sun. He did not spy a single cloud.

"Yes. I felt dampness on my ride. Do you not think it is darker in here today? Perhaps candles would help, or the fire needs to be built up."

Darcy shrugged. The room seemed as bright as any sunny day. Blake's voice was low and flat, which was unusual since, by his own nature, he was cheery in the mornings, weather notwithstanding. He watched him pretend to eat while keeping his head down.

Blake returned his cup to its saucer. "Agh! The coffee is as cold as the eggs." He pushed his plate away and then rose in a single swift motion. "Excuse me. I need to make arrangements for the journey." His napkin dropped on the table's edge before it fell to the floor. Blake glared it although his gaze seemed unfocused. He ignored the crumpled linen and rushed out, his eyes again downcast, his lips held tightly together.

Darcy had seen that expression on his sweet sister, Georgiana. Like her, Blake did not attempt to conceal his severe sadness. Damn. What happened? Did she say no? Did he offer marriage or, my God, did he... Darcy spent breakfast alone preoccupied with the change in his friend.

On the ride to London, Darcy pondered many scenarios for Blake's despair; none he supposed even came close to the truth. Occasionally, Blake glanced back towards Meryton, each time Darcy caught sight of the unchanging despondent expression. Heracles proved to be an adept horse without the need for any direction from a rider who did not attempt to guide him. Blake's thoughts were elsewhere—he had not bared a single smile nor shared a pleasant word to man or beast.

Darcy announced to the empty carriage, "Finally, going home where our families and friends are, and where we can concentrate on business. Nothing will interfere or distract us now."

***

Rawlings entered the cigar and wine shop on Bond Street and waited patiently while Mr. Cuffage finished his transaction with a customer. Once the gentleman departed, Mr. Cuffage led Rawlings to the back room.

"I have made arrangement for you to stay at the Westchester Hotel in lower Manhattan, off the Bowery Street, at 341 Broome Street. Here are the documents and letter of introduction for Mr. Astor. Remember to take them to him upon your arrival in New York."

"What does the gentleman look like?"

"He is a typical German. He is blond and blue eyed. He is tall man, a slender build. He dresses well, and everyone grows quiet when he enters the room, the admiration for him is obvious. He is a most gracious fellow.

"Did you send word to him?"

"Of course, sir. He expects you in five weeks. Do not dawdle. He is leaving for a long journey to the western frontier soon thereafter."

"Can you share any peculiarities he might have?"

"He hates the aristocracy. Do not talk about your father or Lord Blake."

"Excellent. I believe a gift would be appropriate. Are his habits familiar to you? Does he smoke or drink?"

"Both. Here are his favorite cigars. He does not like French wine at all. Shall I send your selection to your house? Oh, wait! A most wonderful new wine arrived yesterday, which he may find agreeable."

"Yes, please. Oh, here are the papers for you to sign and a copy to keep. Send a signed one with my package, which allows you sufficient time to consider the terms."

Rawlings left the shop. Cuffage went in the back and quickly scribbled his name on the documents and packed them with the cigars. He immediately sent the other copy to the Falcon and a short note declaring all was ready.

***

Darcy arrived late afternoon at his townhouse in London after a restless journey. He had in the past enjoyed traveling in his carriage, away from the servants, the friends, the family members. Here he might scratch his nose if he wished and read a book uninterrupted. This four hour trip, he spent his time in solemn contemplation mulling over many concerns.

Blake separated from the traveling group while he continued towards Grosvenor Square. At the turn of the road, he spied his residence—a three story white and reddish tall building glistening in the late afternoon sun. The limestone used for the structure had come from his mines in Derbyshire and gleamed in the sunlight contrasting with the terra cotta bricks embellishments.

"At last!" He sighed, throwing his unread book on the cushion. "It is good to be home."

His butler and housekeeper, the Geoffries, waited for him to disembark from the carriage; they had been with the Darcy family for twenty years. He bounded up the steps and stopped to offer a few polite words before seeking refuge inside. Each wide stride drew him to the staircase and then he sprung up the steps until he reached the floor landing for the music room floor.

"Georgiana?"

When no answer came, he spun around, bumping into Mrs. Geoffries.

"Miss Darcy is not here." She had caught up to her master just when he had turned. Before he could speak, she explained, "She is visiting Lady Victoria, sir. Colonel Fitzwilliam is home, and your aunt and uncle invited her to spend time with her cousins."

"Thank you. Have a tray sent to my room. A simple meal will be sufficient." He smiled at the brandy bottle on the table next to his favorite armchair, beside the window overlooking the busy Grosvenor Square. "Ah, it is so good to be back. I shall not be selfish that Georgiana is staying with the Fitzwilliams. They have been good to her."

Warmed by the fire, he stripped off his jacket, untied his cravat, and even removed his boots. Invitations had been placed on his desk for his examination, which he tackled, discarding those he deemed were from persons only interested in his appearance to raise their social standing. The acceptance pile was short in comparison.

A young servant entered his room carrying a large tray, and then, without looking up, bid him a good evening and left the room almost as invisibly as she had come in.

Darcy opened the brandy. He poured himself a glass and leaned back in his chair. *Damn, I wish I took pleasure in cigars like Rawlings. He is so relaxed after he finishes one.*

He jotted a quick message to his sister. He also penned notes to Rawlings, Kent and Bingley. Even though he had invited Blake to dinner, which his friend agreed to, he doubted the words registered. Darcy hesitated for a second before scribling him a note too. Darcy drafted a list of the many unfinished details left in advance of his other friend's journey to America. Rawlings seemed anxious to leave for America.

Darcy rang for a servant. "Send these immediately. Do not remain for an answer. One moment." Darcy found the message to his sister. "Wait for a response to this one." The man nodded and left in haste.

Ah! Home. Tomorrow, I will visit White's. Meryton's Black Bull Tavern is no substitute for a London club and especially not White's

Chapter Two

Darcy arrived at White's at the exact time specified Where Blake was the only friend waiting for him. They spoke about their reception, and both men expected a fuss. They ascended the stairs together.

Many men clustered around them the moment they stepped in the room. Neither man had anticipated the magnitude of questions. Several older gentlemen, who remained in their comfortable seats by the fire, lowered their newspapers before muttering to each other about the impertinence of the young.

Darcy and Blake stood in the center; the eager members crowding around them and peppering them with questions.

"I lost a bundle, Darcy. I had thought you would be the victor," one gentleman complained.

"Lord Blake, is the stallion as wonderful as they say?"

"Who is this Bingley fellow? And where is Netherfield Park?" Several other members inquired, their voices rang loudly.

Darcy and Blake spent two hours answering every inquiry. Drinks flowed from the well-wishers to them. Finally, the questions ceased and the men moved to the billiards room. They taught those interested in Twenty Points, and were surprised to find that this tidbit had not been included in the papers, unlike everything else. The two friends had begun to narrate the golf match when the members crowding around the billiard players gave way to a tall fair-haired noble approached the table. His icy gaze emitting from the blue eyes found their target—Blake.

"I need to speak to you," the Duke of Charnwood said.

"Now?" Blake glanced at the cue stick in his hand.

"Now," His Grace demanded. His stare was cold, dark, and unflinching. The other members stepped back, lowering their heads and staring at their boots.

Blake's shoulders slumped slightly when he followed behind his father. He overheard Darcy beginning a new account of the games as he walked away.

Father and son found a secluded corner table from which to sit and talk. The club's servants quickly placed a wine carafe before them and then promptly moved to guard their privacy.

"Congratulations on winning the stallion." His Grace said abruptly and without the slightest hint of excitement. "You are late. I expected you back in town two days ago."

Blake nodded and braced his nerves. Any conversation his father started so brusquely was never a happy occurrence. "You did not indicate the reason for the urgency."

"A rumor is floating around that you are involved with another unacceptable woman." He leaned closer and whispered, "My God, son. A country lass with nothing to offer. Is she why you delayed your return to town?"

"Do not worry, father. It is in the past." Blake drew back away from him.

"Good. I am pleased you thought about your duty and ended this affair. Must I get involved?"

"No sir, there is no need for any recompense. Our relationship never went that far."

"Just toying with her, I see."

"No. I did not toy with her. Perhaps at the onset, but then I desired much more the longer I stayed."

"You were wise, then, to end the flirtation before she sought a further connection." His Grace paused, sipping his wine. He did not speak until his son glowered at him. "The dinner party has been arranged. You will attend."

Blake scoffed, and then pushed back into his chair. He covered his glass when the servant attempted to fill it. "Who is she this time? More importantly, how much money does she have?"

"Her fortune is ample, and she is exceptionally attractive. She is the type you like: silly and empty headed, concerning herself with clothes and gossip. Such the flirt, too..."

"I daresay if you know her, she must be experienced in the arts and allurements women use to flatter a man. I assume if she has survived your inspection, then she is cunning too."

"Do not speak so. You forget who I am."

"Impossible. So, what do you wish for me to do? Do I just flirt and toy, or do you desire something more?"

"Son." His Grace sighed. "I am attempting to help. You need to be married and produce an heir. I will not be here forever."

Nor will my inheritance. Blake glanced over to watch Darcy speaking animatedly to the group. *He is fortunate.*

"I want you married this year."

"Time is your enemy. The best ladies are taken."

"You mean you want your hands on a fresh supply of funds." Blake clenched his teeth again. He glimpsed at the men in the club, laughing and sneaking glances his way. "The members spoke about your latest misfortune. You bet on Darcy!"

"Everything was in his favor. No one expected you to win. Not one person. All your friend had to do was come in fourth. I went with the odds. This was not about who I wanted to see win the horse."

"I understand what gamblers do; I have had a lifetime in the subject. Calculate the odds and bet accordingly." Blake leaned forward and in a half-whisper said, "You care not for anyone except yourself." His eyes narrowed. "You never cared for my well-being. God, how I hate you."

"Your words are unkind. The risks I take are for you. I am forever trying to increase my holdings… for you." His Grace reached to pat his son's arm.

Blake jerked his arm away, lowering to his lap. "No, Father, you do not. You gamble because you seek the thrill, not the winnings. Your entire being stays focused on the activity, regardless of the danger or surrounding conditions. Every muscle in your body is tense. A ruffian could hold a knife at my throat, and you would bet on the outcome. Dinner is often late or your attention is absent whenever you are involved in a wager. You speak persistently about your winnings; you never discuss your losses." Blake leaned forward. "Father, you do not think about my future when you bet yet another portion of your fortune."

"I have not given you leave to speak to me in such a way. What caused this change in you?" He maintained his smile when he lowered his head, and with his nostrils flared and his glare from his icy blue eyes boring into his son, said, "I give you fair warning. You will be at my dinner party in four days time. You are to arrive before seven." Standing up, the duke towered over his son. "I insist that you consider this lady seriously." Blake nodded, and his father left for the card room.

Darcy approached Blake with a drink in his hand. "I thought you might need this."

"No. I thank you. Drinking will not solve my problems. Blake stood. "If you do not mind, I prefer a ride."

"Heracles?"

"Yes. He is a beautiful horse. I am grateful you cannot putt." Blake winked to Darcy. "At least in that I may be happy." His smile faded.

"Another skill I must learn. One day I will beat you at chess. We may be in our old age, but I will be victorious. I am a ready challenger at anytime."

For the next few minutes, they continued to speak in more relaxed, friendly manner. Blake realized Darcy stared at him as if he was searching for a five-syllable word to describe what he saw. Blake had no need to admit how sadness had overcome him. He was sure his missing enthusiasm was obvious to anyone looking past their own self-centered thoughts. Darcy was not selfish when his friends were involved. He hoped his friend believed his father was responsible and not Miss Elizabeth Bennet, although he would not acknowledge the reason why.

Blake glanced at the door. "Before I forget, I want you to know I have renamed the horse." Blake said.

"Oh?"

"Netherfield. Of course, I will not correct anyone referring to the horse as Heracles. I wanted you to be aware that I will occasionally call the horse Nether."

Darcy started. "I remember you named your filly Chesterfield after a favorite… place. Netherfield was a favorite place?"

"Yes. Very much so." Blake responded, his voice dull to his own ears. Following the visit from his father, the questioning from the crowd of admirers, and the scrutiny by this friend, he no longer cared how he sounded or if he lived up to anyone's expectations.

The two men soon departed White's, followed by few other members desiring to glimpse the magnificent white Andalusian stallion.

***

Darcy returned home desirous of finding his sister. Her response yesterday to his message had been short, while meaningful. She would arrive in time for dinner today. He experienced a strong yearning to find someone who had been successful in overcoming heartbreak and he hoped she fit his need.

Geoffries informed him that Georgiana had yet not arrived, hiding his disappointment until he spied his sister as she was coming up the front steps. He pulled his lips back to reveal a tooth-filled smile. He knew his servants had never witnessed his delight expressed so candidly before; nonetheless, today he cared not what they thought. His heart raced. She had grown so tall and she was smiling. Smiling! His joy weakened when he saw his cousin, Richmond Fitzwilliam, escorting her up the steps. At least the colonel had brought his congenial ways with him.

"Welcome home, Georgiana." Darcy lifted her off her feet and swung her around. "You too, Richmond." They exchanged warm welcomes followed by customary inquiries about the health of the Richmond's family —Darcy's uncle and aunt, Lord and Lady Cheswick, and his other cousins, Brandon and Victoria. The Fitzwilliams were his only living relatives and he felt close to them since his birth. His mother named him Fitzwilliam following the same custom that used when Lady Cheswick's gave her family name to her second son, Richmond.

"How is it possible you did not win, Darcy?" Richmond asked. "I had a large wager on you. All our friends did, in fact. I daresay you may not be popular with the *Ton*. They lost a bundle."

"I was at White's today and heard their complaints. I am sorry to disappoint you, nonetheless, I knew I was defeated the moment Bingley announced his game. Speaking of which, he and I will play a golf match next week at Royal Blackheath. Perhaps you may like to join us and show me how putting is done?" Darcy aimed his smirk at his cousin, his brows raised.

"Unfair, unfair. You know I have never played."

The banter between the two men grew and the servants all took note. Darcy had invited Richmond to stay for dinner, which he did so with alacrity. Georgiana, having gone to change for dinner after the initial welcome, arrived last in the dining room.

"Georgiana, you look lovely tonight."

"Thank you, brother. Victoria assisted me in choosing a few new gowns. I want so for you to like them."

"If they are all as pretty as this one, then yes I am sure I will." Darcy patted her hand. She sat to his right. Darcy turned his attention to Richmond after he took his usual seat on the left. "You did not mention your sister earlier. How is she doing?"

"Victoria is quieter these days. I prefer to speak on happier subjects. In fact, I am more interested in hearing about your trip. Tell us about the Tup Running! I wager Blake was surprised at your choice. Did he really grab the tail?"

"Yes, he most assuredly did! Quite amusing." Darcy entertained them with stories about all the games. They barely ate while he spoke, enthralled by the competition and his description of the Andalusian stallion.

"Ah, I wished you would have won." Richmond sipped his wine. "I would have secured him from you with our own contest!"

"Humph. And what would you have chosen that would best me?"

Before either man answered, Georgiana shouted out, "Flirting! Richmond would win easily."

"Was there no flirting to be had in Hertfordshire?"

Darcy felt the heat rising on his face and, by his cousin's smirk, Richmond had spied the color change spreading upwards from his neck.

"You did not, man, I do not believe it! Well, did you or did you not engage in a little flirting? Do tell. I am most anxious to learn if there was any sweet lady watching you grab that ram!"

"I am sorry to disappoint you, cousin, no. No one twirled a rose at me."

"Surely there were a few pretty ladies. London does not own them all!"

"Yes, of course, several women were attractive. The Bennets are the local beauties. The eldest two especially."

"Eldest? How many are there?" Leaning back in his chair, Richmond maintained his gaze on Darcy.

"Five."

"Five?" Richmond sat upright, his jaw dropped, his brows lifted high. "All pretty? I must take a trip to Mr. Goulding's horse farm soon! I am in need of a stallion myself. Apparently there is more in Meryton than fine horseflesh. Now, how many sisters are out?"

Darcy sighed. "Unfortunately, all five. Only the eldest two would interest you. Their manners are impeccable; the youngest require stern direction."

"Miss Elizabeth Bennet is pretty, I am positive." Georgiana hid her giggle behind her napkin.

Richmond turned his stare at her. "What do you know?"

"I lately read, and in my brother's own hand, how beautifully Miss Elizabeth Bennet plays the pianoforte, and sings too! He has rarely heard anyone that gives him more pleasure. Is that not true, brother? She giggled aloud when Darcy rolled his eyes. She leaned towards Richmond and with a conspiratorial smile, added, "And she is witty and reads the best books."

"I must hear more about the pretty Miss Elizabeth Bennet that plays and sings so well."

"Humph. Georgiana, you best finish your meal. I wish to hear you play and sing. I missed it very much." Darcy swallowed the remaining wine remnants and offered no further comments about the witty and pretty Miss Elizabeth Bennet. A long time passed before his normal coloring returned, which his sister and cousin also used to tease him.

***

Darcy finished his dinner, had a few drinks with Richmond, and then allowed Georgiana to retire early when his cousin left. He sat alone in his study reminising about a pair of fine eyes when an image of two sad one glared at him. He imagined different possibilities for how Blake was coping until Rawlings' arrival interrupted his reflections. He shook away his thoughts and jumped up. "Let me pour us coffee."

"Damn blasted, arrogant curs."

"Please sit down and tell me what is causing you such distress."

"The Four Horse Club." Rawlings grunted after he plopped into the chair.

"Why would you be so angry with them?"

"I am no longer a member."

Darcy raised his brows. "Not a member? How can that be? You helped start the blasted club. You have raced with these men since Cambridge. What caused the problem? Surely the competition did not result in this!"

"No. The members' attitude did." Rawlings sipped coffee. "I cannot remain with such self-important men. I must admit they opened my eyes wide today. I understood Sir Paxton's usual unsympathetic attitude, but Buxton—my closest neighbor—looked down upon my friends. How dare a man without his own impressive lineage sneer at my friends! The same goes for Mr. Annesley!"

"I believe they both belong to the gentry, which cannot be said about Kent or Bingley." Darcy waited. He sensed the problem.

"All my life I was taught to think less of those beneath me, especially tradesmen." He glanced at Darcy. "Do not look at me that way. You and Blake received the same instruction. You remember what they said: You are better than others. You have a right to walk about as if you own the world because, well, you do. He did not speak those exact words; however, the meaning is unchanged. My father taught me to take from tradesmen; never give. Certainly I should not entertain them in my home. I do not know how many times he warned me that they only want our money and our connections. Do business as one would do when purchasing gloves. They are shopkeepers; I am the purchaser. Damn. I believed him."

Darcy frowned. He recalled his own upbringing and remembered hearing those exact phrases. He wondered if his father would have permitted his alliance. No. His father would never have approved. He returned his attention to Rawlings, who paced the floor spouting vile curses.

"Rawlings! Calm down. Tell me what happened."

Rawlings glared at the crystal decanters on the side table until Darcy poured two glasses, one brandy and one scotch whiskey. Rawlings sipped his drink and settled back into the comfortable overstuffed armchair "Kent and Bingley were snubbed, given the coldest shoulders I have ever witnessed and by every member. They had been welcomed for five minutes until I introduced them. The damn newspapers had exposed their backgrounds at endless length. I understand the tradesmen were the subject of many dinner parties."

"Did you truly anticipate any other reaction? Blake foretold of his club's attitude. I wanted secrecy; at least until we were so well established. What did you expect would happen?"

"I expected my desires to be respected. If I desired to sponsor Kent and Bingley in the club, then my opinion should have sufficient value to accept them."

"Surely you exaggerate their reactions. Come, come Rawlings. These unwritten rules covering class distinctions safeguard our place in society, and you have known this all your life. Do you remember when Kent had said we owned all the land and all the resources? Well, we do! However, our attitude is not stopping their class from trying to push us out. I believe we must give them room, or they will uproot us completely."

"Do not be such an officious foot-licker. How will they do that?" Rawlings scoffed. "Perhaps they might win it card games!"

"No. We are on the path to hand it over to them. I have said it before; I cannot rest on my laurels. Look about, Rawlings. Who has the energy these days? Not our class. You are the one who said we spend out days gambling, drinking, and seducing. All the while, we disown any hard work, preferring for our stewards make the effort. We are not the ones with the new visions, they are."

"I suppose you are right. I did not truly believe what I said, although I accept it as true now. Rawlings sat for a few minutes staring into the flickering fire. Sweat dripped from his forehead. He admitted that the warmth came from the brandy he had been gulping not from the flames. Still, he asked for another.

"Damn, I hate to think about Blake. If I am this angry at my treatment, he will be worse."

"How so?"

"He will back down. He does not possess the strength to go against these people."

"I am not so sure. Hopefully, he may surprise us both."

The two continued to discuss the alliance and found convincing reasons including tradesmen's sons would prove invaluable in the end. After Rawlings calmed down, they discussed the problems with the *Lively*, which had delayed its leaving. They continued long into the night, drinking and discussing the trip.

In another house a few streets from where Darcy and Rawlings sat, two other men discussed the incident at the club while playing their on-going Twenty Points competition.

Kent took his shot. "You understand my position now. Do not deny it."

Bingley sighed and remained quiet.

"Phew! They will never let us enter their little club. You know it. Why did I believe otherwise this past month?" Kent took his next shot. "Two points!"

Twirling his cue stick, Bingley gazed into the distance and then spoke calmly. "Well, Rawlings quit. He glared down at them, and then resigned. You can see he, at least, is committed to altering the way things are done. And I trust Darcy."

"I was surprised by his actions. He started the damn club, yet they threatened to kick him out." Kent leaned on his cue stick while his friend took his shot. "You did not include Blake as someone to trust, which brings up another question all together."

"What?" Bingley stood erect. "Blake is trustworthy and has always been honorable in his dealings, much more so than many tradesmen. My father kept a list of the cheats and robbers."

"And his father? Forget them. We could do this alone. Do we actually want to continue the connection and do business with Blake, Darcy, and Rawlings? He was so angry today, all the same what happens after his relatives intervene? Do not stare at me; the Earl of Wolverly will intercede. Blake will never stand against his father."

"I believed you no longer felt isolated or left out. Remember this is a good opportunity for us as well as them."

I do not need them to be successful. They need my connections more than I need them, as they need yours. Your family owns the Baker rifle."

"Do not be foolish. We have signed the partnership agreement. I do not go back on my agreements. Do you?" Bingley sighed. "No, you do not. Everyone respects your word, Kent. Do not lose that now. You are becoming the man you despise."

Kent cringed. "Sometimes I let my anger flow out my mouth when I do not mean what I say. I have a temper."

"Yes, not unlike another friend." Bingley placed two balls in the corner pocket. "Five points total for me. If you stay angry, I will be a guinea richer tonight. You do not shoot straight unless you are calm." The two men chuckled. Bingley sighed. "I will attempt to talk Rawlings into rejoining his club. He loves driving."

Kent stared at Bingley. "We should start a new one. Rawlings could lead us."

"We would not be allowed to drive in the streets as the Four Horse club does. They have connections we never will. It is just the way life is."

"I will make the offer to Rawlings, and if he chooses not to start a new club, I will not resent him if he rejoins his old one."

The night ended with drinks in the study while Bingley and Kent agreed to do what they could for Rawlings. That was, once a calm Kent collected his guinea for the win.

Chapter Three

The Darcy siblings shared breakfast together from the time their mother passed away until his sister's ill-fated trip to Ramsgate. Since then, Georgiana had found the mornings the most difficult, choosing instead to be alone to face her schedule of busy nothings: dress, eat, study, practice, eat, play, and sleep and in that order. This morning, Georgiana revisited her situation while she waited for her abigail to finish. She sensed her world was changing, the same for her brother. There was something different at dinner the night before—an unnamed perspective or a shifting opinion. She knew the exact moment it changed—it was when she saw the blush rising on his cheeks.

Her brother had often left her unaccompanied for weeks or months at a time. Of course, they corresponded with each other, yet how can words on paper substitute for the occasional smile, the pat on the hand, or the shared jest, now and then? It cannot.

In her loneliness, Georgiana had wished for a sister. William, more devoted and supportive than most brothers, could not provide a womanly bond. A female sibling would give her the freedom to reveal her impulsive feelings for George Wickham. Perhaps then, she would have averted the entire muddle she made of her life.

Foolish. The precise word to describe her actions, and looking back, she had wished that a sister existed, someone who would have taken her hands, and with the most soothing voice, convinced her not to be so imprudent, or perhaps she would have used good-natured teasing to show her the truth. If she had even spoken with the stern Darcy manner to pronounce a forthright but truthful opinion, a sister may have been able to shock her senses back into coherency. An older, confident girl was the type she had envisioned. Instead, guided only by the deceitful ladies' companion, Mrs. Younge, a stranger hired by her brother and cousin, she had convinced herself she was in love.

If not for the commanding actions taken by her dear brother, this morning she, as a discarded, poverty-stricken married woman would have eaten a bowl of gruel in silence without a single melody filling her world. She understood it now. All George Wickham wanted was her fortune.

Her brother's return to London brought it all back again. She had not forgotten his blunt words that unforgettable afternoon. After admitting the plan to him, she had anticipated his grave countenance and expected to hear him speaking in his monotone intonation, yet on that occasion, his calm tone, used when addressing a problem, had deserted him. He had modulated the pitch and beat of his voice, jumping from the crisp and direct sound of his accent to the duller, droning flat timbre resonating in his throat and back again.

Halfway through the discourse, he had mumbled something about turning George into a soprano. Did he think she did not know how that is accomplished? Would he have done that to George? She shuddered at what might have happened if he had arrived the following day, discovering them after they embarked on their planned journey to Gretna Green. In her mind, Mr. George Wickham would have ceased to exist, laid out on a floor somewhere with not a droplet of blood left in his body. Instead, William handled the matter through his usual practice when confronted—by the written word. She had no doubt the scolding was long, direct, and clear in his intent. Most days she wished she had received a letter as an alternative to the verbal education of the adult world he gave her.

She had expected a crescendo to build with his rising declarations; he had astounded her with the opposite. His words, spoken in a harsh, discordant tone and deficient of any harmony, were a dissonance. At the climax of his temper, his nostrils had flared in staccato fashion when his rage possessed his mind. The curve of his ears alternated colors—a red, an unmistakable, bright shade, and a duller pinkish gray. She swore the flashing kept tempo with his thoughts and deepened in hue with the depth of the furrows of his brow. Tiny flashes of fire shot outwards from his eyes causing her to sweat. She recognized that she fabricated the heat from his glare flowing over her cold body, since in truth she did not see a flame. She had witnessed a fugue that afternoon between his eyes, ears, nostrils, and the sound and speed of his words. However, it was not until his dolce-type finale—a melody of expressions so sweet, so soft—that a cloak of shame covered her entire body, crushing her heart and stealing away her breath.

Unable to wipe the haunting composition of her brother's emotion from her memories, she exhausted hours attempting to duplicate the highs and lows on her pianoforte; still, she could not find the right synchronization of musical tones. She had squandered months fighting the wrong harmony escaping through her fingers and overpowering the piece. Every day she advanced a note closer to perfection. Now that he was home, and after witnessing his positive performance with her at dinner last night, she prayed he brought with him the final chord to make her personal sonata complete.

She headed downstairs to join her brother for breakfast and when she entered the dining room, she hummed a tune known only to her.

***

Darcy sorted through the estate and business correspondence bundled up before him. Occasionally, he stopped to recall the contented feeling overtaking from the morning meal with his sister. She had unmistakably overcome her past, and he rejoiced in her success. He now felt comfortable with his plans for her. Returning his concentration to the many tasks awaiting him, he did not hear the doorknob turn until the butler opened the door, loudly clearing his voice.

"Mr. Darcy, sir. Everyone is assembled."

He left for the library, and was pleased to see his housekeeper, Mrs. Geoffries, and his secretary, Mr. Rogers, standing comfortably around the fire. Upon seeing the master enter, they nodded slightly; Geoffries promptly moved to stand beside his wife. Even though Darcy noted the quizzical expressions, he pointed to the chairs, smiling at them as they took their seats. They sat down, silently.

"During the months ahead," Darcy said, "I will be entertaining four gentlemen friends," He said, and then glanced at Geoffries, "who are to be provided entrance without ceremony, unless, of course, I provide other instructions. They may arrive at my door early morning or late into the evening."

Next, he turned his gaze on Mrs. Geoffries. "My friends may also stay overnight without notice." When she nodded, he continued, "Have four rooms made ready immediately and reserved for their exclusive use. Mr. Bingley, one of the gentlemen, shall be given his normal room. Lord Blake, Mr. Rawlings, and Mr. Kent are the others. We will be gathering in the library. I insist you keep the room in an orderly condition; however, neither maid nor footman shall enter unless I grant access. It will be available for cleaning early in the morning or late at night. The door is to remain locked when unoccupied. Post a footman in the hallway."

He took a deep breath, and then turned to Mr. Rogers. "You may be called upon to perform services normally reserved for me. I expect your quick attention to any request."

His steward nodded and rushed to the writing table to scribble down a few words on paper.

"In addition, there may be times we will need your expertise on a matter. Your total discretion is essential." Darcy paused to collect his thoughts before pointing to a vacant space along the far wall. "And I need a large, locking cabinet to be placed over there with five keys, and not one more."

Mr. Roger's brows lifted higher than was normal. Still, he proceeded to make a note of it.

"I hope you did not lose too much money on the competition. It could not be helped. Please inform the staff, I am most sorry for my disappointing finish!" He chuckled when they lowered their heads in an attempt to conceal the rising blush on their faces.

"We did follow the games in the newspapers, and I can assure you your entire staff had been dismayed when you did not win the stallion." Geoffries said. "Among the servants in London society, much wagering transpired. And when you did not win, everyone felt disappointment at losing a supplement to their income, but that did not sting as much as losing our rights to brag." He winked.

After excusing the two Geoffries, Darcy settled into his chair. "What did you discover about Mr. Cuffage? I know I sent you an express to discontinue your investigation; tell me what you had uncovered."

Mr. Rogers' cheek twitched several times. "He was partnered with Mr. Edward Gardiner in the import and export trade."

Darcy nodded for him to continue.

Rogers shrugged. "The partnership has ended. Apparently, there were bad feelings between the two. I hesitate to disparage anyone." Rogers paused. When Darcy glowered at his hesitation, he added, "My investigation is not yet complete. I..."

"Continue with your findings, Mr. Rogers. This is important."

"Well, what I have been able to establish is that Mr. Gardiner took money from the company to invest it in a risky venture. He did so without Mr. Cuffage's knowledge. When the scheme failed, they had to pay out an enormous sum. I believe thirty thousand was the amount."

"And?"

"Mr. Darcy, again I caution you since this information has not yet been verified.

"Go on, what else did you found out?"

"Mr. Gardiner was able to acquire the funds from his brother-in-law. I believe he is a country gentleman, from Hertfordshire. You may have met him. His name is Mr. Thomas Bennet."

Darcy jerked his head. So it was true. Mr. Bennet lost the dowries by his brother-in-law's dishonorable actions.

"Until I can determine the report's accuracy, I recommend you do not do business with Mr. Gardiner. Every word could be a total fabrication."

Darcy nodded. "I have had no plans do so. Just the same, I shall hire a man to investigate him thoroughly. I had heard a similar story from other quarters."

Mr. Rogers nodded. "Yes, sir. this sad situation is known by others and while not the talk of the town, the rumors have been openly discussed."

"I want you to continue your efforts at unmasking the truth about this man. If something different turns up, hire an investigator to probe deeper. I expect you to be discreet when making any inquiries on my behalf. I do not desire anyone to learn of my or my four friends' interests and our involvement."

"Yes, sir." The secretary jotted down a few words.

Darcy gave instructions about the legal documents he had brought with him. This afternoon, he and Mr. Kent planned to meet with his London solicitor on several exporting issues and requested Mr. Rogers to attend. Talk then switched to matters associated with Pemberley and Darcy House. The two men worked for almost a full hour before closing the last account journal.

"Mr. Rogers, please ask Mrs. Geoffries to bring Miss Darcy in to see me in my study."

He did not have time to sip his tea when the two women appeared. Darcy nodded to his housekeeper standing behind his sister. "Mrs. Geoffries, I would like for you to stay as well."

Georgiana twisted a handkerchief in her hands. "You wished to speak with me? You rarely call for me in the middle of the day."

Darcy took his sister's hand in his, patted it several times before leading her to a chair in front of his desk. Mrs. Geoffries sat down next to her. He returned to his seat, and then spoke in a calm voice. "The next few months will be busy ones for me. I need you to act as hostess." He sighed at her fleeting fearful gaze before she lowered head to stare, blinking wildly, at her bunched up handkerchief in her lap. His housekeeper leaned in to support the young mistress. "Mrs. Geoffries will be available at all times to provide assistance. You need not act alone."

"What do you expect, Fitzwilliam?" Georgiana said, spoken tentatively. She raised her eyes and locked her gaze upon his.

"To serve as hostess for dinners for my guests and provide entertainment afterwards."

"Will there be many people?"

"No, my dear. Not at all. Mr. Bingley you know. Occasionally his sisters and brother-in-law will attend. The others include Lord Blake, Mr. Rawlings, and Mr. Kent. They are my particular friends. Oh, yes, of course, our cousin may join us at any time. You are already familiar with Richmond's habits."

"How often will you have guests?"

"It may be every day." Darcy paused when she gasped. "I asked Mrs. Geoffries to assist you. Each morning, I expect you to select the menu; however, I cannot tell you who will dine with us that night." He watched Georgiana's eyebrows lift upwards. "Mrs. Geoffries will offer suggestions. You merely need to make the selections, my dear." He smiled when the housekeeper patted his sister's hand.

"Entertainment, brother? Do you expect me to play and sing?"

"Yes. Georgiana, these are my friends. After a long day involved in weighty matters, they would enjoy relaxing and listening to soothing music. You need not be too elaborate, and sometimes we may play billiards, in which case, you will then be excused." Darcy watched as she fidgeted with the folds of her gown.

He inclined his head towards the hallway, dismissing Mrs. Geoffries with just a look. As soon as his housekeeper shut the door, Darcy sat next to his sister, taking her hands into his. "Georgiana, look at me." He waited until she looked at him. "You will do wonderfully. No one can play better."

"Singing, Fitzwilliam? Must I sing?"

"If you dread sharing your beautiful voice with others, then no, you do not. One day, you will need to display your accomplishments. Regard this time, while the guest list is limited to my kind friends, as an opportunity for you to practice your duties as hostess. If you do not wish to play, then I will have no choice. I shall pull out my violin, for it is the only other musical entertainment available to us."

Georgiana's mouth flew open, and then just as quick, followed with a boisterous laugh. "No, brother, I will play. I would like you to keep your friends. I do not wish to be knocked over as they make a wild dash to the door."

Darcy chuckled before returning to his sympathetic mien and patting her hand. "You can always come to me if you cannot play one evening." He lifted her chin and gazed at her with a tenderness only displayed for her. "Please try."

"I will. Is there anything else, brother?"

"I recommend you speak to Miss Bingley. We all recently stayed at Netherfield Park. She is familiar with all the men's favorite dishes and drinks, and she can offer you excellent advice."

"Miss Bingley?" Georgiana held her breath.

Darcy chuckled. "You may ask her brother to obtain that information from his sister, if you so desire." Georgiana's image and his friend appeared in his mind. Perhaps Miss Bingley is right. Bingley would make a wonderful brother. Bah.

Georgiana rose to return to her studies. Darcy did not miss her subdued manner as she left the room. He had hoped that the smiling, humming young girl this morning was an indication of a more confident sister. He realized she was not and released a deep sigh. He returned to reviewing his papers, and waited for his partner to arrive.

***

Darcy sent word to his sister, informing her that they would have a guest that evening. Kent had arrived to discuss their goals before they met with the solicitor later that day. He would return for dinner.

With the Darcy determination, Georgiana took charge of her first dinner, expressed her relief that no other gentlemen would be attending. She spent the afternoon and early evening meeting with the cook and housekeeper. She selected the menu, chose the music she would play that night, and dressed in the most grown up gown she owned. Smiling at her available choices, she imagined all the shopping trips she and her cousin, Victoria, would need to obtain the proper gowns and accessories as mistress of the house.

The time had arrived; her brother and friend had returned. All was ready and she was prepared for anything. Or so she thought. Kent walked down the stairs with a slow and steady rhythm. His hand was behind his back, which was upright. He did not have the natural grace of movement as her brother did. Georgiana lowered her gaze and the moment he reached the bottom step, she heard his gasp. She twisted the handkerchief in her hands until there was not a smooth area left. He cleared his throat and when she lifted her eyes, he smiled as affably as possible. Her breathing slowed.

"Georgiana, this is Mr. Kent." Darcy said when he entered the hallway. After the two exchanged the appropriate civilities, Darcy offered his arm to Georgiana. They led the way to the dining room.

She had dressed the table in its best: Belgium lace tablecloth, cream-colored French Limoges plates, the Darcy monogrammed silverware buffed to a shine, and Waterford glassware shooting colored sparkles from the light of the candles. Jasmine and hellebore flowers mixed with fresh evergreens filled the table's center.

Darcy leaned in and whispered, "Everything looks wonderful. You have made me exceedingly proud."

Her brother nodded his approval of the chosen wine and she relaxed a little except she dared not look directly across the table at Mr. Kent. Instead, she peeked at him, barely able say thank you when he gave her a compliment and when he smiled at her, she had to place her hand on her chest, almost as if to stop her racing heart. She nodded for the meal to commence the moment Darcy squeezed her hand. Kent turned his discussion to Darcy about exhibits currently at the London museum; still, he took care to include her in the conversation. She snuck a peek at her brother who did no more than nod. Kent made her smile at a little joke about the city air while his greatest success came when he asked about music. She sat upright and became fearless when describing her favorite composers.

"Hayden sounds like Bach to me. Not to mention Vivaldi, Mozart, and Pachelbel, although I admit I do like his Canon in D." Kent sighed. "I cannot tell the difference in their music."

"No, surely you can tell the dissimilarity." Georgiana's face lightened as she offered Kent her biggest smile.

"Have pity on me; I must be tone deaf. I admit, I do like a good melody."

Georgiana giggled. Her brother stared at her.

With his hand on his heart, Kent leaned in to Miss Darcy. "I request you enlighten me each time you play. Otherwise, I will surely name the wrong composer. Only you can save me from myself."

Georgiana agreed by nodding her head. Without looking up she said, "Tonight I have chosen Johann Sebastian Bach. There was also a Johann Christian Bach, his son, although his work is not of the same quality."

"Thank you, Miss Darcy. I shall flourish under your tutelage."

Georgiana moved to the music room while the men remained for the customary brandies. After the briefest of time, the two men joined her. Kent turned the pages as she played.

"You play magnificently, Miss Darcy. I have never heard anyone play so well." He smiled. "I wish my sister Sarah had learned. She is your age and I am most fond of her. I... miss her."

Georgiana watched the young man whose expression had change from joy to sadness. She touched his arm. He attempted a smile, although the previous gaiety was gone. The moment she completed the performance, he took his leave. He had told her he wanted to hurry home and send his sister a letter suggesting she come to London. Georgiana's heart jumped when he asked if he could introduce her. She chose not to warn him, however. Her brother would object. Instead, she nodded and when his eye light up, she smiled.

***

The next day, Georgiana took charge of her first large dinner—all the men in her brother's alliance would be attending. Mrs. Geoffries lead her through the process, and she was able to accomplish a dinner worthy of Darcy House. Her brother had suggested serving a mutton dish for Bingley, and he vowing it was his friend's favorite. He recommended she serve this every time he would be joining them.

That night, her brother again voiced his admiration and quietly pronounced her proficiency as a hostess. The men enjoyed the meal and her choices of wines with the food. Georgiana avoided the lively conversation. Kent tried to include her, unsuccessfully. She was content to watch the as the others ate, talk, and teased.

By listening, she learned much about the men. Being shy did not make her an unobservant person, the opposite, in fact. She discerned Mr. Bingley and Lord Blake were less animated than the other men were. She was not acquainted with the marquess to know if this was his manner. Mr. Bingley's quietness surprised her. He had always been so friendly. Although, he did grin when the footman served his mutton; and she was aghast when her brother laughed at his reaction.

"You said Pemberley, Darcy. You would serve mutton at Pemberley. This is London."

"I still cannot putt. When you have taught me to putt successfully, I will serve you beef."

The men raised their voices at Darcy's jest; Kent leaned towards Georgiana, revealing to her the threat her brother made during the golf game.

"I cannot believe you would do such a thing, Fitzwilliam. Mr. Bingley, this is the last time you will be served mutton, I assure you. I will not be misled again by my mischievous brother!" She cared not at the blush rising on Darcy's face. He finally laughed along with everyone else, promising there would be no more mutton, for a while.

After a time, Georgiana sensed there was a prohibition against discussing certain subjects. Whenever one man recalled certain ladies they met during their trip to Hertfordshire, another would cough and the subject was quickly changed. Lord Blake grew even more restrained at those times.

She did not merely observe the guests throughout the meal. Mr. Kent, having chosen to sit near her, regaled her with his own stories. Now relaxed, she engaged in conversation with him. Once, her brother looked at her sharply when she laughed a little too loudly. Kent had shared a story of one of his sister's pranks.

"Yes, Miss Darcy, Sarah did put a live adder in my bed, but that was not the most horrible part." Kent waited until his young friend pleaded with her to continue. "She put mice in the bed as well. You know snakes eat mice? There was quite a battle raging when I retired that night!"

"Tell me about your sister, Mr. Kent. Is she very young?"

"Sarah is a few years older than you, and she is most mischievous. We both have mischievous siblings! Now, she does not fear anything, which explains how she could handle snakes and mice. It is just the two of us since our parents died."

"Oh, that is the same for Fitzwilliam and me. We share that in common, too, Mr. Kent. I believe she has wonderful older brother too. Where does she reside?"

"She has lived with my uncle and aunt since she was six. That was when our parents died in a carriage accident. My sister will not leave my aunt. They are more like mother and daughter. They even look similar. One day, I hope she will join me in my home and act as my hostess, much the same as Miss Bingley does for her brother, and you do for yours." Kent gazed over Georgiana's shoulder at nothing in particular. Sighing, he sipped his wine quietly. "For the moment, Sarah is contented to be where she is."

Georgiana, experienced at wishful thoughts, allowed Mr. Kent a moment of contemplation. She turned to the other guests and discovered they too were speaking of family.

"Tomorrow I will be shackled to Wolverley House. I have received a command to attend dinner." Rawlings swallowed his wine, and then, inclining his head to the hostess, added, "Now, I would, of course, prefer to dine here, with such a lovely young lady to grace the table." Glancing around, he announced with gusto, "Even the men at this table are more entertaining."

"Will your brother attend as well?" Darcy asked.

"He is our father's shadow. Where the earl goes, Thomas follows. Now he, being such a sycophant, did help me though."

"How so?"

"I was free to roam about unimpeded." Rawlings paused and then laughed heartily. "My youth was educational."

Georgiana caught sight of her brother sending Rawlings a cautioning look directed at her.

"Ahem," Kent said. "Cambridge was an education for us all. I miss those days." Turning to Georgiana, he asked, "Do you attend a seminary?"

"No. I have had a governess and masters, Mr. Kent," she answered timidly.

"Well, I do not miss Cambridge. I prefer a world beyond the books," Bingley said quietly. For the first time, his grin appeared. "Unlike you, I look forward to tomorrow. I will dine with my Uncle Watt."

"I did not know he lived in town, Bingley?" Darcy asked.

"He does not, he lives in Birmingham. He has come to town to speak to the Royal Society, or perhaps it is to listen to a speech. I do not recall exactly."

Blake spoke up. "Tomorrow I also dine at my father's house and I do not look forward to yet another boring dinner. Nonetheless, I am looking forward to dining next week with my uncle, Lord Harrowby. I shall press him about the—

Darcy coughed and glanced around at the footmen. Blake tipped his head. Conversations returned to the more mundane matters normally found at such a dinner. The men even gossiped a little about common acquaintances. The talk turned to business once Darcy sent the footmen from the room and Georgiana had left for the music room, except her curiosity kept her lingering near the door. She fiddled with the flower bouquet wondering what had been left unsaid. Her brother had changed.

"You said you would be dining with Lord Harrowby," Rawlings asked. "Do you think the opportunity will present itself to bring up the gun orders?"

Georgiana caught her breath. Guns? What is this about guns? She pulled a rose from the vase and then returned it to the exact place.

Blake nodded. "Most assuredly. I specifically explained the need to my uncle. He has invited the *crème de la crème* of politics. He then turned to Kent. "You did not mention your family. Are you planning to see them soon?"

"Yes, indeed, it is no different for me," Kent said. "My aunt has arranged a large dinner, which includes everyone in the family involved with the import and export trade business. Of the greatest interest to us, next week I will be dining with an old family friend—Mr. Samuel Galton. If anyone knows anything about distribution logistics for the guns, it would be him."

"Will he be a competitor, Kent?" Rawlings asked.

"No, he is involved more in the slave trade. His guns are inferior. We are not going into that venture, so there will not be any problems."

"Well, Bingley and I will precede with the steam engine pursuits. There are many factories and mines that are not powered by steam engines." Darcy explained they would also spend time discovering more about the improvements and new uses. Kent offered to help, since his late uncle Boulton had been a partner of Bingley's uncle Watt. Boulton had been responsible for the successful selling of the steam engine.

Georgiana gasped. Steam engines, guns! She grew more curious and moved closer to the slight opening of the door. She held her breath.

Bingley nodded agreement with commitments Darcy made for him.

Rawlings gazed at Darcy. "And you? You did not say earlier if you have plans to spend time with your relatives.

"Tomorrow I intend to visit with my uncle, the Earl of Cheswick.

Georgiana smiled. Wonderful. Tomorrow I will visit with Victoria and ask for her opinion. She hurried to the music room when she heard the chairs pushing back from the table.

Chapter Four

The bright sun was unusual for a wintry morning in London, where gray skies blanketed the city most days. Before dressing, it was Darcy's usual habit to drink his coffee and read the London Times. He was fortunate that day; the sunlight streamed through the window behind his comfortable chair, making the fine print easier to read. Considering all the papers published, the *Times* had the most subjects crammed on its four pages. Articles were brief and to the point, limited to the most useful information. And since it rarely provided society news, he considered it superior.

This morning, he quickly scanned the paper, identifying several interesting items.

The Scientific Institution on Princes Street, Cavendish Square, will host its annual lecture Tuesday at eight on the Mechanical Arts by Mr. E Lydiatt. He might reveal something worthwhile to the alliance. Bingley mentioned this man; I will suggest he attend.

The next scheduled meeting for the Directors of the National Society for Education of the Poor throughout England and Wales is Tuesday next at twelve noon at St. Martin's Library. I must tell Mr. Rogers to place this on my calendar.

Darcy read the next article: the rumor of an embargo in the American ports was revived again yesterday. We notice it to say it rests on no foundation. He scoffed. When they make promises like this, it is not true. I shall ask Blake to look into this.

Two important publishing announcements caught his eye. Lord Coke announced the publishing of his second, third, and fourth part of the Institutes of the Laws of England Dealing with High Treason. He read the full article. He supposed he must spend an afternoon reading these laws. He decided to stop in Lincoln's Inn on Portugal Street to purchase the volumes along with the 'Digest of the Statue Law covering shipping and navigation' by John Reeves, Esq. This work discusses the plantation trade and the commerce with Asia, Africa, and America.

Finally, one last item caught his eye; 'The Kiss' by Stephen Clark, Esq., a five-act play he had seen at the Lyceum, was now available for purchase at the theater. This will amuse Georgiana. I am sorry she was not well enough to attend with me last summer. I shall obtain a copy and surprise her.

Not finding anything else noteworthy, Darcy finished his coffee and rang for his valet. His uncle had requested he meet with him today, although he had not mentioned the reason.

His journey to his uncle's house was swift since the traffic on the road was light. He sighed while he recalled Georgiana storming from the breakfast table. He had denied her request to go with him today. No, he shook his head. She was not yet fully grown. She acted as a child would have behaved when denied something. And then, when he gave in and rushed to the music room to tell her, she insisted she needed to practice. Her bottom lip stuck out further with each note she pounded on the pianoforte. Humph. She is still a child.

Although, the night before she did not pout or sulk when he announced he would not be leaving for Pemberley this winter, business responsibilities kept him in town. She had always before made a fuss when he did not spend time with her. This time she argued against going—he needed her in town to act as hostess. She reasoned with a mature argument. But after he agreed she demanded to purchase gowns reflecting her new status. Did she plan the whole scene just to finagle a new wardrobe? She, as are all women, is a mystery. Perhaps she is becoming adept at the female manner of persuasion. His little sister was growing up. He debated this until he reached Cheswick house.

Darcy entered his uncle's home, removed his coat and hat, and headed to the breakfast room where the family was gathered. His uncle and eldest son Brandon were arguing about politics, Lady Cheswick and Brandon's wife were avoiding each other, while Richmond was reading the latest society news in *The Morning Post* and did not look up until his mother cried out—

"William. You are here." Lady Cheswick smiled. "Come, sit down with us."

Darcy found a seat near his aunt and next to "Richmond, Where is Victoria?"

"She is not feeling well, and will not be joining us this morning. In fact, she rarely joins us anymore." He shrugged. "She will not even attend any *at home* receptions."

Darcy was well aware that Victoria was two and twenty, and still unmarried. She needed to marry soon to avoid the whispers of her approaching spinsterhood. She could not meet any prospects without spending time at social events or the theater. Refusing to accept any *at home* reception invites indicated the depth of her unhappiness. Unlike balls, soirees, and parties, where guests remained for the evening eating, conversing and being entertained with music or cards, *at home* receptions required nothing more than milling your way through a crush of people at the host's home before heading to the next one until the wee hours of the morning. The entire effort took no more than fifteen minutes, thereby presenting oneself as available. Many grand homes held their receptions on the same evening, when the full moon allowed the most illumination for roaming the London streets, causing the invitees to scurry from one home to another. Hence, a brief attendance.

"She believes her heart to be broken," his eldest cousin said without emotion. "Your rake of a friend was responsible, Darcy."

"My friends are not rakes, Brandy."

Richmond snicker at Darcy's jest and lowered the paper to observe his brother's reaction.

"Do not call me that. You know I hate being called by my childhood name." Lord Brandon said. He banged his fork down.

"Exactly which one of my friends are you calling a rake?" Darcy asked, using his deeper voice and his face scrunched into a scrowl.

Brandon glared at his cousin. "Lord Blake, of course. He is a seducer of women. I do not think he ever met an unmarried lady that was not to his liking." He relaxed his stare and allowed the corner of his mouth to rise. "Of course, I never minded watching his flirting as he was most entertaining."

Darcy felt his throat tighten. Seducer of women? Another accusation. I must find out what Brandon is referring to. "Oh? I have heard nothing of which you could accuse him. You should not repeat ugly gossip."

Brandon glared at Darcy. "Even if Victoria fell into his trap?"

Darcy jerked his head back and glared at his cousin.

"Yes. Your friend courted her all last season, while you remained at Pemberley. He actively pursued Victoria, staying by her side at every ball, dance, dinner, and card party. However, after attending a private ball at Lord Dembry's, he suddenly stopped his attentions, and Victoria secluded herself in her room, and has been hiding in there ever since."

"What did Victoria say about this? Surely you asked her!"

"Yes, I did ask her if there had been any improper behavior by Blake, and every time I asked, her response was the same. She burst into tears without a single word of explanation. I failed to discover what happened. I suspect he compromised her, or perhaps engaged in another inappropriate behavior. Afterwards, he disappeared from town, I suspect in an attempt to avoid her and her family. By now, I assume he found someone more to his liking, or perhaps a lady with more fortune. "

Richmond fussed with folding his paper and laid it on the table, cleared his throat, and presented Darcy with a grin. "You could solve Victoria's problem."

When it came to his daughter, his uncle wanted a titled husband for Victoria in order to elevate the status for any child and grandchildren born to her. Darcy knew, as an heir to a dukedom, Blake fit the requirements. Victoria would be a duchess and her son would one day be a duke. The entire Fitzwilliam family would rise in the social circles. Lord Cheswick preferred achieving a higher social standing to riches as long as it did not detract from his own fortune.

Brandon, at thirty, had married the daughter of another earl, bringing considerable money into the marriage and a house in London. However, five years after their union, they remained childless, leaving Richmond as the heir presumptive. Although the five-year wait was not unusual for the Fitzwilliams, the couple had hope.

"I was sorry to hear about your second place finish for the stallion," the earl said.

Darcy shook his head. Bingley has no idea the problems he has caused. Did everyone lay down money on me? "Did you lose much?"

"No. I bet on Lord Blake. He always won the competitions when you two were at Cambridge."

"Oh!"

"Do not be daft, boy. I most certainly did place a rather large wager on you!"

"Now, Winnie, do not tease Fitzwilliam." Lady Cheswick glared at her husband. "I am sure he tried his best. Golf is not his game."

"If he wished not to be teased, he should have won. Darcy, please enlighten me as to who exactly is this Mr. Kent"

"He is from Leicestershire. The five of us attended school together and became friends."

"Who is his father? Who is his mother?"

"I believe Kent's parents died years ago. In fact, all of us had lost our mothers before we met in Cambridge, and that loss bonded us together--young men without their mothers to civilize—

"Civilize you?" the countess asked.

"Yes, exactly." Darcy nodded his head and smiled to his aunt.

"Who is his family?" The earl tapped the table with his finger. "I am unaware of anyone of importance by that name. You have been friends with Mr. Bingley for years, and you know I have never been pleased with that relationship. His family comes from trade."

"As does Mr. Kent's family, father." Brandon said and then snickered. "Darcy is expanding his friendships downward."

Sighing, the earl set down his silverware. "Darcy, we need to talk seriously about your choice of friends. Even Lord Blake is a problem; he is not welcome here. You know the Duke of Charnwood is nearly bankrupt."

Darcy furrowed his brow and glowered at his uncle through tiny slits.

"Mr. Bingley is headed in the right direction. He purchased the estate, I understand.

"He was uncomfortable purchasing it with so little information, so he leased it for now."

"Well, that is wise. He has no experience in estate business. Humph. I doubt he will succeed." The earl tapped his chin with his loosely balled fist and then pointed to Darcy. Now Mr. Rawlings is only a second son and quite rebellious, if I recall correctly.

"Richmond is a second son. I count him as a friend as well as a cousin, even though he, too, has been unruly at times."

Richmond scoffed and then returned to hiding behind his paper.

"He is family," the earl said. "You cannot help your connection to him. I would like you to befriend men of superior consequence. You must broaden your social connections. Upwards. Surround yourself with others like us. Otherwise, the friends you keep now will drain you. Heed my words, boy."

Darcy did not choose to argue this morning. If experience proved true, any further debate on the subject would be unsuccessful. Knowing any dissension on his part would merely keep the lecture going, he allowed his uncle to expound his views until the subject was exhausted.

"When do you leave for the country, uncle?"

"Soon. Why do you not join us? The winter season is so dull. With our home so close to Pemberley, Georgiana could spend time with Victoria. She has been most helpful to our girl.

"Georgiana is remaining in town, as am I." Darcy crinkled his nose when taking a bite into his pastry. *These are definitely not as tasty as the cook's treats at Netherfield Park.*

"Well, then, perhaps Victoria can remain in town with her. Oh, yes, I must ask a favor before it slips my mind." When Darcy raised his brows, the earl continued, "Would you escort Victoria to the theater Tuesday? She has expressed an interest in the new play at the Lyceum."

"I have no plans for that night, and it would be a pleasure for me as well. I have not had any superior entertainment in a while. Do you know what is playing?"

"The Rivals."

Darcy sighed. *I am not interested in a romantic play.* "Perhaps the theater at Covent Gardens might be a better choice. I believe Venice Preserved is playing there."

"No. Georgiana has mentioned how they both would like to see this play. It is a comedy and she needs to laugh and smile." The earl leaned forward, and with a scowl, added. "I must also ask that no one else attend with you, especially none of your friends. We need to bring Victoria out slowly, and I do not want her upset. Can I count on you to help her?"

Darcy nodded.

The earl settled back in his chair. "Shall you stay for dinner? I would enjoy spending the day in intelligent conversation. I am interested in the competitions, and am anxious to hear more. And if necessary, I believe the Fitzwilliams can supply you with enough challenges. I heard talk of a new billiards game?"

"Twenty points and my friend Bingley conceived the game."

The earl grinned. "There is no competition I cannot win. All it takes is a little sacrifice, and knowing when to make the winning move. I will defeat you, or my name is not Winthrop Fitzwilliam."

"Uncle, perhaps both Georgiana and I can attend dinner another day. I have plans for tonight; nonetheless, I think I have the time to demonstrate my superior skill at Twenty Points. Are you positive you wish to part with a few guineas? I lost the stallion with a golf club, although I assure you I am formidable with a cue stick."

"We shall see, boy. Now, I wish to offer you a consolation prize to ease your pride in the loss of the Andalusian. Before you arrived, my favorite wine arrived from the Cigar and Wine Shop. I insist you allow me to send over a few bottles. Georgiana has taken a liking to it."

"Why would I decline?"

"I admit my failing to be completely loyal to England. The wine is from the homeland of Le Petit Caporal. I know you have chosen not to patronize anything French at this time. Regardless, they do make the best wine." His uncle winked as he finished his coffee before they left for the billiard room where the earl's sons had sped ahead.

***

Dinner at Wolverley House began precisely at eight. Lord Wolverley was a punctual man, and expected everyone else to be equally so. Rawlings had made it a habit never to be late when his father sent for him, and so he entered the dining room at the exact time requested. He was jolted with the hostility enveloping the room. "No need for a blaze today. The looks you are throwing at me have enough fire to heat half of London."

"Gerald, be seated."

Rawlings nodded to his father and took his seat, sighing loudly as he dropped into the chair. He suspected the meal would not go well, his first visit since his return from Netherfield Park. At least the wine glass is full. His father, along with his elder brother, sat at one end of the table, with him at the other.

"I am sorry you did not win the stallion. I understand it was a fine piece of horseflesh."

Rawlings agreed with a slight tip of his head, his mind racing. It is never good when my father starts out with a compliment. I wonder what it will be this time. Will he lecture me on my drinking, my friends, my lack of competition skills, or on my inaccessibility within the Ton?

Thomas coughed. "Brother, I would have fared better in the chess game, all the same I doubt if I would have bothered with the ram. Your friends are a bit odd."

Lord Wolverly earl dropped all discussion about the competition until the plates were full and he dismissed the servants from the room. He cleared his throat. "Gerald, I wish to speak to you about your friends." He held up an old Morning Post and pointed to an article about Kent, which revealed his background and how he nearly won the stallion. "I am seriously displeased that you are associating with tradesmen's' sons."

Rawlings grabbed his wine glass. "I did not know you read that sorry excuse for a newspaper. I was under the impression you only read The Times."

"Gerald!"

"I went to school with them."

"Yes, the worthless paper supplied that information. Now, Buxton told me about what happened yesterday. Did you really take tradesmen's sons to the Four Horse Club?"

"I invited my friends. They did not disguise their opinion and they treated them in a chilly, condescending manner, as if they were decidedly beneath their notice."

The earl slammed his fist on the table. "It was no more than they deserved. If you wish to resign from the club, do so. Driving is such a wasteful endeavor, and I have heard all about the wild behavior up at Salt Hill—drinking, gorging on food, and gambling beyond control. Now is the opportunity for you to surround yourself with more serious people."

Rawlings sighed. He had heard this before, although not as forcefully spoken as his father did this time. "You wish me to drop all my associations?"

"Do not be absurd. Lord Blake and Mr. Darcy are better choices, and I have no objection to your continued relationship with those two, even if the marquis's behavior is at times questionable. However, your so called friendship with the other two must end today!"

Rawlings sipped his wine while he readied his words and his strength. "You no longer have a say in my life." He returned his father's glare. "I shall choose my friends without regard to you or the society to which you belong."

The Earl pointed his finger at his son. "You have a duty to your family. You know who is acceptable, and who is not. Neither my name nor your brother's can be connected with them. I will not continue to allow you to spend your time with them."

Rawlings put the glass down and sneered at his father. "Why? Why are these men so unworthy to you?"

"We have discussed this many times." The earl shook his head. "Trades people are not honest, they only want you for your money or your connections, and they are probably reformists as well. They want to destroy the aristocracy and that means me. How many French nobles lost their heads?"

"Bah. Do not be so dramatic, father. We are English."

"Still, they wish to take over our lands and steal our wealth. They will not stop until they do." Releasing a long breath, he swallowed a forkful before sharing a smile with his son. "I want to help you make better decisions."

"Father, they have more wealth than I do."

Leaning forward, the earl glowered. "Do not damage your brother in such a way with these connections. If you are not careful, they will force their way into our clubs, our social life, and our business affairs, and who knows how low our standards will sink then."

"Perhaps they would be better at running the country than we have been, as well as all the other activities, including business." Leaning back in his seat, Rawlings smirked. "I know Kent and Bingley are better dancers, and both charm the society ladies quite well." With his attention turned to his plate, he ate the first bite of his dinner.

"They would risk any financial connection with you just to use it later to purchase a big estate and become a member of the gentry. The risk would be *your* fortune and *your* name. They have nothing to lose. They want to be us. "

"You mean gamblers, drinkers, and users of women?"

Slamming his hand down on the table, the earl raised his voice. "You will disconnect yourself."

"I will do as I please." Rawlings noticed his brother smiling at him. "You have your eldest son to play the puppet. When does he marry the fair Lady Christine, and when will it be announced?"

"The wedding is in four months. I expect you to attend."

Rawlings shook his head. "I will be out of the country."

"Where are you off to now?"

"America."

."What has gotten into you? First, you disappear to an unknown parish in the middle of nowhere, now America."

Thomas dropped his fork. "Brother, have you no self-respect left?"

"I plan on finding out what life is like in a classless society." Rawlings patted his lips with his napkin before raising his wine glass to his lips.

"There is no such ideal. They may not have a titled aristocracy; they do have classes. There will always be the distinctions between those with power and those without."

"Well, at least they will not show a penniless duke more respect than a wealthy entrepreneur."

"I forbid your leaving."

"I forbid you telling me what to do. I have my own fortune now."

Thomas cried out. "You mean Margaret's fortune, which would not have been yours had father not secured the marriage for you."

"He did no such thing."

"Yes, he did, my ignorant brother. She would not have you. You are just the second son, and she was after someone titled or rich."

"Like you." Rawlings unintentionally spit towards his brother.

"In her calculations, you were worse than any wealthy tradesman. She had no interest in a penniless second son."

"Stop," the earl yelled. "I will not have you two speak in this manner. This is not the place, nor do I ever wish to discuss what happened. You will not go to America, Gerald."

"Well, it seems this dinner is at an end." Rawlings stood, wiped his mouth with the napkin, and threw it on the table. "Unless you shoot me dead, I will be on the high seas soon." He marched out without a look back.

As he stood on the steps waiting for his carriage, Rawlings thumbed through a book on the American government he had purchased earlier.

"I did not know you were reading these days."

Rawlings snapped his head around at his brother's voice. "I have a long trip ahead. What do you want, Thomas."

"I need to talk you out of this madness. You cannot be serious about going overseas. Why would you go there?"

Rawlings smirked. "I am looking for a place where second sons can be just as important as first sons."

"Do not be such an addle brain. You only need to marry well, and there are many fine ladies available for the picking."

"Perhaps they are what you want—women using you for a title—making them a different sort of whore."

"Gerald. Perhaps your friends find you clever and witty, except to me you are just an ill-bred buffoon."

"Really? You think that? Well, then you should have offered yourself to Margaret. She would have loved your title."

"Do not twist my words, brother. She wanted Darcy, and she ended up with you, which explains why she was so angry that night. I do not understand why you switched rooms!"

"I needed the money, something you do not understand. I know you set Darcy up. Do you wish to confess your sins now?"

Thomas glared back with a wicked smile upon his face. He shrugged, offering no details.

Rawlings scoffed. "May your Christine be everything that Margaret was to me. My next wife will be someone entirely different than an ice maiden of London." He turned towards his brother and looked him in the eye. "Do not bother me again, Thomas. I hope I do not see you for a long time, perhaps even for the rest of my life. I would rather Kent or

Bingley be my brother." He slammed the gate so hard the gilded 'W' upon it shook before he stepped into his carriage and when he looked back his brother stood with his hands on his hips.

"Fool. You will learn the hard way which class of people has the power in this world." Thomas yelled.

Rawlings remained upset when he approached Darcy House. Feeling the need to shake off his premonition that the future was not as bright as it has seemed at Netherfield, he sought his friend's assurance that all would be well. When he arrived, he learned Bingley had shared dinner with the Darcys and had remained for drinks in Darcy's study.

"Good evening, Darcy, Bingley." Rawlings entered the room and instantly frowned when he noticed the serious mien of the two men.

Darcy stood and moved to the sidebar. "Brandy?"

Rawlings nodded.

Bingley sighed. "I thank you for yesterday, Rawlings. Neither Kent nor I expect you to resign from your club."

"Well, I lost my taste for it... or rather the members. I will be off to America shortly, and there is no telling for how long." Rawlings shrugged. "It is of little consequence to me."

Bingley presented him with a slight smile. "Kent suggested we start our own club."

"Perhaps when I return, we can discuss it. Let him know I will consider doing so, as we would surely beat their high-class breeches off. They would never race with us though. They could not afford to lose."

"You have our thanks, just the same."

After gulping down his brandy, Rawlings studied his friends and then chuckled. "What is the conversation tonight? Shall I guess?" Rawlings laughed at Darcy's scowl.

Bingley leaned back in his chair with his eyes directed at neither man. "I mentioned how much I delighted in the Hertfordshire trip. I enjoyed myself more than I ever thought possible and met many fine people."

Rawlings peeked over his brandy glass. "Many, Bingley?"

Bingley nodded. "Well, yes, true. A few are finer than others."

"Prettier too. When will you be going back?"

Bingley's shoulders slumped. "I doubt if I will go back. Darcy pointed out the problems with returning."

Rawlings clutched his glass. "Not return. Why not?" He glared at Darcy. "What is this about?"

"We were discussing the Bennets. I explained that Miss Bennet was merely acting upon her mother's instructions."

"And?"

"Miss Bennet is lovely, and was always polite and well mannered. Even so, I could not discern if her heart was touched by Bingley."

Rawlings glared at Bingley. "What did you think?"

He sighed, his gaze remained down. "She did enjoy our talks, still, it is true she was just polite."

"She gave you a scarf for the race, which is more than being *just* polite."

"I requested it. Darcy and I talked about that. It seems everything between us was at my insistence."

Rawlings moved to Bingley, placing his hand on his shoulder while sending a heated stare towards his other friend. "I disagree with Darcy. She seemed to like you in particular, Bingley." He softened his voice and squeezed Bingley's shoulder. "She is not a demonstrative person. You would be the only one to know how she felt."

"She never was more than polite." Bingley looked up and then shrugged.

"She is a polite girl," Rawlings countered.

Darcy cleared his throat and shook his head. "Her mother—

"Yes, what about her mother?" Rawlings asked.

Bingley slumped further into his chair while the other two men challenged one another. He leaned over and hid his face in his hands.

"Did you not see how she dressed her girls? It was despicable." Darcy said.

Rawlings caught his breath, took another swallow of brandy before returning to his chair. "I am sorry. Was it the quality of the material or the cut of the dress that has you so riled?"

"The cut of the dress! If it was cut much lower—"

Rawlings interrupted. "I beg to differ with you, Darcy. Our own dear Caroline Lamb and the rest of the Carlton House Set have shown more than the Bennets."

"Humph. She only did as her mother demanded, I am sure of it. Mrs. Bennet pushed her daughters on us all. Bingley is just too accepting." Darcy leaned back and crossed his arms.

"I do not understand the problem. If Bingley is happy, and you agree Miss Bennet shows him respect, then your ideals for a marriage have been met."

"Not all. She has nothing to bring into the marriage except her beauty."

"And her manners. They were impeccable. She is not a lively girl, Darcy." Rawlings turned to Bingley. "You must consider her character before you say she is not truly interested."

Bingley lifted his head. "She never, well, she never encouraged anything more than polite talk. Her mother was watching all the time. I think Darcy is correct. She is being forced towards me."

Rawlings moved to the sideboard and poured another drink, this time with twice the amount. The two other men declined when he offered to refill their glasses.

Without looking at Rawlings, Bingley swirled the whiskey remnants around in his glass "I do not wish to see Miss Bennet forced into a marriage in order to please me or her mother." He shook his head. "I could not bear living every day with someone that married me for security. Perhaps if I felt less for her, it would seem acceptable. I could not bear to have a marriage where the love existed on only one side, and I would loathe myself to see *her* compromise herself for me."

Rawlings glared at Darcy. "You are cruel to do this. It is his life, not yours."

"He needs to understand the ramifications of a loveless marriage, and one that does not bring either financial or social advancement to him. He has an unmarried sister, and his choice for a wife does matter."

"Miss Bingley would find her way. She should not be a part of this discussion."

"It is not a factor, Rawlings. I will not hurt Miss Bennet by making an offer she cannot refuse. With her dowry, she will be able to find someone more to her tastes."

"Dowry?" Rawlings tilted his head with his right eyebrow raised. Darcy merely shook his head and flashed a warning stare to him. Rawlings was not aware Miss Bingley had kept the Bennet loss from her brother. He presumed she did so because she believed her brother would have immediately proposed had he heard the news. She joked often about how as a child, he was always bringing injured kittens and puppies to the nursery. He would love them back to health.

"Well, I do not believe you, Darcy. Have you not learned anything from my marriage?"

"That is exactly what I am trying to save Bingley from—a loveless marriage arranged by a mercenary mother."

"Mrs. Bennet is not the most mercenary mother by far. In fact, she waited until her girls showed an interest, and not the other way around. And if she was mercenary, she would have foisted a daughter on you or me. As I recall, she never pushed any girl your way. In fact, I believe Mrs.

Bennet could not stand the sight of you. That is not the definition of a mercenary mother."

"Did you not see their dresses? Did you not see what they displayed?"

"Yes, a mere suggestion of nipple. So? I found it quite seductive. And besides, you could only catch a glimpse when they exhaled and their skin separated slightly from their gown. Is this what you are referring to?"

"Yes, precisely. She put her daughters on display as if they were—"

"Whores. No, they are not. They revealed only a sliver, not so uncommon should you take the time to notice. The ladies of the *Ton* do so all the time. I suspect they even emphasize them somehow. Why is it you have just noticed this about the ladies. Whose nipple were you looking at?"

Bingley's gasped. "You were looking at Miss Bennet, Darcy?"

"No." Darcy scoffed.

"No, Bingley, he had no interest in *her* nipple. I myself fancied a younger one. She exhaled often, and I was able to discern it was quite pink." Rawlings turned to Darcy. "Bingley will tell you that this is not the first one he has spied from a neckline."

"Rawlings can we change the subject." Darcy said, blushing.

"Bingley, make up your own mind." Rawlings gulped his drink and slammed it down on the table. "I have had my fill of the machinations of higher society. I know my way out." Rawlings left before either man could object.

Bingley fidgeted in his chair. "What if you are wrong, Darcy? Would I not be also hurting her if I do not return?"

"You will have to do exactly as Rawlings said. Make up your own mind. I gave you my views; he gave his. Now *you* must decide. Since you are the only one who ever spoke to her alone, you would know if she gave you that special look or treated you differently than us. I am just saying I did not see any indication she favored you."

Bingley drank his whiskey slowly. After he was finished, he informed Darcy he would see him the next week. He did not wish to be rash in his decision.

Darcy stirred the fire and thought about the many different looks Jane had given to Bingley. Could I be wrong? Could she care for him?

His thoughts drifted away from Miss Bennet to her sister. He imagined her eyes sparkling in merriment at the squirrel burying the nut. The remembrance of a lavender scent that he had noticed at Netherfield

Park filled his nostrils and then again when he had his lone dance with her. Images of the supper at the ball invaded his thoughts, and he felt a desire to pull her into his chest and kiss the top of her head, banishing all of her embarrassment.

Absentmindedly, he continued to stir the fire as his thoughts drifted to the other members of the Bennet family: the absent father, the scheming mother, the silly flirtatious younger sisters and then finally, the dishonest uncle in Cheapside.

"Impossible. I cannot attach myself to them."

Chapter Five

Blake studied the guest his father had invited, and found himself, for once, in agreement—she was definitely beautiful. Her hair was dark, although in his mind, not dark enough. It was also straight, which was another problem. He preferred to see bobbing curls brushing his neck. Blake maintained his blank epression. Who was responsible for suggesting a man prefers a woman with no thoughts of her own? He did admire her figure. Her gown displayed it expertly with the most expensive silk, and her neck sparkled form the jewels, large and pretentious. He imagined seeing a simple red cross around *her* neck and scoffed.

The Duke of Charnwood introduced his son.

"Lady Eleanor, it is a pleasure to meet you." Blake bowed, keeping his focus on her as she performed the perfect curtsey. She did not raise her eyebrow in silent inquiry, nor present him with a mischievous little smile. Her expression appeared as blank as models in the fashion magazines. Perhaps if they hired better artists, the women would show a little emotion on their faces. His father nudged him to escort her into the dining room. He stepped closer and detected a delicate fragrance about her. Wrong flower, my dear. You cannot win me with jasmine.

Blake offered his arm, and once she accepted, they fell behind his father. When His Grace glanced back at him, he nodded and he responded by presenting the same vacant look his partner did. Blake chuckled with sufficient volume to cause everyone nearby to turn.

"I beg your pardon, I was—

His father interrupted. "Enough, son. Let us sit."

They found their places at the table and waited for His Grace to signal the footmen to pour the wine.

***

As the final hour ended, the door to Darcy's house opened to find an inebriated Lord Blake standing on the step. The butler blocked him from entering.

"I need to speak to Mr. Darcy."

"My master is not available." Again, he put his body in such a way as to blocked the entrance.

"I demand a word with him."

"Sir, perhaps you should return home. Mr. Darcy will contact you in the morning."

Blake rose to his full height and glowered down at the butler. "I insist you announce me immediately. Inform him a problem has arisen that requires immediate resolution."

"My orders were explicit, sir. *You* are not to be admitted, not tonight nor any time, until further notice."

"Tell your master I need to speak to him now!" Blake pushed his way into the house, his hands clenched into fists. He glared at the servant, challenging him to touch his body in any way.

"Very good, sir. Please wait here." The man pointed to the chair in the entrance hall as he moved swiftly to inform Mr. Darcy of his unexpected visitor.

When Darcy arrived shortly thereafter, Blake stood to greet him, expecting a welcome smile from an old friend, instead he gasped at the furrowed forehead and downturned mouth. He noticed the glower aimed in his direction, but before the marquess could speak, Darcy landed a right fist along his jaw.

"Throw him out," he shouted to Geoffries, whose feet seemed frozen in place and appeared as stunned as the gentleman lying on the floor was shocked.

Blake propped his body up on one elbow. "What the hell this is all about, Darcy!"

Darcy walked away, stopping only to instruct his man to kick him out if need be, when Blake yelled in his loudest voice—

"Do not turn your back on me. I demand to know what my sin is to deserve such a greeting. I will call you out if need be."

"Ah." Darcy turned to the man stretched out the floor. With both his hands held ready to perform bodily damage and every muscle in his body taut, Darcy stepped closer to Blake. His neck muscles remained tense as he stood over him.

"I beg you to explain what happened. What is my sin? If I am to put to right this alleged wrong, then you must divulge the reason for this sudden aversion to me. I insist!"

"As you wish. Take Lord Blake to the study." Darcy barked as he turned to his butler. "You are to return in one hour, and unless I say otherwise at that time, you will throw the blackguard out and never let him grace my house again. Bring as many men as you might need. Big men. Mean men."

The butler assisted Blake to his feet and grabbed his arm.

Darcy quickly reached the study and held the door open for them. "Throw him in the chair over there. No need to be gentle."

Blake collapsed into the seat, gasping for air.

"Are you drunk?" A startled Darcy bellowed when he heard a hiccup. "This is unlike you."

Blake groaned. He slumped further down in the chair, resting his forehead upon his hand.

"Breathe deeply. I want you alert when I charge you with your despicable behavior. And it is despicable, I assure you. I want you sober when you are tossed out like this morning's refuse."

Blake's breathing was heavy, his eyes moist. "I am going to become a monk."

"Humph. I heard this pronouncement every time you had a problem with either a lady or her parents." He poured himself a whiskey. "All this time you treated me as a fool! Do not show such false pretense with me."

"You are wrong, Darcy. I do not understand at all. You caught me off guard, and I cannot recall a single action of mine that would cause such a reaction."

"I am tired and weary of men like you. Why must your breed always find their way to my doorstep? You may have the family name and even wealth, unlike another person I shall not mention, but you are both rakes." Darcy spit out the words before dropping into his chair. He fixed his stare on the man sitting across from him.

Blake leaned forward, his hands on his knees. "I implore you to please just tell me what you have been told. I assure you I do not deserve this... impertinence."

"What do you say about your dealings with Lady Victoria Fitzwilliam? I have heard the most immoral accusations."

Blake sat upright. "Victoria? What about Victoria?"

"Lady Victoria or I shall thump you again?"

"Yes, of course, Lady Victoria. What do you believe happened? I will share with you my story if you first tell me exactly what is it that you think I did." Blake waited, and when Darcy did not respond, he said, "Now I am the one not to be trifled with, because only a falsehood made against me would cause you to behave so boorishly."

"Boorishly? I will defend my cousin no matter who harms her. Tell me you did not use your *bloody charm* to trifle with her feelings." Darcy bent forward, grabbed the chair arms, his body slightly raised and his face drew near to Blake's. "Blast it, Blake, tell me the truth."

"Trifle – I did not trifle. Is that what you heard? Then Lady Victoria is no lady."

"Be careful, Blake," Darcy squeezed the arms. "A pummeling would do you good."

Blake massaged his chin. "You are wrong. It will not help me at all. So what exactly did I do to Lady Victoria?"

"Trifled with her feelings, broke her heart and then moved on to your next victim—I know it all—first, Lady Victoria, and then, Miss Elizabeth. Why do women fall for rogues like you? You and your father are nothing more than scoundrels."

"Miss Elizabeth, did you say? How is she involved with my affair with Lady Victoria?"

Darcy jumped up. "I was correct. You did trifle with Victoria." He stood over Blake. "I shall send you from this house immediately!"

"Darcy, calm down, calm down. I will tell you the truth if you are willing to hear my side." Blake leapt from his chair. The two men glared unblinking at each other. A spark from the fireplace sputtered towards them, breaking their gaze.

Blake kept his eye focused on Darcy who had relocated to his familiar, comfortable spot – the window overlooking the courtyard. His body remained taut. Blake spied his own image reflected in the glass.

Blake rushed to the side table and poured a brandy. He needed fortification, not to aid him against Darcy, but against himself.

Darcy called out while maintaining his stance looking out the window. "Did you name a horse Cheswick after her as well?"

"No, I did not. What has caused you to be so angry, Darcy? Ask any question about Lady Victoria. I will tell you anything you want, since I have done nothing that I am ashamed to reveal."

Darcy turned to Blake. "Tell me about your flirtations with Lady Victoria."

"Would you be willing to listen to the *whole* story and not interrupt or attempt to pummel me?" Blake chuckled. "I will defend myself next time you try."

Darcy nodded, and with his hand pointed to the chairs, inviting Blake to sit. Darcy accepted the scotch poured for him as they sat across from each other. Blake waited. Darcy sipped a small amount, set the glass down, and crossed his arms. "Go on."

"Well, my father is a failed and broken man. Yes, I admit it. I had to remain silent as he plundered the family vault, sold items secretly to pay for his gambling, and even his seductions and debaucheries. Were you aware he keeps several mistresses?"

"No. I did spot him with inappropriate women at times and I am fully cognizant of his habits at White's." Darcy relaxed his shoulders slightly, although his arms remained crossed.

"Well if it was just White's it would be a simpler problem. He has racked up gambling losses in White's, Waiter's and even at lowly Crockford's. Do you know what it is like to belong to such a family? No, do not answer. I am as well aware of your background as you are of mine."

"I suppose there is probably more to this story than the bare facts my cousin revealed. All he indicated was that you trifled with Victoria's feelings, left her broken hearted. He implied that you had compromised her at Almack's. Is there more?"

Blake nodded.

Darcy held up his hand, moved to the door, and informed his servant that under no circumstances were they to be disturbed. He returned to his chair and encouraged him to continue.

While he composed his thoughts, Blake stared at the glass as he swirled his brandy.

Darcy tapped Blake's arm and spoke in a half whisper. "Please, go on. I promise to hear you out completely before I pass any more judgments."

"Thank you, I do not ask for more." Blake lifted his head, leaned back into the chair. "Where was I? Oh yes, my family. When my mother passed away twelve years ago, my father—who to my knowledge had remained true to her; however, I could be wrong—took up companionship with an actress. An *actress*, Darcy. She connived to gain jewelry, bonds, a house, a carriage and continued to bleed him dry. He gambled at her direction. I suppose my father was grieved; I believe he truly loved my mother."

Darcy whispered, "Yes, I am sure he did. I remember your mother, and how your father doted on her."

Blake sipped his brandy. He slumped in his chair. "Father was a typical eldest son that inherited great wealth—arrogant and selfish to all his wants and needs. This is the way with every eldest son, with Bingley the possible exception."

"Excuse me, Blake. You find me arrogant?"

"Yes, you are. You come and go as you please. You look down on anyone not of your circle. Think about how you treated the society in

Meryton. I do not care. You have a right and good reason to be proud of your heritage and to be aloof to those beneath you. I understand your attitude better than most; these people generally only speak to you to gain favor. They always want something. If not money, it is the connection. I fear the day my father discovers I partnered with tradesmen. My God. He despises them. All my life, he berated them. Called them scoundrels and cheats. He has not let a tradesman on our property. I digress; allow me to continue with my story."

"Please do."

Blake glanced at Darcy, caught his breath, and mumbled, "What should I say?"

"The truth," he answered.

"As I said, my father spent years gambling away the family fortune. He has not the talent for creating wealth, just spending what already existed. Many of his tenants left for the cotton mills and other industries in the country months ago. They have, in a few cases, improved their lots and in others fared much worse." Blake paused and then stared at Darcy. "You have faced the competition for the laborers, I assume?"

"I have. Please continue."

"Very well, I know this cannot be delayed. We are near bankruptcy as Rawlings suggested. My father married off my dearest, sweetest sister to a viscous Austrian commoner. Of course, he obtained a fortune for her hand and no doubt, it was extensive. I suppose in my father's mind, daughters could marry anyone if there was a large enough fortune. My father is more selective for me. Well, the Austrian received a pound of flesh for every pound given to my father. Did you know she died last summer?"

Darcy shook his head and sat quietly while Blake composed himself.

"No one was permitted to visit her. I suspect the secrecy was to conceal her bruised and broken body. Her husband monitored all her letters, incoming and outgoing. Her maid snuck word to me, still it was too late, or perhaps my knowing was the reason my sweet sister succumbed to the final beating. At least she endures no more pain or misery." Blake sunk further into his chair

Darcy gripped his arm. "I am most sorry for your loss, Blake."

Blake nodded. "Well, the money kept us afloat for quite a while. When my brother Edward married Miss Thornsby, as arranged for him, cash appeared. Yes, money can be made through land, trade, banking, industry and marriage. Again, my father cares not the pedigree for his younger children, only the fortune. Madeline was at least of like mind. She, a baron's daughter, thought she was marrying up. Unfortunately, now she has no funds to spend on gowns, jewelry, or balls. My wonderful younger brother spends more on his mistresses than on her and what he does not spend, my father does. He follows father around as close as a shadow attached to his feet. Margaret has the social connection she wanted. I often wonder how she likes her arrangement now. My family is incapable of making money, except through marriage. I suppose you can figure out where this is heading?"

"I suspect Victoria was to be your arrangement? She possesses a grand fortune."

"Before we get that far in my story, let me explain a little about me, well, maybe just a little. At Cambridge, I studied hard and I tried to fashion myself after the most successful students. You were one. I noticed how everyone always treated you with the greatest respect, although many feared you as well. That fear was due to your wealth and standing in society. One bad word, one cut from you, and many trying to improve their status would lose their acceptance in the *Ton*. Overnight. Did you know that, Darcy?"

Darcy furrowed his brow, yet did not speak.

Shrugging, Blake continued. "I doubt if it ever crossed your mind. Well, I tried my best to be as you are—honorable in all your dealings, and desiring the truth above all else. You are my ideal of the best of men, even with your faults." Blake chuckled when he added, "We all have faults. Do not look so shocked."

Blake paused as the breath he inhaled caught in his throat. He strode over to the sidebar and poured yet another drink, which seemed to have no effect on his mental awareness. Darcy continued to wait. Blake stared at the fireplace and noticed the embers were growing dim. He tended the fire, collected his thoughts, and sent Darcy a slight smile as he returned to his seat.

"Yes, you did surmise correctly. He demanded I ally myself with Lady Victoria. You must believe me when I confess I did not want to do this. Yet, you know how it is in our society. Marriage agreements are made all the time. I was a coward, too. I had never gone against my father in my entire life. He can be quite formidable. They instill in us that we must honor our parents. No one ever adds to that commandment that we only need to honor them if they remain decent. Nevertheless, he said I was to marry a reputable lady from a respectable family and one with a fortune. He arranged for my introduction to Lady Victoria. With the thought that a marriage to her would make *you* my cousin, I agreed."

Darcy sat up, tightening his grip on his glass. "Go on, and I want the whole story, regardless of my earlier reactions."

Blake nodded. "I attended the same parties, balls, and every theater event. I presented myself to her family as a man in pursuit of marriage. Yes, I did everything in order to court, woo, and win Lady Victoria. She is beautiful, charming, and worthy. Believe me when I say this. At no time did any improper actions take place between Lady Victoria and myself. Not one kiss, not one misleading word, not even a hint of impropriety. Once, I stood a little too close to her at Almack's and cast my gaze over her body in suggestive manner. That was my worse offense. There was one problem, however."

"And that was?"

"One day I asked myself what you would do in this case. You understand, I had no desire to actually marry her. Lady Victoria is a pretty, young girl. She has acquired all of societies' requirements of what a lady should be. Please stay calm. You may not like what I say next."

Blake waited until Darcy nodded.

"I find her shallow and empty headed, and with not a single thought beyond anything she reads in the fashion magazines or society pages of the newspapers. I want more than this from a wife. She admires all the wrong people, merely because of their status." Blake paused and composed his thoughts. "Like my father for instance. I no longer hold him in high esteem contrary to you and your family. In fact, as the Duke of Charnwood, everyone does. No one cares that he has ruined the family and brought us to near bankruptcy. The situation has become so horrid now; perhaps we have even lost that."

Darcy looked away as he recalled his uncle's admission the previous day.

"Well, lately I would rather a tradesman was my father than him. Perhaps then, I would have been used to veiled disgust thrown my way. In the end, I told Lady Victoria the truth. I did not love her, and I only courted her because my father deemed the alliance desirable. I even told her he was after her money. I swear to you, I never desired her fortune. I am only guilty of being a dutiful son. Now hate me, if you will, for disappointing her dreams. It was done for the best. Lady Victoria needed to know the truth, and one day, I pray she may just find the right person. It is not me."

After a moment's pause, he leaned towards Darcy. "What was this you said regarding Miss Elizabeth? You alluded that I was trifling with her."

"I was wrong. Forgive me, Blake, about my accusations concerning Victoria. Miss Elizabeth is a different story. You pursued her and, yet, you concealed your designs. You would not admit to me what your plans were, leaving me to doubt your intentions were honorable. Until this moment, I had suspected you wanted an arrangement that did not include marriage. Why did you hide your intent from me and lead me to think ill of you? You did it deliberately, and it caused me no end of worries."

"First, what I do is truly none of your business, nor is Miss Elizabeth under your protection. It was you who was causing no end to my worries. I was desperate for you to remain disinterested and allow my ruse to work. I had forgotten how you take responsibility for your particular friends and acquaintances. Sometimes, Darcy, you overstep your authority and take charge when it is not appropriate, whether it is Cambridge or Netherfield Park. To answer your question, and I did agree to be truthful and forthcoming, my father was the reason for concealing my attachment to her."

"Oh?"

"If one single whisper about my attentions to Miss Bennet reached his ears, he would have arrived in Meryton with the purpose of badgering her to seek her future elsewhere. He would threaten her in any way he found to be successful. I refused to place her in that situation. He can be most formidable."

"I do not think she would have cowered from him."

"You do not appreciate how vicious he can be. If she proved unmovable, he would hurt her family. Mr. Bennet is not, shall we say, commanding. No, he could not withstand the demands of a duke pounding at his door. My father would do anything to stop the marriage. Even her seven thousand pound dowry would have been deficient for him, not to mention her lack of those connections he deems necessary for his heir. Neither connections nor fortune matter to me. I had to maintain a sort of duplicity; my pretense protected her. I required that no one believed I would pursue marriage. I only thought of her, and I care not what anyone thinks about me. Let them call me a scoundrel or rake or any other disrespectful name. I know the truth, and when we wed, all suspicions would have disappeared."

"I witnessed how attentive you were to her and how she responded. I am surprised you did not express your intentions to her."

"We had plans to meet the day after Bingley's ball at a secluded spot, away from protective friends. Remember, you interrupted us on the balcony as I was about to reveal my feelings to her, and then you opened the door and I made alternate plans."

Darcy sensed the heat rising on his cheeks.

"I waited all day for her to arrive. I intended to offer marriage. I was ready to explain the situation with my father. I had hoped she would, with the blessing of her family, marry quickly, or even elope. Once done, my father would have little recourse. I would have even given up my title for her. I care not to be called Lord Blake if it meant she was my wife."

"Oh."

"I often dreamed she called me Robert. I do not believe titles were important to her. Of course, when my father dies, his title will go to me. Until then, I could be content to while away the hours in her company. I needed nothing else—not money, title, nor business."

"May I ask what happened?"

"She never came, so I went to Longbourn late that afternoon."

Darcy sat upright.

"She ran away from me. Her mother explained how she left for London with her father that morning to avoid something. Me. Blake's voice faded out on the last word.

Darcy opened his mouth, paused, and chose instead to hold his words back when Blake continued to speak.

"I had planned to propose marriage in front of her mother. She would not allow Miss Elizabeth to reject my offer. For the second time in my life, I was found to be unworthy."

"Second time?"

Blake nodded. "Lady Beatrice from Chesterfield."

"Oh."

"I never had the opportunity to propose to her either; a friend divulged my intentions to my father, and he immediately took charge. I refuse to forgive Lord Atterton for his officious behavior."

"What happened with Lady Beatrice?"

She did not have the fortune my father deemed necessary, hers was a mere twenty thousand pounds. He sought her out and informed her that she was not acceptable, and that he would never condone or approve the marriage. He threatened to take away my title and remove me from his home, without ever revealing my own holdings. He convinced her she would be better off seeking another. She had cared for me, but she sought security over happiness. My father threatened her family until they relented. Today, I am glad I did not offer for her. I was young and inexperienced. She turned out to be just like all the other

London social climbers. This is why I know what he would have done to the Bennets."

Darcy winced. He glared at the flames dwindling down and hurried to rekindle the fire. He pushed the poker around for several minutes.

Blake interrupted the silence. "It is all for naught."

"Are you positive she would refuse you if you spoke directly to her?"

"Yes. There can be no other explanation. She clearly understood the reason for meeting me the next morning."

"You may be wrong. Why not seek the truth from her? If she is in town, what keeps you from seeking her out?"

"I assumed she discovered my family situation, and then coupled with her own financial loss, I suspect she just avoided having to give me an answer. I had never revealed my personal wealth. I have broken off any connection with her, and I do not wish to see her again."

"I have doubts about her running away. I witnessed how she gazed upon you whenever you entered the room and how delighted she was when you two spoke."

Blake held up his hand. "Do not say another word about her."

Darcy approached him, and placed his hand upon Blake's shoulder.

"By your expression, Darcy, you appear to want to ask me something further. Is there anything else you need to know?"

"I would still like to call you friend. Will you call me one as well, even though I know I do not deserve the name?"

Blake saw the sincerity in his countenance and quickly nodded. He massaged his chin. "I hope never to be in fight with you again. You should have chosen boxing as your game."

His servant returned precisely one hour later; Darcy waved him away and then turned to Blake, "Why did you come here tonight?"

"To report to you that my father is demanding I drop all association with Kent and Bingley."

"Is he aware of the alliance?"

"Not that he said. He did read about the games in the newspapers, which identified Bingley and Kent and their backgrounds. I swear my father was mad, almost insane, at the mere thought I would attach myself to tradesmen. He belittled them ever since I was a toddler. He calls them cheats and liars to their faces. He hates tradesmen of any sort. And that was not the only issue that upset him; he had heard rumors of my attraction to someone there. He was adamant even before the ball that I return home and then after someone passed along a report I had danced the Waltz, his demands became more threatening. He was anxious to introduced me to this new lady he had arranged for me. She is a wealthy woman who fits his criteria for a perfect match."

"What will you do?"

"I decided to ignore my father and create my own fortune. I needed the thirty percent I won. I demanded it because I thought only of her. I wanted to give her a dukedom. I wanted all the things wealth could provide. I wanted to see her in the jewels and gowns a duchess should wear. I did not want anyone to speak ill of her. She... "

"But you said you had sufficient wealth."

Blake sighed. "When the heir to a dukedom makes an offer of marriage, everyone expects it to be backed up with enormous wealth. I could not bear seeing Miss Elizabeth as a future duchess living in a small country estate. I wanted to offer her more, much more."

"Will you be leaving our alliance?" Darcy asked, his voice shaky.

"No. Even now, even without her, I understand how important it is to support my title with wealth. I always comprehended what duty and obligation involved, at least in my mind. Now I am acutely aware what the responsibility embodies. This is why I will remain a partner and do so without regard to or complaint about the tradesmen's sons." He hesitated. "Mingling in business is just not done. My estate is producing well enough, but even you fear for the future. Trade may be beneath us, yet it can be good and honorable."

Darcy nodded. "Bingley and Kent are perfect examples of that presumption."

"I understand you would prefer not to be involved with tradesmen, and as such, must conceal the partnership from our peers. We are above them, and that is what makes this so difficult. Listen, Darcy. I warn you, I cannot withstand much more adversity."

"And the lady your father selected for you?"

"Oh, and I will not marry this latest dressed up bag of coins. That is definite. Unless I find another woman as worthy as Miss Elizabeth Bennet, I will not marry at all.

Chapter Six

Bingley approached the Somerset House, home of the Royal Society, where James Watt was attending a meeting of its members or Fellows as they called each other.

In 1660, the crown and parliament had sanctioned the *Royal Society of London for the Improvement of Natural Knowledge*, now known as The Royal Society. All great men of science belonged to it and shared their current successful pursuits, and on occasion, their failures as well. The Society met weekly where the members met to discuss the exciting discoveries of the day or serve as witnesses to experiments.

He imagined his uncle standing in front of all these other men of knowledge expounding on the future benefits of steam. He could not hold back the chuckle at the, thought of how his uncle could ramble about any subject.

Standing in front of the generously proportioned building with its copious windows, he imagined what it must have been like when it was the home of the Queen many years ago or when lavish parties and entertainments for the royal court here. He had heard many stories about the goings on. He surveyed the massive neoclassical palace that housed the Navy Board and the three principal learned societies: the Royal Society, the Royal Academy of Arts, and the Society of Antiquaries.

Entering the door on the east side of the building, Bingley climbed the staircase where upon reaching the top he tried to remember which apartments were used by the Royal Society and which were occupied by the Antiquaries.

"Sir, may I direct you?" A well dressed, yet somewhat disheveled, gentleman appeared. His arms were full of papers and journals of which any number of them was ready to tumble to the floor.

Bowing, Bingley said, "Royal Society, kind sir. May I help with those?"

"I am heading that way." The gentleman pointed to the left with his head as he handed a couple of the journals to the young man.

The two men moved to the left leading to the meeting room. Bingley opened the door allowing the scholarly fellow to proceed in first. Once inside, he abruptly stopped to glare in awe of the room. Perched along the back wall a man sat on a throne-like chair and directly in front of him stood a long bench filled with strange looking objects. Apparently, Bingley thought, there is to be an experiment today. Rows of benches, similar to the pews in church adorned each side of the room, filled with a wide variety of men. A few were dressed in the highest fashion, others, without regard to the latest cut of the clothes or tie of cravat.

Two rows of portraits of distinguished looking men hung on the walls of the oversized room and the many chandeliers' light highlighted a clear view of their images clearly. He recognized several men in the paintings, including the uncle he had come to see; 'however, most of the subjects were nameless faces of men of a different era.

Bingley handed the journals to someone who had quickly come to aid them. Now empty-handed, he searched the attendees for his uncle until he spotted him sitting alone in the third row. James Watt, at that exact moment, turned towards him and waved him over. Bingley joined him as the presentation commenced, not aware of the subject under discussion. The topic was unknown to him and he did not understand what was happening. However, his uncle was enthralled and did not speak for a full hour until the experiment ended and the presenter spoke the final word. Uncle and nephew snuck away for refreshments and conversation at a coffee shop located not far from the Royal Society.

"Did you see those strutting peacocks, walking around as if they were true men of knowledge? Bah."

"Pardon me, uncle? I do not follow you."

"I beg your pardon, my boy. When Sir Joseph Banks became president, he allowed wealthy amateurs full membership along with their pretentiousness filling the air and subjecting the true Fellows to unquestionable drivel and poppycock.Sir Joseph thinks we need patrons. I know we do, my boy, we do. Allow them to think they are equal? We will never do that regardless of our need for money." Watt caught his breath. "None of us is able to conduct our experiments without a great deal of money. The presentation today will cost too much for any poor man of science to cover. Fortunately, there was no drivel spoken today; today a man of knowledge conducted the experiment. Did you understand what he did? No, well he was demonstrating the possibility of an electric light. So many patrons believe gas will light the world, instead I prefer to think it will be electricity. Then again, Ben Franklin championed that concept and expounded upon it in his letter to the

Lunar Society." Watt paused and gazed at his nephew. "Beg your pardon. I do go on sometimes. Why did you wish to see me today?"

"Now that you have mentioned the Lunar Society, Uncle James, I... would... like..."

"Charles, take a breath. Spit it out, boy. You have not spoken so slowly since the first time you gazed upon a young lady with a man's mind.

"I would like to bring Lord Blake and Mr. Darcy to your next Lunar Society meeting. I understand you will be holding it in London this month."

"Did you say you want to bring gentlemen to the meeting?"

"Yes, sir. Lord Blake and Mr. Darcy. They are my friends."

"I have heard you often refer to Mr. Darcy. I do not recollect a single mention of Lord Blake." Watt studied his nephew's reaction. "I fear the other three members may object. You know we are a bunch of old Whigs! I am positive they are Tories."

"We do not discuss politics. Not since our Cambridge days. Mr. Darcy and I are friends I assure you, sir. Lord Blake may at times be conscious of his higher standing; still, he has never shown anything other than friendship to me."

"You were in an educational environment, where the barriers between students are often blurred. You know, Charles, men born of rank are not always willing to socialize with those below their station. Will he not look down upon my group? We are not of the nobility, nor are we estate owners. We do not belong to those circles."

"Lord Blake has never shun or cut me at any ball or other social function. Lately, we have all been together at Netherfield Park."

"Oh, yes, I read about the competition, and I was prudent not to wager on my own family member."

Bingley lowered his head to conceal a fast spreading blush he felt was rising on his cheeks.

Watt grinned. "You know, my boy, I may risk funds on uncertain endeavors of scientific nature, but I never risk it on games of chance. Now tell me, what else occurred at your country home? You went there primarily on business, I recall; something about the rifle."

Bingley proceeded to explain what had transpired during his stay in Hertfordshire. He laid out the entire enterprise and the roles for each of the members. He announced they had signed agreements for a true partnership, and grinned when he revealed how desirable his friends had found the Baker rifle.

Watt remained quiet as Bingley spoke, occasionally smiling at the stories of the games, and even releasing a snort of pleasure at the description of tup running.

Bingley felt himself gradually transforming back into the quiet man with slumped shoulders, downturned lips he had become lately, and had assumed his eyes had grown as dull and lifeless as he saw the world. He could not push himself back to his old self. He did not try too hard.

"Who is she, Charles?"

"No one, sir."

"Nonsense. You are sporting that forlorn expression again."

Bingley sighed. "Her name is Miss Bennet. I am only dismayed because she did not return my feelings."

"I am sorry, my boy. I hope she was at least gentle when she turned you down."

"You mistake me. She did not turn me down since I did not make her an offer. I would never put her in an awkward position of that nature. I... respect her too much."

"Oh?"

Bingley sighed and returned to staring at an invisible point far away. "She is the most handsome lady of my acquaintance. She deserves a marriage to someone of higher status. She is a gentleman's daughter and possesses all the grace and beauty of a countess. I am nothing more than a tradesman's son."

"Perhaps you are mistaken in your understanding of her feelings. Her inclination may be aligned with yours?"

"I have little hope. I assure you, there is one unmistakable influence... her mother."

"Oh?"

"As my friend Darcy said, she is as mercenary as any huntress anywhere. She pushed her daughter towards me at every opportunity. Miss Bennet was always polite and never..."

James Watt fiddled with his cup of coffee as Bingley retreated even further into himself.

"Invite your friends to the next Lunar Society meeting, Charles. In particular, you should encourage Mr. Darcy to attend." Noticing his nephew's countenance had lightened and his grin returned with his approval, Watt patted his arm. "However, I warn you not to get your hopes up. I suspect they will be busy with a previous commitment or have ready another excuse for not attending."

"I believe they will come."

"Perhaps you should not mention it is a meeting, and just invite them to a dinner party."

***

Kent glanced around the area surrounding his Uncle Daniel's home. The streets were clean, the houses well maintained and the neighbors were all successful tradesmen. His uncle's home was near the Kent family warehouse in Cheapside. Kent's home, left to him when his parents died in the carriage accident, was a few houses further down the street. It was not a great house but a comfortable, well-kept home. One day, he promised himself, he would live on Grosvenor Street in a grand house with many servants, and then he would purchase his own Andalusian stallion to parade through Mayfair.

His father's will specified that his son could not take charge of the business until he was thirty, and demanded instead for his son to enjoy life before assuming the heavy burden of responsibility. Until then, his father's brother, Daniel, would manage everything. However, Kent, not a man who favored leisure over work, chose in its place to spend his free time working alongside his uncle in preparation for assuming his place, now only two years away.

The Kent family was on the rise with a significant fortune increasing daily. They all appeared to prefer working to leisure as they gathered strength from the business dealings and contracts made. A member of the Kent family dominated in every aspect of commerce: import, export, shipping, textiles, manufacturing, architecture, and most recent, transportation enterprises. A Kent was involved in the building of the canals and improvement of the roads after a family member had convinced the politicians of the necessity for upgrading the highways and the profitability of doing so. Ever since he and Darcy rode the *Catch Me if You Can* train, Kent recognized rail as the solution for the future of transportation, and had considered building his own line to Leicester.

In two years, Kent would inherit the largest of the family fortunes. His family referred to him as *the heir,* and since his position within the family was well known, every tradesman in England treated Kent with proper respect. He, in turn, maintained the honorable and trustworthy reputation his excellent father had established.

Throwing his shoulders back as he strode inside the house, Kent steeled himself for the coming arguments he knew his family would foist upon him. Tonight, he was dining with the most vocal believers of the reformation of society—his uncles, Daniel and Milton and their families.

Dinner discussions always turned into a heated debate over individual rights and the problems with class distinctions. Entering the parlor, he spied one of his uncles quickly approaching him.

"Good evening, Uncle Daniel." Kent bowed, relieved when he noticed his smile. Good! They have not yet begun their bickering.

"Good evening to you, Son. Pour yourself a drink. Your Uncle Milton is helping himself, I see." Daniel nodded his head towards the far wall, where two men stood—one older gentleman and one young man nearer his own age, his cousin Elliot.

He joined his uncle and poured himself a full glass of whiskey, just as Milton's eldest son slammed his glass down. "I do not want to think of commoners in complete control. They are unschooled and ignorant in the way of the world," Elliot shouted.

Kent leaned back and listened. He was in agreement with his cousin.

Uncle Milton poured his son another whiskey and shoved it to him. "Whigs do not want to go that far, Elliot. You must own property in order to participate."

"True." Elliot shook his head. "Yet the Tories have been in charge for a long time and have accomplished much. Are we not the world's greatest nation? Why do you not praise them for our standing in the world?"

"How the hell did I raise a son to be a Tory? And you…" Turning, Uncle Milton directed his stare at Kent. "Are you a one as well? My God, the word for outlaw in Ireland is Tory and they are right. Yes, sir, they do indeed steal from everyone."

Kent caught his breath and took a large gulp of his whiskey before responding. "I believe what Elliot says has merit. You must admit that the Tories have accomplished a lot." Kent offered his uncle a slight smile. "Forget the Irish. In Scotland, Whiggamore means raiding party! I suspect the Whigs do want to raid the Tories of their power."

The men held a staring contest as Uncle Daniel suggested they finish their drinks in comfortable chairs.

Taking his seat, Elliot crossed his legs and glared over the top of his glass. "Father, unlike you, I am not a Tory. I do not wish to destroy them."

Milton smirked. "No. You merely want to use them to elevate your own status. We have watched your ambition to become members of highest circles of society increase each year." He turned to Kent. "You are the same—just like your cousin."

Kent raised his brows. "Is that wrong? I wish to advance myself to a better life. I cannot find fault with it."

His cousin Elliot nodded in support.

"You two do not understand. They will never let you join."

Elliot sat tall in his seat, with his chin raised, imitating the same haughtiness he witnessed from many of his university friends. "All it takes is money. I plan to enhance my earnings in such a way that I will be rewarded by acceptance into their world. I will work with the Tories who will help me advance."

"They will use you, Son. They will take all your hard efforts and leave you with nothing. As I sit here today, I can guarantee you will never be invited into their world."

Kent cleared his throat. "Well, there are other ways to be accepted."

"Marriage? Do you speak of marriage?"

Kent nodded his affirmation.

Milton shook his head. "In order to obtain their acceptance, you would have to connect yourself to someone in the upper levels of society. They would never let their daughters marry a tradesman, mercantilist, or industrialist like ourselves. It is just not done."

"There are a few more open to inclusion of men of fortune. Many aristocrats are Whigs, is that not true? You cannot place all the blame on the Tories."

"Saving the plight of the poor and opening the doors to the Catholics is vastly different from bringing us into their homes."

"I am not poor, and I am not Catholic." Kent replied.

"No, and you are not gentry either."

"I will prove you wrong. I have made friends—"

"Bah. The men you have been associating with will leave you behind. They might occasionally include men such as yourself for activities such as this competition I read about. Tell me, have you been invited to their homes when they are hosting an important dinner?"

Kent remained silent.

"Have they introduced you to their marriageable sisters or cousins? Or do they keep you separate from that part of their world."

Again, Kent remained silent. An image of Miss Bingley sitting on a bench in a far away garden came to his mind. He had made a similar warning to her.

"You understand you are not on their level. They included you in a shooting party in a meaningless place; they allowed you to compete in their competition only because there was no opportunity for you to connect yourself to their families. And you did not win which cost us all a bag of coins."

"Lord Blake was the better rower."

"Do not tell such a falsehood, Kent. What was the meaning of letting him win? The papers were riddled with stories how you rammed into Mr. Darcy's boat. What did the Lord say to make you do his dirty work?"

"Bah! Blake won. If Darcy believed that he would have taken his revenge out with his fists. See, no bruises." Kent turned his head back and forth.

"I will never believe you, an experienced rower, lost. You gave it away. Did you enjoy leaving important work behind for your sojourn to the country for fun and games?

"Perhaps the trip to Meryton was not all leisure?"

"Ah ha! So they did bring their sisters! I must assume we can announce your engagement any day now."

"No. I referred to other opportunities."

"Nephew." Daniel glared at him. "Are you doing business with these men?"

Kent shrugged.

"Unless you have a signed contract protecting you, they will steal everything you own. Never do business with them. Always do business for them." Daniel tossed back the rest of his wine.

Milton added, "And even then you must understand that they may not pay on time, or if they are a member of the noble class, they may not pay at all." The two uncles laughed. "Remember you cannot bring charges against anyone in the House of Lords. They are above the law."

"You mean they are the law." The older men guffawed.

"I have no fear of my dealings with my friends. Even Lord Blake has invited me to his estate."

"For what, sport? Has he invited you to a ball? You need not answer. I see the truth on your face."

"I do not believe you understand the young people of today," Kent said, his voice rising. "This is the nineteenth century, and times have changed. Bingley and I attended Cambridge, their university. We were included in their group, and now in their business. And we will be invited in their social life as well. You are too old and cynical, Uncle."

Milton shrugged his broad shoulders. "I am just experienced. Hmmm. Business you say?"

"Yes, tell me more. Is there any way we can benefit?" Daniel asked. "Is this why you questioned me regarding trade laws?"

Kent relented, against his better judgment, and explained their plans.

Daniel, the uncle in import and export indicated there might possibly be honorable actions on the part of his nephew's young friends and agreed to help him.

Milton, remained silent, and Kent noted that his uncle was taking in every word as if he was trying to memorize the conversation. His manner so disturbed him that when the evening ended, Kent covertly followed behind him. Milton gave the address of a house on Grosvenor Square. Why would Uncle be going to see the Falcon? Kent processed this information, yet he could not come up with a satisfactory answer. He worried that he had revealed the alliance plans, but he was thankful he had held back on the global trading scheme. He vowed to discover more before he informed Darcy.

***

"Good Morning!" Rawlings announced as he sauntered into the breakfast room at Darcy House. In front of him were two men deep in conversation—Kent was talking, and Darcy listening with intensity.

"Join us! Did you just arrive?" Darcy asked as Kent nodded his acknowledgement.

"Straight from breakfast at Cavendish Square." Rawlings patted his pocket. "I have brought with me the signed contracts from Mr. Cuffage. What is the plan for today?

"Kent and I are headed out to view a few warehouses, meet with importers, and visit an official from the East India Company."

"What do we know about the company other than they are the referred to as the mother and father of all trade in the East Indies and beyond?" Rawlings filled his plate and joined his friends.

Kent placed his fork and knife down. "What is it you wish to know?

"Will we need to be involved with them for our trades?"

"Most definitely. We will not be successful in the worldwide plan until we employ a strategy for trading in the East Indies and China. We must deal with the East India Company."

"Do they have a monopoly?" Rawlings took a bit of ham. "Darcy, I am disappointed there are no sweet pastries this morning."

"You finished eating them yesterday, except for this one." Darcy bit into the treat he held in his hand, and then smiled as he wiped his mouth. "Mm. This is one of the best tasting pastries of all. Extremely good, really. Lemon filled."

Rawlings jerked his head toward the doorway, causing Darcy to look. Rawlings speared the pastry with his fork and popped the uneaten portion into his mouth. "Yes, Darcy, quite tasty. Now what were you saying about the monopoly?"

"The East India Company is more complicated than just being a monopoly. Kent is the best one to explain."

"The actual transactions are between the company and merchants." Kent sighed. "I suppose that is why I have such an extensive knowledge. My family has been dealing with them forever."

"Well, Kent, go on. I suspect I may need to be fully educated on them before leaving for America."

"True, even America cannot avoid them. They came into existence in 1600 when Queen Elizabeth provided a charter to a select group of merchants and businessmen with the express purpose of breaking the lock held by rival Dutch and Portuguese trading companies."

"What did they purchase back then?"

Kent held up his forkful of eggs. "Spices. The charter empowered the company to build forts and trading posts, properly referred to as factories, maintain armies, and even conclude treaties with Asian rulers. They control all the trade since they own the factories, creating a monopoly in a way. If any merchant wishes to establish an export arrangement in India, they must do so through the Company.

Darcy set down his coffee cup. "Could not another country take over one day and compete with the British posts?"

"Perhaps. However, the East India Company also controls competition through pricing, since they are the only ones that do not pay custom tariffs. And they, in fact, make money through taxation of the land within established territories, and can tax any amount to a competing seller.

"I presume that is why there are such riches to be made in Indian goods."

"Cotton, silk, indigo dye, saltpetre, and tea are the main commodities, all of which are exceptionally profitable. China tea is the most sought after of all teas. The East India Company does have one product available for trading desired by the Chinese. I doubt if you wish to participate in that occupation."

"What is it?" Rawlings asked.

"Opium. It is banned by the Chinese government and has to be smuggled into the country. Nonetheless, vast fortunes can be made from it."

Darcy cleared his throat. "I am not of a mind to enter the drug smuggling world. There must be a way we can break into the China trade. Kent, perhaps you can do further research.

Kent nodded. "My Uncle Daniel is well versed in China; however, I will admit, we have not been successful yet."

"Does the monopoly still stand?" Rawlings asked

"There are efforts in Parliament to open up competition."

"Blake!" Rawlings and Darcy shouted in unison and then shared a laugh.

"I will ask the highest paid partner to query his uncle for help," Darcy announced.

The men finished breakfast and headed out to meet with an official at the East India Company. They planned to apply for the necessary trading license. The official was pleasant, and methodically explained the process for trading with the Company, repeating much of what Kent had said earlier. As the men listened, Kent kept his eye on the assistant sitting behind the official.

Darcy filled out the required papers after the others agreed. The official carefully placed the documents in his desk drawer and waited patiently until the three men departed. He summoned his assistant and handed him the application, although Kent had remained at the entrance to the official office with an alibi to his friends of having to retrieve his gloves left behind. He hid behind the door, listening to everything said.

"Take these documents to this home at Grosvenor Square." The official handed a packet to his messenger. "Do not allow anyone to detain you. This is most urgent.

The assistant read the address and said, "Yes, sir. Immediately."

When the assistant left the room, he nodded to Kent and closed the door. They moved down the hall where Kent inspected the address. "The Peregrine? The Falcon is interested in us? What is inside?"

"Yes. The Falcon is paying for any information concerning you. This is your application."

Kent handed the man a guinea, his mind pondering why the Falcon was pursuing him. He sent the clerk on his way. He caught up with Darcy and Rawlings outside the building. He did not reveal what he had learned. The three men spent the afternoon visiting with other tradesmen in Cheapside. Kent introduced him to the persons handling goods from, Russia, British America, the West Indies, and Africa. Kent's connections were located in every port in the trading world, with the exception of China. Kent took them to all the best warehouses, including the East India Company Warehouse, where the three men spent the rest of the day browsing and making notes of the types of products sold.

"Will you both stay for dinner? " Darcy asked as the men headed back to Grosvenor Square.

Rawlings shook his head. "I am sorry, but I cannot. I must finalize my affairs before I leave. I received word from the Captain we will sail on Tuesday, next week."

"Well, I accept," Kent said. "I need to record a few thoughts from today's outing in our journal. If I wait, I will not be able to remember anything of importance.

Darcy nodded. "Dinner will be a little early tonight. I am taking my sister and my cousin to a play."

"Which one?" Kent sat upright.

"The Rivals at the Lyceum."

"I am not familiar with it." Kent watched as Darcy stared at his hands. Kent wondered why he would not look at him. He coughed. Still, Darcy glanced anywhere except at him. What is he hiding?

The carriage remained quiet as it moved through the busy streets, first stopping at Rawlings' home and then winding its way to Grosvenor Square, where the two remaining men separated for a time: Kent left for the library; Darcy to his bedchambers to prepare for the evening.

"Miss Darcy! You look lovely tonight." Kent bowed, and as he raised himself upright, he cast his gaze on another lady descending the stair. He offered a small smile before returning his attention to Georgiana.

"Oh, Mr. Kent. How are you today? Did you keep my brother busy all day, or did he tire you out?"

Kent nodded. "Your brother never stops. I will admit I am famished and look forward to dinner tonight." He glanced again at the other lady walking towards them.

"Oh, I do not believe you know my cousin. Let me introduce her to you." She turned to the lady dressed in a manner that contrasted with her olive coloring. Victoria stood next to Georgiana. Victoria had dressed in a pale blue silk with tiny pearls outlining the neckline. A five-sapphire necklace encircled her neck and her hair was pinned up with small sapphire and pearl pendants. Georgiana looked sweet in a pink dress covered with a sheer white nearly transparent layer along with a neckline appropriate for her age. It gave the impression of an angel. . May I present Lady Victoria Fitzwilliam? Victoria, this is my brother's friend, Mr. Kent of Leicester."

Kent bowed as Lady Victoria curtseyed. He snuck a peak at Georgiana. She winked at him causing him to stutter.

"Mr. Kent is an expert on piano composers." Georgiana raised her brows and released a giggle.

Kent smiled widely while tipping his head towards Georgiana. "Any knowledge I have is because of you, Miss Darcy. I am hopeless without your help." Kent bowed and rewarded Darcy's sister with his practiced smile before glancing at Victoria. "Lady Victoria, are you an expert on the pianoforte, too?"

"No, Mr. Kent. No one is as proficient as Georgiana. Do you play at all?"

"I believe I can honestly say I cannot play one note! My endeavors are limited to the turning of pages."

"That I can do as well!" Victoria laughed. "Georgiana is favored then with two page turners, while we are privileged to hear her beautiful playing."

Darcy joined the threesome. "Oh, thank you for entertaining the ladies." He smiled at his sister and cousin. "Dinner awaits." The group moved to the dining room led by Darcy and Victoria. The dinner discussion remained focused on music, composers, and humorous childhood stories. Kent continued to draw out Georgiana, but Victoria as well.

At the end of the meal, Darcy rose from his chair. "We must be off, if we are not to miss the first act. Kent, you have the library to yourself."

Kent rose from his chair, bowing politely as he watched the three depart. His uncle's word booming in his ears: "Do they keep you separate from that part of their world." The longer he stood, the more flush his face became, the deeper his brows furrowed, and the colder his stare became at the closed door. Nostrils flaring, he snarled aloud through a jaw clenched tight, "And perhaps, *Mr.* Darcy I should build the fire, clean the floor, and empty your chamber pots. Or, perchance, I will one day leave you standing alone while I go off with the ladies. Well, not tonight."

Chapter Seven

The Darcy carriage pulled to a stop at the entrance door of the Lyceum. Drury Lane Theater had suffered a fire two years earlier and temporarily leased this building, known for exhibiting Madame Tussaud's waxworks. The repairs would take another year with improved subscriber boxes and, more importantly to Darcy, the alternate private entry. Tonight, he glanced around the entrance, chuckled when he imaged all these lords and ladies turning into wax creatures and frozen in place with their mouths open.

Darcy turned to assist his sister and cousin. When Victoria stepped down, the murmuring increased. This was her first outing in many months and sine he was gentleman escorting her, the tongues flapped, reviving long forgotten suppositions. Her gown's tightness, even with a high waistline, clearly suggested a small waist lay underneath, which further added to the talk among the theatergoers.
Georgiana kept her head down while Victoria examined the crowd, stopping to stare whenever a fair-haired man smiled her way. Darcy led the ladies towards the door, returning nods to acquaintances while they walked without stopping to talk. Once they settled into their seats, and searched the audience for friends, Richmond burst into the box. "Good evening!"

"Welcome!" Darcy said. He caught his cousin's signal for a private conversation, and hurried to the hallway, but when Georgiana admitted her fears to Victoria about her début, Darcy held Richmond back. He listened outside.

Victoria responded with a few humorous stories related to her coming out. Georgiana revealed her discomfort was not of the presentation but of being around gentlemen who would flatter her.

Victoria patted her cousin's hand. "You appear at ease with Mr. Kent."

Darcy could see a smile appearing on Georgiana's face.

"Victoria, if you would be so kind, would you share your opinion of him?"

"I believe he is most charming, and he does make me laugh, which I have not done in such a long time. He studies a person whenever they respond to his questions. He is polite, well mannered, and is educated in gentlemanly affairs. Now, it is your turn to tell me more about him."

"He is a great friend of Fitzwilliam's. They seemed to be involved in something together, although they have not revealed what. Oh, Victoria!" Georgiana sighed. "He is smart, very intelligent, and I enjoy hearing about his family. And Mr. Kent is kind, do you not think?"

"Yes, he does so."

Georgiana leaned closer to her cousin and whispered, "And so handsome."

Darcy jerked upright. He furrowed his brow and ignored Richmond who was tapping his shoulder. He waved him away.

Victoria nodded. "Yes, quite. He has a disarming smile, which he uses often."

"He tells the most humorous stories. I know you agree since you laughed many times."

"I cannot deny it. I could not contain myself about his sister's pranks." Victoria sighed. "Unfortunately, we will not meet her."

"Why?"

"Georgiana, you must guard yourself from… well… persons not of our sphere."

"Humph! You sound like your brothers. Did you not find Mr. Kent worthy?"

"Mr. Kent is a friend to your brother, and we know how discerning he is; still I do not see any other type of connection for you with him."

"Because he is not titled? Or that he has no estate? He is kind, handsome, and wealthier than another particular gentleman acquaintance. Mr. Kent has no other faults, except who his parents are. You should become better acquainted with him, and you will see he is suitable for any lady."

"Be careful, my sweet young cousin. If you are not careful, you will lay yourself open to all kinds of rakes. You must listen to your elders if you wish to secure your future."

"Who has to be careful? It seems we both have made mistakes." Georgiana rapidly fanned herself before snapping the fan shut and glaring at the attendees below.

Victoria lowered her head, as did Georgiana. The two ladies spoke no more.

Richmond finally pulled Darcy away, only stopping where the crowd had dispersed. "I am worried. We need to leave immediately, before this damn first act starts."

Darcy lifted his brows. "Why are you so upset?"

"Do you know anything about this play?"

"No. What is the problem?"

"The plot is about a young girls' elopement with a deceitful military officer—a man disguising his true self. Sound familiar?"

"Oh, God. I did not know. You are correct. Georgiana must leave before the curtain rises." Darcy turned and took long strides across the lobby towards his box, not stopping to acknowledge anyone along the way. They reentered the box and immediately felt the unhidden tension between the two silent young women. The girls sat with their backs toward each other while they searched the audience. Georgiana smiled and waved to someone just entering below. Darcy noticed the man returned the wave and then rushed to his seat, slumping into it, and stared at the stage.

Darcy tapped Georgiana shoulder. "Ladies, I beg your pardon but we must leave."

"Why, brother? Is someone ill?"

"No. I… am unsure of the suitability of this play."

"I prefer to stay. I know about the particulars and… I must see this play, please. I assure you, brother, I am fine."

Darcy gazed at his sister while holding her hand in his. He squeezed it once and smiled when her tiny hand squeezed his in return.

"Victoria?"

"We have spoken about the story, and I wish to remain as well. I have heard it is an amusing play, and I do so long for a little light-hearted wit."

Darcy relented, and the two men took their seats behind the ladies.

Richmond tilted his head towards the boxes across from them and whispered, "The Falcon is here tonight. Should we speak with him?"

Darcy turned his head and spotted the elderly gentleman staring at him from the box directly across from them. Darcy nodded, acknowledging him, and then quickly returned his focus to the stage. "No. Georgiana needs me here tonight. You know how he enjoys telling stories about his prowess. I am more concerned about Georgiana than keeping up appearances and paying my respects to—"

Richmond interrupted, "the damned old buzzard."

Darcy grinned. "Yes, precisely, although he is a harmless old bird. I will remain here with my sister." He leaned forward trying to locate the man who had waved to his sister. The seat was now empty.

***

"Tonight I must be successful. I cannot afford to fail. My thirty percent depends upon it." Lord Blake rapped on the imposing door at 39 Grosvenor Square until a highly starched butler admitted him inside. His uncle's invitation to dinner indicated important political leaders would be attend including the most influential of the men—Lord Liverpool, the Secretary of State for War.

Blake hoped he would find an opportunity to approach Lord Liverpool with information on the Baker rifle. The servants removed his outer coat, gloves, and hat while he contemplated several opening tactics: Sir, why are you letting the brave soldiers use slingshots when a superior firearm is available? On the other hand, I could say, I wager the poorest marksman in the Army can become England's best with just one shot from this rifle! He considered going back home to get his rifle and then returning to the party to shoot the main course. Lord Liverpool would not ignore the gun then. He chuckled aloud while a servant led him to the dining room.

Lord Castlereagh, a previous Secretary of State, had chosen the chair to his uncle's left. The most notable Tories and their wives were seated at the table along with one pretty, young lady. When his Uncle Harrowby tipped his head at the empty chair next to her, Blake was pleased to discover that he would sit next to Lord Liverpool. He tipped his head to his uncle.

"Blake, have you met everyone?" When he indicated that he had not, Harrowby introduced the men and their wives.

Blake glanced at the other influential men and realized that he did have the best connections just as Darcy had suggested. These men held power over every area of life.

Harrowby continued his introductions with a few special remarks about the only unmarried woman. Blake nodded to her, but then turned his attention to the two men across from him.

Lord Sidmouth warned his friends the Luddism movement in Nottingham had spread to Yorkshire, Lancashire, Leicestershire, and Derbyshire. The men broke into factories at night, destroying the new weaving machines. Blake made a mental note to question Darcy about how this might affect exporting their textiles.

Blake's aunt tapped her fingers on the table. "Has anyone has seen *The Rivals* currently playing at the Lyceum.?"

"Much too frivolous for me." Lord Sidmouth responded, and returned the conversation to politics, which lasted throughout the meal regardless of their wives attempts to divert the talk elsewhere. They sent each other what Blake supposed was long-suffering looks.

Blake consumed his meal while he listened, attuned to any news affecting their business, whether positive or negative. It was the first time he had been interested in politics. He reminded himself to pass on information about a frame-braking act to Darcy. *He is heavily involved in the cotton industry up north, and this would be important to him. I wonder if he knows about the Luddites.* He noticed his uncle gazing at him with a curious expression.

The time arrived for the ladies to disappear to the drawing room while the men remained for the traditional after-dinner brandy. Blake recognized his opportunity had arrived once a discussion about war began.

"Lord Liverpool, I am a curious fellow. How do our soldiers fare? I have been in the country, and have not followed our efforts."

"In the country? Yes, we all know where you have been, Blake. Did you perchance ride that stallion over here tonight?"

"Not tonight. I came by carriage. However, if you would like to see him, I will gladly make arrangements for you to inspect him," Blake bowed his head.

"Inspect? I prefer to ride." Liverpool chuckled. "His name is Heracles, I understand."

"That is the name given to him by my friend, Mr. Bingley."

"Bingley? I know that name and the image it brings to mind is not a young man," Lord Castlereagh said.

"I suspect you remember my friend's father. The Bingley family has developed an impressive new rifle for the militia and before Mr. Bingley died, he had offered it for sale to the Army." Blake glanced at them. Several of the men had attended his father's shooting parties. Smiling, he added, "Bingley's family has modified the Baker rifle in such a way, even I can hit the lead bird in flight."

"You? I do not doubt your word, but this is something I must to witness for myself," Lord Liverpool exclaimed. "Your prior proficiency is legendary."

Blake laughed with the others. "I admit, I never was a good shot. Sir, this rifle is amazingly accurate, and quick to reload. I would never again consider competing against anyone without it." Blake nodded and smiled at the chuckles heard throughout the room. "

Liverpool swirled the brandy in his glass. "Is the offer for the rifle still standing?"

"I believe so. Mr. Bingley passed away before the rifles's latest improvements were finished. The price has risen. I am well acquainted with his son, whom I met at Cambridge. He has taken over his father's role of selling the rifles. I could arrange a meeting if you desire."

"Yes, yes! And remember to ride over on the stallion. Send a message around next week."

Blake sighed. Darcy was correct again—deals are made over brandy and cigars.

The other men joined in on the discussion of the stallion and the competition. Several men slapped Blake on the back and demanded stories. Most had wagered and won bets. The conversation moved onto the war on the continent, taxes, parliamentary reform, and the Catholic issue. Blake felt comfortable with these men. The Tories were a conservative lot, preferring life as it was now. They would never consider any other system for ruling and managing a country and would fight to maintain their hold on power.

When the guests departed, Blake's uncle pulled him aside and asked him to remain. Blake found a comfortable chair in the study while Harrowby poured two glasses of his finest brandy.

Blake glanced around the familiar room. For someone so involved in the parliament and the complexity of any law or regulation, his uncle kept his desk in pristine condition, in fact, the desk seemed unused. A hand-drawn silhouette of his aunt as a young girl graced the desktop. Blake studied the volumes lining his bookshelves—laws, essays, histories, and war strategies. Neat and organized, he thought, and then he turned his attention onto his uncle. He is as fastidious as I am. I suppose I take after him in that regard. He examined the pattern on the rug, wondering what was so urgent or important.

Harrowby cleared his throat several times until his nephew looked up. "It is good to see you again. I was impressed when you pulled out the victory for the horse. Beat that tradesman's son, this Kent fellow."

Blake nodded, but remained silent. They had discussed this earlier with the other men. He was curious where this was heading. One trait he had acquired from studying Darcy was to remain quiet when others were attempting to attain his opinion.

His lordship slid into the chair opposite his nephew. "I won a small fortune on the golf game. When the papers revealed the final game was golf, it was hard for me not to conceal how well it suited you. The men who bragged earlier only mentioned their winning bets on the rowing race. They did not know your skill at golf and had bet on Mr. Darcy for that game."

"Had Bingley chosen another sport, I do not believe I could have overcome the point deficiency."

He held up his glass. "Well, a toast to you. Good show." While his nephew sipped his drink, his uncle continued, "I hope you enjoyed the dinner tonight. I had expected you to be more interested in the sweet young girl sitting next to you. Tonight you showed more interested in the politics."

"I found the talk exceedingly informative. I did not follow everything, but enough in order for me to enjoy the evening."

"Perhaps you may wish to engage yourself in this type of life?"

"I view it as a spectator sport. I leave it to the better men." Blake saluted his uncle with his glass.

"Nonsense. You would do well, since politics is a competitive sport, although the stakes are higher and will affect more people. However, I warn you, passions run high at times. We were fortunate the talk about the Catholic issue did not result in fisticuffs. Sidmouth and Castlereagh do not see eye to eye on that matter."

Blake set his unfinished brandy aside and attempted to stand to leave.

Harrowby tapped Blake's arm when he moved to the door. "Sit for a moment more. I… " He waited until Blake returned to his seat. " I asked you to stay to give you a fair warning."

"Fair warning, sir?"

Harrowby nodded. "You are no longer a little boy with little boy's interests. This business about the Baker rifle sales caught my attention. Apparently you are attempting to make a life for yourself; one separate from your father. I applaud your decision to seek a change, and you would be wise to act quickly. However, as I said, I do give you one warning."

"Lock up my money when father comes to visit?"

"Do not be coarse. I caution you to deliberate sensibly about your connections. The news accounts addressed the backgrounds of Mr. Bingley and Mr. Kent. I imagine your young friends regularly espouse the social underclass arguments. There are many groups attempting to overthrow our system of government. You must be careful with whom you socialize, boy. These are dangerous times, and only the most naïve will fail to understand."

"We never talk politics. They are no more interested in the subject than I am."

"Just a warning, and…" Blake waited for the next unwanted advice to come. "This country miss—"

"Do not speak of such things." Blake rose abruptly. "I grow tired of all this attention to my social activities. I wish not to discuss it beyond my assurance that there is no country miss. The reports were mistaken, sir." Blake stomped towards the door. "Please do not raise the subject again."

"Very good."

Harrowby caught up to him and gently grabbed his shoulder preventing him from leaving the room. When Blake turned to face him, his uncle used his smile, which could disarm the angriest man debating any issue in Parliament. "I, too, would like to get a glance at Heracles."

"I renamed him. He is called Netherfield now." Blake realized once he revealed the new name, his uncle would understand. He had professed his love for Lady Beatrice to his uncle and discussed his anger at his father's behavior. Harrowby had convinced him to accept the situation and, when he did, his uncle presented him with the auburn-hued filly and suggested he honor his feelings by naming the horse after the location of his flirtation instead of her name.

Harrowby patted his nephew on his back. "Your aunt is planning a dinner party next week. Will you join us? I promise I will not pressure you into political service. Not yet, anyway. Perhaps afterwards you can tell me all about your trip and your friends."

Blake nodded and departed for home. He felt an ache throughout his body when he spied his crest on the carriage before he climbed inside seeing insead the letter E engraved on a crystal knight.

Elizabeth. Oh, Elizabeth, why? Why did you run away from me? What frightened you?

He dabbed a single tear escaping his eye catching it before it trickled down his cheek. However, it was not until he had arrived home had he realized his right foot had been repeatedly crushing an imaginary chess piece with his foot.

***

"Shall I explain that for you again, Bingley?" Darcy nudged him with a light tap. The morning was cloudy and the air was cold. Darcy feared the warmth from the fire was causing his friend to nod off.

"Excuse me; I was not attending at all. My mind is elsewhere today. Does town seem dull and boring lately?"

"You can always hold competitions in the park outside." Rawlings pointed to the window. "We could fence each other, or better yet, we could partake of a few boxing matches. We did not do that at Netherfield Park," he said, and just as quickly muttered, "Damn."

Bingley responded with a long sigh.

Darcy stood. "Bingley, put the work away and play a game of Twenty Points."

Unresponsive, Bingley continued to stare out at the street until Blake bounded into the library. "Darcy, I have excellent news."

"Would you like to join us in a game of Twenty Points? Rawlings and I were just trying to tempt Bingley in a game."

"Not today, thank you. Bingley, I am pleased you are here. I wish to share my news with you which will interest you the most."

Bingley sat upright and gave Blake his attention..

"We have a meeting next week with Liverpool to discuss the rifles. I have no doubt it will be a big order and I will have succeeded in my part of the agreement."

"So soon? We just arrived in town," Rawlings asked.

"The letter I sent to my uncle from Netherfield Park..."

Bingley moaned again.

"… that you delivered it when you took that short trip to town. I had asked for his assistance, and last night he arranged a dinner with all the appropriate politicians. Lord Liverpool was there."

"Excellent." Darcy said. "Bingley, will you be able to attend to this matter next week at Liverpool's office?"

Without looking up, Bingley answered in a monotone voice, "Yes. I would like to include my Uncle Watt. Would that be a problem?"

"No, that would not be a problem. However, he has asked me to ride the Andalusian, so you will need to arrive separately."

The men began to sketch out the particulars for the meeting. After fifteen minutes Bingley was almost his old self. He even joked about Blake claiming to hit the lead bird to the politicians. Once the specifics were completed, Bingley stood, excused himself, and departed.

"I have never seen Bingley so despondent. Do you know why?" Blake asked.

Rawlings leaned further into his chair. "I believe he is missing the excitement, as he said. London does seem dull and boring."

"Perhaps. I have other news." Blake stood and walked over to the fireplace. He pulled a packet from his pocket and held it up for friends to see.

"Insurance papers."

"You have been a busy person," Rawlings said. "Are they life policies on us, Blake? Should we be afraid to be alone with you?" He laughed. Blake shook his head and sighed.

"No. These are examples for drafting our liability insurance policy, although it was used for fire insurance, which is the most similar. I have taken the liberty of marking up a policy."

"Good work. You always did your assignments quickly. If you leave the papers here, I will review them tonight. Do you mind if I share these with Mr. Rogers, my secretary? He has an experienced background in this area."

"Yes, if you are sure of his secrecy. I would not want this to be shared with anyone."

"I trust him."

A knock caused all the men to turn their heads towards the door.

Before any announcement, Kent walked in, holding several hefty bound documents, fat with pages of information. "Good morning."

"What are those? Not our reading material for today, I hope. You could take a lesson from Blake. See, that is his contribution." Darcy pointed to the three-page document on the table.

Kent laughed. "Well, apparently being succinct is not a Blake family trait. These are the laws regarding importing and exporting. I believe his uncle was involved in drafting them."

Rawlings thumbed through the information. "Our politicians have been busy. Blake, perhaps politics is the profession for you since you are a busy man as well. You might teach them how to economize on their words. No wait! Mr. Bennet did not find your chess tournament rules succinct. In fact, he complained about the verbosity. Yes, verbosity was his word."

"Where did you get these, Kent?" Darcy asked.

"My uncle was kind enough to lend them to us. He also offered his services."

"Does he know about our alliance?" Darcy asked.

"I revealed only enough of our plans to elicit his help. He provided a little guidance for dealing with importers from America. Trade is currently sporadic. He did say the potential for profit is great once our countries differences are resolved. However, if the situation worsens, we might suffer untold losses. America has the resources and the ability to manufacture any goods we do, and would need us less than we might need them."

"I believe working with John Jacob Aster will resolve that problem." Darcy picked up the contract Rawlings would take on his journey.

"Perhaps." Kent shrugged.

The men spent the morning plowing through the mounds of papers on Darcy's library table. In the afternoon, each man went his separate way, returning for dinner.

"Miss Darcy, another beautiful table," Kent said as he led Georgiana into the dining room. "From the fragrance in the air, might I guess we are having roast beef tonight? My favorite!"

"Yes, we are." Georgiana lowered her head to hide the rising blush she assumed was appearing on her cheeks.

"I hope *The Rivals* proved appealing."

"The play was… interesting. The central character, Lydia, had several suitors for her hand with one man pretending to be something he was not. I found much to like and much to dislike."

"Perhaps one day another play will live up to your expectations. I will be on the lookout for one to recommend."

Georgiana fell quiet for the remainder of the meal.

Darcy had noticed that her head remained bowed, even when Kent attempted to include her in the conversation. The play had left her cheerless. He had worried that the plot of the young girl's romantic desire for elopement with a penniless military officer would be too difficult for his sister. In hindsight, he should never have allowed her to attend, or at the least, they should have left once Richmond warned him. His sister had not smiled since the play.

Darcy reminded himself to contact his aunt without delay. His sister needed an older, wiser companion or governess, and this time he would rely upon any recommendation she would make. He and Richmond had failed when they employed Mrs. Younge. That horrible woman worked with Wickham to deceive them. This time, he would let Richmond's mother assist with locating a worthy lady. He was jarred back when Rawlings tapped the glass with his knife.

"My friends, next week is Atterton's ball. Do not forget, a person who never takes time off from work becomes boring, as well as bored. What do you say? Shall we attend?"

Blake and Bingley declined. Miss Bingley had petitioned her brother to escort her to a soiree. Blake had indicated he had other plans, the details he did not provide.

Kent agreed quickly, as did Darcy, although with more reluctance.

When Georgiana left the dining room, Kent noted her slumped shoulders and subdued parting words. He leaned toward Darcy, and in hushed voice asked, "Did I say anything to upset her tonight? I am truly sorry if I did."

"No. She is a little tired after the theatre last night. She will be herself again after a good night's rest." Darcy spoke calmly, yet even he could tell his words did not sound sincere.

Kent frowned. "Please convey my apology if I caused her any uneasiness."

Chapter Eight

The men rushed to complete many activities during the week, and much remained to be accomplish. Each day more pieces of the world-trading puzzle fell into place. Kent's Uncle Daniel was instrumental in everything except the China trade, which proved to be more difficult than anyone expected. The officials at the East India Company had not responded to their request for a license, but at the meeting, they suggested the alliance's wish to be involved in Chinese trading would cause a problem. England controlled all such trade through its East India Company licenses and to date they had not granted access to any individual or company. Darcy considered scrapping it, but realized it was the critical leg in the worldwide strategy. They continued to pursue the approval.

The men stayed busy with their assigned undertakings convening at night to report any progress over drinks and dinner. With Kent's continued gentle coaxing, Georgiana grew more communicative since the play. Her hosting skills improved with each passing event. Having taken the time to learn all the men's favorite dishes, she discovered Bingley was the easiest man to please; he savored everything, except mutton. Like her brother, Kent and Blake favored the beef selections; Rawlings showed a partiality to the simple meals and fancy ragouts, revealing his own contradictory personality.

So it was, Georgiana's selection for an early dinner—a stewed beef rump—was chosen since Rawlings was scheduled to sail the next morning for America. While the men partook of their usual after-dinner brandy, they enlightened each other on their accomplishments in more detail. Darcy announced that he had found sufficient underwriters, and Blake said he had finalized the insurance policy. Bingley had worked on the sale of the modified Baker Rifles, while Rawlings and Kent had pursued many tradesmen in Cheapside, although they reported that Mr. Cuffage urged them to avoided meeting with Mr. Gardiner or visiting his warehouse. He had given them a list of other tradesmen they should avoid.

Rawlings, having grown tired in-depth business discussions, refilled everyone's glass, and lifted his drink in the air. He led the now familiar salute, thereby ending the serious conversation. "To the Alliance!" The men rose, repeated the toast, and then gulped the liquid down in one swallow. Darcy felt a shiver run through his body. His inner sense nudged him. For an unknown reason he worried this toast may be the last one they drank together.

Edward Atterton's party was that night. Bingley left to escort his sister to another function, Blake, not yet forgiving of the man for his interference with Lady Beatrice years ago, declined and returned to his home. The remaining men prepared to leave for party.

They arrived late and, unfortunately, so did everyone else, causing a crush of people attempting to gain entrance at the same time. Edward Atterton had spied them through the large window overlooking the driveway, and with unusual promptness, led them inside. He did not know Kent, except by the news accounts of the competition, but he and Rawlings had been friends at Eton.

While they climbed the stairs, Darcy experienced a sense of déjà vu. He sniffed the air filled with the scents of roses, lilacs, and jasmine. He could not detect any lavender. Once the men gathered at the top, they entered the ballroom together.

Those assembled suddenly hushed at the sight. All three men were handsomely dressed and appeared stately in their manner. The most important information floating around the room was that they were unattached, rich and had recently participated in a grand competition in the country. Every matron quickly moved to her unmarried daughters, chastising them to stand up straight, shoulders back and, of course, to display their most pleasing smiles.

Rawlings led the men to the refreshment table. Kent, taking his drink, left to attend to several acquaintances beckoning him to join them. "Darcy, when we entered the assembly hall in Meryton Sir William came to welcome us. Tonight, Atterton rushed to greet us. I believe you did not appreciate Sir William's effort, at least not as much as you valued Atterton's."

Darcy pointed his head to the host. "Yes, but unlike him, Sir William is a... a—"

"Hobnail? Clodhopper? Perhaps, but Sir William acted for the best reason. His goal was to put us at ease in a room full of strangers."

"Humph! His goal was for one us to meet and marry his daughter. Atterton has never pushed his sister on me.

"Why then did Sir William introduce Bingley straightaway to the Bennets? I agree, there is a little bit of the buffoon about him, but he is a gentleman underneath. Did you call Atterton a clodhopper? No, but yet, he also possesses the same foolishness in his manner."

Darcy glared at him. "What are you doing? Why are you bringing up a country dance? What do you wish to lecture me on today?"

"My friend, I plan to introduce you to the Meryton society in this fashionable party in London."

Darcy attempted to leave; Rawlings held him back. "Hear me out first, and then make up your own mind. I shall not force you to socialize if you are apprehensive about talking with others; but I wish to show you the world through my eyes."

Darcy shrugged. "Very well."

Rawlings pointed out a well-dressed older lady standing in the corner with two young maidens. "Do you recall Mrs. Long and her two nieces, Eunice and Diana? Surely you remember them." Rawlings waited until Darcy fixed his stare on the women in question. "Do you not notice how she fusses over the girls, and how she tries to puff herself up as the social leader there? She is the same as Mrs. Long."

"Humph."

"I am well acquainted with her boring and insipid manner. Her two daughters are so much like the Long nieces. I can attest they own little understanding. They limit all discussion on fashion. You did not dance with the Long nieces, but I did and the conversation was the same, I assure you."

Rawlings next directed his friend's attention to a well-built older man to their left. "Is he not our Mr. Goulding? His conversations are horses, horses, and more horses. Mr. Goulding breeds and sells the animals while he buys and stables them—no real difference between the two. When did he ever speak to you about anything else?"

When Darcy laughed aloud, many guests turned to stare. "You have a point there. Still, this is not Meryton. These people are not as crash or rude."

"Take note, my friend, we cannot do as we please, even here in sophisticated London, we are scrutinized. Members of the *Ton* are not as loud as the Meryton society, but guess what they are whispering. He is Mr. Darcy, my dear, and he is worth ten thousand a year. He is standing next to Mr. Rawlings, a younger son of the Earl of Wolverly, but I understand he is building his wealth. Mr. Kent, over there, almost won the stallion. He is rich, to be sure, but he is not even gentry! Only the poorest gentlemen would allow his daughter to marry that tradesmen's son."

Rawlings took a breath when a mother walked by with a younger lady in hand and whispering. "Dear, one of the gentlemen may appreciate your practicality, and may even prefer quality to the shallowness of the other girls."

After they walked passed, Rawlings turned Darcy, directing his attention to another mother and daughter. "Without a doubt, that was Lady Lucas with Miss Charlotte in hand!" He glanced at a group of ladies approaching them. "Ah. Here comes the pièce de résistance." Rawlings bowed. "Why, Lady Maria, you look lovely tonight, as do all your daughters. Are you acquainted with my friend?"

"No, sir. We would be most honored with an introduction."

"Lady Maria, may I introduce Mr. Darcy?"

"It is a great honor to meet you. May I present my daughters: Miss Margaret, my eldest, Miss Felicia, my second, and finally Miss Rebecca.

While the girls curtsied, Darcy figured out which family they represented before Rawlings asked if there any more lovely ladies at home.

"Oh no, Mr. Rawlings. How kind of you to ask. I have yet another girl, but she is dancing." Lady Maria pointed with her head to the dance floor. "She is my youngest and most lively child. Would you like to meet her, I can send one of the other girls to fetch her?"

"No, ma'am, I beg you not to interrupt her pleasure."

"My daughters are well schooled in all dances."

After waiting a few awkward moments for a response that did not come, they daughters left and with an ill-disguised whisper the mother exclaimed, "Humph, they are not quite so desirable to us, my dears."

Mr. Rawlings announced, "That was Mrs. Bennet! Although she has only four daughters, they are all out. Well, shall we play cards tonight? I have not noticed anyone lively enough for me to dance with, and I realize none of your usual dancing partners attended tonight."

"I do not dance as a rule anywhere if I can help it."

"But you did demonstrate your skill at the Netherfield Ball. Tonight, let us be old men and spend the evening with a deck of cards." The two men approached the card room in silence. After a few moments discussing the Netherfield competition, they found opponents for whist, and stayed engaged in many games..

Darcy did not utter a sentence longer than three words. The similarities between the two societies hounded his thoughts and his attention to the cards suffered. Rawlings seemed not to care even though they continuously lost. Occasionally, Darcy would lean back in his chair, gaze into the ballroom while the dancers drifted by. He studied the women making their turns. London twins. They are all the same. Still, they are a class above the Meryton women.

He lost interest in whisk after only two games. Rawlings said he sought the quiet of a comfortable room and suggested they return to Darcy House for a few drinks. This would be the last time they would be together before he sailed. When they informed Kent, he chose to remain at the party to continue his flirting and conversing with his new acquaintances. Darcy offered to send the carriage back for his use when the party ended.

Upon arriving at Darcy House, the two men headed straight to the study where Darcy poured the drinks and Rawlings paced the floor.

"Sit down, please, Darcy. I must speak with you."

"I wish not to debate you on the merits of London society and Meryton's lack of anything notable." He crossed his arms. "Have you not said it all tonight at the party?"

"That was just the first act in this drama."

"Drama? Which play does this resemble? With you, it should be a comedy; perhaps *A Midsummer Night's Dream*."

Instead of a laugh, Rawlings picked up his pace muttering until he plopped down in the other chair. "The similarities between the two societies I showed you tonight were the first of my warnings."

"I understood completely what you did, but I hold a different opinion. Meryton cannot compare to London. I grant you there was a little truth, but the two places are not equal."

"I did not say equal, Darcy, you mistake my point. You should not overlook opportunities because of perceived imperfections."

"Are we speaking of business or pleasure?"

"Business especially, but do not dismiss the possibility for happiness in your personal life. You, my friend, are in danger of marrying merely for the sake of your family fortunes."

"I have no thought of marriage to anyone. Nor have I ever."

"Bah! Did you not focus your attention on Lady Victoria the first two we were at Cambridge. She visited often enough to raise eyebrows among your friends. I realize that she did not return once Richmond had graduated, but I also noticed tension between you two. And now I heard you escorted her to a play recently."

"I did consider her, but we discovered we were too much like sister and brother. Nonetheless, she is an example of what I desire: a good family, impeccable manners, skilled in the arts, an excellent manager of servants, well read, and sophisticated sufficiently to tread the London swamps. She must have the background to aid in Georgiana's debut. In addition, I wish to have a large family, so she must be healthy and bring a little fortune into the family to bestow upon the younger children. She has no equal in Meryton."

Joining your life with another should be more than a business alliance. Damn it, Darcy, do not seek merely increased wealth or connections when there is someone who can provide you with a deep source of joy. Happiness in life should not be traded away."

"Humph. I know whom you are referring too. Her mother is mercenary, Rawlings. The same holds true for her younger sisters."

"How can you be so positive? You rarely spoke to any of them."

"I have witnessed how venal Mrs. Bennet is."

"Oh. Would you be so kind to enlighten me?"

Darcy moved to the fireplace where he stoked the fire in silence; his angry jabs with the poker sending orange embers flying up the chimney. Since the sparks had done little to subdue his demons, he moved over to the window, his reflection clear in the dark panes while he stared bleakly out into the night.

"Are you angry or pained?" Rawlings rose from his chair, but Darcy held his hand up to halt his progress.

"I do not know which it is. A little of both I suppose."

"Tell me. I am a willing listener. There is no friend here to interrupt us tonight."

Darcy recalled both times when he tried to share his thoughts about Miss Elizabeth Bennet, but the sudden presence of others had delayed any discussion. After giving instructions to one of his servants, he closed the door. "We will not be interrupted."

Rawlings brought the brandy carafe closer to their chairs. "I will not joke or tease. I am your greatest supporter, perhaps your truest friend, for I will not hold back my opinions."

"I know." Darcy glared out the window. The townhouses across the square gave off only pinpricks of lights on this starry evening. With the study situated at the front of the house, he could easily watch the movements of his neighbors. He found it entertaining to see which carriages drove past each morning and who returned home each night.

More importantly, he could discern who was calling upon him before the doorman opened the door. Darcy's shoulder's slumped.

Rawlings set down his drink. "What is on your mind?"

Darcy, raised his chin. He spoke to the blackness outside the window, but loudly enough for Rawlings to hear. "You were aware of Blake's attraction to Miss Elizabeth."

"Of course. I believe we all knew of it. He was not the one hiding his interest."

Darcy shot him a black stare. "Did you know he was planning to offer marriage?"

Rawlings shook his head. "No. But my conversations with him left me to believe he was debating the consequences of connecting himself to such a low family. When I heard the Bennet girls had lost their dowries, I assumed he had dropped the connection. He cannot afford to marry without regard to fortune."

"He has sufficient wealth bestowed upon him by his mother. His situation is not as dire as we had believed… he had every intention of proposing to her the day after the ball." Darcy slowly shook his lowered head. "I will admit to you that I am not sorry he never made the offer, although I regret that his reason for not doing so only confirmed my beliefs."

"Which are?"

"Mrs. Bennet is of the most mercenary type. Her daughters are no match for her. They will do as she says. Do not forget, pushing Miss Bennet on Bingley is another example of her nature. And I am convinced had I shown the slightest outward interest in any of her daughters, Mrs. Bennet would have compelled her daughter to show an interest in me that she did not experience."

"What did Mrs. Bennet do?"

"I interrupted Blake and Miss Elizabeth on the balcony at the end of Bingley's ball."

Rawlings sat up in his chair. "I do not understand. How does her mother figure into this?"

Darcy took another deep breath. "Once I appeared, Miss Elizabeth left quickly, but I stayed to question Blake about his intentions. No, that is not true. I challenged him to think about what he was doing. I even revealed that Miss Elizabeth had lost her dowry."

"But how does this prove your belief that the Bennets were fortune hunters? Did Miss Elizabeth say something that made you think she was after his title?"

"No, not at all. And I confirmed my suspicions that Mrs. Bennet pushed her daughters on rich men." "

"How could interrupting Blake and Miss Elizabeth do that?"

After moving to his chair, Darcy dropped in it and leaned forward, both arms resting on his legs. He gazed at his fingers while he fiddled with his hands. "On the balcony Blake faced me with his back to the ballroom. I was positioned in such a way that I could see the door from the corner of my eye. What happened next proved my beliefs about the greedy, opportunistic Bennets." He sighed.

"Hardly. You never held a good opinion of them before. But go on." Rawlings settled back in his chair, sipped his drink, and scoffed at Darcy's glare.

"Mrs. Bennet opened the door as we were talking. At that time, I..." He jumped up, gulped his brandy, and moved to the fireplace, where he stirred the fire with a poker with force. He did this for a few moments, sighed, and turned to face Rawlings. "I was reminding Blake of his financial troubles by emphasizing his father's calamitous state of affairs. Upon hearing this, Mrs. Bennet left abruptly, believing Blake to be penniless. After she left, Blake disclosed how he was well situated financially. He could easily afford a wife and family."

"I do not see how this makes Mrs. Bennet a mercenary?"

"Blake waited for Miss Elizabeth the next day. She never appeared."

"Perhaps there was a problem. She may have been ill."

"Blake thought so too. After waiting hours, he became concerned and set off for Longbourn. Mrs. Bennet informed him that Miss Elizabeth had left for London with the expressed intention of avoiding him."

"That does not seem possible, even for her, but even if it is true, you still have not satisfactorily explained to me how this makes Mrs. Bennet mercenary?"

After throwing the poker into the stand, Darcy plopped into his chair and crossed his arms. "Do you not understand?" He glared at Rawlings's shrug. "Mrs. Bennet believed Blake to be poor, and no longer a preferable match for Miss Elizabeth. She must have insisted somehow that her daughter not marry him. You must have noticed Mrs. Bennet pushing Miss Elizabeth on Blake at every opportunity. You cannot deny that. He was no longer sufficient for marriage to her daughter. That is why I believe she is purely mercenary."

"But how did you learn of this?"

"Blake told me the whole story one night, when I had accused him of horrible goings-on. I am fortunate he did not call me out. Of course, I would have chosen pistols if he had."

"Did he not seek her out in London? You both returned to town early."

"No, he did not. He believed Miss Elizabeth ran away from him. He did not care to discuss it."

Rawlings sat still. Darcy listened to the fire flickering and crackling in the stilled room. It was several moments before Rawlings spoke.

"I doubt the truth is known regarding the whereabouts of Miss Elizabeth Bennet. I most definitely think she would have rejected Blake herself. She would not have run away. She is not a simpering lady! Furthermore, I suspect her mother was merely trying to protect her daughter from poverty." Rawlings blinked his eyes before flashing Darcy a cold stare. "I believe *you* thought this out as well." Rising from his chair, he raised his body to its full height. "You did not challenge Blake's understanding at all, did you?"

Darcy dropped his head, "I tried, but Blake did not want any arguments. He was decisive when he stated he had broken all connections with her. I... suppose I could have insisted futher, but I..."

"I am surprised by Blake, but I know full well why you offered no objections. By remaining quiet, you saved her from marriage to him. Well, now Blake has removed himself from consideration, are you planning to pursue her?"

Darcy rose again, this time retreating to the window. Placing one arm against the frame, he traced an imaginary figure on the glass. "I think of her often. Honestly, I do not live a single day without wondering where she is or what she is doing. I can smell lavender regardless of the flower in a vase. Her fine eyes appear before me every night before I fall asleep, and are smiling at me when I wake. I have tried hard to focus on business. Still, I cannot shake her image from my mind. I miss hearing the sound of her voice.

"So are you?"

"What?"

"Planning to pursue her, now?"

"No! I do not plan to seek her out. I will not." His voice trailed off, "I cannot."

Rawlings leaned forward. "Is it the low connections or the lack of fortune? You are not in want of either."

Darcy turned back towards Rawlings. "She would not be accepted by the *Ton*, or more importantly, by my family. Georgiana's future will depend heavily upon who I connect myself to."

"Bah! Do not use your sister as the excuse. Even Bingley refused to consider Miss Bingley's in his decision. What exactly is it you seek in a wife that Miss Elizabeth does not offer?"

"All I want is a respected person to guide Georgiana and bring the Darcy name honor. Increasing my holdings is an important consideration, as well."

"You mean to say forty thousand pounds would be acceptable as a reason for connecting yourself to a woman for life? If so, my friend, you are a fool, and in light of your confession, perhaps I was as well." Rawlings stomped to the sideboard.

Darcy sat stone faced.

Rawlings poured another brandy. "I should have let you be saddled with Margaret. You would then have a different opinion of the beautiful, witty Miss Elizabeth. Of course, if you married Margaret then you would have to worship Elizabeth in secret. Oh, pardon me. You worship her in that manner now. Do not be a fool. You have a chance to achieve your greatest desire."

"Saddled? Was it so horrid?"

"Yes, it was. The events of four years ago are seared on my brain and I think of them with hatred."

"I have always wondered how Logan discovered her plan."

"I do not know. He does not reveal his sources. I never told you that the ball, supposedly to reward my graduation from Cambridge, had been arranged to ensnare you. Do not look so shocked. My family is one of those good connections to which you are always referring."

Darcy gripped the chair's arms. "Your family wanted to ensnare me in a trap with Miss Stevens? I do not understand."

"I never wished to reveal it to you, but now I think I must in order to save you from yourself. Let me enlighten you. My brother, the real mastermind behind the plan, convinced my father to hold the ball. I should have known immediately Thomas had a deceitful purpose. When has he ever shared any of father's attention with me?"

Darcy was about to speak when Rawlings jumped up and sent him a disapproval look. He carried his brandy with him as he paced around the room.

"Logan sent word during the later that evening. I had not deemed anything amiss they gave you a room in the family quarters. I was so pleased to be shown such attention that I overlooked several danger signs." Rawlings paused, careful not to gulp his drink. "Logan sent word to me during the ball—and he was specific—you were the target of a compromise. I sent word to switch all your belongings into my room and a few of my personal possessions into yours.

"Your brother planned this? Why did you think it was him?"

"Him and Margaret. Their entire plan crystallized in my mind upon receiving Logan's note. I had observed her cuddling up to you and all the time sending sly smiles back to Thomas."

"I always felt you and he were more like relatives than neighbors since you visited your grandfather's estate so often. Damn, we played together when we were young, although thinking back on it, your brother and Richmond teamed up against us. I cannot believe this."

"Logan had barely completed making the switch when my brother escorted our dear little Margaret to your room. Of course, neither of them knew it was now my room."

"Nor did I. Why did you not tell me that night?"

"I was mindful you were confused, but we had to act fast. I had little time to explain. What happened that night, I shall never forget. I entered... "

Rawlings dropped into his chair, leaned back, crossed his leg, grabbed the chair arms, and stared blankly to no place in particular. "I entered a darkened room—no fire in the fireplace, no candles lit and the drapes shut out any evening light—I felt secure in my own plan. In fact, it was so dark, I could not see my hand when I closed the door behind me. She demanded I not light a candle, or she would ruin me forever by screaming loudly. I did as she said, all the while smiling at the wench. I had my own plan. She forced me, although it did not take much effort, to remove my clothing. You understand, I allowed her to do these things. Logan was prepared to stop the fiasco upon my word, but I allowed her to continue beyond what was necessary for a compromising situation."

"But why? Why would you do such a thing?"

"I had my own agenda. I am a second son. You do not understand what life is like for one not born an heir. My choices were the army, the navy, or the clergy, and none held my interest. Perhaps I was not as spoiled as my brother was, or even as you had been, but I did live as leisurely life, which dissipated the moment I graduated. I had finished my studies at Cambridge so my father expected me to move on with my life. I had planned to join the army, but when Logan sent word about Margaret's plan to entrap you, I set into motion a way for me to continue this gentleman's life."

Rawlings gulped his brandy. "From the second I entered the room, I realized my scheme would work. We are the same height and weight and since we both favored wearing black at the balls, we dressed similarly that night. My straight hair was a problem, yours is too damn curly. I used my hands to tossle my hair. I was sweating—I have never compromised a lady before—so I hoped there woud be a few ringlets. I believed the blackness of the room would conceal my eye color. Otherwise, she would not know my true identity. We do look like brothers, as everyone has teased."

"How far, Rawlings, how far?"

"As far as you can imagine. I took her in my bed. I wanted no dispute. She was totally compromised. Once I had finished, I shouted for Logan, who brought another servant in the room carrying enough candles to light up Almack's. It was entertaining when, Margaret saw my green eyes and instantly realized with whom she had bedded. She screamed, of course, and, therein aggravated her problem. My brother charged in the room dragging her father with him. I only assume he had a pretense for being nearby. He expected you to be mostly undressed and her in a torn gown. She could still pretend to be untouched that way. But, I must say she had not been timid about the act nor was she inexperienced. She did things no lady should even know."

"I suspect there was a scene? I only wished I had known. Rawlings, I have a way to protect myself. This has been tried before, and my man is well trained to handle such things."

"Bah! Logan had found your man drugged and unconscious. They were determined to succeed, regardless of the risks, and my brother would not allow anyone to stand in her way."

Darcy sighed. "I did piece together a little of what happened the next morning. I assumed she schemed to entrap me. I should have never switched rooms. The guilt has hung heavy on my heart. But why did you not tell me later?"

"I did not wish you to think ill of me or my family. It was that duty and obligation you always worry about. So, I preferred you confused than knowing the truth.

"I felt used somehow although I could not identify how and I was angry at being kept in the dark. Why did you keep your distance?"

"I could not avoid the guilt I carried. It was my family, Darcy, who tried to compromise you. I could not look at you. I could not look at myself in the mirror for years. The invitation to Netherfield Park was my chance to regain your friendship.

"I am truly sorry you felt that way, but why did you not just reveal what they were up to?"

Rawlings's voice cracked. "The true question is, why did I compromise her? I needed the money, the lifestyle, but mostly I needed to move on with my life. I believed upending my brother's scheme was my best recourse." He paused, staring at his hands, his head hung low.

"But you could have found another bride, someone more suitable. You did not have to do this."

"Bah! You show your ignorance when you say that. You do not realize how the ladies react once they discover a gentleman is not the heir. You have never seen the way their expressions change, and believe me when I say the transformation is quick and decisive. Unless a second son is a man of means in his own right, the ladies swiftly excuse themselves, not caring if their actions are impolite. My mother did leave me with a small house and a little fortune, but not enough to build a gentleman's life on. I needed more, or so I thought. You…"

Darcy raised his brows.

"What I am about to say is not meant to inflict further guilt but to save you from a wretched existence. When she screamed, she had no other choice. She had to marry me. Can you imagine her shock? She believed the entire time she was in your room, engaging in inappropriate activities, which she seemed to enjoy greatly. She assumed she would soon be the Mistress of Pemberley. Instead, she ended up married to a second son with little money and no estate. Of course, my father had to pay for the indiscretion. In addition to purchasing my townhouse at Cavendish Square, he provided a yearly stipend to ensure Miss Nobody Stevens would not suffer financially, although without our little *tête-à-tête* she would have not married any better."

"Were you able to forge a life together?"

"Life? Well it was one atypical for men of our status. I took my marital rights during the first several months. She laid on the bed, fully dressed, motionless while I did my best to create an heir. She took her joy by shouting *your* name at my climax. After two months, the situation changed."

"Oh?"

"I found the door between our chambers bolted and nailed shut. I assumed I had achieved a successful coupling and created an heir. I no longer needed to cross the threshold into her room and I was not sorry for it. But the goddess of fate had not finished with me yet. An heir was not to be. She lost the babe. She unbolted the door a month later, but I never returned. Not once in the remaining three years she lived. I lost all desire for a child if it meant having to join with her again. Instead, I spent my evenings at taverns and pubs."

"Ah. Now I understand your skill at skittles."

Rawlings chuckled. "Yes, but I had not played Quoits often enough to beat Bingley or Kent. If I had, the stallion would have been mine!"

"I assume your drinking habits changed then as well?"

"I suspected you noticed. Well, yes. I refused to drink alone, so I had my drinks either at the tavern or in my bedchambers. Several times, Logan drank with me at my insistence, of course. He spoke of his heartbreak too. I presume he made it up just to ease my mind."

"But I heard your wife died in childbirth. I must have misunderstood."

"No, you did not. Margaret did die giving birth to a son and my brother mourned for months."

Chapter Nine

"Gerald!" Lord Wolverly called out as he moved up the gangway, taking long strides with every step. The tall masts of the *Lively* rose above the other ships, and with its 114-foot length, had made it easy for him to locate the ship that would take his son across the ocean.

Rawlings turned around at the sound of his name. "Father! What are you doing here? It is too chilly for you."

Logan ducked below deck as soon as Lord Wolverly caught up to his son.

"Son, I was afraid you had sailed, and I would not reach you in time. I cannot believe you are going." He leaned against the railing, panting in deep breaths. His face was flush and sweat had formed on his brow.

Rawlings handed his father a handkerchief. He placed his hand on his back. "I am leaving, sir, and nothing you say will cause me to change my mind."

"I do not understand why you insist on taking this foolhardy trip. You have sufficient wealth to live comfortably without resorting to sailing to the wilderness." Lord Wolverly wiped his brow, and then grabbed his son's arm. "This is dangerous, Gerald. Did I not secure your future?"

"Bah! You only concerned yourself because of our family's embarrassing situation." Rawlings' gaze bore into the pleading man with the blackest stare he could muster. "You and Thomas attempted to ensnare my friend! My God, Darcy was my guest in your house, Father. I will never forgive you for such deceit." His father's firm grip on Rawlings' arm impeded his effort to walk away.

"I did nothing, other than provide the financial means necessary for a union between you two. You behaved like a rake, son. You trapped her for her money and your friend helped."

"What a ridiculous idea. Darcy is an honorable man, as am I!" He yanked his arm free.

"Honorable? You? How is that possible when you were the one who compromised that poor, innocent child? Thomas told me Darcy had asked Margaret to join him in his room, which she did. She expected him to come to her. You and Darcy ruined that poor innocent girl."

"Bah! She was neither innocent nor a child. I was not her first. I acted only to save my friend from a wretched life."

"Thomas said she loved your friend, and perhaps she was no longer innocent because Darcy had been with her before. I had no part in any deception. I only wished to help you, since I believed you desired her to be your wife."

Rawlings voice trembled as he spoke louder. "Thomas tells lies when he wants something he cannot have, and you know me well enough to understand all was not as it seemed."

"I am not as ignorant and accepting of what your brother says as you think! I watched Margaret entice Darcy, and he did, he did, I swear, return her attentions. He danced with her and brought her drinks. He rarely left her side all evening. I make no judgments of a gentleman's behavior; trysts happen all the time. Your friend is not immune to a pretty face."

"Not immune? You do not comprehend his character at all. He is a true gentleman, and she used his good nature to monopolize him. I am positive it was Thomas who suggested you to watch Margaret and Darcy. That was part of his plan."

"You should have told me the truth."

"I have held back telling you because I could see no point in causing you pain. Father, Thomas, and Margaret planned their trickery after you declared she was not acceptable as a Countess. With our Derbyshire estate adjoining Pemberley, Thomas intended to pawn her off on Darcy, and keep her nearby. Convenient for assignations, do you not agree? Moreover, with Margaret becoming a Darcy, they would spend many social evenings together. You knew her well enough to understand she would never allow herself to be hidden away in a nearby cottage like a common courtesan."

"Your brother had no such designs on her."

"Well then, Father, why did Thomas mourn her so deeply? Can you not guess? My wife carried *his* child, and when she died in the process, he drank to an excess even unknown to him. I heard him calling out to her in the night amongst his sorrowful moans."

"I do not believe you." Lord Waverly glared at his son. "Thomas—"

"He is the father. I swear!" Rawlings bellowed.

"Stop. This conversation is not solving the problem before us. You do not need to run off to America. You belong here."

"I am going." Rawlings crossed his arms against his chest. "I will not discuss my leaving any longer. I sail today."

Lord Waverly turned away and grabbed the railing. "I failed you," he mumbled. "I failed Thomas, too, but I most definitely let you down."

"You did no such thing, sir. I sought the marriage, regardless of how it came about, but Thomas' role should not be kept from you."

"I will piece together the truth if I must hold a flintlock to his head."

"I own a modified Baker rifle that would work better. A most accurate shot." Rawlings laughed quietly.

"But if what you say is true about their ruse, then I am truly sorry. I should not have forced you into marriage."

"No one is to blame. It is the second son's plight."

"If only." Lord Wolverly shook his head, closed his eyes, and gripped the rail tighter. His knuckles turned white. Holding back a sob, he waited to speak until his control had returned.

"Let us not run through the *if only* scenario again. Thomas was born first. He is the heir, and is entitled to everything."

"He behaves much in the same way as his mother did—selfishly and with an exaggerated, self-important air. Perhaps, if I had remarried after her death, then Thomas would have had a more kindhearted attitude to you and your friends."

"Such as Bingley and Kent?" Rawlings forehead furrowed, and his eyes turned dark until his father lowered his head.

"True. I own that fault as well. But tradesmen, Gerald? Can you trust them? Believe me when I say I speak from experience when I emphasize the problems with associating with them. Bah! You will do as you want which as has been your behavior since your mother died."

Father and son leaned against the railing, staring at the horizon and did not speak until a sailor interrupted their reverie.

"Mr. Rawlings, sir? The Captain invites you to dine with him tonight."

"Tell him I accept." Rawlings brushed his jacket and straightened his cravat.

Lord Waverly squeezed his son's shoulder. "Gerald, I... do wish you the best."

"Thank you, sir."

"I... will worry for your safety. Is there anything you need, or something I can do?"

"No. Logan is traveling with me. We will be fine. All is well."

Lord Wolverly wiped his eye. "Damn salty air."

Rawlings studied his father with a fresh mind. He discovered gray strands nestling among his thinning hair, deep-set wrinkles framing his eyes, and large brown freckles dotting his father's hands. And he did not stand as tall as he had remembered. When did he get so old? He felt his throat tightened and quickly reached and squeezed his father's shoulder. Why is his breathing so shallow? Is he ill? Should I stay?

The two men spoke in calm, hushed tones for a few minutes, each man gathering strength from the other until they ran out of impersonal topics to discuss. When Lord Wolverly approached the gangway to depart the ship, he turned for one final look at his son. "Write as soon as you arrive."

"I promise. Take care, Father." A lump in Rawlings' throat burned. He failed to utter the words he wanted to say and the Lord wished to hear. As his father walked down the gangway, he felt the urge to run down and hug him just as he had done as a toddler. Instead, he grabbed the railing when his father turned, waved, and then got inside his carriage. Rawlings watched the horses pulling him away, returning his father's wave too late. He spied Darcy's carriage pulling up, he tried to swallow the lump in his throat and quicky wipe away the mist in his eyes.

Logan rejoined Rawlings on deck and waited for the men to alight. Long before boarding the ship, Rawlings had decided to introduce Logan as a gentleman acquaintance, and planned to call him Mr. Logan throughout the trip. The subterfuge was for Logan's protection from the British Royal Navy. However, he did expect Logan to perform usual duties, albeit in secret. Logan had agreed to the plan.

Darcy stepped out first, and located Rawlings standing on the deck near the gangway. Bingley and Kent followed close behind. Darcy and Bingley headed towards Rawlings while Kent sought out Captain Pierce.

"Is everything as I requested for Mr. Rawlings and Mr. Logan?" Kent nodded towards the gentlemen on the starboard side.

"Everything is in order, Mr. Kent. Although your friends have been given the best, I worry the staterooms are not what they are accustomed to having."

"Fear not. They do not expect luxury." Kent turned his gaze upon his friends. "Both gentlemen will take the voyage without complaint, being pleased they could travel on this marvelous ship that crosses the ocean in forty, and not the usual sixty-two days."

"Yes, the *Lively* is fast, which may cause bouts of seasickness."

"Well, it is good then, that it is such a short journey."

By the time Kent caught up with the travelers, Blake had arrived. The five men exchanged their final goodbyes. Many months would pass before Rawlings was due to return home and they felt it keenly.

Bingley patted Rawlings on his shoulder. "You will miss my dinner party. When on their best behavior, the invitees can be exceedingly interesting."

"Who are these interesting people?" Rawlings asked.

"James Watt is one. You could have shared your negative opinion of the steam engine and the locomotive, and then he would have enlightened you on the future of transportation."

"I am sorry to miss an evening of pistons and governor things." Rawlings winked to Bingley.

"They are called flyball governors," Bingley grinned. "Never let him discover you do not understand his life's passion. Uncle Watt would expound up the subject you until you could describe the intricate workings of one. I speak the truth. I was cornered over a discussion of flyballs years ago."

"I am sorry to miss the party just the same."

Bingley turned to the others. "I invite you all on Thursday night to the dinner for my family and friends and a few members of Kent's as well." He eyed Darcy and added, "Oh, and my Aunt Watt will be my hostess, so please bring Miss Darcy. I can assure you, it will be a different conversation, an enlightening evening."

"I must decline," Blake answered quickly. "I have dinner plans with my Uncle Harrowby. Lord Liverpool will be there, and I should attend, with the rifle sale proceeding. It will be a much different conversation than yours, but I imagine an enlightening as well."

Bingley grinned. "I understand. Perhaps next time."

Blake turned toward Rawlings. "Oh, Uncle Harrowby warned me of the likelihood of another war with America soon. He is working on avoiding future hostilities, but until then be on the lookout and watch your backside over there. Heed his words—these are dangerous times."

"Thank you for the caution, Blake. Let us hope your uncle is successful. I do not know if England is able to fight two wars at the same time, and to be honest, victory over Napoleon is our first priority. I suspect nothing will happen in America until we finish with the *little corporal.*"

"Darcy, will you be able to attend?" Bingley asked.

"I, too, have plans."

Rawlings noted Bingley's grin fell into a frown when Darcy declined, and once everyone spoke their parting words, he requested Darcy remain behind to clarify something about Astor. Blake bid Rawlings God speed and disembarked with Bingley and Kent.

Rawlings turned to Darcy. "Bingley is your loyal friend, and meeting his family meant a great deal to him." Rawlings eyes narrowed into tiny slits and sent the heat from his glare towards Darcy. "Do not treat him this way."

"I cannot attend, Rawlings." Darcy stood straighter and returned Rawlings' glare.

"When will you stop being so damn haughty, and cease to look down your nose at people beneath you? You need to lower your chin, Darcy, and raise your attitude towards those not in your sphere. Would it be so difficult for you to show the tiniest particle of respect to your friend? Must you always treat him as an unequal? He admires you, and when you decline his invitation *without* attempting to provide a sincere explanation, such as Blake did, then you are not as convincing. He detected your mendaciousness, as did I. How is that for a four syllable word?"

Darcy said nothing. "You are correct. I do not have plans, but I declined for my sister's sake. I do not wish to expose Georgiana to strangers. She... is shy, even with acquaintances. Without a doubt, she cannot find comfort in conversing with different kinds of people." He glanced at the docks where Kent just shrugged in response to a comment Bingley made.

"Perhaps that is true, but you have no excuse. I warn you as a friend, you must address this facet of your character before the Bingleys of the world look down and reject you. One day they will rule us all!"

Reluctantly, Darcy nodded and the two spoke about the looming voyage and the business aspects of the trip. Afterwards, Darcy returned to the dock, where the other three men were waiting.

Rawlings, accompanied by Logan, watched his friends talking on the dock. Logan, however, focused his attention on the stranger hidden by the crates, acting in a clandestine manner, and pointed him out to Rawlings. The person slinked into the shadows.

Darcy, Bingley, and Kent waved goodbye and climbed in the carriage as Blake mounted his stallion. The men headed towards different locations.

Rawlings waved, again too late. He turned to Logan. "Shall we partake of some food? I believe they have refreshements in the dining compartment for the passengers. Perhaps we might meet the other passengers making the trip."

***

Darcy's carriage pulled up at the Custom House where Kent and Bingley planned to discover the procedures and proper documentation for trading a variety of products. Custom House, two hundred feet in length and consisting of two floors caught Darcy by surprise. He had expected a less imposing structure, something to match his perception of the subordinate role of trade. Alas, this was the opposite, a most significant structure.

Kent and Bingley climbed out of the carriage and headed inside while he continued on to the Royal Exchange in search of insurance underwriters. They ascended the staircase in search of the customs officers in the Long Room. All British custom offices are so named even if the actual space was a short, small, and cramped room. Nonetheless, this one lived up to its name, running the length of the building. They located the appropriate custom agent and spent several hours becoming proficient in shipping activities.

The Custom House may be the home of the shipping documentation, but the Royal Exchange is the centre of the country's shipping industry. Darcy ventured up the staircase to the Lloyd's Room. open to underwriters and brokers. Having himself been involved in underwriting ships over the years, Darcy was well known by the patrons. He spent the afternoon drinking coffee and cajoling two particular underwriters to join in his new venture and was confident of their secrecy, having worked with them before. Several other gentlemen showed an interest in the bundling of different types of insurance. They expressed the necessity to be first group to do so. Lloyd has had a reputation for being first. By the day's end, he was satisfied a sufficient number had agreed to underwrite their shipping and liability insurance.

He left in search of Blake, who had also traveled to Threadneedle Street to the Stock Exchange where the buying and selling stocks and raising the money for new enterprises took place. Just as Darcy approached the Stock Exchange, Blake emerged from the front door.

"Were you successful?" Blake asked.

"Exceedingly. I have found six underwriters. They asked to be kept apprised of our plans as we go forward. And you?"

"An old family friend educated me in the financial world and has been most helpful in explaining the best methods to raise money. He offered to help, but before I accept, I need to know what can be shared."

"I suppose everything except the fur trade. We must keep our plans with John Jacob Ascot a secret."

"Then, I will fill him in on the efforts that I concealed earlier. Perhaps, he will prove to be helpful in other areas, as well."

"My thanks, Blake. I am headed back home. Do you care to join me?"

"Sorry, I cannot." Blake threw a look over his shoulder to the upper floor of Stock Exchange. "He invited me for dinner tonight, and after his help, I felt obligated to accept."

The two men parted after agreeing to meet along with Bingley and Kent the next day.

***

Darcy, sitting alone in his study after returning from the docks and a full day of business, mulled over Rawlings' warning. He ignored the rudeness of his friend's words; instead, he focused on his own behavior. Was it truly necessary to refuse Bingley's invitation so quickly? Did I do it to protect Georgiana or myself? Am I avoiding associating with these people? He retrieved writing materials from his desk and penned a note.

> Bingley,
>
> Good news. My appointment has been postponed and I am available to attend your dinner party. I look forward to a stimulating evening of pistons, cylinders, rotary engines, and flyball governors. I researched each one, and I promise I will be able to withstand any challenges thrown at me by your illustrious family and friends. I shall not embarrass you!
>
> Unfortunately, Georgiana must decline. She thanks you for the invitation, but other commitments keep her away.
>
> I shall arrive at seven the night after next.
>
> FD
>
> PS. Will Oban be served? I seemed to have nothing left of my consolation prize.

He handed the letter to Geoffries with instructions not to delay the delivery and then rushed to join Georgiana in the music room, where he was startled to find Kent sitting beside her, turning the pages. The two smiled constantly, shared sidelong glances, and laughed repeatedly. Kent leaned closer to whisper in her ear, but stopped when he spotted Darcy standing in the doorway. His wide grin switched to a smug smile.

Darcy decided to be more attentive to the growing friendliness of his friend and his sister.

Chapter Ten

"Good Morning." Darcy smiled at his sister sitting in her usual chair, buttering her toast. "You look lovely today."

"It is a lovely day. I merely dressed accordingly." Georgiana returned his smile.

Darcy filled plate with a touch of eggs and only one slice of toast,.and then took the seat at the head of the table. He patted his sister's hand. "What are your plans for today?"

"Study and practice." Georgiana sighed. "It is always the same. But, I really do wish to be proficient, so I must practice." She giggled. "Now if you had ever learnt, then you would have been proficient just by putting your fingers on the keys. All the music in the world would flow instantly from your head and heart, without missing a single note. You are Aunt Catherine's favorite, are you not?" Her smile grew wide as her brother coughed into his napkin.

"You are in excellent spirits today. May I ask why?"

"We are going to a party tonight."

"What?"

"Mr. Bingley's dinner party. I am looking forward to attending."

His neck muscles tightend. He fidgeted in his chair. "I do not believe this party will be to your liking. No one you know is attending."

"Mr. Bingley and Mr. Kent will be there. I know them."

"But the others are all strangers and I... am not sure you should be introduced to any person I have not met."

"Humph! You and Richmond think of me as a little girl."

"Georgiana. You are still young."

"Too young to make my own decisions, I know! I know!" She threw her napkin down on the table and jumped up prepared to run out of the room, but dropped her head and spoke in a half-whisper. "Will I never be forgiven?" Her shoulders slumped as she rushed away.

Darcy sighed and pushed his plate away. He was sipping his coffee when he noticed a letter from his Aunt, Lady Cheswick. Without delay, he tore the seal and scanned the words. How fortuitous, she has found a governess for Georgiana. Mrs. Annesley? I hope she is someone who can handle my sister's outbursts and sudden changes in attitude. Why can she not be more like me? Why can she not see how childish she is at times? Humph. I do not understand her at all! Returning his attention to his breakfast, he spread blackberry jam on his toast. Kent! He must have told her about the party!

***

The full moon, in addition to the light from the flickering candles inside, lit up Bingley's townhouse. Darcy climbed the steps, peered into the house and relaxed. The attendees seemed animated, but when a burst of laughter erupted, he worried about the conversations to come. Flyball governor! What is that contraption, again?

Bingley greeted him and ushered him into the drawing room filled with men and women engaged in passionate arguments. Darcy felt he was attending a verbal boxing match and not a debate of technical theories. With most of the words foreign to him and the direction of the talk beyond his understanding, he was relieved when they stopped talking when he and Bingley approached them.

"Mr. Darcy, may I present my uncle, Mr. James Watt, and his friends, Mr. Keir, Mr. Edgeworth and Mr. Galton." While the men exchanged civilities, their wives joined them. Several young daughters and nieces trailed behind. It was not long before the next generation of inventors joined the crowd. Everyone had heard of the Mr. Darcy from Bingley and Kent over the years.

Although Darcy was anxious when the guests surrounded him and felt the invisible hand tightening around his throat, he spoke quietly to the men, and answered many questions, including those he would not normally answer. He discovered they were skilled at obtaining information from a reluctant source. Perhaps that is because they seek answers to all things and seem especially skilled when faced with an unresponsive challenge. He considered his friendship with Bingley and realized his friend had whittled more personal information out of him than anyone his acquaintance did. Had he been Bingley's challenge? He grinned at the thought.

When Kent arrived, Darcy puzzled over how familiar he was with these men of knowledge. He turned to Bingley who explained that Kent was related to the Boulton family. Still puzzled, he looked around the room and asked, "Who exactly is Boulton, and how is he connected to this group?" Darcy felt the heat rising on his cheeks when he heard gasps by several guests.

Mr. Keir joined them and offered Darcy a friendly smile. "James Watt, Bingley's uncle, and Matthew Boulton, Kent's uncle, teamed up years ago for the production of steam engines." While Mr. Keir spoke, Darcy glanced over to Bingley, who had now joined Kent, and realized they had become engaged in the technical discussions with several other men. "Mr. Darcy, your friends have been thrown together for years, and both are well indoctrinated in these type of conversations."

"Thank you, Mr. Keir. I was not aware of the relationship between the families. I met both at Cambridge where we shared living quarters, but they never mentioned their connection." Darcy studied the rotund, older man. He was dressed in black, which highlighted his red hair. Scottish! He assumed this explained Bingley's taste for Scottish whiskey. He was surprised several men appeared to be from Scotland. *Do they breed men of science there much like I breed sheep?* The thought amused him for a moment.

"They speak with immense fondness of their university days. Well, Bingley does. Kent is more private, but do not mistake his quietness. His mind is always turning, and one day we all expect *The Heir* to do great things."

"The *Heir*?" Darcy asked, startled by the level of respect this man assigned to Kent.

"Yes. His late father accumulated a great fortune and became the... king, so to speak, of the tradesman world. No one was more forward thinking than Mr. Kent. No type of business existed which he avoided, and he was successful in them all. He sponsored many endeavors. Kent is the prince, or as we affectionately call him, *the Heir!* Now if you excuse me, sir, my wife is waving for me. I suspect she is trying to defend my opinion of the density and viscosity of gases."

Darcy stood alone, lost in his thoughts. *How did I never hear about Kent's background? The Heir? The Prince?* He never mentioned his father's success. He had just released a long breath when Bingley's cousin, James Watt, Jr., collared him and spoke with unbridled urgency about the exigency for a steamship to cross the ocean. Darcy barely had the opportunity to say he agreed. He too had previously considered the ship's value and finally was able to indicate his own desire to invest in one. They spoke at length on the need for the enterprise until several others joined the group to state their opinions. Those expressing arguments against the endeavor were as unwavering as the ones for it. Men of science are certainly an opinionated lot, yet, no one was offended at being opposed. Darcy chuckled. They seem to thrive on owning a different viewpoint. Their favorite expression was 'You are wrong!' Darcy could not imagine any other place where such a rude remark would be allowed to stand. These men, and the ladies, did treat it as a challenge and fought back by responding with the same phrase preceded by a No!

When a servant announced dinner, all the guests made their way into the dining room, continuing their various heated discussions while they found their seats. Darcy sat next to Bingley's Uncle Watt and his son, James, Jr., and their wives. Sitting directly across from him were Mr. Edgeworth, Mr. Galton, and Mr. Keir. Bingley, Kent, and the young Mr. Boulton sat together. The wives and daughters scattered in vacant chairs around the table. No one seemed concerned by the absence of a planned seating arrangement or the mixing of the sexes. There appeared to be an uneven number of males and females. At any dinner he had attended before this would have been considered a failure on the part of the hostess.

"Mr. Darcy. I understand from my son you have an interest in steam engines?" the elder Watt asked.

"Yes, I do. I use them in my mines in Derbyshire. I also look forward to seeing how they will improve over time. I cannot imagine a mine operating without a steam engine."

"We all expect grand things from these engines, which will be used to power many activities in the future. If it pleases you, I will be honored to show you the latest versions."

Darcy nodded, pleased at the offer made by this congenial man, and they spent the next several minutes discussing a various issues. When Darcy learned that patents were an act of parliament, he offered to help attain any new ones through Blake.

"I understand another one of your friends is traveling to America. I hope he finds the time to ride on the Claremont," James Watt, Jr. said.

"Yes. Mr. Rawlings just set sail, and I can assure you he has been so ordered to take that trip by Bingley." Darcy glanced towards his friend.

"I only suggested it." Bingley looked down at his plate.

"And provide a report!" Darcy laughed when Bingley blushed, but not before releasing his recognizable grin. Since meeting the elder Watt, Darcy understood his friend better. *Ah! Bingley gets his amiable manner from him, twisted smile, and all.* Darcy resumed eating, content to listen to the conversations around him, and did not speak again until he heard someone mention the Society.

"Bingley has mentioned a society of gentlemen in science before. Is this the Royal Society?"

"You speak of the formal one, Mr. Darcy." Mr. Watt looked around the table. "We... have been privileged to belong to a smaller group."

"Lunatics they are!" Kent exclaimed.

Darcy's mouth flew opened.

"Do not worry, Mr. Darcy. That is merely our nickname, but lunatics we all are as well." Mr. Keir laughed along with the other members. "The last of us are here tonight. In addition to myself, there are only three others." Mr. Watt nodded to each man as he spoke his name. "Mr. Edgeworth, Mr. Keir, and Mr. Galton."

Mr. Edgeworth set down his glass. "At one time, the society had fourteen members, and a few correspondents, Mr. Benjamin Franklin from America was one. We meet once a month when the moon is full so the way home would be brighter; therefore, safer. Thus, the name Lunar Society and eventually our friends and colleagues named us lunatics. So, you see, it is really a compliment to be so labeled."

"We just let you think that is the reason." Mrs. Keir laughed along with the other ladies at the table. The men mumbled.

Darcy turned his attention to Mr. Keir. "I understand your work was with glass and chemicals."

"To be honest, I made my money in soap. Cheap soap to cleanse the body."

"Clean up society, you mean. You tried to do that too." Kent winked to Mr. Keir.

"Well, soap did not achieve that. It would take parliamentary reform before that happens."

"Out of order!" Mr. Watt exclaimed.

James Watt, Jr. leaned in to Darcy and whispered, "Talking politics is not allowed at a Lunar Society meeting."

"This is a meeting?" Darcy brows rose.

"Did Bingley not explain this to you? Each man may invite one guest, which you are his tonight. Bingley first petitioned to include you several weeks ago, and we have been looking forward to tonight."

Darcy felt a chill run through his body when he realized how close he had come to disappointing his friend. He vowed to thank Rawlings one day.

"Is there something other than steam that interests you, Mr. Darcy?" the elder Mr. Watt asked.

"Everything new interests me. Lately, I have become fascinated with gas and with something called electricity."

"Ah, that is my field, and one day electricity will be the main power source—not steam!" Mr. Edgeworth pronounced, followed by loud objections of several men at the table, led by the Watts. "Now, I also have experimented with telegraphy. Imagine sending messages across the country in seconds."

"I cannot imagine communications so quickly. Do you believe it will also cross the seas and oceans?" Darcy considered such easy communication with Rawlings while he traveled around in America.

"No, I do not, since the sound is transmitted through wires. There is not enough wire in the world to stretch across the oceans."

Darcy sat back in his chair while he listened to Edgeworth speak in terms that only the others could understand. But when the inventor touched on improvements in agricultural machinery, he sat up straight and asked, "Do you need a place to test the equipment?"

Everyone teased Darcy about gaining the advantage over his neighbors. They explained many wanted to test their experiments without purchasing or investing in the machine.

"I understood you have tested a firearm recently," Mr. Galton said to Darcy.

"I am sure it was not yours, Samuel," Mr. Keir smirked.

Mr. Watt laughed. "No, it cannot be Galton's, since this rifle is accurate and does not misfire!"

Samuel Galton's company was the largest supplier of cheap and sometimes unsafe muzzle loading muskets for use in the slave trade. Although his purpose for the firearms disturbed the Lunar Society members, Galton's interest in science overcame their objections and, in the end, they had not blocked him from joining.

When the conversation and laughter ended, Kent's aunt, Mrs. Boulton, caught Darcy's attention. "If you ever travel to Birmingham, please stop by the Soho Manufactory."

Darcy listened while she and her son explained about the factory. Kent's cousin had taken over the business when his father had died. They made gilded decorative objects such as clocks and candelabra as well as silverware, and the cheaper Sheffield plate wares, an affordable alternative to silver for the growing middle-class. Mrs. Boulton pointed out the manufactory's true worth, although well known for its products, was their humane treatment of the workers.

"I will be honored, and shall make a special trip. Perhaps, he can join me?" Darcy looked over to Kent, who was staring at him.

"At your service, Darcy, and I promise you will have much to see and much to learn."

The butler entered the room. "Mr. Murdoch."

James Watt stood and greeted the man, then turned back to the dinner guests and announced, "Tonight we shall not need the moon, for Mr. Murdoch has brought us all bladders and pipes."

When everyone laughed, the younger Watt took pity on Darcy and explained the joke to him. "A few years ago, on a dark cloudy winter's night, Mr. Murdoch questioned how he would be able to reach his house over such bad roads. But as you will learn, he is a creative person. He went to the gasworks where he filled a bladder, which for an unknown reason he had with him, and placed it under his arm like a bagpipe. He lit the stream of gas emitting from the stem of an old tobacco pipe, thus enabling him to walk in safety to Medlock Bank. That is how the Gas Light Company began."

"Gas Light Company?" Darcy's face lit up.

"Yes." Watt, Jr. spotted the interest in Darcy's eye. He continued, but in a lower voice. "I understand there has been a slight delay in proceeding, but it looks like everything is back on track now to light the world. Mr. Murdoch's sponsor has provided significant funding; two hundred thousand pounds, I believe. A great fortune, but his sponsor is determined to light London."

"Ah. Then I will look forward to the day I can read a book easily in the darkest night. Does he need additional monies? I may be interested in an investment of my own."

"His sponsor would never allow anyone else to participate. He is a powerful man, and I would caution you to not attempt to get in his way."

"Do I know him?"

"He is well known, but Mr. Murdoch is not at liberty to identify him. Initially he had found a few generous investors and had begun work, but was forced to seek help elsewhere when the funds did not materialize. He does not care for his current sponsor at all, but, unfortunately, he is the one with the sufficient money to succeed."

Although unhappy with the warning against investing in what he viewed as a profitable venture, Darcy hid his discontentment, and spent the evening enjoying the conversation. He may not have understood the discussion, but he was at least able to follow a little. Laughter was scattered among the heated opinions as joking and teasing relieved the tension between the guests. To his surprise, the wives and daughters participated in the complex discussion; the opposite of the dinner parties he routinely attended.

Expecting the traditional after dinner music or poetry readings, Darcy was shocked when experiments comprised the evening entertainment. Each man had brought with him his latest efforts or the materials to test a theory.

Mr. Murdoch began with a rudimentary experiment. When he pressed a button, a loud sound rang out. They all looked at him quizzically until Murdoch announced, "It is a doorbell."

As one man examined the doorbell, Mrs. Boulton asked, "Whatever for? We have men standing at the door to announce any visitors!"

"Nonsense, this will be welcomed by the lower classes. Just imagine. Someone comes calling, rings the bell and you will be able to hear it anywhere in the house."

"A nuisance I think." Mrs. Boulton said as all the ladies clapped in unison. "A doorbell will not keep anyone away. They would just keep pushing that button until someone answers the door."

"The lower classes cannot afford doormen. A doorbell will fit their need perfectly," Murdoch said brusquely.

Darcy discovered that scientists did not handle criticism well when someone based a claim on feelings and not on methodical reasoning. Standing away from the others, Darcy pondered how valuable a doorbell could be and agreed with the ladies—more a nuisance than help. Astounded that the women would voice their opinion so easily, and the men accepted their comments matter-of-factly, left him mute. Fashion and gossip were the only conversations his female acquaintances engaged in, but he did not object to hearing these ladies' ideas. Perhaps, I should add to the list that the accomplished woman must include the ability to articulate scientific opinions.

Darcy's thoughts shifted to an image of girl with fine eyes, twinkling at the exuberance of this dinner. He imagined her joining in the conversation, although he doubted she had any exposure to inventions and their inventors. But, he had no doubt she would have felt at ease with the teasing conversation, and would have found a way to lob a few volleys of her own. He studied the ladies' faces, and was quick to notice they all possessed a twinkle similar to Miss Elizabeth, but without her flecks of gold shimmering in her brown eyes or even the adjoining raised brow and slight smile.

Feeling isolated, Darcy glanced around the room and decided that the young, attractive ladies seemed more interested in the experiments than in him. His saw one particularly attractive young girl whispering in Kent's ear. She glanced his way, but immediately shifted away while the color on her face darkened.

I wonder who she is. With her dark hair, she might be related to Kent or perhaps, she is more intimately connected? Her figure is light and pleasing. Darcy felt a stab in his heart as he imagined another light and pleasing figure. He sniffed the air and sighed when the only fragrance he could detect was roses. He breathed deeply, allowing lavender to fill his head. Miss Elizabeth, where are you tonight? What are you doing for entertainment? You should be here with... He shook his head. .

Mr. Keir was next to present his experiment. All the guests, including Darcy, stood nearby while he placed salt in a circle on the tabletop.

"Tonight, I plan to test the theory that a spider will not walk across salt." Mr. Keir pulled a leather bag from his pocket. He opened it up and held up a raft spider, dangling the creature in front of the ladies. It was the largest spider Darcy had ever seen, and was amazed the women did not faint, call for smelling salts, or run from the room in tears. In fact, they passed it around from one another and assessed the worthiness of the creature. Finally, Mr. Keir retrieved his eight-legged arachnid from the young lady that had whispered to Kent earlier, and placed it in the middle of the table. It was not a full minute before it left the circle and disproved the old myth. Salt did not intimidate this particular spider. Mr. Keir pulled out another spider, this time a common house spider. It, too, fled across the salt.

Everyone clapped. Darcy noticed a few men exchanged coins. Ah. Wagers find their way in this society as well. I wonder if they hold their own Olympics. They are, after all, Bingley's relations!

"Mr. Darcy, this is routine for us," Mr. Edgeworth said. We experiment and test many theories. Nothing is beyond our consideration. I remember when Benjamin Franklin wrote that he was going to fly a kite in a lightning storm just to prove to the world electricity could be harnessed. He did it too. Proved me wrong. I have been obsessed with electricity ever since. I miss my old friend, Mr. Franklin. We corresponded until he died."

When Mr. Edgeworth moved to the table to present his experiment, the elder Watt joined Darcy. The two men stood slightly apart from the rest. Before Darcy could ask for more information about the steam engines, Watt changed the subject.

"Charles does not seem to be himself these days. You were with him recently, Mr. Darcy, is there something amiss? Is there something you can do to cheer him?"

Darcy glanced at Bingley. "Well, I am planning to play golf with him next week. Perhaps that might return him to his grinning ways."

"I suggest you skip the putting. Demand, good sir, that the hole is finished when the ball reaches the putting area!" Watt laughed.

Darcy bowed. "And do you play too? Perhaps you have the time to join us?"

"Not my game, sir. Not my game at all. I doubt I would even manage to hit the ball!"

"Perhaps one day."

"Mr. Darcy, I do seek a favor of you when you enjoy your golf outing with my nephew."

Darcy nodded.

"You need to explain to Charles that he is a worthy suitor. He has wealth, manners, charm, and is loyal to all those he loves. He is second to no one. He will believe you."

"I believe you refer to a certain lady from Meryton. He is everything you say, but he is not the problem. Her mother is."

"Do you think Charles should cower from a matchmaking mother? Damn. Find me a mother that is not mercenary,. Women cannot work. They must make the most secure marriage that is possible. Will you at least convince him to at least call on the girl?"

Darcy stood rigidly, thoughts flashing quickly through his mind, mostly on the opposite of what Watt proposed. He preferred Bingley seek a lady who could help him rise in London's society. If the business succeeded, then his friend would be in a better position to advance. He continued to defend this internally, fighting every impulse to agree to do what Watt requested.

"I believe your silence tells me what I need to know. Well, I know what to do." James Watt moved away from Darcy and headed towards Bingley, where they spoke quietly.

The guests spent the evening trying different experiments as they argued and teased each other over their theories. Sitting with Bingley and Kent, Darcy, for the first time, found himself envious of the two tradesmen's sons. The gathering had proven far more interesting than he had anticipated, and one he would have regretted missing. I must write to Rawlings about this evening. He would have found something witty to share about these people.

Darcy and Kent remained to share a few glasses of scotch with their host, who was busy pouring the Oban in his study. The room, decorated in dark wood, seemed to match Bingley's mood lately.

"Where was Miss Bingley tonight?" Darcy asked. "I was surprised she was not in attendance."

"She had other commitments. And truthfully, I suspect she would have created one if necessary, for she truly hates these meetings. She would rather not be included. My Aunt Watt serves as hostess whenever we hold a meeting here. I wish it were more often. They usually meet in Birmingham."

"Still, I was surprised." Darcy stared sheepishly into his glass.

"Your attendance was a secret." Bingley grinned.

Darcy nodded. "Ah. Well, it was a most interesting evening. I thank you for inviting me."

"I was honored you came; however, I am sorry your other engagement was delayed."

"Do not worry yourself. I should have immediately canceled that engagement upon your kind invitation. I assure you this was more rewarding. I have never been so intrigued by a party."

Kent peered over his glass as he sipped his scotch. "It was a shame Miss Darcy was otherwise engaged tonight. I had hoped she would have been able to come. It would have been beneficial for her to attend this dinner party." He did not remove his gaze from Darcy.

"Georgiana is still young. I would not want to put her in a situation that would cause her undue stress." Kent opened his mouth to speak when Darcy held up his hand. "And no one should be concerned with her social schedule except me."

"I beg your pardon. I did not mean to suggest I know better what she should do. Perhaps, a much smaller introduction into science would be wise. This was a most boisterous evening, and if one is not used to the enthusiastic discussions, one can be easily intimidated."

"Now that we have finished explaining our sisters' absences—"

Kent interrupted. "Not true, Darcy. We have not discussed my sister."

"And where was she this night? Off to a ball or party?"

"She was here. She seemed intrigued by the experiments," Bingley answered quickly for Kent. "She dangled the spider over Kent's head.

"I am sorry. I do not recall meeting another person by the name of Kent." Darcy said.

"I must ask your forgiveness, Darcy." Bingley tilted his head to the right and shrugged his shoulders. "I should have introduced her. I forgot you had not met her before."

"I assumed you had been introduced. I arrived late," Kent said.

"Well, perhaps we will have another opportunity. I suggest we discuss our current activities." Darcy handed his glass to Bingley. "You recently returned to the Custom House, and I have a few questions."

Bingley and Kent satisfied Darcy's questions. They talked excitedly, making recommendations to which Darcy agreed. He, in turn, gave details of his visit to Lloyds. He indicated he had found the underwriters for portions of their planned activities, and even a few men showed an interest in the liability insurance. Before long, all conversation faded away. Bingley refilled everyone's drinks, sat down and stared at the fire. He had lost his earlier enthusiasm. His glum look returned. His shoulders slumped, and he barely participated in the conversation about the play Darcy had seen at Lyceum Theater. With no other business subjects left to discuss, the three men sat in silence. Darcy glanced at Bingley, and then towards Kent, who shrugged. Bingley released several loud sighs.

Darcy refilled Bingley's glass. "What are your plans for the winter?"

Bingley sighed again. "I believe Caroline and I will be here until late February, when we will leave for the north to spend time with family. Tonight, Uncle Watt invited us to visit. I will, of course, pursue other avenues of revenue for the alliance." Bingley turned his attention to the popping sound in the fireplace and stared at the shimmering flames. "We will depart after Lord Dembry's ball. I... do not expect to return until summer. Perhaps as late as July."

"You will not return for the Season?" Darcy was surprised by Bingley's plans. He had never known Bingley to miss the society of the ladies during that time. Every year a new group of young females appeared, and every year Bingley attended the balls and parties with pleasure each time.

"No. I have no interest this year. I would rather spend time focused on business." Bingley continued to stare at the fire. "London seems dull and boring to me."

"I will remain in town this year," Darcy said and then thought how he had hoped they could leave Meryton's lovely ladies behind and find others to fill their thoughts.

"I expected you to go to Derbyshire."

Darcy shook his head. "The alliance business will keep me in town. I will not be heading to Pemberley until July. You and your family are welcome to join us then." Darcy turned to Kent. "You are invited as well. In fact, it may be a good opportunity to reconvene. Rawlings will have returned.

Both agreed—Darcy noted that Kent did so enthusiastically while Bingley's responded with indifferent nod.

Darcy sighed. "Do you suppose Rawlings had such an enjoyable evening?"

Chapter Eleven

"Hold your head over the side, Logan. Do not be sick on me." Rawlings pulled Logan's upper body above the railing, supported him while his valet released his meal, heaving until there was nothing left. "Do not return to the stateroom. You will just become seasick again. Stay here. I will get you blankets."

Logan slumped against the railing. Another passenger, suffering from the same ailment, slithered down from the railing and joined him on the damp wooden slats of the deck. Their moaning continued, muted but not so quiet the other man could not hear.

The stranger laughed between moans. "Thank God this is only a forty-day journey."

Logan nodded. "But, sir, we still have more than four weeks to go. This nightmare cannot dissapate soon enough. I have decided I prefer a slower moving, and less choppy, ship—one that sails only in sunlight and during calm seas."

"I, too, prefer to never board a boat again." The stranger winked.

Rawlings, returning with an armful of folded up blankets, spied the other man who was shirvering alongside his valet. He handed him several blankets as well. "Good evening, sir. Please accept these. It is much too cold today."

"Thank you. I am exceedingly grateful." He draped the blanket around his shoulders, and placed a folded one on the deck for him to sit on. "Oh, excuse me, let me introduce myself. I am Francis Cabot Lowell from Boston, Massachusetts. I have desired to speak to you since we boarded, but I did not expect it to be under these circumstances."

Rawlings introduced himself and then asked the two seasick men if they needed water. When both men waved away the request with one hand and covered their mouths with the other, Rawlings found an almost clean spot on which to sit. Logan had not kept any food down in two days and it worried him.

Today the ship swayed more than any day since they departed. Those not able to control the churnings in their stomach had found their way to the railings. Rawlings and Lowell had exchanged a few more words when the seas finally calmed and a moonbeam broke through the gray sky. After four days of agitation, the ship sailed on top the water without a lean to the right or left. The two seasick men breathed evenly.

"What brings you to America?" Lowell asked.

Rawlings clutched his woolen blanket tight. "Business. We are seeking new ventures. What brought you to England? Is your family still there?"

"None that I know personally, but, yes, a distant remnant still resides somewhere." Lowell paused to breathe deeply several times before continuing. "My family is engaged in import and export trading."

"Ah. You are a good man to know. We, too, are in the same endeavor. Perhaps fate serves us well."

"I will be pleased to provide you with a letter to give to my father. I, however, am seeking a different occupation. I spent considerable time in Manchester, studying weaving methods."

"We have a friend in Derbyshire who is involved in textiles. Perchance we can return the favor. Are you planning on setting up mills in America?"

"Yes. In fact, I seek to establish a cotton factory in Waltham."

Perhaps it was the kindness he had shown or his approachable manner that allowed Lowell to reveal his plans to Rawlings without fear.

"I have a particular loom design in my mind. I plan to build a working model as soon as I arrive. I hoped to convince a machinist friend to aide in the endeavor. He is an expert in building mechanical devices."

"Is his name by chance, Mr. Bingley?" Rawlings asked.

"I beg your pardon, but no. Should I know this Mr. Bingley?"

"He is a friend whose family is mechanical as well. But are there not other mills in America; or does the mercantile system limit itself to exporting the raw materials to England for us to manufacture?"

"Mostly we send our raw material to England. There are a few mills in America performing a few functions, but mine will handle the entire operation. I want to convert raw fiber into cloth without having to rely on others for any aspect."

"Is that not done now?"

"No one has set up an operation of this magnitude. Not even in England."

"I wish you good fortune, Mr. Lowell. I hope you find the success you seek. And some profit!"

"Mr. Rawlings, by handling the entire operation under one roof the profit will be great. And if England does not relent in the trading prohibitions with America, a war will come, increasing the need for finished products. My finished products, I hope. During a war, the seas will become too dangerous, and all trade between our countries will stop, which would increase my sales immensely."

"Do you think there will be hostilities?"

"Yes, I do. The Whigs are in power now and they will not allow this trade prohibition to stand without retribution. And, I warn you, that they will never stand for the way England boards our ships and takes our men. But then, as I said, war would help me reach my goal."

"Whigs? I suppose you have your reformist party too! Do you need the war for your business?"

"Not so much since a trade embargo exists. If it remains for a period in the future, then my mill will not face competition from England. It is your finished products that I would find difficult to compete against."

Rawlings sat quietly and vowed to remain vigilant in learning all about business in this new land. He silently thanked Darcy for giving him purpose in his life. In addition to traveling to a new country, he felt an excitement that did not come from the gentleman's life. He enjoyed business. It was as if he had joined a secret club, and he knew the secret handshake. He belonged, and they accepted him simply because he dared to dirty his hands with trade. This man beside him did not weigh his worthiness based on his family status. In fact, he had not even questioned him on his social standing.

With the continuing calming waters, Lowell and Logan regained their equilibrium and agreed to return to warmer quarters. The three men made their way to the dining room, where Lowell pointed his head towards two eye-catching young ladies. "My sister and cousin are here. Come, let me introduce you."

"You are looking better, Francis," the prettier of the two girls said while keeping her gaze on Logan. Lowell's sister preferred to check out Rawlings. She sent him a slight smile.

"Mr. Rawlings, Mr. Logan, I present my sister, Miss Marie Lowell, and my cousin, Miss Christina Long," Lowell said.

"It is my honor," Mr. Rawlings said quickly. He nudged Logan with his elbow. Logan, who had been staring at Miss Long, neglected to respond. Any ability to employ civil manners had been lost, overcome by the most seductive smile ever sent his way.

Logan bowed. "Miss Long, Miss Lowell. I hope you have fared better than Mr. Lowell with the storm."

"Yes, unlike Francis, we do not grow ill over a little tossing and... rolling. Please join us." Miss Lowell pointed to empty seats at their table. "We were just enjoying tea and biscuits. I daresay they are helpful in weathering the storm, as my brother should have learned by now."

The men took the seats and heartily agreed to tea. Rawlings was the only one, however, who accepted the biscuits.

"In what part of England is your home?" Miss Lowell asked Rawlings. When she saw Rawlings raised eyebrows, she added, "Your accent. It is British. Although," she turned to her brother and added, "after a year in England, you sound exactly like them."

"I live in London, but my family home is in Staffordshire. Have you traveled in that area?"

She shook her head. "No. We did not go beyond London." Miss Lowell glanced at her cousin. "We attended a friend's wedding."

Rawlings remained quiet, but stole peeks at Miss Lowell while the group discussed London society and found her eyes to be, well, eye-catching. Having seen blue, green, and brown eyes many times in a pretty face, he now found them all ordinary. Miss Lowell's eyes were violet. She constantly turned to him, casting him a small smile when she did. His tongue felt glued to the top of his mouth, and his palms had begun to sweat. He felt uncomfortable in this setting, and did not have the confidence to engage in small talk. Miss Lowell did not seem to mind, nor did she seem surprised by his reaction.

"Tell me about American society. Do they have one?" Rawlings said, regaining his composure and his tongue. He smiled when Miss Lowell feigned a hurt expression.

"Sir, New York City will be to *your* liking. It is full of old aristocrats."

Rawlings reacted with surprise at this pronouncement. Lowell laughed. "We still call it Colonial America. They still think themselves as either British or Dutch, depending upon their background."

"Even now that a quarter century has passed since the revolution?"

"Yes, and they still believe they are superior!" Miss Long exclaimed, blushing quickly when she realized her comment was rude. "I am sorry, I spoke without thinking."

"Do not worry. You only spoke your mind. Nonetheless, it is understandable for these men to think this way. Why the British are superior!" Rawlings winked to Lowell. Logan's started. This was the first time he had ever witnessed Rawlings' humor in company. He had always assumed his master had shared this trait with him in private.

Lowell patted his cousin's hand. "Our new friend is jesting. He knows who won the war!" Everyone laughed aloud and returned to their tea and biscuits.

Rawlings leaned forward, and in a lower voice said, "I understand you to imply then, that Boston is different from New York."

"Most decidedly not! They are the same," Miss Long exclaimed, but her opinion was disputed by the Lowell siblings. Smiling, she added, "And we Americans are the superior ones."

Miss Lowell tilted her head and gazed at Rawlings with her violent color eyes sending a gaze that burned into his. "The old aristocracy may hold sway in the New England states, but that is only with the old generation."

Amused by their brashness, Rawlings' attention darted from Miss Long to Mr. Lowell and back again to Miss Lowell. "And the new generation, what holds sway with them?"

"All that is truly needed to be in the upper crust is money, hordes of money!" Miss Long interrupted.

Rawlings laughed with the others, and smiled at the Bostonians. They fit his likeness of Americans. Brash, energetic, excitable, interesting, honest and above all else, accepting of others, especially second sons.

The group talked about America for the next hour. As time wore on, Rawlings found the cousin, Miss Long, to be a bit flirty, as well as outspoken. She was not afraid to speak her mind or bat her lashes to win an argument. Rawlings watched Logan's reaction to the group, and decided to tease him later. He would call him Darcy, Jr. He rarely spoke, and when he did, it was short and abrupt in tone. Rawlings thought about the similarities between Logan and Darcy, when he suddenly comprehended Darcy's manner was due more to shyness, not haughtiness, and that was what caused him to act in such an aloof manner. He was astonished he had not discovered this before.

Miss Long turned her charms on Logan. She spoke in sweeter tones and cast long simmering glances his way. Rawlings was concerned over her overt actions and his valet's reaction to her. He, on the other hand, could not completely stop himself from sneaking peeks at the violet eyes aimed at him. *Oh, Miss Lowell, you are lovely, exceedingly lovely.*

The time arrived for the ladies to bid them all goodnight. Lowell offered to escort his sister and cousin to their cabin, but asked the men to stay for further talks. They both understood he meant they would enjoy something stronger to drink upon his return. Logan gave his regrets, announcing his desire to rest after such an ordeal, and left for his cabin. Rawlings offered to escort Miss Long, and smiled inwardly when Miss Lowell attempted to conceal a pout.

"Mr. Rawlings," Marie Lowell whispered. Rawlings leaned down nearer to her face and whiffed the unusual fragrance. He was not familiar with the flower used in her perfume. He looked closer at her eyes, and discovered they became a deep purple when candlelight displayed them.

"I must apologize for my cousin. She is overly friendly, but she is a fine lady."

"There is no need. I took no offense at anything she said." Rawlings presented her with his smile, well practiced to appear welcoming and charming. "Nor you, Miss Lowell. I respect the devotion a person has to his or her home, however long they lived there."

She smiled up at him. "It would be my pleasure to introduce you to Boston, should you find your way there. My brother would like that. My cousin will, I am confident, have other activities to fill her time." She accepted her brother's arm. Miss Long slid her hand around Rawlings's and spent the short walk to her cabin in blatant flirtation.

For the first time in his life, Rawlings seemed to be the hunted, and he was intrigued. He decided he would make time for a trip to Boston. Perhaps he would visit there once his business with Astor was finished.

***

When attending his Uncle Harrowby's dinner, Blake hoped for a quiet evening of honest discussion about politics without so many guests; but Lord Harrowby's life was social as well. Tonight, many fine families and their unmarried, young daughters graced his home for dinner and an evening of entertainment—music and card playing. The latest amusement was whisk and Blake's uncle and aunt partnered together and won often.

Harrowby had invited the Godwin family, including their beautiful, unmarried daughter, Avery Anne. He had known them for years. Forty years earlier, his and Mr. Godwin's fathers had worked together on Lord North's India Bill. Although the Act had not been perfect, the bill gave greater parliamentary control over the East India Company, and for the first time, made a distinction between commerce and ruling the territory. Today, Mr. Godwin had taken his father's place, and followed his lead by remaining involved in the Company, albeit as an advisor to the current Lord Harrowby. Mr. Godwin cared about the commercial aspect, while Harrowby concerned himself with the governing side.

Blake bowed and spoke politely with each lady when presented to him. A few were tall, others short, all were thin; but it was not until he was introduced to a redheaded vision in a shimmering gold gown, that he paid the slightest notice. Her beauty first caught his interest, as did her green eyes, but her ability to hold a conversation was what drew him to her. In addition, she did not smile as much as the other ladies did. In fact, she barely smiled at all. As he led her into the dining room, he remembered Darcy's comment about Miss Jane Bingley. She smiled too much. Perhaps he was right. Perhaps all the smiling that the ladies did was just another trick. Even I prefer women that do not flirt and smile at me. Lady Beatrice was the first, Miss Elizabeth the next and now I meet this serious Miss Avery Anne Godwin.

Lord Harrowby watched carefully, pleased his nephew was engrossed with his friend's daughter. She was a better orator than her father, who was standing across the room, also intrigued with the two young people. The two older men shared a glance, indicating their hopes for a future alliance. Blake and Miss Godwin chose to sit together at dinner, spending the time in close discussion.

"Do you have political leanings, my lord?" Miss Godwin smiled before biting into her roast beef.

"I have recently become interested in politics. I find the Tories want the aristocracy to hold onto power, while the Whigs wish to give others opportunities."

"My lord, surely you cannot believe anything a Whig says." In a deliberate motion, she placed her fork down as sparks flew from her glare to his.

Intrigued by the fierceness of her words, Blake was thankful he was of the same political party. He supposed, if allowed, she would have purchased a modified Baker rifle and shot any reformist that stood in her way.

"You have been misled by your friends."

"If they are Whigs, they have not informed me," Blake answered. He slowly brought the rice to his mouth as he glanced sideways at her. He stifled a chuckle when she gulped her wine.

"Mr. Kent's family is full of Whigs. You know him."

"We never discuss politics."

"Just games, competitions, and horses," she said without concealing her smile.

"Mostly. There are a few other topics gentlemen discuss when left on their own too long."

Miss Godwin placed her hand upon her chest. "Such as the ladies, I presume."

Blake raised his glass. "Drink. We argued once over the best wine to serve and brandy to drink." Blake tried to conceal a slight smile as he brought the glass to his lips.

"I am assuming the wine was not French!" Miss Godwin spit the words out.

"No. My friends did drink Scottish whiskey." Blake chuckled when she gulped her wine. "I do not care for that drink, and was content to have won the stallion and not the Oban."

"Mr. Kent's family is involved in all matters of industry." She leaned closer and spoke in a whisper. "If you are not careful, your friend will push for control, and turn you into a... tradesman."

"The industrialists and entrepreneurs are the ones creating the wealth. Perhaps they should be in charge." Blake chuckled at her raised brows.

"In charge?" Her surprised look switched into a glaring stare and bore into him so sharp that Blake leaned away from her.

The two continued to banter back and forth all through dinner. He would make a comment, and she would react with more passion than Blake assumed existed. Neither paid much attention to the other guests. By the evening's end, Blake had smiled more than he had thought possible when he arrived. He noticed his uncle and her father repeatedly glanced at each other, nodding their heads, but he did not care. He enjoyed his evening.

Blake was pleased when the ladies removed to the music room to prepare for the evening entertainment. He wondered if Miss Godwin would be displaying her talents and if her passion spilled into other activities. While he sipped his brandy, he attempted to guess which musical piece suited her. Perhaps either Hayden's *No. 44* or a piece from Mozart's *Idomeneo*. Those pieces are certainly sudden with violent dynamic effects, much like her.

***

Kent spent the morning working at Darcy House. He had rechecked all the cabinets for two important documents, not seen since Netherfield Park. One document laid out their plan for how they would circle the world in trade, and the second one covered the strategy to obtain agreement with John Jacob Aster for the fur trade. Kent made a mental note to discuss the missing documents with Darcy.

"Good afternoon, Mr. Kent."

Kent whipped around to see a young lady dressed in the softest blue colored gown and smiling at him with her hands gracefully folding in front. "Miss Darcy! Good afternoon to you." He bowed deeply when she approached him to curtsey.

"Will you be staying for dinner? We are having your favorite."

"Veal?" Kent asked and broke out into a grin when she nodded. "Will anyone else be attending?"

Georgiana moved even closer and whispered so quietly, he had to lean down to hear. They shared a few more words huddled together, but before Kent could step away, Darcy entered the room.

"Kent! I did not know you were working here today." Darcy's brow tightened until deep vertical lines appeared, a warning Kent could not miss.

"I have been busy all morning." Kent snapped upright. "Thank you, Miss Darcy. I will attend."

Georgiana nodded, squared her shoulders, and then slipped out the door without saying a word to her brother. Watching her leave the room, Darcy released a deep sigh.

Kent returned to lock the cabinet.

"Attend what?" Darcy asked.

"I would rather not say." Kent said, his voice sharp.

"I would rather you did."

"I gave my word."

"To my sister?"

"Yes."

Darcy approached Kent until they were standing eye to eye. Both men stared until Kent lowered his head.

"Do not be such a bloody idiot, Darcy. Your sister is planning a surprise dinner party for you tomorrow. It is your birthday, is it not? She wanted to have a nice dinner and torment you about your growing old."

"Oh! I..."

"I know. You beg my pardon." Kent walked toward the window. "You seemed to be doing that a lot lately. Now, I have broken my word to your sister."

"I will be surprised, I promise, and frankly, I am. I... am only trying to protect my sister. But, I will say no more except I would like for you to attend."

Ignoring the request, Kent returned to staring out the window. "What do you do when you stand here? I have been trying to figure it out for months now."

"I think."

"Does the motion outside the window distract you?"

No. I do not see anything.

"So that is all you do? Think?"

"And deliberate as to what I will say. Sometimes I decide not to speak at all. I have a temper."

"I noticed. I believe you once admitted having such a trait to Miss Elizabeth Bennet." As Kent turned to face him, he caught his breath when he noticed Darcy had startled at her name. Kent flashed an understanding look. "Yes, I will attend, and I warn you, I will assist your sister in tormenting you."

"Perhaps I should have moved to the window before I spoke to you. I…"

Kent held up his hand. "Please, no more. Do not beg my pardon. We are friends, are we not? I do not need an apology for every little mishap."

Darcy nodded and then departed, leaving Kent alone in the library, where Georgiana's dinner party replaced business issues in his thoughts. He imagined the opportunity before him—a social evening with an Earl's family. He wondered what his Uncle Daniel would have to say to this.

***

Although Georgiana had sent cards to the Fitzwilliams, the Bingleys and Hursts, Lord Blake, and Mr. Kent, only six people entered the dining room that evening. Lord and Lady Cheswick had left town for their country home and Richmond was busy with his military responsibilities while his brother and wife had left for Bath a day before the invitation arrived. The Hursts also sent their apologies. Victoria could attend, but she explained to her young cousin she would accept on the understanding that Lord Blake did not.

Fortunately, the marquis made his excuses, choosing to spend the evening at his chess club instead where several gentlemen had sent challenges to him.

Georgiana was grateful for his foresight, since she needed Victoria to round out the party with three men and only two other women in attendance.

Darcy and Georgiana led their guests into the dining room. Darcy reacted with surprise at the table decorations and the presents lined up around his place.

"Happy Birthday, brother," Georgiana whispered.

"Hear, hear!" The others exclaimed.

Kent escorted Lady Victoria, while Bingley and Caroline followed. Darcy sat the head with Lady Victoria, Kent and Caroline along the left side, Bingley sat on the right side next to Georgiana.

"Thank you, all. As I look around the table, I have never been so pleased to be one year older and to celebrate with such good friends. Thank you, again."

Studying the wrapped gifts, Darcy concluded they were all books except one. He opened the first one, *The Lives of the Most Eminent English Poets with Critical Observations on their Works,* in three volumes, by Samuel Johnson.

Lady Victoria laughed. "Volume one uses long abstract words which I suspect you know each one; volume two is sufficiently haughty, but comprehensible to anyone that uses only three syllable words, and volume three is an essay on Swift."

"Thank you, Victoria. I have searched many years for these books."

"My father found them months ago. All the Fitzwilliam's have been looking ever since the last Twelfth Night celebration when you mentioned your desire for them."

Darcy selected Kent's book next.

Kent nodded to Georgiana. "I was asked to choose a book dealing with science and I believe this provides sufficient guidance to experiment on your own.

Darcy read the title to everyone. *"Experiments and Observations on Fermentation and the Distillation of Ardent Spirit* by Joseph Colier. Why thank you, Kent, but now you will have to test each batch! You come from a long line of experimenters!"

Caroline smiled when Darcy picked up the book from her, although it was mostly handwritten pages tied together with ribbon. A titled page on top read, *A Collection of Poems* by Major Henry Beekman Livingston, Jr. "Livingston? Is he a new poet?"

"No, but he is not well known in England. Our families have been friends for generations. They now reside in New York, but we have maintained contact through correspondence. I am positive that one day he will be recognized as a great poet."

Darcy untied the ribbon and gently handled the poems, stopping to study several of the intriguing titles. *The Dance, The Progression and The Vine & Oak,* and one he assumed was written for children entitled, *Account of a Visit From St. Nicholas.* He began to read it aloud.

> Twas the night before Christmas, when all thro' the house,
> Not a creature was stirring, not even a mouse;

The stockings were hung by the chimney with care,
In hopes that St. Nicholas soon would be there…

Everyone clapped when he had finished reading the entire poem.

"What a wonderful tradition. Neither the Burning of the Yulelog tradition nor Boxing Day will compete with this for the hearts of children. Has it been published in America?"

Caroline shook her head. "He sent them to my grandmother and then several more poems arrived a year ago. He gives this poem to many people. He wrote it when his children were young, and it became a tradition for our father to read it to us every Christmas. It is his favorite. I had forgotten about these until Georgiana requested we all bring a book as a present. I know you collect first editions, and while it is not bound, it is the originals. Perhaps one day you could continue my family tradition and read the poem to your children."

"I will. Miss Bingley, this is a wonderful gift." Darcy thumbed through the poems, his brows lifted when he spied the title on the last poem, *Epithalamium: A Marriage Poem*. Feeling his cheeks burning, he nodded to Bingley's sister and carefully retied the pages together and set aside. "I will treasure them always, Miss Bingley. I am exceedingly grateful for your thoughtfulness."

"Mine next." Georgiana handed him her book.

Darcy ripped the paper with enthusiasm and read the title aloud. *"Rules for Angling, Parts I through V* by Richard Bloom."

"Perhaps now you can catch that old thirty pound diligo." His sister giggled.

Kent questioned her with his look until she answered, "Latin for prize. My brother has been chasing this one old carp ever since I can remember. What did you name him?"

"Busillis." When everyone turned their gazes on him and waited, Darcy continued, "Latin for baffling puzzle. He has been one ever since I caught him and he slipped through my fingers. I was sixteen. I have not come that close since then."

Bingley laughed. "Perhaps I should use that nickname for you, my friend. You have baffled me often. Now you have one gift left, and I will admit that it is not a book."

Darcy picked up the box and removed the ribbon and as he opened the top, Bingley cautioned him to be gentle with the contents. Darcy removed a few strange objects and shook his head. "I am at a loss for words."

"You usually are, Darcy." Grinning, Bingley moved towards his friend. "Let me show you how this works. Mr. Keir sent this to you. It is called an arc light and a man named Humphrey Davey invented it. These two wires attach to something called a battery, and this charcoal strip hooks across the two wires. Now watch."

Bingley connected the wires to the battery and then asked the servant to blow out the table candles. He attached the strip forming it in an arc. A light detonated, burning a brilliant white glow much brighter than any candle. When Darcy leaned in to get a closer look, the beam of light disappeared. Bingley laughed and then handed Darcy more charcoal strips.

"This is amazing, Bingley. I cannot thank you enough."

"Mr. Keir enjoyed discussing electricity with you the other night. When I informed him of your approaching birthday, he had this sent to me right away. He said you mentioned that you longed to have a bright light for reading at night."

"But it goes out quickly."

"Unfortunately, all progress takes small steps to begin with. You will learn it takes much effort just to achieve the smallest change. And not everything runs smoothly either. Sometimes everything you have been taught is for naught and you must learn to accept what you thought was not possible."

Darcy lifted his glass. "A most delightful party, everyone. I cannot begin to express how happy I am..." He gazed around the table at the group assembled and continued, "And to be surrounded by my friends has made today the best celebration held in Darcy House."

Darcy signaled for the meal to begin and as expected, Caroline monopolized the conversation by sharing the latest talk about the town. She also complimented Georgiana many times on her exquisite taste in table decorations and meal choices. She repeatedly admitted to everyone how she adored veal. Soon, the others drifted off into conversations with others, leaving Caroline to eat in silence. On occasion, Kent and Bingley brought her into the conversation, but she was rarely able to add to their discussion. They discussed Bingley's dinner party, and the various characters that had attended.

During a lull in the conversations, Lady Victoria turned to Kent. "Pray tell us, good sir. Are there any wonderful tales you can share about Darcy from his Cambridge days?"

"Are you wishing for his boisterous laughter, wild storytelling, or yodeling in the middle of the night? I know it all!"

"Yes, please tell all."

All the conversations ceased as everyone's eye turned to Kent. Darcy revealed a slight smile and nodded to Kent to continue.

"I am sorry that is not possible. He was just as he is today. Quiet. Not even an entire barrel of ale could affect him. As a sober and thoughtful man, he was a friend to me and to all the newest students. I must admit, I would not have stayed had Darcy not taken charge and kept me from making foolish mistakes."

"You forgot about his birthday celebration, the one at the Boar's Head Tavern." Bingley smirked.

"My God, I did!"

"What happened? You must not leave this room without revealing the whole story." Georgiana exclaimed. "Something did happen. My brother is as red as Victoria's necklace." Everyone compared Darcy to the ruby pendant, and began to argue over which one was brighter.

"Do not divert us. What did my brother do?"

Bingley laughed. "After being forced to celebrate at a local inn, he rode back to our lodgings on his horse, facing backwards."

Kent wiped his eye with his napkin. "It was the funniest sight. He held on to a few strands of the horse's tail, and he would not stop saying giddy up. We called him giddy up man all the next day."

"How is it possible? Would he have fallen off? Would the horse go forward?"

Kent patted Lady Victoria's hand. "I rode alongside and led his horse, although it was not easy. I do not know how he fit on the saddle. And then Darcy kept smacking the horse's rear as if it was his neck."

"And one time he did fall into its tail," Bingley added.

Darcy shrunk down in his chair, shaking his head. "I hope you have learned to like mutton, Bingley."

Georgiana sighed. "I wish I could have witnessed it."

"Do not forget, Kent, he hummed and sang all the way. Something from the *Marriage of Figaro*. I could not keep him quiet. When everyone bolted out of their homes and yelling at him to be quiet, he started singing, 'I beg your pardon, I beg your pardon.' He would bow and sing. He must have lost his beaver five times. Do you still have that dirty crumpled old hat?"

Darcy shook his head.

"When we handed it back to him, all he could say was 'Thank you, my good man,' as if we were his servants." Kent rose and bowed to Darcy, who was sighing deeply.

"He tried to dismount but became confused. It seems he has a habit of placing his hand on the horse's neck when he dismounts, but he could not find it."

"How did he get off?"

"Fell right into the dirt. Slid right off the back end. He kept singing 'I beg your pardon, sir' in a strange womanish voice as he stared up at the underbelly of the horse.'."

The laughter died down after a few moments, and the room grew still as they sheepishly peeked at Darcy. His face was hidden his hands while making sobbing sounds. Georgiana's eyes grew wide, but the second her hand touched his arm, his head shot up and the loudest laugh she ever heard escaped his mouth.

Darcy smiled as he reached for his glass. "I wish I could have witnessed it too! And now I will accept bribes from my friends and family to maintain my silence, because I also have a large stock of stories, and I can tell much better narratives than that sorry little tale."

They spent the evening sharing embarrassing moments, including ones Bingley knew about Caroline, and when the dinner neared its end, Darcy rose and held up his glass.

"I offer a toast to my wonderful family and friends for providing me with the most enjoyable dinner to celebrate my birthday." Darcy bowed. "Thank you, my good men and thank you, my good ladies."

His smile grew even wider as the woman with fine eyes who had hazily appeared to be sitting at the other end, holding her glass up in a birthday toast to him. Her right brow lifted and her eyes twinkled while her mouth curved slightly upwards. She nodded her head. However, just as suddenly, she vanished, leaving him feeling unaccompanied in a room full of people.

Chapter Twelve

Invitations to the Lord Dembry's Twelfth Night ball had been sent around town with 1811 now ending. He jestingly called it *The End of It All* since it was the last event before the remaining families would depart for their country estates. London would not come alive again until Parliament opened and everyone returned to start the Season. Although Lord Dembry invited the Netherfield Park friends, Rawlings was sailing towards America and Kent spent his night sharing dinner and discussing his own personal business with his uncle.

Waiting for the time to leave, Darcy sat alone in his library shuffling papers on his desk. He abandoned any reading using the excuse that the candles did not provide enough light. He had spent a few minutes looking for several documents that had been missing. He made a mental not to ask Kent about it. or perhaps Rawlings took them to show Astor.

He paced the floor before stopping to stroke the fire. He poured himself a brandy, his scotch whiskey long depleted. He nestled into the soft cushion of his favorite chair swirling the amber liquid in the bottom of his glass. He could not erase the woman in his thoughts. Her speckled brown eyes twinkled at him while he swallowed his first sip. Humph. I must not think of her. I...

He ignored his own command, and closed his eyes. Her face took form and then her neck. He felt his body burn as his imaginations traveled down the neck to that pinkish sliver where fabric met skin. His hands tightened on the chair arms when he allowed his mind's eye to go behind the material, and licked his lips and leaned forward. His head snapped up. Damn. He gulped his drink, rose, and poured another one.

He forced himself to find a different subject for his thoughts. "The Rivals! Now what were the names of those books the actress mentioned in the second scene?" He jumped up and hurried to the bookcase where he fingered several of the titles. *The Reward of Constancy.* That was one. I am a constant sort of fellow, so where is my reward?

Darcy studied his own collection and questioned if the books in the play were real. He moved further down the bookshelf, tapping the tomes as he went.

Oh, the second book was *The Fatal Connection.* Darcy threw his shoulders back and stood upright. "True, any connection to Elizabeth would be fatal. My uncle would never approve, nor would Aunt Catherine. I would be better off dead then face them. Humph."

When the next title penetrated his consciousness, he allowed his body to slump and his head to drop. *The Mistakes of the Heart.* That was the third book. "Can there really be a mistake of the heart? How can a person ever be a mistake when desire is so strong?"

Well, I believe I am living the last book, and then shouted, *"The Gordian Knot!"* Even though the room was empty, Darcy looked around sheepishly. He returned to his chair, contemplating his intractable problem as he drained his glass of the fiery liquid. He mulled over his situation for a full hour until the time arrived to leave for Dembry's ball.

Darcy and Bingley had agreed to ride together. It did not take long before they spotted Blake who had arrived first and stood against the wall, waiting for them to arrive. He was gazing at the dancers while they turned and swayed to the music. Darcy wondered why Blake was not dancing since he rarely missed an opportunity to flirt with the lovely ladies. He and Bingley made their way through the crowd. The three men were speaking quietly to each other when the whiff of a familiar scent— lavender—startled Blake and Darcy, both catching their breath. They jerked their heads around only to discover the fragrance was wafting from an old matron..

After a few minutes of silence, Darcy pointed his gaze towards the dance floor. "I am surprised you two have chosen to watch rather than participate. I believe that is my role at these affairs."

"Do you not find the music rather mediocre?" Blake stared at the musicians. "Their music is…"

"Yes, it seems a bit off to me too." Bingley nodded. "And no beauty has caught my eye."

Darcy surveyed the room, filled with enough beautiful, stylish, and fashionable ladies for the most demanding of men. Although many ladies had departed months ago, every woman attending this ball knew how to walk, hold herself, smile behind her fan, and even speak in the right tone. The not-so-important gentlemen fluttered around the women, pretending to be more notable than they were.

"Well, why are you not dancing, Darcy? You usually partake of a dance or two at balls where everyone is known," Blake asked.

"It is dull and boring tonight." Darcy winked to Bingley, who just sighed loudly in response.

"Perhaps we should play cards. Is that not what most gentlemen do when they do not dance? You would know, Darcy."

"I do not play cards at balls. I would rather—"

"Discuss books?" Blake interrupted, and then followed it with a shallow laugh.

"Oh. Who is that lady?" Darcy asked as the crowd made way for a beautiful redhead. The green silk was of the best quality. She wore a contrasting ruby pendent, which reflected the candlelight as she roamed around the room. The sparkles had a mesmerizing effect upon anyone gawking at the precious stone cradled in the white of her bosom. She searched the faces until they landed on Blake. She moved forward.

"Miss Avery Anne Godwin."

"I am not surprised that you would be acquainted with the loveliest woman in the room. Where did you meet her?" Darcy asked.

"At Uncle Harrowby's dinner almost a fortnight ago."

The men stood taller when she approached. She curtseyed, and then reminded Blake he had promised to dance with her at the next ball. Blake offered his arm, she accepted, and they left with the other two men wondering more about her. Before Blake and Miss Godwin could find a place in the line, a gentleman approached Darcy, requesting a private moment. He suggested they speak in the library, further piquing Darcy's interest.

Once they arrived, the gentleman paced the room, touching a few books on the shelves. Darcy waited patiently in a comfortable chair, not offering any conversation. He drew circles on the chair arms with his finger matching the path of the man. He had he known him for his whole life, and his father had conducted business with this man in particular. Their estates touched Derbyshire. Unable to guess the reason for the discussion, Darcy cleared his voice until the gentleman stopped and looked his way.

"Mr. Wilcox, is there something you need? Is there anything I can do for you?"

"Good gracious, no. First, I must thank you for your kindness during last year's harvest. Without your help, I would have lost my crop and fallen on hard times. I did not reveal it then, but I had borrowed money; and had you not provided the assistance when you did, my property would have been forfeit. You saved my estate, young man. Your men worked diligently, Darcy. The man I borrowed from would have never shown any mercy. I am only sorry you wish to keep your kindness a secret. Why, if you—"

Darcy held up his open palm, stopping the older gentleman from further discussion. "I suspect you have something else you wanted to say?"

"Yes, you are correct. I came straight from the country to warn you."

Darcy sat up. "Why? What concerns you?"

"Several months ago, a man had been discovered on my property. He was seeking information about you. He would not reveal for whom he worked, and unfortunately, the local magistrate declined to take action. I do not know why."

"What information?"

"At first I found it more curious than alarming. He sought any morsel about the help you gave me last autumn. He asked many questions about your men, and in particular about how you compensated them. He made notes in a journal, but he either destroyed or hid it away before he was brought to me. I thought the man was seeking information to use against me not you, but since my brother visited me last week, I have come to believe that I am not the target."

"I will be on the look out. I thank you for the information." Darcy glanced at his fingers. *I am always a target.*

"There is more!"

Darcy looked up.

"Someone has been questioning many tradesmen in London, and in every instance, they are asking about your involvement with them over a business venture. My brother emphasized that the rumors are spreading rapidly among them."

"Do not fear. There are always rumors where I am the topic."

"No. I have not explained myself well. They are being warned not to deal with you, and they are... afraid. I do not know what you are involved in, and I make no judgment, but I did want to inform you. I would not like to see you harmed."

"Do you have information about this man? Is he the same man who was found on your property?"

"No, it is a different man. I doubt he uses his real name, but the talk is about a powerful individual is behind these actions, and you are the target."

"Thank you, Wilcox. I will alert my man and begin an investigation."

"Well, that is all I wanted to say. I wish you well; and do not hesitate to call on me for any assistance." Wilcox bowed as Darcy rose from his chair.

Slapping the man on his back, Darcy thanked him again and they spoke of the coming winter before they parted company. Wilcox left the premises, and Darcy returned to the ballroom, where he found Bingley sitting alone.

"Darcy, if you do not mind, I prefer to leave. I have no interest in the ball tonight, and I find I am not the best of company." Bingley said.

"If you wait until the dance set is finished, we can take our leave of Blake. I, too, find nothing of interest here."

Bingley agreed, and the two watched as Blake and Miss Godwin continued their dance. "They appear to be arguing. Well, she appears to be arguing. Blake merely smiles at her and nods his head. That seems to make her argue more."

"He does seem to antagonize her." Darcy studied Miss Godwin's face, searching unsuccessfully for a raised brow. He watched helplessly when he imagined her red hair turning dark and several curls bounced along her neck. The green of her gown faded until it appeared almost creamy in color. When the woman in his vision held her arms open to him, Darcy shook his head, clearing his mind of the image of Elizabeth. He turned to Bingley. "Yes, there is nothing in this room that interests me.

"You seemed deep in thought. What holds your interest so intently?"

"I... I was wondering what Blake said that has caused such a reaction in her." He wondered how it was possible his friend could so easily flirt and transfer his attentions so quickly. Blake did appear pleased to be dancing with her. "Did he mention this lady before?"

"Not to me."

They waited silently for the set to end and took their leave when the dance was finished. Blake and Miss Godwin remained, but instead of dancing, Darcy noted they disappeared into another room. Humph. Perhaps another balcony!

***

"Now, is that Beethoven's?" Kent asked while listening to the sonata Georgiana played.

"Yes, he is a new composer. Did you recognize how he uses pieces full of sharply articulated phrases, staccato declarations, and accented chords?"

"To be honest, no. I do not even know what that means. Truthfully, it was a guess. You had mentioned him the other day and I... assumed you would play his music soon." Kent dropped his head but barely concealed his chuckle..

Shaking her head, Georgiana released a deep breath. "You are a difficult student, Mr. Kent. But you do turn pages wonderfully."

Darcy had entered the music room quietly; he stood in the doorway listening to their conversation and cleared his throat when they shared a smile. While pleased to see Georgiana's mood less somber, her growing interest in Kent raised a few concerns. For years, Kent had sought out the most ignored ladies in society. Of course, they were titled or from an established, old family, but had neither the money nor the beauty to warrant attention from someone of a higher station in life. Hence, the opportunity existed for the tradesman's son to improve his social standing. Since Kent's behavior did not affect him personally, Darcy had never concerned himself with the manner in which he, like other social climbers, operated—until now.

When Georgiana spotted her brother, her face turned such a deep shade of red, so dark he could see the spreading color across the room. But when she lowered her head and whispered something to Kent, he decided not to delay any longer. He would ask Geoffries for a daily report about their interactions. Since his butler would be discreet, he doubted Kent would realize he was under surveillance.

"Good evening. That was lovely, Georgiana. Kent, I did not realize you were here tonight," Darcy said through a forced smile.

Kent straightened his cravat. "Miss Darcy has been instructing me on composers; however, I believe I am a lost cause. They all sound alike to me." Kent glanced towards Georgiana, who lowered her head and stared at the keyboard.

Darcy drew closer to her, leaned in, and said, "It is nice of you to help my friend, Mr. Kent. I admire your willingness to help someone so hopeless. I realize it must be impossible with one so tone deaf, and so out of his echelon."

Georgiana giggled at Kent, who was pretending to glare meanly at her brother. Kent's exaggerated manner did not amuse Darcy, and the lightheartedness in the room dissipated.

"What shall I play for you, brother?"

"I must apologize. Kent and I have business to attend to this evening." When Georgiana's smile faltered, he added, "I desire to hear my favorite Bach piece later tonight, and if Kent wishes to partake of our late night dessert, he will have to guess which Bach it is!"

Georgiana smiled to her brother. Kent looked back and nodded his thanks when she began to play his favorite tune as he and Darcy left the room.

Once inside the library, Darcy pounced. "I was surprised to see you here tonight."

Not intimidated by the sharpness of Darcy's words, Kent pulled the letter from his pocket and handed it to Darcy. "I left my dinner early with a message from my uncle. I believed the purpose was too important to delay. I was awaiting your return when Miss Darcy took pity on me sitting all alone in the library. She offered another lesson in composers. I must say, though, it is as hopeless as you said."

Not amused at his attempted jest but willing to ignore it for now, Darcy focused his attention on the letter. "I see, you are summoned to appear at the Custom House. I wonder how they discovered we were considering shipping rifles to British America." Darcy stared at Kent when he spoke.

Kent shrugged. "I am just as surprised as you. Perhaps someone in Bingley's family revealed it."

***

Sitting in his study, Bingley stared at the documents on the desk without comprehending a single syllable. He had no desire to read the words, let alone act upon the request. Lately, his thoughts had often returned to the wonderful time spent in Hertfordshire. He glanced around the room before opening a locked drawer and caressing the vivid blue topaz pendant retrieved from within. "I was going to give this to her as an engagement present. Mother's eyes sparkled so when she wore it."

Assessing the room filled with mahogany furniture, and walls covered with deep green paper, he decided it matched his mood: dark, dull, and boring. The blazing fire kept the study warm, still a feeling of coldness ran through his body. His mind returned to another fire in another room—Mr. Bennet's study. The only image he recalled from that day was the cameo on the desk; perfectly crafted, so even he could discern it was Jane. He had stared out the window into the garden hoping to catch a glimpse of her. If she could welcome me into her life, I would be content. If only she wished it too.

Bingley returned the pendant to its place in the drawer, and then walked to the window. He finally understood Darcy's need to separate himself from everything and gaze at nothing while he thought. He realized Darcy stared more inwardly than outwardly now that he had become accustomed to the same endeavor. Ignoring the reflection on the glass pane, Bingley brought to mind every word and gesture Jane had made. He compared her to the manner in which Miss Lydia would frolic and flirt and then tease the redcoats.She was not like that. Jane was a lady.

He had always been aware Mrs. Bennet pushed her daughter towards him whenever they were in a room together. He remembered how his angel would lower her head to hide the blush. Was it embarrassment for me? He shrugged. Was she merely dutifully doing as her mother required, or did she care for me at all? Was it just for money?

Bingley tried to identify a single change in her actions after learning her dowry was lost. When did they lose it? Was it gone the entire time? Is that why her mother pushed her so? Bingley could not detect any alterations in her attitude from the moment they danced the first dance at the assembly until their final goodbye as he handed her into the carriage on the 26th of November, the night of his ball.

Forty days have passed without a single spark of sunlight in my heart.

When Jane had danced with Rawlings, he remembered how his own hands had twitched uncontrollably. Bingley recognized from the beginning that his feelings for her were different from those he had experienced with other ladies. He had felt the intensity of her hand whenever they came together, his skin burning at her touch. Holding his hand up to his face, he attempted to stare heat into it. This is my curse. Every lady since Jane has the coldest hands. I cannot stand to touch them. He shook his hand and returned to peering into the darkness with both hands now clasped behind his back.

His recollections centered on her dainty smile. It was the same. She smiled with the exact smile she used with Darcy, Rawlings, Blake, and Mr. Goulding as she did with me. He covered his eyes with his hands.

Bingley meandered over to the chair closest to the fireplace, hesitating before he sat down as he conjured up his beautiful lady sitting near the fire all bundled in blankets. When she stayed at Netherfield Park, he had witnessed what his life would be like today, if only Jane had loved him.

Plopping his head back against the chair, he dreamed of his beautiful angel pouring him tea. He studied the conjured up likeness of her hands as she held the teapot and the strainer. He had always admired the graceful way she picked up the cup and saucer. He reached out to accept it from her when his mind returned to the present. He checked around the room to see if anyone had witnessed his foolishness.

He leaned further back in the chair. His mind wandered to the competitions. He pulled the scarf from his pocket. He drew it near his nose to inhale its fragrance. It no longer held the rose scent he had come to love, yet it smelled as strongly to him as the day she handed it to him. He remembered how it covered up that spot on her breast. Not even I believed the Bennet girls all had freckles in the exact same spot. I wanted to rip that dress and discover the truth of that tiny sliver. I wanted to taste her and touch the silkiness of her skin.

Bingley returned the scarf to his pocket. Tonight at Dembry's ball, he realized there was no one else whom he wanted to ask to dance. The ladies were elegant, sophisticated, witty, and beautiful. Having always enjoyed the female sex, he found them all to be insincere and untrustworthy now, and none of them represented his ideal of an accomplished woman. Always before, they had agreed to the dances, not out of any interest in him, but for his fortune, and he could no longer accept a lady's attention based on money. He wanted something more; he wanted a woman that wanted more than wealth. He stared at the fire and announced to the empty room, "I want Jane."

Slowly he rose from the chair and moved to the desk. I suppose I should concentrate on the rifle sales. Lord Liverpool is counting on my getting this order correct. Perhaps I should speak to Darcy. He needs to know that Liverpool sent word to the Custom officials about the shipment of the rifles to British America. If the United States boards the ship and seizes the weapons, the alliance could be in major trouble politically.

Bingley prepared the note, and wondered how Rawlings was faring. He should not be arriving in New York for another few weeks, and he supposed the ocean trip could be just as dull and boring as the ball had been earlier.

***

"Take that man." The sailor pointed to Rawlings. "I heard him speak. He is a British citizen. "Are you trying to desert your duty and your country, you lowlife?"

Logan stood between the sailors and Rawlings, defying them with his stare.

"Do not dare touch us, you mewling fen-sucked bugbear and…" Rawlings turned towards the other man approaching Lowell. "And you, you little cullionly, fat-kidneyed lout, do not dare place a hand on me or my friends."

A man hurried off to find the captain, and when they arrived, Lowell cried, "You must do something."

Captain Pierce threatened the sailors and waved a letter he pulled from his pocket.

After reading the message, the leader yelled, "Release him. Our apologies, good sir." When the other sailors looked at their leader, he merely said, "His father is Earl of Wolverly." The sailors let go immediately, but maintained their hold on Logan and Lowell. As Captain Pierce decried their action, Rawlings held his hand up and shouted,

"These are my companions. You cannot take them."

"The letter made no mention of the others, sir. We have our orders from our captain. All able-bodied British subjects are to be returned to the Royal Navy. These men are British deserters."

Lowell paled at the thought. "I am an American, you simpleton. My father is a powerful leader in Boston."

"Makes no difference to me. You sound like an Englishman to me."

Rawlings tapped Lowell on the shoulder, held his finger to his lips and shook his head. "Take me to your captain. I need to speak to the man now."

The leader escorted Rawlings to the British ship. Nothing Captain Pierce said changed the clasp the other sailors held Logan and Lowell. In fact, the more Pierce spoke, the tighter the grip became, until finally, Lowell begged the captain to quiet down lest his sister and cousin hear.

After a moment, one sailor asked another one, "How much do you suppose it will cost him to buy these two here?"

"I suspect more than you make in a year."

Lowell looked at Logan. He nodded to show agreement with the sailor. "A captured man might be freed with bribery money. Rawlings had planned for just such an incident for me."

"But not me! I must speak to their Captain."

Mr. Lowell, I suggest we wait until Mr. Rawlings returns."

The hostages and sailors remained in their same positions while they awaited word from the British ship. They did not have to wait long. Rawlings returned with a wide smile upon his face, sauntering along the deck with a casual gait. "Enjoying the night air, my good sirs. It is a bit chilly for a walk about the deck. And I see you have become cozy with our new friends while I was busy visiting our neighbor across the water. Should I be hurt?" Rawlings handed a note to the Captain and demanded the sailors release the men.

Logan sighed in relief. However, Lowell was confused until the British leader nodded to release the men after the Captain handed him the note. The sailors left shortly afterwards, and without taking any prisoners. The captain returned to the bridge. Lowell and Logan waited for Rawlings to explain himself.

Rawlings took his time straightening his cravat and smoothing out his waistcoat, but he did offer a smirk when he looked at their confused faces. "I know the Commander well, or rather the Lieutenant-Commander. We attended Eton together. He, too, is the second son of an earl. The commander succumbed to cholera, and my friend took control."

"I assume then our freedom was... free?"

"Let us just say I only had to pay half the going rate, or rather, I received two for the price of one. My friend has to pay the sailors, and our friendship would not overcome what is due. Now he does apologize for the disturbance and offers to escort us to safer waters. In fact, he demands it. Unfortunately, it will not be New York. He has his orders to detour us to Boston."

"Boston, why that is my home!" Lowell exclaimed. "Did I hear correctly, Mr. Rawlings, you are an earl's son? Moreover, what are you, Mr. Logan? The son of a duke or a prince?"

"He is my friend. He—"

"I am his valet." Logan interrupted.

Rawlings shrugged. "You have been a poor sort of valet this trip. Why, I had to care for you! Perhaps though, you can be the earl's son and I shall be the valet. We are heading to America, and I suspect I will be received better with your background than with mine."

"Not true, Mr. Rawlings. Many will want to meet you and not your valet." Lowell turned to Logan to apologize when Logan held his hand up.

"Call me Rawlings. I have grown tired of titles," Rawlings said as the men approached the railing to watch the Royal Navy return to their ship. "I suppose it is the custom in America for friends to call each other by last names."

"Or first names. We do not hold any particular custom. You may call me either Francis or Lowell."

"Lowell it is then, and this is Mr. Logan." Rawlings smiled at Logan's sighs.

Logan grabbed his stomach. Rawlings guided him closer to the railing. "Shall I hold your head again?" He did not speak. He merely did what one did when one could no longer put off a natural urge to relieve oneself of dinner. Rawlings was somewhat surprised when Lowell stood beside them.

"When we arrive in Boston, how shall we introduce you, Mr. Logan? As a gentleman or a valet?"

Logan turned to Lowell, shared a grimace before leaning over the rail again.

Chapter Thirteen

"As a valet, please." Logan looked worn out when he answered Lowell's question. He did not wish to return to the role of gentleman, and now that the British had boarded the ship he realized it was safe to reveal his status without fear of being taken. He had always enjoyed being in the background, and believed his life worked better from that station. The three men had returned to the warmth of the dining room and talked for a while about the situation.

Rawlings grew concerned when Logan abruptly excused himself to head back out to the deck.

"I am sure he will be fine." Lowell's gaze followed the queasy looking man as he disappeared from the dining room. He was about to speak again when Rawlings held his open palm up.

"Traveling as a gentleman is safer. As a valet, the British would falsely claim he was a deserter. Nonetheless, my own countrymen should have treated me with more respect, but I suppose the Navy trusts no one these days. The number of deserters increases daily."

"You two speak as friends. I do not have a valet, and I am curious. Is this the usual way between a gentleman and a manservant?"

"Not usually. Logan has been with me since I was a mere lad of sixteen and I sought a friend at that time. He complied with my request. I was surprised to discover your elevated status in Boston. You come from a prominent family? You surprised me when you told him your father was a powerful man."

Lowell laughed. "We are a pair, trying to hide our pristine family connections." He breathed in deeply as the ship lurched forward in an attempt to make up lost time. Lowell supposed that was what caused Logan to return to the railing. "Our talk the other day did not reveal your true plans. You, however, discovered mine."

"I belong to a group of young men, partners really; two tradesmen's sons, one marquess, and one highly esteemed gentleman farmer, who put us together. He is the one with interests in milling."

"A gentleman farmer? Is he involved in any other industry?"

"Mining, shipping, insurance. In fact, he insured this ship, and will be delighted I was able to earn him his profit," Rawlings said.

Having learned more about the congenial man sitting across from him, Lowell relaxed as the two spoke about the the alliance. Rawlings explained what they were attempting and Lowell provided him with a solid understating of how business worked in Boston and New York. Much to Rawlings' surprise, the American offered to provide letters of introduction for him. Lowell emphasized that the Livingston family in New York would be the most beneficial family to meet, and in Boston, the Perkins and Forbes families could offer insight into the China trade.

The two men shared a few drinks and talked well into the night, touching on many topics including similarities and disparities in the politics and the social realm between their two countries.

When a silent pause occurred, both men agreed to turn in for the night. Returning to his cabin, and while preparing for bed, Rawlings dwelled on the friends he had left behind in England. He wondered which activities were keeping his friends busy—business or social. Bingley, he supposed, was still mourning the loss of his angel. Kent had returned to the place he preferred, as would any social climber.

When Blake and Darcy had returned suddenly from Hertfordshire, he concealed his unhappiness at not being able to return to Netherfield Park. He had planned to seek permission to court Mr. Bennet's youngest daughter before leaving on this voyage. Now the opportunity was lost.

Rawlings took in the emptiness of the room and realized how he longed to hear Lydia's laughter and again receive the teasing looks she had sporadically cast his way. He should have returned to Meryton and announced his intentions. Then, Mrs. Bennet would have kept George Wickham away. Tonight he would be resting easier instead of fighting this sense of foreboding. The arrival of the Bingley family in London ended his opportunity to secure her. He pulled the coverlet back and gazed at the vacant bed. He wondered if Miss Lydia was dreaming of redcoats or had the waltz changed her thinking in any way.

As he climbed into bed, his thoughts turned from Lydia to Bingley and then to Blake, wondering whether the two friends had overcome their recent heartbreaks, or if Darcy had admitted the truth of his desires. Thoughts of his partners faded as the likeness of Lydia Bennet came into view, but just before he succumbed to sleep, the faces of Miss Long and Miss Lowell appeared. He clutched his pillow tightly to his chest. A hunted man, indeed!

***

Three weeks had passed since his sister's surprise dinner party. Darcy's schedule was so busy, he had not had time to read any of his books, but he made plans to make his first batch of distilled spirits for Kent's birthday in July. A servant placed a pot of tea on the table where Darcy sat, fingering the collection of poems given to him by Miss Bingley. He studied the paper, deciding several of them were old. The pages numbered fifteen, and contained cheerful prose, but only a few went beyond odes to family members. Still, he recognized that Miss Bingley had given him a unique gift.

Sipping the tea, he read one of the more interesting ones: *The Procession*.

> The legislators pass along
> A solemn, self-important throng!
> Just raised from the common mass,
> They feel themselves another class.
> But let them in the sunshine play
> For every dog must have his day.

He placed the poem down and finished his cup of tea. *Just raised from the common mass.* Hmm this speaks of Kent or even the men of science. *For every dog must have his day.* He mulled over the words until a knock interrupted his thoughts.

"Enter." Darcy looked up as Mrs. Geoffries and another woman came into his study.

"Mr. Darcy, Mrs. Annesley has arrived for your interview."

Darcy rose and moved towards the neatly dressed and poised woman. "Mrs. Annesley, how good of you to come this morning. I was most impressed with your experience, and Lady Cheswick has recommended you highly."

"Mr. Darcy." She curtseyed and sat in the chair he indicated. Mrs. Geoffries left the room, closing the door behind her.

"I understand you are seeking a governess or lady's companion for your young sister."

"Yes. She is sixteen. Her mother died when she was an infant, and by the time she was ten, her father passed away. She has been in my charge for almost five years now, along with my cousin, Colonel Fitzwilliam. She spends her time studying languages, art, history, and music. She plays the pianoforte with great skill. I secured masters for her in each subject and she has excelled in them all. Help with her accomplishments is not what she needs. I am seeking a woman's guidance for this time of her life. Neither my cousin nor I are best able to address her concerns."

"Sixteen. I understand. I suspect you have witnessed an emotional outburst or two."

"Yes, precisely. But how did…"

"I was that age at one time myself." Mrs. Annesley chuckled. "In the teen years, excessive sensitivity is not uncommon nor is it unusual, and in one respect, a right of passage into adulthood. Has she acted in any way that was not proper?"

"No, but… almost a year ago there was an experience that left her a little insecure."

"Should I be aware about the particulars?"

"I choose not to divulge the incident for now. If after working with my sister you find the need for information, then we could talk again. I would prefer Georgiana determine if she wishes to reveal the story."

"Very well, sir. Is there any other situation of concern I should know before I accept this position?"

"She is a sweet girl, but easily upset, and unfortunately she can be swayed by others who use their charm on her. I expect you to keep a close eye on anyone befriending her. I would like you to help her understand how to judge people and their attentions to her. But mostly, she requires someone to guide her through this period in her life."

"What are her habits?"

"She is inclined to practice on the pianoforte for several hours daily. I would not like to see a change in her routine."

"I studied intensively when I was young. I look forward to being around music again. My last charge was not so inclined. Her talents leaned towards drawing and painting. With the information you have provided, I have no reason not to accept the position as lady's companion. I would like to begin immediately if possible. My prior commitment is now complete, and with that young lady's recent marriage, my companionship is no longer required."

"Excellent. I will expect regular reports on her progress." Darcy rose. "I will direct Mrs. Geoffries to provide you with a tour of the house and your private chambers." Darcy rang for the housekeeper. The two ladies departed with his secretary standing in the doorway.

Darcy waved him in and invited him to take sit. "It was good you came, Mr. Rogers. I wanted to talk to you about a pressing matter. Have you discovered any new information regarding Mr. Cuffage?"

"No, sir. All the talk around town has died out. I doubt if I can uncover anything that we do not already know. Shall I hire an investigator?"

"Yes, but a more pressing issue requires attention. A man digging into my affairs has approached many local tradesmen recently. His goal is twofold. First, he wants information about the alliance, and second, he has warned them not to do business with me."

Mr. Rogers jerked upright. "Yes, sir, right away. Do you have any particulars on what the man seeks?"

"A little, but I prefer to tell the specifics directly to the investigator. Have him see me in the morning."

"Yes, sir. Is there anything else?"

"Nothing else, except to address what brought you here."

"Your shipping business. I came to report that the latest ships arrived in Nova Scotia safely. I received this message from the captain."

After dispensing with the note, they spent the next hour discussing his business. They had just finished when Mrs. Geoffries knocked. Mr. Rogers departed.

The housekeeper approached her master, her hands wringing. "Mr. Darcy, I need to speak to you about the upstairs maid. She is with child, and will not be able to continue.

"Is someone available to take her place? If not, hire a new girl."

"It is just… "

"Just what?" Darcy asked, impatience creeping into his tone.

"I fear what will happen to the young girl. Her husband died in a carriage accident in late summer, only a month after they wed. He had worked for Lord Dembry. She returned to her old position as a chambermaid shortly after his death. She is a hard worker, and presented no trouble now or during the three years previously. And apparently she did not know her condition at the time she returned."

"Does she have any family to assist her?"

"None, sir. She is so frightened about her future that she has stopped eating in an attempt to hide her situation."

"I will have none of that. Is she willing to move to Pemberley? I know an older tenant, a widow, who would welcome companionship, and I am positive she would be delighted with an infant in the house. It is a small cottage, but there will be enough room. I will pay a small fee while she lives there; but, I will expect her to take up her duties at Pemberley when the time comes."

"Yes, sir. Thank you. I know she will accept willingly. May I tell her now?"

"Yes, and please feed the girl. Tell her I insist. And send in fresh tea."

Darcy picked up the poems again and headed for the chair next to the window. The late afternoon sun offered a bright light for reading. He selected the poem titled, *The Vine and Oak, A Fable.*

> A vine from noblest lineage sprung
> And with the choicest clusters hung,
> In purple rob'd, reclining lay,
> And catch'd the noontide's fervid ray;
> The num'rous plants that deck the field
> Did all the palm of beauty yield;
> Pronounc'd her fairest of their train
> And hail'd her empress of the plain.
> A neighb'ring oak whose spiry height
> In low-hung clouds was hid from sight,
> Who dar'd a thousand howling storms;
> Conscious of worth, sublimely stood,
> The pride and glory of the wood.

Darcy caressed the paper. Elizabeth, are you are the empress of the plain; am I the neighb'ring oak? I do hide from you and yet, I do not know why. *Pride and glory of the wood.* Am I so prideful? Am I so conscious of my own worth? He put the poem away when the servant arrived with the tea, promising to finish reading the rest later.

***

"I am afraid you must share." Mrs. Gardiner opened the door to her largest guest room. Having had her fourth child, the available rooms for her visiting nieces had dwindled. "Rest for a while. Dinner will be early. The children wish to see you again."

Elizabeth assisted the maid with unpacking her trunk and waited to speak to her sister until the servant left.

"Jane, did you bring your heavy cloak? Town is colder than I remember. I feel a chill."

"I believe it is downstairs." Jane touched Lizzy's head. "You are warm. Lie down before it gets worse."

"I am fine. I am only tired from the trip. But are you well? Your complexion seems pale, even for you."

Jane sighed. "I am more anxious than ill. Do you... do you think...?"

"Yes, I think Mr. Bingley will be pleased to learn you are in London."

"And Lord Blake? Perhaps he will be calling on Mr. Bingley when I visit Miss Bingley. Shall I mention your being in town?"

Elizabeth remained silent as she twirled a curl around her finger. Jane folded her arms across her chest and tapped her foot. Elizabeth sighed.

"I only wish to discover why he left without taking his leave, but I fear the answer."

"You said his father had called him home. Perhaps he could not wait another day, and you must admit when you did not appear, he had no reason to delay his return to London. He must have thought you did not wish to hear what he wanted to say. You must see the reason in what I say."

"I agreed to travel with you to London because I want you to have the chance to speak to Mr. Bingley. I have no hope of seeing Lord Blake."

"And I wanted you to have a chance to find out why Lord Blake left. I have less confidence in Mr. Bingley than you do."

"I suppose we came for each other... as well as for ourselves." Elizabeth climbed in the bed as Jane covered her with a blanket. "Such wretched irony."

"What will you say if you have the opportunity to see Lord Blake and he offers you marriage?"

Elizabeth sighed. "I do not know. I have not let myself imagine being married to him."

"Why not?"

"I have no fortune and the only connections I have are so beneath him. And the way our family behaves, I am almost ashamed to be called a Bennet. Did you not see Lydia and Kitty running about at the ball? Did father not embarrass Mary, who should not have exhibited herself in such a way? And mama! You did not hear her remarks. I could not look at Lord Blake. I could not look anywhere except my plate."

"I do not believe it was as horrible as you make it out. You have many charms."

"I have no fortune, and our connections are a tradesman and a lawyer for uncles. How could any man of his position connect himself to me? I have nothing to offer."

Jane patted her sister's hand. "Perhaps he did not mind. He did request a private meeting."

"At first I assumed he wanted to propose, but Jane, why did he not come to the house? Why did he not take his leave properly?"

"You do not believe he would make a dishonorable offer? I do not believe that of him."

"But he gave up so easily and if he wanted marriage, he would have never left without speaking to me. Hand me the handkerchief in my personal box. Yes, that one."

Jane brought the item to her sister. She had often caught her fingering the cloth, and once had nearly caught her opening it, but Lizzy had never shared the contents.

"This is what I found that morning." Lizzy unwrapped her keepsake and studied her sister as Jane tried to make out the contents. "A broken chess piece, a white knight. He had my initial etched on it and his family coat of arms. I assumed it was a wedding present because he had said a white knight is honorable and good and protects his queen. But surely you can see he was angry enough at my absence that he smashed it to pieces."

"He must have been hurt deeply, Lizzy. Imaging what his emotions were when you did not appear. I do not think he acted only in anger. He is an important man, and your absence must have surprised him and made him believe he was unimportant. Perhaps our family's behavior did give him worry, especially our youngest sisters."

"I can only imagine his opinion of the entire Bennet family, and I can hear the words he might think. I know he must believe any connection would be a degradation, and I cannot conceive what his family would say or do. His father is a duke! His uncles are earls. Surely, they would object to his connecting with someone without titles, connections, or fortune, and to a woman with a family that acts in total want of propriety and acts as if it is the correct behavior. I cannot bear to recall the ball at Netherfield Park. They confirmed every suspicion he may have had.

"Well, if he is that squeamish, and cannot bear to be connected with a little absurdity, he is not worth your regret." Jane patted her sister's arm.

Pulling the blanket up to her chin, Lizzy settled into the pillows. "He would never say so directly. Lord Blake is a gentleman, but he would think it, and although we would never discuss his true feelings, the disgust would fester with every reunion with the Bennets." Lizzy patted the bed until Jane sat beside her. "Now the question is why did Mr. Bingley not return? Unlike Lord Blake, there can be no mistaking Mr. Bingley's opinion of you, dear sister, or that of yours for him."

"Oh, dear. Have I behaved in an improper manner when I was near him?"

"Not at all. Charlotte believed you did not show your feelings except we know you well, that is why your admiration for the man was obvious to us. I thought it was obvious to him too. He did stay close to you every opportunity. Now, admit your feelings for Mr. Bingley?"

"I like him; that is true, but… "

A knock on the door interrupted Jane. Mrs. Gardiner peered inside and informed the girls that dinner would be at six, but if they so desired, they could have trays sent up. Both agreed they were not too tired.

The two girls' discussions turned to clothes, fashion, and weather, but before they left the room for dinner, Jane and Elizabeth made a pact not to tell everything to Mrs. Gardiner.

***

Blake trotted towards Bingley's house. The two men had spent several evenings together under the pretense of work. They, however, met to commiserate their lost loves. Although they shared no words on the subject, each man understood the other's sadness. They would discuss anything other than the Bennet women or Netherfield Park. Just like their time in Cambridge, they leaned on each other when flirtations failed. Today Blake needed Bingley's companionship. He had spent another fitful night imagining what his life could have been. A vision of a queen wearing a cloak marked by his coat of arms appeared. She was holding a chess piece, a knight, and it switched from white to black and then back to white again. Oh, Elizabeth! Why did you trifle with me? Why did you flirt, tease, and cast those bewitching eyes on me. Was I not rich enough?

Turning into the street, he was startled when he spotted Miss Bennet leaving Bingley's house. He carefully examined her countenance. She was definitely sad. Her shoulders slumped, she kept her head low, and every so often, she dabbed at her eye. I suppose Bingley made his decision. I wonder if he is aware how dreadful she feels. Is it the loss of money or my friend that causes her such grief?

The recognition hit him that he did not know where the Bennet girls stayed in London. He decided to follow behind and discover the whereabouts of their uncle's home. He had only known it was somewhere in Cheapside as Miss Bingley had pointed out many times. He could not remember her uncle's name or never knew what he looked like and without either he had no way of searching for him. He had frequented the warehouses in Cheapside hopeful he might find Elizabeth there but to no avail. Miss Bennet's appearance gave him hope.

Blake patted his horses' neck. "We are fortunate today. Perhaps we can find out where Miss Elizabeth is staying."

Twenty minutes later, and with the rumors he had heard concerning her uncle's dishonesty were filling his thoughts, he watched Miss Bennet climb the stairs of a modest, but relatively new townhouse. He noted how the property was well cared for by its owner. When a properly attired doorman opened the door, he did not identify any common signs of financial distress. Usually, these particular servants were the first to go, and yet this person was opening the door as another servant left the house on an obvious errand. This puzzled him. He stopped a young lad running down the street and asked who lived there and when indicated it was the Gardiners he recalled it was the name of the uncle. Yet, the family did not seem downtrodden.

After the door closed, he glanced around the vicinity and memorized the location. He felt disappointed when Miss Elizabeth did not greet her sister's return. He fought the urge to bound up the steps and bang on the door. He preferred a private discussion. Instead, knowing her propensity to walk outdoors, he assumed if she was visiting, it would not be many days before she would leave the house. He would wait each morning for her, and when she stepped outside, he would seek the answer to the question nagging at him daily. *Why did she run away from me?*

He remembered his meeting with Bingley and, trotted away. The production of the rifles was near completion. His Uncle Harrowby and Lord Liverpool had been successful with the military order and he needed Bingley's signature on several documents. The customs official was satisfied with the documentation for the shipment to British America. England was concerned about the continuing escalation of hostilities with America, and the British government believed the rifles were necessary to protect those lands.

Blake returned to Bingley's house, only to discover his friend had left to search for him at White's. Bingley would not find him there; he had not entered his club since his initial appearance upon his return from Hertfordshire. Since his father spent his afternoon's there, Blake decided not to follow Bingley to the club, instead turning for home to make plans to seek out Miss Elizabeth. He could not move on with his life until he learned the truth. She haunted his nights, and now that he had seen Miss Bennet, he knew she would stay on his mind all during the days, too.

For the next week, Blake sat atop his horse, hidden from view from the residents of the Gardiners's home on Gracechurch Street. The air did becoming warmer with each morning, and there were days he swore his breath froze in the air. The temperature should have been hotter, the calendar showed spring was soon to arrive. He did not leave his position for hours while he hoped she would appear on the front step. Four small children, one servant, and Miss Bennet ventured out each morning for a short walk down the street. Not once did a dark haired beauty join them. He concluded Elizabeth was not in Cheapside, and with a melancholy heart, he gave up his quest. She was not there, and he doubted he would ever see her again.

***

"Lizzy, drink this." Mrs. Gardiner held her niece's head up. "Please."

"What is it?"

"A dear friend sent this over. She promises that you will be better in a day or two. You have been ill for over a week now, so drink this. I insist."

"What is in it?"

"Oh, it is flavored water. I boiled ginger root, cardamom seeds, turmeric, and garlic. Lizzy, dear. I am worried. Nothing has worked yet. Your fever has not abated. You must drink this."

Elizabeth sat up on her elbows and swallowed the concoction. Jane wiped her sister's forehead with a cool, damp cloth, and Mrs. Gardiner covered her niece with a fresh coverlet.

"Oh, Jane," Mrs. Gardiner whispered when Lizzy fell back asleep. "Thank you for helping with the children. They have enjoyed their walks each morning, but today I wish you would stay with Lizzy. Watch her carefully. If she is not better by tonight, I will send word to her father."

Jane nodded and sat with her sister for the entire day. Lizzy slept soundly but every once in a while she would wake just long enough to sip the cold remedy.

At eleven that evening, Lizzy woke up smiling. Her fever had broken and she informed a drowsy Jane that she was hungry and tired of lying in bed. Careful not to disturb Jane when her sister fell into a deep sleep, she slid out from under the covers and ventured down the stairs with the intention of sneaking into the kitchen. She wanted something of substance having spent the last ten days sipping broth.

"Who goes there?"

"Uncle, it is me, Lizzy."

"You are well?" Mr. Gardiner approached his niece, touching her forehead with the back of his hand. "No fever."

"I am well. The potion aunt gave me worked wonders. Now, I am surprised to find you here."

"You found me out. I regularly sneak in here for a treat before I retire for the night. How much will it take to secure your silence?"

"The truth."

Gardiner felt his neck muscles tense. Holding a pie, he found a knife and several plates and pointed to two chairs. "Your dowry money?"

"How did you know?"

"You have been mumbling in your sleep. Your aunt was worried."

"Yes, I seek the truth since I do not understand how my father lost the money."

"Mr. Cuffage worked with an inventor who appeared to have discovered how to create light without candles, well, more precisely, with lamps that glow from the burning of gas. The inventor needed two hundred thousand pounds in order to light the streets and houses throughout London. He had applied to Parliament for a patent for his invention, and presented a proposal. Mr. Cuffage found a banker to loan him the money and your father and others provided the collateral for a percentage share of the business. Alas, the inventor spent all of the funds in materials and labor while they waited for the patent and the order to proceed. When Parliament did not approve, Cuffage called the loan and your father was required to make full payment. The company dissolved, and with it went any hope of recovering your dowries."

"Oh. And had the patent been approved, Father would have seen a profit?"

"The proposal to light London would have resulted in your father more than doubling his investment. However, the true profits would have come from the patent to produce all the gas lighting needs for England. You father risked your dowries for potentially enormous wealth and unfathomable fortunes for his daughters."

"We were content with what we had."

"He wanted to do more, but he had no money of his own. Everything belongs to the estate and with it entailed away, he feared Mr. Collins would confiscate the profits for himself. In order to invest, he had to use your dowries, the one source of funds out of Collins hands."

"Did you invest?"

"I did not, but only because I needed to expand my own business. Mr. Cuffage had collaborated with me on several successful ventures in the past, and that is how your father came to know him. Since then, I have discovered he cheated me on several contracts, although I do not have the proof. One day I will find the evidence and send him to Newgate prison, regardless of whoever is shielding him."

"Someone is shielding him?"

"Yes. I suspect he is a powerful man. Perhaps he is the banker. I do not know."

They ate their pie in silence until Lizzy thanked her uncle and returned to her bedchambers. For the first time in weeks, she would venture outdoors in the morning.

***

Darcy entered the music room to find Kent turning the pages of the latest composition from Beethoven at Georgiana's side. He switched from one foot to the other while the couple whispered together, their heads in close contact. His brow furrowed when his sister giggled and the lines on his forehead grew deeper when Kent blushed. Darcy's gaze drifted onto a beautiful white flower tied to a note resting on the pianoforte. Darcy immediately recognized the ribbon wrapped around the items as the same one Kent had used to wrap his birthday gift. He also had not miss how Georgiana moved quickly to drape sheet music over the flower before flashing a signal to Kent that her brother had joined them.

He doubted either one would be willing to share their secret. A pattern had emerged. Every time he had entered the room, they returned to an upright proper position and gazed everywhere, but at each other.

"Kent, I need to speak to you in the library." Darcy turned sharply, not waiting for an answer; his long strides covering the hall carpet with ease. Darcy paced about the room, deliberating what to say and how to not cause offense.

"Darcy, is something upsetting you? Is there something wrong with the shipment of rifles?"

"No. Everything is proceeding as planned. I… have other issues on my mind."

"I would be willing to help if you need it. I have been busy securing agreements with tradesmen all week. I believe we are approaching a full cargo for British America. Only one or two more orders are needed."

Darcy moved to the window. "I assume Bingley informed you Lord Liverpool was the person behind the Custom Office inquiries about the guns to British America?"

"Yes, and he and I handled the matter to everyone's satisfaction." He waited quietly while Darcy continued to stare out the window without offering any further conversation. Unwilling to allow the silence to continue, Kent cleared his voice loudly enough to cause Darcy to turn his head. "I hope you are thinking about the enormous profit we will be making once the ship arrives."

Darcy turned around and faced Kent. "Did any tradesmen shy away from your business?"

"No. Why do you ask?"

"Did they realize I was a partner?"

Kent remained still while he composed his words. "I did not reveal any partner, as you requested. Should I have?"

"No. It will be best not to do so. They only need to know you are placing orders for a company."

Kent's gaze darted from his friend to the floor and then back again to his friend before fixing his glare on the floor. His hands twitched as he squirmed in his chair. "I have been careful to maintain the secrecy you, Blake, and Rawlings desired, and have the tradesmen deal only with me. Although I suspect we have not achieved complete secrecy."

After a moment spent in careful observation of his friend, Darcy returned to looking out the window. "Well, never mind. We only sought a delay in revealing the membership until we established ourselves. I cannot find several important documents mapping out our strategy. Do you have them?"

"No. Perhaps they have been mislaid. Blake could have needed them for gaining political backing."

Darcy turned away from the window and shrugged. "Perhaps so or even they may be with Bingley. Rawlings might have taken them to present to Astor, as well." When no response was forthcoming, he slid into the chair across from Kent. "Well, let us discuss a more interesting subject. I would like to make our plans for the trip to the SoHo Manufactory in Birmingham. You aunt was gracious in the invitation, and I would like to visit the facilities. I am desirous of meeting your family's other business partners."

"Excellent. I am available at your convenience. She is looking forward to the visit, as is her son. They will treat you royally."

"That is not necessary. I will not be able to leave until I return from my annual trip to my aunt's home in Kent."

"All things named Kent are good," his friend chuckled.

Ignoring Kent's lightheartedness, Darcy continued, "The trip to my aunt's is planned for the last day of March." The two men identified which day was convenient for them and set the date shortly after his return one week later. Kent promised to inform his aunt to make arrangements, and as there was nothing else to discuss, he promptly set out for his home.

Miss Caroline Bingley arrived. Her pretense was to visit with Georgiana, but once inside the house she sought out Mr. Darcy. He was sitting in his study staring at the papers on his desk. He had not read a single word since he was contemplating the growing relations between Kent and his sister. Unprepared for a discussion about Jane Bennet's visit to the Bingley home, he responded in short, crisp answers.

"Miss Bingley, how may I assist you?"

Caroline spared no ridicule in her description of Miss Bennet's unhidden hopes to see her brother. She informed Darcy that she, of course, had not informed Jane of her brother's whereabouts and quickly hurried her out the door.

"I do not think you acted properly, but Miss Bennet should not expect to be reacquainted with Bingley whenever she calls upon you."

He barely heard her say she would not tell her brother about Jane's appearance. He merely answered, "Do what you think best, and I agree not to inform him either. He does not need to be reminded of her while he is still disheartened." Yes, he thought, if he sees her now, he will succumb quickly. Bingley will not listen to reason.

Miss Bingley left to visit with his sister. Darcy rose from his chair and walked toward the fireplace. He felt warm, even though the flames were dwindling. After restoring the fire to full force, he moved to the sideboard. He reached for the bottle of Oban Bingley had sent over and filled a glass, shaking his head. Mrs. Bennet must be desperate. Neither Blake nor Bingley has returned and all of Meryton must know of their misfortune by now. Did Elizabeth come to town as well? He shook his head. Forget her. Protect yourself!

***

Although the afternoon sun was bright, the air still maintained its winter nippiness. Having reached its destination, the carriage stopped, and Kent stepped down. He had spent many outings over the years along the paths in Hyde Park, cultivating relationships with the regular attendees. He had always acted in the appropriate manner, not wishing to be a party to any scandal. He believed his future depended upon a pristine character. Darcy may abhor scandal, but he feared it. He could ill-afford to be tainted by it and any decision he made whether business or pleasure rested on it. Thus, he worried about his connection to Blake whose father was indeed a scandal bubbling up.

Money was one talisman to London's upper echelon, and his wealth could purchase him a worthy lady; although he had no doubt the particular ladies that might be interested in him would not enhance his property. In order for his acceptance, her family would need to be near insolvency, but her financial status was of no concern to him. He wanted the invitation into the inner circles of the best families. If a lady lacked the desired connections, she would not be worthy, or so he thought. She needed to be young and unmarried and he preferred her to be a little attractive. That was important. Over the years, several ladies matched his criteria, but those flirtations had not worked out. His heart had not been touched, which was the final ingredient for marriage. He needed to feel something for the woman he wed. And now he knew it be true, he felt something for her.

No more than a quarter hour passed before he spotted Georgiana and her cousin, Lady Victoria. He startled a little when he spied a well-dressed gentleman escorting them down a familiar path. He was not tall enough to be Darcy, and was huskier in build. Both ladies laughed while they walked, another indication it was not him. Moving to a parallel path and walking ahead, he was able to study their expressions. This man shared a certain intimacy with them and, for the first time in months, he worried he would have competition after all his hard work.

He approached them speedily and yet quietly, trying to hear their conversation before they discovered him, but to no avail.

Georgiana looked up and exclaimed, "Mr. Kent. Oh, please join us."

Kent nodded and eyed the other two walkers. He bowed to Lady Victoria and to the gentleman moving quickly to Georgiana's side.

As her escort leaned down and whispered to her, Georgiana blushed and looked down at the path. "Richmond, I would like to introduce you to Mr. Kent. He is my brother's friend. Mr. Kent, this is Colonel Fitzwilliam, Victoria's brother."

Kent released his breath and smiled to the two ladies, but eyed the colonel suspiciously. He offered his arm to Georgiana, but the colonel directed him to assist his sister. The four walked on, their talk covering the competitions, Darcy's inability to putt, and shared acquaintances. Kent felt the colonel's gaze boring into him with every interaction with Georgiana. The colonel glowered when he caught him winking at her and she, in turn, smiled widely at him, but it tuned into a full scowl when she enthusiastically listed his many good qualities to Lady Victoria.

Chapter Fourteen

Darcy shuffled through the morning's post, examining the mail while he ate his breakfast. Every day brought the same routine. After checking each piece of correspondence, he divided the letters and invitations into separate piles, letters of urgent nature in one stack, and the rest set aside for later consideration. The mail presented to him did not include everything; his secretary separated out the unimportant and less urgent mail and placed those on his desk in the study. They consisted of requests for money for a charity, or other pleas for help. While the wealthy received this type of request daily, Darcy was sent more than most Londoners. His family had supported many charities, and the newest master had become well known as the most generous of all.

Piled next to her plate, the servant had organized Georgiana's correspondence with the letters not from family members placed on top. She, having been tutored her whole life, was without any friends of her age to share a young girl's dreams; therefore, she rarely received any correspondence except from family.

The habit of the siblings was to open her letters first and share the contents. Her mail included invitations needing a response and letters from relatives, most recently her cousin. At three and twenty, Victoria was her closest female relative in years, but their age difference still created a slight chasm between them. Georgia, at sixteen, was just entering into the grown up world, whereby Lady Victoria had several years of experience and held different opinions. What was giggly and romantic to Georgiana was boring and dull to Victoria. At Lord and Lady Cheswick's insistence, however, the two young ladies spent more time together.

This morning Darcy was so distracted by a particular letter sitting on top of his own stack, that he did react when Georgiana slyly slip a piece of correspondence in her lap and hid it under her napkin. Although he witnessed it, his concentration was focused on his own letter. He vowed to ask her about the letter later.

Both brother and sister were preoccupied with wanting to go off to read their own interesting letters, the two ate quickly and agreed to delay opening their other mail until later that afternoon. Georgiana remained seated when Darcy grabbed his messages and left for the study.

He settled into his favorite reading chair, the one located close to the window beside a cloth-covered round table where the servants had just placed his morning coffee next to the stack of books and journals. He picked up his cup and sipped before he opened up the letter that had caught his attention. He was anxious to hear what Rawlings had to say.

> Darcy,
>
> We have arrived in America, although the British Navy was so kind as to escort our ship to Boston instead of New York City. I had always wanted to visit this provincial little town, and they were pleased to accommodate my wishes.

Darcy stopped reading, and grew pale at the thought the *Lively* had been boarded and Rawlings and Logan might have been abused in any way. His muscles tightened, although he realized Rawlings had arrived safely, otherwise there would be no letter. He returned his attention to the handwritten words.

> I have learned on the crossing how to be a valet. Our Mr. Logan learned how to lean over the railings and not make a mess of everything. Had it not been for the most polite British navy seaman that helped hold Logan ever so tightly, he would have made a complete untidiness of the deck one cold night. Being a well-bred gentleman, I immediately boarded the HMS Whiting, a beautiful sloop of war with its three masts and eighteen oversized guns, and profusely thanked the Lieutenant in Command for his men's kind attention to my friends. He told me not to thank him, but he had received orders to divert our journey. Apparently, they left England a week before we did, and had been patiently waiting for us.

Darcy shuddered. He gingerly rubbed the letter as he realized Rawlings had been taken to the British ship. He and Rawlings had spoken several times about the possibility of the *Lively* being boarded. He returned to reading the letter.

> The lieutenant was cordial in the usual way. You know how young, ambitious upstarts are with a presumed wayward British subject. He offered to return me to my homeland, and to secure a wonderful room at the Newgate Inn. I assured him the hotel was not up to my standards, and we revisit Eton, in order to complete my thrashing of a particular new student.

Darcy laughed as he remembered the boy assigned to Rawlings as his fag. In addition to making the boy clean, cook, and run his errands, Rawlings had whipped the boy to remove his supercilious attitude. Afterwards, Rawlings took him under his wing and ensured his success. They became great friends, even after Eton. If it were not for Rawlings, the boy would not have been able to do so well. He recalled the young man did join the Navy. A more relaxed Darcy again picked up the letter.

> Of course, the fag has learned how to tease since school, and I did compliment him on his attempt to do so. I advised him, quite loudly too, given that he appeared to be growing deaf, my friends were enjoying the warmth of sailors hugging them close in the chilly evening air, the warmth of their cabins would be preferable at this time of night. I suggested my concern that others would misread the kind actions of his men, thinking perhaps they had been at sea too long, and were looking for a special type of warmth themselves.

Darcy laughed aloud, shook his head, and then continued to read.

> Needless to say, he signaled to another young upstart to have his men return to the HMS Whiting without any new companions. After agreeing to dine the next day with him, of course, not without a cost, so I provided a little of my wealth for the privilege of eating without restraints. I returned to find my friends telling the British sailors such funny stories, and in such animated ways.
>
> You are a clever fellow. Did you wonder at the word 'friends?'

Darcy leaned back in his chair. He knew Rawlings would not wait to tell him about this new person or persons.

> We are fortunate to have journeyed with a young Bostonian. He and Logan were sharing space at the railing when I first met him. After spending time in England, visiting near Derbyshire, studying milling, he now plans to open a cotton mill in Massachusetts. He is ambitious, and reminds me of another friend of mine. His father is a powerful man in Boston and, he is well established in the import and export business. I believe he may be the China connection we have been seeking.
>
> I am thankful I was the one that took this journey, for I had no trouble sharing the blanket with what appeared at the time to be a person of decidedly lesser status.

Darcy reread the sentence and placed the letter down. He rose from the chair and rekindled the fire. Once the flames were licking merrily against the logs, he paced about the room until he stopped at the window. He looked back several times to the letter lying upon the table.

Georgiana knocked and entered the study. "William. Come and hear my newest sonata. I need you to tell me if it is worthy to play for Mr. Kent. He will be here later."

Darcy forgot about the mail, and left with Georgiana for the music room. While she played, he vowed to have a word with Kent. He worried Georgiana was letting her innocent heart rule her actions again. With the possible scenarios completely engaging his thoughts, he did not remember Rawlings' letter until much later that night.

***

"My compliments to your beautiful wife, Lowell," Rawlings said. "My ability to express my thankfulness is beyond my meager capabilities. The trip would have seemed empty, had I not had your family activities to enjoy. I am sorry Mrs. Lowell was needed elsewhere this morning. Please convey my thanks, and share with her it has been a most wonderful and rewarding experience."

"We have all enjoyed your visit, even the children. One day you should have your own houseful. You were most entertaining." Lowell noticed Rawlings placing letters inside his coat pocket. "Has Logan gone?"

"He is overseeing the arrangements for the trip to New York. This reminds me, I must thank you for the letters of introduction." Rawlings patted the coat. "They will be most helpful. I cannot thank you enough."

"Well, Rawlings, it is little repayment for my freedom. I cannot imagine how my family would have endured my captivity. Instead, they can now think kind thoughts of our neighbors across the ocean; although I do not think the good feelings will last."

"Nor do I. Let us hope then it is merely a hiccup in the eventual friendship involving two great nations."

The two men continued to discuss the possibility of war and the ramifications that were sure to follow. They had agreed to remain correspondents, and provide any help they could during any hostilities between their countries.

"I wish you well with your cotton mill," Rawlings said. "I wrote to my friend, Mr. Darcy, who I believe will provide assistance with anything you may need. It is my desire for the alliance to conduct business with you in the future, and I hope you desire the same."

"Yes, I do, as does my family."

Rawlings and Lowell had entered into a financial agreement. Lowell had determined the preferred way to raise funds for his cotton mill was to sell stock in the company. Both Rawlings and Logan purchased a significant amount of shares. If Lowell was successful, they would realize an enormous profit. Rawlings had also asked Lowell to put aside shares for the Alliance. He must obtain his partner's permission before making a purchase for them.

"I understand my father has offered to provide trade assistance?" Lowell asked.

"He has, and I am most grateful. Your neighbor, John Forbes, offered his help with the Chinese *Houqua*. Without these connections, I doubt we could be successful in our trading in that part of the world."

The two new friends stood silently as Lowell's servant helped Rawlings with his outdoor wear, and just as he turned to step outside, a young girl came running into the foyer, crying openly.

"My dear Mr. Rawlings, please do not go."

Miss Marie Lowell rushed in behind the youngster, catching her breath while Rawlings gave his attention to her young niece.

"I must, my little Countess." Rawlings turned and smiled at the precocious eleven-year-old beauty staring at him with a large tear streaming down her cheek. He pulled a kerchief from his pocket. "Remember what I taught you about keeping your emotions in control." Rawlings lifted her chin up, wiped her tear-streaked cheek and said softly, "It is not proper to cry so in front of others. When you cry, they believe you to be weak, and we both know you are a strong girl."

She stood a little taller and wiped the falling tears with the back of her hand, even though Rawlings handed her the handkerchief. She clutched the linen cloth to her chest with her other hand before hiding it behind her back.

As she smoothed her dress, Rawlings turned to Lowell and whispered, "You should be relieved she has another few years to go before she is out. Otherwise, you will need that modified Baker rifle I told you about to keep the hunters away."

"I do not dread that day. In fact, I am impatient for it, for I enjoy all forms of entertainment." Lowell lowered his head and whispered, "I have planned many surprises for any man that comes to call." Lowell glanced over to his sister, and suddenly smiled widely. "Including men calling from across the ocean."

Rawlings eyed Miss Lowell, and bowed deeply to her. "Miss Lowell, I cannot thank you sufficiently for the introduction to Boston. Your brother has been most kind to permit you to guide me. I have made many new friends and enjoyed all the parties and dinners this past fortnight. You made me miss my home considerably less." Lifting her hand, he kissed it with the slightest touch, squeezed it, and chuckled at the younger girl pressing herself closer to him.

Rawlings noticed the small hand raised in the air. He leaned down and kissed the young girl's hand. He smiled when she blushed and said quietly, "Remember, you shall be my little Countess for as long as there is a King of England."

With misty eyes, he stood quickly, nodded to Lowell and was off.

***

Darcy slipped under the bed sheets and opened Rawlings' letter. Having first spent his morning with Georgiana, and then in conversation with Kent, Lady Victoria filled his afternoon when she called upon him and his sister, He was pleased to see a growing relationship between the two cousins. He wondered at Georgiana's whispers to Victoria, and promised to speak to his cousin about their secrets. He would also ask her to help keep Georgiana from unworthy men seeking advancement, and then thinking about Kent, he decided to solicit Victoria's aide in monitoring the growing friendship between his sister and his friend.

Now that night had arrived, it was the first private moment he had had to finish reading his friend's letter. Feeling the letter in his hand, his thoughts returned to Rawlings. "Let me learn about his new friends."

Darcy marveled at Rawlings way with words, wishing he were equally skilled. He pulled the candelabra closer to his bed until satisfied that enough light shone on his bed for reading. The Gas Light Company cannot launch themselves soon enough for me. I shall be their first paying customer, and the first lamp will be here in this room. Or the electric light. I care not which one wins the competition!

He leaned back into the pillow, and found the place he had earlier stopped reading. Ignoring the offending sentence and moved on to the next paragraph.

Boston proved a treasure trove of future business partners, the merchants agreeing to align with their alliance and assist with the China trade. Darcy released a long sigh. Even Kent had difficulty with this aspect of their plan. Rawlings was the perfect man to go. He comes from the best of families, and yet he is comfortable among those that are not. Britain had granted a monopoly on all trade with China to the Honorable East India Company, making it impossible for the alliance to trade directly. Rawlings' new coalition of tradesmen would overcome that particular obstacle.

As he continued to read, he had to look away when his friend asked about Bingley. *What would* Rawlings think if he knew Miss Bennet visited Bingley's house? He must agree Mrs. Bennet was desperate to send her there. Nevertheless, he will surely not be pleased about how Miss Bingley and I conspired to conceal her visit. Darcy finished the letter and laid it aside, but the offending sentence repeatedly whispered to him.

'I am thankful I was the one that took this journey, for I had no trouble sharing the blanket with what appeared at the time to be a person of decidedly lesser status.'

In an attempt to block the thoughts invading his conscience, he focused on the next phase of Rawlings' trip. I wonder if he found New York City just as rewarding as Boston? He blew out the lights.

***

The hired driver pulled the horses to a standstill in front of a four story red brick townhome. "This here is the Westchester. Used to be a home, but during the revolution, our great hero George Washington arrived here and set up his war office over there. Now, when Washington showed up, the owners of this house sold it, and they moved back to England. I will wager George Washington slept here.

"Are you sure?"

"No, sir. Just jesting. An American joke, I suppose, or else the man slept anywhere but his own house. Everyone claims he slept at their home." After curtailing his laugh, the cabbie pointed to the street and the surrounding area. "Now, you can see that Bowrey Street is turning itself into a commercial boulevard. Only families lived here before. They are mostly gone, and the inns and business have taken over."

"What changed?" Rawlings asked as he paid the fare.

"Fours years ago, the political bosses had mapped out new streets in this area into square boxes. That is what all the activity is around here: building streets and businesses and townhomes and look at the rubbish everywhere."

"Boxes?"

All the roads will intersect into these perfect boxes. Square boxes! Organized it is. They call them things blocks. Have you ever heard of such a thing?"

"No, I have not." Smiling, Rawlings tipped his hat to the cabbie as Logan assisted with the trunks. The carriage driver waved goodbye as he pulled away along a slightly crooked road. "Shall we register?"

Logan nodded, and followed behind Rawlings as they entered the Westchester Inn and approached the desk to give their names to the clerk, who informed him the hotel was full.

"Sir, what exactly do you mean? We do have reservations for this hotel. Here is the written confirmation." Rawlings stood defiantly and shoved the confirmation letter Mr. Cuffage had supplied him at the desk clerk, using his most intimidating stare, a mimic of Darcy successful glower.

"There is a grave misunderstanding," the clerk said while he examined the document. "This is not our stationery. I fear someone has perpetuated a falsehood, and I can assure you, good sir, it was not *this* establishment.

"Nevertheless, might we register today? We are tired from our journey."

"All the available rooms are taken. In fact, all the rooms in all the hotels have been reserved for well over a fortnight for our annual year end celebration."

Rawlings released a long sigh, his every muscle tightened, and he knew if he had possessed any energy, he would have punched the man in the nose. His training on proper behavior took over. "Pray, tell me, sir. How do I find transportation?" Rawlings glowered..

"To where?"

"Mr. Livingston's home in Manhattan." His scowl increased.

"Mr. Robert Livingston, the Chancellor?"

"Yes. We are scheduled to meet with him tomorrow, but I suppose he might be the best one to locate a fine establishment for us for the night."

"Excuse me for a moment." The clerk scurried to the back room, and within a minute, a well-dressed manager appeared.

The manager looked the two men over from head to toe. "I beg your pardon. My clerk is mistaken. We have your room ready. It is the best suite we offer. Again, I beg your forgiveness for his error. I will take you to your rooms. Please follow me."

Logan appeared with the trunks, and Rawlings spoke quietly to the manager, who found a servant to handle their luggage. Rawlings grinned at Logan and waved him along as they made their way up the three flights of stairs.

They examined the rooms, and agreed that while it was not equal to Lowell's guest rooms in Boston, it was far superior to the cabin onboard ship.

"It appears we have the whole floor to ourselves." Logan said as he opened the first trunk. "

"I suppose Mr. Livingston is a powerful force in New York. Meeting Lowell was providential. Let us hope our good luck continues." Rawlings lifted his trunk and placed it on the wooden stand for the luggage, but when he began to open the lid, Logan raced over.

"Sir, I will take care of your clothes."

"Rawlings! Call me Rawlings, not sir! I will finish unpacking my trunk. I have grown accustomed to performing valet duties. In fact, I would rather work than sit and watch you stay busy. There is nothing else for me to do. I am hungry, and waiting for you to unpack both trunks will delay my meal. So move away."

Logan relented, and the two men quickly dispensed with the unpacking and headed down to the inn's dining room. Once the food arrived, the two men devised a schedule for the next day. Recognizing the first stop would be to find John Jacob Astor; Rawlings pulled out the documents and circled the location on the page Mr. Cuffage identified as Astor's home. Rawlings emphasized that he could not afford any mistake tomorrow, as the global strategy was riding on collaborating with Astor. They finished the meal and headed out to a tavern recommended by the desk clerk. Rawlings was disappointed it did not possess any pub games, but realized Kent and the alliance could happily correct this situation. America caused Rawlings to bubble up with ideas; everywhere he looked, he found an opportunity.

The next morning, the manager sent up a breakfast tray for the men, and they ate while Logan prepared his master for the day. Rawlings teased him about his preference for his valet duties, and reminded him in America, anyone could be anything. With an unspoken anxiousness, the two men finished dressing and left the room.

The clerk, apologetic about the previous day's episode, located a hired carriage for them and they headed towards the address they had for Astor.

"Burned down?" Rawlings searched the area for any building still standing.

The carriage driver laughed. "You are looking at the remains of the old Morris Warehouse. I heard tell it burned down four years ago. I thought you knew."

"We were informed John Jacob Astor's establishment was here." Rawlings squeezed his hands into fists. "Do you know where the man might be found?"

"I only arrived in New York two months ago. Sorry, mister."

"There is a good fee if you can help us locate him." Rawlings held up a bag of coins.

The driver nodded, and headed to a tavern where his brother worked. He suggested several places, none of which proved to be successful. Apparently, many residents had heard of Astor, but none knew where to find him. The last place on the list was Staten Island, although it remained largely unsettled, but a few families had moved there ever since a ferry service had begun. Thinking it was worth a try, they headed to the embarkation point.

A strapping young lad of sixteen or seventeen approached them while they waited for the boat. His gaze swept over the two men standing before him, and did not bother to conceal his curiosity, since his glance seemed to weigh the men's importance. The young lad kept his surveillance on the men while he prepared the ferry for the trip to the other end. Once his tasks were completed, he sought out the pair.

"Is there anything I could do to help you, sirs?" He waved the two men towards him so he could steer the ferry while they spoke. The boat lurched forward just as Rawlings and Logan joined him.

"You are young to be running the ferry. Is this a family business?" Rawlings asked.

"Yes. It is if you count one as a family. Well, my mother did lend me the money, but it is my business."

"You! This is your ferry?"

He nodded. "Yes, and I do a good business, too!" He waited a moment, and when no one spoke up, he asked, "You are from England? You appear to be gentlemen."

Rawlings sized the young man up. "Let me introduce myself, I am Gerald Rawlings from Staffordshire, England, and this is my associate, Mr. Logan." Rawlings attempted to bow when he noticed an ungloved hand thrust his way.

"We shake hands here, sir. I am Cornelius Vanderbilt."

Taking the lad's hand in his, he felt the firm grip the young man had. "I shall remember that name. If you are successful at such a young age, I can only imagine where your life will take you."

"Shipping. I plan to expand my business to ships—schooners and steamships. Have you heard of them sir?"

"Yes, in fact I have. Are you also planning to build a railway, too? They use steam engines."

"Railways?

"Steam powered trains that move over the land on tracks."

"How do you know about this?"

"I am acquainted with the nephew of the gentleman who invented those engines. He promises it will change transportation in the world. I even saw one in London."

Cornelius stood silently for a moment, reflecting on the railway possibilities until a wide smile stretched across his face. "We are nearly there." He inclined his head towards the shoreline.

"I must beg your leave. We are in need to find a gentleman who we believe resides on this island."

"Perhaps I know him. I have lived on Staten Island all my life, and I am acquainted with every family. What is his name?"

"John Jacob Aster."

Laughing, young Vanderbilt shook his head. "No one named Astor rides this ferry. You will not find him here. I do not know where he lives, but, I believe the man you want took control of a large estate and house from Aaron Burr a few years ago. He subdivided the property, and I heard tell that he granted the tenants a twenty-year lease. Richmond Hill House is located on Varick and Charlton Streets in Greenwich Village. Just ask any hack to take you to there. Did you know General Washington had his headquarters there somewhere when we gave your kin a thrashing? Why he even slept at Burr's house, I believe." Cornelius laughed unabashedly.

Ferrying back to the embarkation point, Vanderbilt and Rawlings discussed the future of steam and mechanical inventions. They promised to correspond and share information about the progress made in their own countries. Rawlings and Vanderbilt shook hands.

Pleased his hired carriage had waited, Rawlings gave the man the new address, and his driver found the location easily. The home, however, was empty. Discouraged, the two men agreed it would be best to meet with Mr. Livingston and hopefully, as Chancellor, he would know Astor or have people able to locate him for them.

Pulling up to the Livingston residence, Rawlings was impressed. The spacious townhouse with a white portico supported by four large wooden columns could rival any found in fashionable London.

Two doormen, immaculately groomed and expertly uniformed, stood guard. The older one accepted the letter of introduction, and left Rawlings and Logan with the other doorman waiting on the top step. The cabbie pulled up further along the street, curious if the doorman would permit entry, He did not wait long before the two gentlemen went inside.

"Mr. Rawlings, Mr. Logan, please come in. You are most welcome here." Livingston said excitedly. "My good friend, Mr. Lowell, had sent an express earlier, and we have been expecting you. Where are you staying?"

"The Westchester"

"Oh no. That is a mediocre inn at best."

After Livingston led them into his study, Rawlings thought living here seemed remarkably similar how it is across the ocean. He felt like he was at his father's home. The furniture was of English manufacture. The books along the wall included the Greek and Roman classics, British history, and even a few novels. He noted the wine carafes were filled, and with a quick study, he assumed that the landscape paintings on the walls must have been painted on the Continent. He admired one scene of a beautiful stretch of land alongside a river.

"That is the eastern bank of the Hudson River. The brick home in the painting was burnt down by your countrymen during the revolution, but I had it rebuilt, and perhaps we can take a trip up to see my home before you leave."

"You are most generous, sir. And forgiving."

"And you, sir, saved my friend's son from capture."

Livingston demanded they tell the whole story about the boarding of the *Lively*. Rawlings, a great storyteller, made the event seem much more exciting than it had been. Lowell had informed him Livingston enjoyed drama, and so it was a dramatic story he told. Livingston was enthralled, and poured drinks continuously as the story unfolded. When it ended and the conversation turned to the reason for the trip, Livingston was stunned.

"Astor? You have come to see John?"

"You know him? You may be the only one in this whole town. We have been searching all day. I had been given Water Street as his address."

"He worked there years ago. I am surprised the hired hackney was so ignorant about the man. Astor travels out west often, so I do not know if he is in town. His wife, Sarah, and his son, William, handle the business while he is gone. I am not aware what his eldest son does, but his second son is in charge of the business while he traveling. Sarah is the backbone behind that business. She has run it for years.

"Might you share where we may seek him out?"

Livingston provided directions, but suggested, since night was approaching, to wait until tomorrow to seek him at Water Street first.

When it appeared his guests were about to leave, Livingston invited them to dinner. He would ensure they met with Astor, or at least his wife, the next day, he even offered to join in their pursuit. "And if you desire, you may reside here during your stay. Even George Washington slept here." Livingston laughed aloud while Rawlings sighed.

At dinner, Livingston learned the reasons for the two men were visiting America. He offered to arrange a special trip on the Claremont, and to set up a private meeting with Fulton. In fact, he announced he would host a party, at which they would be the guest of honor.

Rawlings and Logan returned to the hotel, and informed the manager of their change of plans. They would be leaving in the morning, and requested someone transfer their luggage on the carriage Livingston was sending. Back in their room, Rawlings and Logan settled into their chairs with their evening brandy.

"I fear nothing Cuffage imparted to us was truthful."

Logan refilled both their glasses. "I do not doubt he fabricated his friendship."

"I no longer hold a good opinion of the man at all. I doubt he ever met Astor."

"Do you also doubt Cuffage was Mr. Gardiner's victim? The Bennets did put the blame for their misfortunes on Cuffage."

"Damn. We must have been hoodwinked there, as well. But what purpose did he have to deceive us? My God. The entire global strategy rests on Astor, and it appears we have been targeted for misdirection, but why?" Cuffage had nothing to gain or lose by inventing a relationship with Astor. I cannot find a reason."

He and Logan spent the night ruminating over possible scenarios, none reflected in Mr. Cuffage's favor.

Chapter Fifteen

During his uneventful trip to Water Street, Rawlings considered New York City as a budding and emerging London. The wealthy lived on the cleaner side, with the other parts of the city serving as home to ill-dressed residents and broken down buildings, with rubbish everywhere, and dead horses rotting in the streets. The stench smelled similar to the east end of London, and Rawlings had no doubt that disease was as rampart in the untended part of New York City as his own hometown's dirtier sections. When asked, Livingston explained how Yellow Fever had claimed the lives of many off and on during the years. He cautioned them to stay clear of the area, as another plague was spreading.

The carriage stopped. The men exited, and stood in front of a store with a large sign, which read: Musical Instruments. The inside was well organized; not an item out of place. Rawlings smiled. Good old German neatness! As soon as Mrs. Astor greeted them, Livingston asked after John; she nodded, returned to the back room, and reappeared with the man in question on her arm. Rawlings gasped, the hair on his neck stood up, and his palms began to sweat. He used his handkerchief to wipe his hands. Cuffage said this man was blond and blue eyed. Another lie. Where does this end? Who is Cuffage?

Astor offered his outstretched hand to Rawlings as he had done with Livingston. Not accustomed to shaking hands, he followed up the American custom with a proper English bow. The more rampant the disease in a city, the less individuals should touch each other in public, and with Livingston's talk about the plague; he wondered why they continued to shake hands without the protection of gloves.

Everyone followed Astor to the back room, where he pointed to a closed door. "We can be more comfortable upstairs in my old home."

Rawlings trudged up the steps. "Are your ballrooms upstairs too?" Astor and Livingston glanced at each other with puzzled expressions. Rawlings admitted all dancing took place on what they would call the upper floors in England. Livingston said that while most did follow that lead, not everyone did, and his, for instance, was on the ground floor. Rawlings turned to him with a wide smile. "You, sir, are an intelligent man. I only hope the architects across the ocean do the same.

Mrs. Astor served tea. Logan took a seat next to Rawlings. He had shaken hands, but did not speak beyond the normal civilities. While the conversation ensued, he listened, and studied everyone with great interest.

Astor questioned Rawlings about his purpose for the visit. When he mentioned Cuffage, Astor gazed at him with a blank, unreadable expression. Mrs. Astor indicated that they had not heard of the man.

Nodding, Astor agreed. During their conversation, Rawlings and Logan discovered an unpleasant fact. The man sitting with them, who supposedly had a relationship with Mr. Cuffage, had, in fact, stayed with a Mr. Edward Gardiner when he resided in London prior to his move to America. Gardiner assisted Astor in securing his passage, and he was the tradesman currently handling his trading deals in England.

"Did you say Edward Gardiner? Of Gracechurch Street?" Logan asked.

"Do you know him, sir?" Astor asked.

Rawlings shook his head. "No. I have only heard gossip surrounding his foray into an unsuccessful venture. I am beginning to doubt the rumors were true." Rawlings turned to his valet. "I believe we have been deceived by Mr. Cuffage."

"What does this Mr. Cuffage look like?" Astor asked.

Rawlings began the description with the man's height—short. By the time he finished drawing a picture of the man and explaining the purpose for their connection, he felt a wave of uneasiness flow through his whole body as Astor continuously shook his head and repeatedly uttered one word-no, no, no. Logan remained stone-faced, but Rawlings understood he, too, was concerned.

Astor scoffed. "Cuffage? No. I know the man and he is not honest. He cheated my friend Gardiner." When he identified the man, Rawlings surprised every person in the room with his loud gasp.

With a tremble in his voice, Rawlings asked, "Please, are there writing materials I could use? I need to send a message to my partners immediately. I also need to find the fastest ship headed to England. This is of the direst urgency."

Mrs. Astor handed Rawlings paper and a perfectly sharpened writing pen. He scribbled the note and address it in great haste. "I only pray this letter arrives to Darcy in time."

"And Gardiner is not destroyed, as well as your friends," Astor remarked.

The men left without further delay. Astor and Livingston accompanied Rawlings to the dock, and they located a ship heading towards England the next morning. Livingston spoke to the captain. "This message must be given the highest priority, even if the British come aboard. It is urgent this letter find its way to Mr. Fitzwilliam Darcy, London, England." Rawlings handed the captain additional coins to pay a messenger upon docking."

"You are fortunate because you are looking at one of the new sloops. It travels across the ocean in less than a month. Before long I will be the captain of the *Pacifica,* a ship which will require no more than a fortnight to go the distance! Imagine crossing the ocean in fourteen days! Alas, for now, your mail will take over three weeks."

Comfortable with the captain's assurances, the men returned to Water Street to map out a strategy. As the day was growing late, Astor invited everyone for dinner in his new home. Livingston declined, but indicated he would make his carriage available for Rawlings and Logan to leave at their convenience.

The men spent a long night hammering out the details necessary for collaboration. Impressed with the wit and intelligence shown by Rawlings, Astor remarked that he liked the man because he was not as haughty as most men of his status. Logan, he concluded, was a valet masquerading as a gentleman, but he added that he did not care. In America, anyone could climb the social ladder, regardless of parentage— even a music instrument maker turned fur trader.

"Did you say your second son would take over your business?" Rawlings asked with raised brows.

"William is not feebleminded, and in America, I am free to leave my inheritance to any my children or I may divide it in any manner amongst them." Astor learned forward. "I am a third son of a butcher, and I do not hold to the practice of leaving my estate to the eldest. My wealth shall be given to whichever child earns the right to manage my inheritance, and that would not be my eldest son."

Rawlings laughed. "I believe my father thinks like you, but the law of primogeniture in England is specific. My brother will inherit everything and against his desires."

"Your journey brought you to the land of opportunity, as many second and third sons discovered upon arriving on our shores."

"I noticed the same pioneer spirit in Boston as well."

Astor sat upright. "You made connections in Boston?"

"Indeed. Frances Cabot Lowell was gracious in introducing us to the prominent families there. We met Lowell when we crossed the ocean together." Rawlings turned to Logan, who nodded in agreement.

Astor furrowed his brow and stared at Rawlings through narrowed slits. "Are you are speaking the truth about Lord Blake and Mr. Darcy partnering with tradesmen's sons."

"We signed documents to back up our partnership, all five of us. While not the usual practice in England, we need each other to be successful in our alliance." Rawlings found Astor to be a little brusque at times, but he discovered it was because the man did not suffer fools or foolish talk gladly.

"Would your partners object to adding my friend, Gardiner, to your alliance?"

"Once they learn the truth, they will be knocking at his door with their hat in their hands." Rawlings laughed, and then his face turned somber. "I pray the letter reaches Darcy before any harm is done. He must act quickly."

"If you believe Gardiner will be added as a partner, then you may include me in your plans. I am attempting to open a trading post on the other side of this continent. It will make the global trade route complete. You see, I, too, had the same vision." Astor picked up his pen and prepared a letter of recommendation for Rawlings to take to his old friend. "Please convey my good wishes when you see him."

While Astor was busy writing, Rawlings prepared a list of the terms for a partnership. After studying the requirements, Astor agreed to have his lawyer prepare a written contract. By the end of the visit, they had hammered out all the details for establishing a partnership. Between the Boston contacts and Astor, the global strategy was now complete.

***

The first action the captain of the sloop took upon landing in Liverpool was to summon a messenger. His ship had made it across the ocean in six weeks, without interference by the British Navy but delayed by the weather. He waited for the messenger and enjoyed the unusually warm air for the first day of March. It was not long before he handed over two letters to the courier, and instructing him to deliver Rawlings' letter first. He gave the man a shilling, which was only one quarter of the funds Rawlings had given him for the express post. The captain, then as now, believed the amount given exceeded any normal payment, and reduced it accordingly. He, of course, pocketed the difference. He also pocketed the coin given to him to deliver a different letter to a different man, also one noted as urgent.

After placing one letter in his satchel, the messenger had to squint at the scribbled address on the second one before he glowered at the captain, who shrugged and exclaimed, "Do the best you can," and then promptly walked away.

The messenger carried the unreadable express for several days. He did do his best to decipher the address, but after several unsuccessful delivery attempts, he placed the letter back in his satchel. He forgot about it until a fortnight had passed and a courier sent by a Mr. Bingley handed him another post. The writing was also undecipherable, but at least the courier had told him the address. He delivered Mr. Bingley's post that day and, noticed the similarities in the address with the earlier letter. He pulled it out and compared them. The scribbled addresses seemed to match. He handed both letters to Darcy's doorman and hurried away.

And so, after days buried in a satchel, Rawlings' letter now found its home on the silver holder in Darcy's study, along with other non-urgent mail. This now somewhat crumpled and dirtied missive stayed on the top of the letters on the silver holder until the next day, when the maid hired to replace the pregnant servant accidently knocked the tray over and scattered the letters everywhere. She was too new and needed the position to tell anyone what she did. She put the letters back in what she hoped was their original sequence, but Rawlings' letter had slipped behind several rarely used journals, where it remained unopened, unread, and forgotten.

***

"My lord, Mr. Cuffage has arrived and he indicated he had urgent business to discuss with you."

The elderly man nodded, and handed the young maiden's merlin to the falconer and turned to her. "My dear, your little pigeon hawk is training well. You must study Frederick II's *The Art of Falconry.* Everything you need to learn is contained within the covers. Now, I would like to stay and provide a few more suggestions, but please excuse me, I am obliged to see to this problem."

"Of course. When you return though, my hawk will win." She glared at her great uncle with a slight curl of her lips.

The old man laughed. "You need to practice more before your bird can beat mine. Remember, I am the champion. However, you showed your true spirit just now, and as I have said many times, if you wish to gain what you want out of life, do not cower or grovel around any gentleman. Do not speak about fashion and clothes, instead offer a challenge to the young man. If you do, one day, you will be a duchess." The Falcon smiled before walking away to meet Mr. Cuffage.

"My Lord." Cuffage bowed. "I have disturbing news that just arrived from America."

"Shall I retrieve my champion Peregrine? Do I need to identify you as his target today? He will attack small vermin, such as rats and mice upon my command. I do not like disturbing news." The old man smiled as Cuffage flinched. "A jest. Do not look so worried. What have you learned?"

"Mr. Rawlings has established connections with a prominent Boston family. The diversion away from New York did not prove successful."

"Humph. How did this happen? The purpose for landing in Boston was to provide a delay long enough for our agent to reach Astor first, not to assist him in finding trading connections in a different city."

"I have just received word from America." Cuffage pulled the letter from his coat pocket. "Mr. Astor had been on a trip out west, and was not available for several weeks. We have no one in Boston to undo the arrangements made between Mr. Rawlings and Mr. Lowell. I understand the Lowell family trades with China. "

Turning to remove the shadow falling over the letter, the old man read the words written on the paper. He folded it up and handed it back to Cuffage. "China is the most important key to completing their global strategy, as made clear in their documents that Whitson stole from Netherfield Park. This is distressing news, but... perhaps Mr. Rawlings can be persuaded to remain in America, where opportunities are plentiful, and abandon Darcy's alliance. Surely the Lowells would do business with a man they know rather than strangers across the ocean. Are there any other issues?"

"Darcy has discovered our warnings to the tradesmen. I have called off our man for now."

The lord nodded, and waited to hear the next problem he sensed was coming.

Cuffage did not disappoint, although he stepped backwards before revealing it. "Mr. Kent has been obtaining contracts and agreements with the tradesmen."

"I assumed he would be the one Darcy asked to do exactly that, so what is the problem?"

"The contracts are made with Mr. Kent, and not a single indication the alliance or Mr. Darcy appears in the signed documents. I suspect he has his own agenda."

"Well, he is his father's son."

"Apparently so."

The old man directed Cuffage's attention to his bird of prey just landing on the falconer's arm. "Do you know what they say is the most impressive skill the Peregrine has?" The old man laughed. "It is able to kill two birds with one mighty swoop."

His grand niece could hear the laughter several hundred yards away.

***

On a bright, crisp, mid-March day, the butler opened the door and peered at the man standing in front of him, fashionably dressed for the early spring weather. The man handed his card and watched while Geoffries studied the front and back before nodding his head and disappearing inside.

Geoffries entered his master's study. "Mr. Darcy."

Darcy held his finger up in the air until he finished the sentence he was writing. Geoffries handed him the card as soon as he put his pen down. Reading the name, Darcy shook his head. "No. This man is not welcome here at any time. My door is closed to him."

Geoffries started to leave when he turned around. "He indicated he had important letters for you from—"

Darcy held up his open palm. "I am not interested." He spoke in a tone that Geoffries understood. On this matter, his master would brook no discussion.

Rising to his full height, the butler nodded, and returned to the man waiting at the front door. He handed his card back. "I am sorry, sir. Mr. Darcy is not available at *any* time. He is not interested in your letters."

Mr. Gardiner sighed, shook his head and departed, taking Rawlings' messages with him.

***

The last week of March arrived, causing a scurry of activity at Darcy House. His trip to Rosings the following morning was bad timing. Darcy assumed Rawlings had reached New York City by now, but he was waiting for confirmation. Bingley had left for the north to be with the Watt family. A somewhat somber Blake had become more involved with his Uncle Harrowby. Finally, Kent continued strengthening his friendship with Georgiana.

On any given day, they were in the music room or the library. Nevertheless, Darcy admitted he had neither witnessed anything inappropriate in their behavior. He could not decipher if Kent was being friendly or flirting with his sister. Most days, friendliness won the argument.

Still, his concern grew, and their guarded closeness suggested they were keeping a secret. Darcy's thoughts often returned to last summer and, in retrospect, the signs did seem similar in Georgiana's demeanor, but this time there was a difference. Kent was wealthy, had no need of her dowry, and did not seek any revenge. While that was in his favor, Darcy understood fortune hunters hunted not just for money. Social status was the other reason unmarried persons from the highest circles of London society were pursued. The interlopers were all around town, but everyone considered climbers a worse match than an insolvent peer. Family connections, even impoverished ones, opened doors, and doors opened opportunities. Social climbers brought nothing to the marriage, except money.

Darcy kept busy while he waited for Victoria's regular morning call. With the impending trip, he needed to secure her assistance in keeping a sharp eye on Georgiana. Mrs. Annesley indicated his sister seemed to share her secrets with her cousin and suggested he elicit her help.

"Fitzwilliam. You wanted to speak with me?" Victoria peeked through the partially opened door.

"Yes, come in and... Mrs. Annesley, please come in as well, and close the door behind you." Darcy rose from behind the desk and moved to the two chairs in front of the fireplace. Mrs. Annesley busied herself with studying the books on the small table next to the window.

Victoria slid into the chair across from her cousin. She waited while Darcy fiddled with his hands and composed his words.

"Victoria, I seek your help."

"I, of course, will do anything I can. Go on."

"Georgiana—"

"I have witnessed no problems. Do not tell me something has happened?"

Darcy shook his head. "No, but I am concerned about her growing friendship with Mr. Kent."

"Mr. Kent? Do you oppose him as an acquaintance?"

"I do not. However, I am worried where their friendship is heading."

Victoria laughed aloud before covering her mouth with her gloved hand. "Do not worry. They are merely friends. Georgiana told—"

"I see the situation differently. You have not viewed them as I have when they were alone in the music room."

Victoria glanced at the chaperon. "Mrs. Annesley is with them. There has been no evidence of improper behavior by either one." She leaned forward and spoke in whisper. "Darcy, you should be ashamed to think of your friend in that manner."

"But Georgiana did exercise poor judgment last summer. I cannot allow her to make another similar mistake."

"Mr. Wickham's behavior was above only that of a callous rake. But, are you aware of a deficiency in Mr. Kent? I would like to be informed if there is anything dishonorable about the man. I have seen only goodness in him. He is pleasant, charming in fact. He is not for want of fortune. His single defect is he was born the son of a tradesman. If he had been a lord, you would not react this way. Would you react this same way if Mr. Kent showed similar attentions to Anne or me?"

"Yes, I would. I am surprised at your change in attitude. He is... not—"

"Not what? A marquess? Or are you hoping for a duke for your sister? If she were to choose, Georgiana could not find a better partner in life. Do not be so ostentatious, cousin. Your Fitzwilliam side is showing. He is a good man."

"So you will not help me?"

"No. I will not break a confidence with Georgiana, as she would never break a confidence with anyone, including you, Mr. Kent, or myself. I will not spy on an innocent friendship. In truth, Georgiana is only—"

Darcy threw up his hands. "Enough. Perhaps I overreacted to the situation. I did not mean to cause you any distress. I will withdraw my request."

Victoria rose and squared her shoulders. "If I discover him too forward in his behavior, I will let you know. Mr. Kent should not worry you. Your sister has grown this past year, and I think you should allow her to continue along that path." Victoria lowered her voice. "Do not break her budding spirit."

Darcy nodded, but when Victoria stormed out of the room with Mrs. Annesley following behind, he called for Geoffries. Darcy was prompt in his directions. His butler was to provide a report on the activities of Mr. Kent and his sister. He expected full details of their interactions, and if there was any hint of impropriety, he demanded an immediate express. He recalled the letter his sister had hidden in her lap one morning. He added the report must identify a list of every letter his sister received, every letter she sent, and if there was a reply. He warned Lady Victoria must not discover what he was doing. Geoffries nodded his agreement and departed, leaving Darcy to mull over his order. Women. Why can they not reason like men?

***

His trunks were loaded onto Darcy's carriage before Richmond bounded up the steps, two at a time. When he reached the top step, he turned, enjoying the spring morning. After a cold February, the warm air had arrived early this year.

Geoffries opened the door, and indicated the family was enjoying their breakfast. Richmond walked quickly through the house, entered the small dining room, and loaded up his plate with his second morning meal of the day. He nodded to the servant to pour him coffee, and took his usual seat at the table.

"Good morning, Darcy, Georgiana. Father and Mother send their greetings." They nodded politely. Richmond continued, "They also suggested Georgiana stay with them."

"She will visit from time to time, but she has made known her desire to remain here. We will only be gone for a week." Darcy glanced at his sister, who was sitting erect gripping her fork.

"One week? Excellent. I was afraid that Aunt Catherine would force us to stay for a month, well a fortnight at least. I will be able to spend a few agreeable evenings, before I must report back to the regiment."

"I have urgent business here, that is why the shortened visit. I have made plans for a trip to Birmingham to visit a manufactory."

"Darcy, do not tell me you are giving up your estate and becoming a... a tradesman?" Richmond held up his hands, horrified, as though he was repelling the Devil himself. "We are ruined."

"I do not see what is so awful about tradesmen?" Georgiana asked with a sharp edge to her voice.

The two men stared at her. The room was quiet for several moments, until Darcy broke the silence. "Although Richmond's comment was in jest, what he said had a bit of truth. It is acceptable for a little intercourse and a guarded friendship, but it must not exceed that. It is best to connect ourselves with only those enhancing our position. This is the way it is."

Looking down at her plate, Georgiana did not respond. As her mood changed, Richmond remembered his walk in Hyde Park. He did not bother to control his scowl when he recalled her defense of Mr. Kent, even then. He relaxed and leaned back into his chair. "Seven days is the perfect for me. And since it is so terribly short, shall I remain here instead and guard our little girl?" He hid his smirk behind his napkin.

"I am not a little girl, cousin. I am sixteen." Georgiana raised her gaze from her plate and bore into him with the Darcy stare.

"True. But I believe you need guarding from all the ogres and trolls under your bed and hiding... "—Richmond ducked under the table— "here!"

"Phew. I have not been afraid of them for years." She dropped her head under the table and wailed, "You treat me like a child."

"Perhaps you should stay with my parents."

Georgiana clasped her hands together. "Please, Brother, I prefer to practice on my pianoforte, than on Aunt's. It is horribly out of tune. No one plays there. Victoria will visit daily; she promised."

Unbeknownst to Richmond, Darcy had discussed having Georgiana stay with the Fitzwilliams. His uncle had agreed it would be safe enough for Georgiana at Darcy House, and at the same time, it was an opportunity to get Lady Victoria to leave her bedchambers. Georgiana was the only person able to encourage her to do so lately. His uncle promised faithfully to keep an eye on his niece.

"You may stay," Darcy announced in what he had hoped was his most authoritative voice and all discussion regarding Georgiana ended.

Breakfast finished in friendly banter; although, Richmond appeared more subdued than when he first arrived. Soon, the two men climbed into the carriage and left for Rosings.

With her guardians gone, Georgiana scampered to her bedchambers, penned a message, and gave it to Geoffries for immediate delivery. Geoffries wrote the name of the recipient in his journal, and had a footman deliver it to Miss Sarah Kent. He thought the request was neither improper nor worrisome, since Mr. Kent had brought his sister to meet Georgiana more than a month ago. He had assumed Mr. Darcy was aware of her visit.

The carriage ride began in silence. Darcy carefully shuffled through his papers, trying not to damage the handwritten collection of poems. Richmond pulled out the newest novel written by Rosa Matilda.

Darcy glanced at the title, *The Passions.* "What, another tale of suspenseful, passionate love set in haunted ruins or an abbey surrounded by wild landscapes?" Shaking with an exaggerated shiver, Darcy laughed aloud. "Oh, the burning desires, the horror, the fear! Is that not reading material for little girls and old dowagers?"

Richmond shook his head. "If you ever thought about what the delightful ladies of the *Ton* read, then you would realize this is our training instructions for advancement on that particular battlefront. I will lend you my book since you could use a little suspenseful, passionate love in your life."

Darcy shook his head. "As for reading the book, I think not, but let me not keep you from planning your next campaign." Darcy studied his cousin when he relaxed and reopened his book. Curious, Darcy asked, "Have you identified a specific battlefield?"

"No, that particular territory has yet to be defined. But, I must be prepared when one appears, and so should you."

Darcy opened the lone communication he had received from Rawlings. He chuckled aloud and caught Richmond peeking over his book at him. Until he refolded the letter, his cousin had kept up his surveillance, silently. But when he glared out the window and sighed loudly, Richmond reacted.

"What concerns you so?"

Darcy shrugged. "Nothing. I have been meditating over a friend's despondency of late." he released a large breath followed by a deep sigh. "I had to step in to ensure an unworthy marriage did not take place. I am afraid it is taking longer than usual for him to overcome his infatuation."

"Unworthy? How so?"

"Mercenary in every respect. He was unable to see the truth." Darcy paused and recollected another friend in a loveless marriage. He promised himself that he would never again allow any friend to suffer Rawlings' fate. He realized his cousin was still staring at him, awaiting further explanation. "The lady would not do for him. He could choose more wisely. One day, he will understand it was for the best, and I am sure he will thank me profusely."

Richmond merely shrugged and returned to his book.

No further conversation occurred until they neared the boundary of Rosings' property. Richmond stared out the window, showing a curious interest, and unaccustomed to anyone looking forward to a stay with his aunt, Darcy broke the silence. "What interests you, Richmond? You remind me of Georgiana on her birthday, waiting for her present."

"Oh. Did I not tell you? No, I imagine not, from that puzzled look." Richmond paused since he enjoyed having information that his cousin did not. When Darcy's glare did not abate, he added, "Anne writes that the new parson has taken a wife and she has a visitor."

"By your interest, I can only assume it is a young lady. Do I presume correctly?"

Nodding, Richmond smiled. "A beautiful and witty one, according to Anne's last letter to Victoria. I believe she is a little envious of her, and more than a little intimidated by one so independent of thought and mind.

"Do you know her? Where is her home?"

"Hertfordshire," Richmond smirked.

Darcy's expression changed from boredom to curiosity. "Which one is from there, the wife or the friend?"

"Both. Anne remarks often at Mrs. Collins' grace, poise, and wit. She is clever."

"A clever lady?"

"Yes, and she has beautiful, expressive eyes, and is not afraid to express her opinion even to our aunt. Black hair that is spun in curls is another feature. She plays the pianoforte and sings with such tone. She has a sister that is fair haired."

"When did they marry?" Darcy held his breath.

"Oh, not long after you left Hertfordshire. She was forced to marry him, I understand. Something about an entailment and someplace called Longbourn."

Darcy gripped the sides of the cushion. "Her name?"

"Mrs. Collins."

"No. What name was she known by in Meryton?"

"Let me see. Either Elizabeth or Charlotte."

"Which one?" Darcy leaned forward, his voice rising.

"Oh, wait. I was incorrect. The beautiful and witty lady is the visiting friend, Miss Elizabeth Bennet. Mrs. Collins was Miss Charlotte Lucas. I believe you know her? You spoke of her excessively to Georgiana and me at dinner that night upon your return."

Releasing a deep sigh, Darcy nodded his head in the affirmative and then smiled. He explained he had the privilege of being in her company at Netherfield Park and at several social gatherings. She was exactly as Anne indicated; she was witty, forceful in her opinions, most attractive, and played the pianoforte with much feeling.

Richmond chuckled at his cousin's smile every time he said her name, and he laughed when Darcy peered out the window in search of her and nearly leaned his whole head out of the window to get a clearer view when he spotted someone. Shaking his head, Darcy sighed, and leaned back in his seat.

"Darcy, Let us plan to wait on the new parson and his wife soon. It is the proper thing to do."

"Yes, quite right Richmond. A visit would be proper."

"And Aunt Catherine would expect us to show respect."

"I agree."

The carriage stopped in front of the main doors, and when they entered the house, they were informed that Lady Catherine and Anne awaited them in the drawing room. They visited until time arrived to dress for dinner.

Darcy, pent up since Richmond's revelation, climbed the steps two at a time, entered his bedchamber, and shut the door behind him.

Miss Elizabeth's likeness swirled around in his mind. She is here, and Blake is not around to catch her attention. He fidgeted when a vision of Blake materialized, staring directly at him, his glare burning. Moments later, the form of Bingley appeared alongside Blake, and he, too, stared, but his gaze was blank, dull, and listless. As quickly as the images appeared, he dismissed any concerns he felt.

He gazed out the window and located Hunsford over the trees. Tomorrow, Miss Elizabeth, until tomorrow, he thought. I will not let this opportunity pass. He suddenly turned, and with a smile on his face, left his room and descended the stairs for dinner.

Chapter Sixteen

Speak up man. Darcy glared at Richmond and Miss Elizabeth chatting in the parsonage's parlor. How can this be? He is talking to her and I am here listening to a discussion about the garden? Ignoring the one-way conversation Mr. Collins was conducting, Darcy kept his sight on the small curl bouncing on her neck as Elizabeth smiled, laughed, and shared words with his cousin. Get up and speak to her. Do not let yet another bloody charmer claim her time. Get up.

When Miss Elizabeth glanced towards him, Darcy could not make his lips smile, even though he tried. His neck felt not just damp, but so wet that trickles oozed down his back. Richmond shrugged at something she said. He watched her tilt her chin, raise her brow, and, with the slightest curl of her lip, she turned her head toward him yet again. Forcing the muscles in his legs to react, he pushed himself upright, not realizing the inane parson was in the middle of a sentence until he became vaguely aware of the man's apologies. He moved closer, with a deliberate intent to speak to Miss Elizabeth, and disregarded the grating tone of the toady man who was almost clinging to his arm. Ten minutes, and I have yet to show proper civilities.

"Good morning, Miss Bennet. How is your family? I hope they are well."

Elizabeth answered in the usual way and then sat still while she waited for his response. When he did not respond, she raised her brow. "My eldest sister and I have been in town these three months. Have you never happened to see her there?"

"I did not have that pleasure." Well, I did not actually see her. Miss Bingley informed me she was in London.

"I hope your friends are well."

Darcy moved his weight from one foot to the other. "Yes, they are all well."

"Do you engage in competitions in town, or have all your friends retreated to the countryside?

"Lord Blake, Mr. Kent, and I have remained in London. Mr. Bingley is visiting family in the north and Mr. Rawlings has journeyed to America."

"America? Well, I wish him well. And the stallion; does Lord Blake ride him still?"

"Yes. All our friends wished to see the Andalusian, and he has been busy showing him off. It appears everyone in London was interested in the games."

"I was interested in you winning, Darcy." Richmond laughed, and smiled at Elizabeth when she turned towards him. "I believe all the Fitzwilliams were paying attention to the golf game, since we had all wagered on him." He tipped his head towards Darcy.

Darcy rolled his eyes.

Richmond returned to his discussion about Rosa Matilda's newest book, but when Elizabeth offered her own lively opinions about the nonsensical purpose of gothic novels and cited *The Passions* as an example, Darcy chuckled loud enough to cause his cousin to turn and glare at him. He retreated to the sofa, happy to let the parson take control of any conversation, while he kept his attention focused on the colonel and the lady engrossed in friendly banter.

His cousin spoke at length, while she nodded and more than once snuck a peek towards his side of the parlor. The moment the room grew quiet, Darcy stood, making it known it was time to leave. Richmond conceded, and the two left for Rosings.

"Darcy. You were restrained, even for you. I had expected much more talk from you, since you are acquainted with Miss Bennet. If she had not testified to your acquaintance, I would think you spoke a falsehood before. I believe you like her."

"Humph." Darcy continued to march to the house with uncommon speed, his long strides pulling him away from both the parsonage and the irritating colonel. He felt the hairs upon his neck standing straight up.

"Have I touched a nerve, dear cousin?" Richmond said.

Darcy entered the house without speaking, bounded up the stairs two steps at a time, and rushed toward his bedchambers. Richmond tried to follow, but with shorter legs, he failed to reach the door before Darcy slammed and locked it shut. His cousin's laugh could be heard as he walked down the hall to his own chambers.

Darcy paced the room. Damn charm. Blast! Why does she not see beyond the fine words of charming men?

He needed to think, and his feet carried him to the window where he moved the drapery back and peeked out over the front lawn, concentrating his stare on the forced landscape design.

Goulding, Blake, Wickham, and now Richmond. Darcy slumped into the chair and tapped the arms with his fingers. He recalled her appearance while she gazed upon the other four men.

The image of her laughing with Goulding struck first; her eyes flickered when she spoke, her head tilting to the right. Darcy shook his own head when he realized it was leaning to the left. She never tilted her head when she spoke with me. He returned to tapping his fingers and conjuring up images until he could not sit still any longer.

He poured himself a glass of wine, and wondered why his aunt did not provide brandy. He would tell his man to fill a carafe and keep it filled for his entire stay.

Why must that invisible hand squeeze my neck everytime I am around her? "You look lovely today, Miss Elizabeth," Darcy said aloud and then ran his hand through his hair. Why could I not have been a little charming?

He gulped his drink and settled back down into his chair. She did not tilt her head sideways at all with Blake; why she gazed up to him with her head lowered. Even now, he felt his hand itching to reach for her chin. He wanted to lift it up, gaze full square into those eyes, and amuse her until the tiny gold and sometimes green flecks would appear. Her eyes had always turned a subtle, shiny emerald color when she cast them on Blake. No wonder the man waited all day for her. He shook his head.

"Damn you, Blake. Why did you take a liking to her? You filled her head with…" Darcy paused, gulped another sip and added, "flowery words. Did you give her flowers too?" He remembered she had worn wildflowers in her hair at Sir William's party, twirled a garden rose at his Tup Running game, and adorned tiny rosebuds in her curls at Bingley's ball. He felt a stab when another image of a flower appeared, this time a marker in what he assumed was a secret passage in the book Blake gave Elizabeth at Netherfield Park.

Darcy rose and began to walk around the room again, stopping and holding his breath until the footsteps he heard in the hall faded away. With only a single hour of privacy left, he had no desire for company. Richmond can deal with Aunt Catherine and Anne this trip.

He poured his third glass of wine, not hesitating as he drained it. Pulling the drapes back, he envisioned a different world outside. Little children with beautiful black curly hair pranced on the lawn with makeshift wooden horse sticks, each with the Darcy crest emblazed on their bridles. He leaned closer to the windowpane when the little girl gazed up to his window, smiling all the way to his heart.

But when the girl's eyes slowly transformed into those of a grown up woman in a pale yellow ball gown, he stepped back from the window, closing the curtain in an unsuccessful attempt to block out the vision. Her eyes grew increasingly dark until they were black as an unlit night sky. He shuddered as he heard her call out, "blinded by prejudice."

Unable to stop the words from ringing in his ears, he raised his hands to each side of his head, attempting to block out her taunts. His actions made no difference, as he could still hear her say, "He has been unlucky to lose your friendship, and in a manner which he is likely to suffer from all his life."

Another blasted charmer. Wickham must have been at his best to convince her to defend him so. Did he woo her too? Damn him and his blasted charm. 'Lose his friendship' What did she mean by that? 'Prejudice!' Humph. If she only knew the truth.

He smoothed his clothing. Richmond will be talkative tonight. How does he think of such frivolous subjects, and why do the women always listen and laugh? As Darcy approached the door, the sight of an animated and laughing Elizabeth speaking to his cousin sprung into his mind. Damn blasted charm.

**

The week continued along the same pattern. Darcy woke early, ate breakfast, and went for a morning ride. He returned to find Richmond and Anne chatting about impractical things while they ate their meal. His aunt always had her breakfast tray sent to her room. After spending the day on the estate problems, he spent his late afternoons listening to his aunt expound on the virtues of Rosings and its female heir. He appeared both attentive and noncommittal, and continued this charade through dinner and evening drinks. Every evening, the four played cards; Richmond paired with their aunt and Darcy with Anne. Only his superior play allowed them to remain competitive.

All during the week, Richmond appeared to be enjoying Darcy's situation, sending him secret smirks whenever possible. Late at night, they met for several games of billiards. Darcy had introduced him to Twenty Points when he had first returned from Hertfordshire, but now preferred not to play that game or to engage in anything remotely connected to Netherfield Park, in general, and Longbourn, in particular.

Drinks in Darcy's bedchambers followed the billiards and then Richmond would retire, leaving him to spend a restless hour or so before succumbing to sleep. He tossed and turned, falling asleep late in the night. Nothing he did, be it drinking or thinking, could shake her likeness or her fine eyes from his consciousness.

He had not returned to the parsonage since that early morning almost a week ago; however, the Sunday Services brought about a change in the pattern. The day before, Richmond had not joined Lady Catherine and Anne for their normal afternoon visit, and his whereabouts were not revealed until he came to Darcy's room for his brandy later that night. He had spent the entire afternoon with the Hunsford ladies, and the majority of his time in deep conversation with Miss Elizabeth.

Darcy squeezed the arms of the chair each time his cousin deliberately and methodically shared a word or a look he had received from the beautiful Elizabeth. Richmond withheld nothing in painting a picture of her lovely smiles, whispers, glances, and even an accurate description of the flashing golden and green specks.

When his cousin retired to his own bedchambers, Darcy paced back and forth between his bed, the door, and the window until the wee hours of the morning, all the time arguing with himself over all the men in Miss Elizabeth's life: Richmond, Wickham, Goulding, and Blake. He steadily drank the entire carafe of brandy. He debated the merits of a country girl without money or connections and having an unfortunate family. Finally exhausted at one in the morning he fell into a deep sleep until three hours later when he bolted upright in bed.

"She saves her most serious looks for me. Why it is me—I am sure now—she *loves* me."

Darcy did not return to sleep, choosing instead to jump out of bed, light a candle, and stand at the window, staring at his reflection flickering in the glass against the blackness of the night. His hair was tousled; his nightshirt twisted and wrinkled.

The timepiece on the mantle indicated the sunrise was more than an hour away. He had time to determine what his next step would be.

"She loves me, I am positive," Darcy stood before his reflection in the window, rubbed his chin, and glared at his face.

She does not want Blake, or she would have met with him the day after the ball. She had never even pretended she wanted Goulding, no matter how fond there were of each other. They would be engaged by now if she did. Darcy thought of Wickham. I must warn her somehow of his evil side. But his mouth curved into a smile as he remembered her stay at Netherfield Park. All the time flirting with Blake; she tried to make me jealous! Why was I so blind? She sent me sly looks often, and I was a fool not to know. What must she think of me?

"It cannot be helped, but I will show her I understand now. I will attend to her, and it will not be with childish words or pretty flowers. My Elizabeth has more depth than that." My Elizabeth! His deep-set dimples and the crinkled skin beside his twinkling eyes were easily discernable in the window's reflection. He grasped his hands behind his back. "I will treat her with proper respect and decorum."

Darcy mentally listed ways to court her attention. He did not believe she needed much encouragement. He was rich, and after evaluating the image on the windowpane, decided he was handsome enough to tempt her. Yes, she is discerning in her choice.

A knock interrupted his reverie, and when he opened the door, he was startled to find Richmond fully dressed for a sunrise ride.

"You are up and about early."

"Are we not leaving today? My trunks are ready, and I came to see if a morning gallop was to your liking before the long carriage trip back to London after church services."

Darcy froze. I cannot leave now. He shook his head. "Oh, I beg your pardon. I will be staying another week, but if you wait, I will happily change into riding clothes and join you."

When Darcy moved toward the dressing room, silence ensued. Richmond did not speak until they returned from their ride and, the only words he said were a curt and abrupt, "Good ride."

Darcy, busy contemplating the new revelation about Elizabeth, did not consider the change in his cousin, although it did register as an urgent matter on his mind. Today his only interests were in Elizabeth. After giving him a slight nod, he left to prepare for church service. Only his best would do, for today he would signal to Elizabeth his desire for a closer acquaintance.

***

Darcy's gaze never strayed from Elizabeth the entire time he sat in his aunt's parlor that evening. He was unconcerned when she spent most of the time conversing with Richmond. He overheard her words: Rosings, Hertfordshire, traveling, books, and music. His cousin had said nothing of any consequence, or anything other than his usual brainless chatter, and Darcy sighed, but was content, knowing they were becoming friends. While his aunt rattled on in the background, he anticipated what future meals would be like at Darcy House and Pemberley. He envisioned Richmond and Georgiana laughing and sharing secrets with his Elizabeth, while he oversaw their friendship from the head of the table. His Elizabeth would sit, not at the other end of the table, but to his right. His palm felt a spark as he imagined his hand caressing hers.

Lost in his reverie, he paid no attention to his Aunt Catherine until she demanded attention be paid to her. Mr. Darcy awoke from his dreams when she asked him to concur in her pronouncement about practicing to Elizabeth. A little ashamed of his aunt's ill breeding and condescending manner, he made no answer. There will be none of that when we are.... Darcy's chest tightened as he held his breath. Married, I was about to say married. My feelings have gone beyond the desire for friendship. But now I must mull this over more carefully, more rationally, and with logic and practicality. From the raised brows on Richmond's face, Darcy feared he had displayed his reaction to his thoughts and realized he would have to guard his emotions more closely.

Later, after he had retired to his bedchambers, Darcy did what had become commonplace for him; he paced. He would pause, pour a drink, take a big gulp, and then continue his long strides around the room, concentrating on the Bennets and other issues. How can I even consider connecting myself to such a family?

Darcy slid into his chair at the writing table, pulled out a blank sheet, and with a sharpened pen began to list the problems.

Father. Mr. Bennet hides away in his library. He shows no respect to his wife or silly daughters, but he does look upon his eldest two with fondness. He has shown a lack of judgment on business matters, but that is immaterial to me. He would not be included in my business ventures.

Mercenary Mother. Yes, Mrs. Bennet is mercenary, but Rawlings pointed out all mothers are thus. He scratched the word from the list.

Silly and ignorant sisters. Visits could be arranged at my convenience, not theirs. I can determine the best time. One day they will marry, and I will never have to deal with them again. Darcy drew a bold line across the words.

Friends. Elizabeth did not meet Blake. He was not her choice, so he should not... Darcy returned to window. He cannot fault me. He... he had his chance. He has found another now. His thoughts turned to Bingley. I am sorry that Miss Bennet did not care for Bingley. He could have been my brother. Well, perhaps he would be a good match for Georgiana. They are both gentle people. He returned to the desk and crossed out the word. "My friends will rejoice in my happiness."

Duty. My father and mother directed me to marry someone who would enhance my holdings or increase my standing in society. But why? I have more wealth than is required if I was to have ten children. I am my own man. I can choose anyone I please. I am satisfied with my circle of friends. That will not change when I take Elizabeth for my wife. Again he took his pen to the paper and drew a line through the word.

Darcy froze as he glared at the next word on the list.

Family. Here is a problem. Aunt Catherine would never approve of anyone other than her daughter to be my wife, even if they had wealth and stature, let alone a no-name country miss from an unknown parish named Meryton. What do I owe her? I will never marry Anne. I need an heir. She cannot argue against that! Darcy jumped up and made his way to the brandy carafe. He poured another drink, but this time he merely swirled the amber liquid around in the glass before putting the drink down without a single sip. He returned to his desk, and glowered at the offending word again. "Family!"

My Uncle! Of all my relatives, Richmond's father would be the hardest to persuade. He is rigid in his opinions. He would never accept Elizabeth. Never. When he discovers she has an uncle in Cheapside…

Darcy abruptly spurted out, "a dishonest uncle in Cheapside." He ran his hand through his hair and then rubbed his chin. How can I overcome that obstacle? Will I be asked to bail the man out of debtor's prison? Will he try to con me out of my money? How can I keep Elizabeth away from him?

"Oh, Elizabeth," Darcy whispered as he laid his head in his hands. "My dear, sweet, Elizabeth."

Saying her name brought back the memory their only conversation since he had arrived at Rosings. He had smiled at her impertinence while she had played the pianoforte, and frowned when he recalled how Richmond sat next to her in a chair, placed too far for turning pages and much to close for merely listening.

She raised her right brow when she said, 'You mean to frighten me, Mr. Darcy, by coming in all this state to hear me? But I will not be alarmed though your sister does play so well. There is a stubbornness about me, which will never be frightened at the will of others. My courage always rises with every attempt to intimidate me.' She had teased me in a way no other woman had done before, showing herself to be intelligent as well as witty.

"Why did he encourage her to tease me more?" Darcy said aloud, when Richmond said, 'Pray let me hear what you have to accuse him of. I should like to know how he behaves among strangers.'

She answered him while playing notes and peering up at me, both the music and her countenance was so sweet. 'You shall hear then—but prepare yourself for something dreadful. The first time I saw him in Hertfordshire, you must know, was at a ball—and at this ball, what do you think he did? He danced only four dances! I am sorry to pain you—but so it was. He danced only four dances, though gentlemen were scarce; and, to my certain knowledge, more than one young lady was sitting down in want of a partner. Mr. Darcy, you cannot deny the fact.'

Darcy sipped his brandy and smiled at himself for being able to reveal something private about his character. 'I certainly have not the talent which people possess, of conversing easily with those I have never seen before. I cannot catch their tone of conversation, or appear interested in their concerns, as I often see done.'

His willingness to share his faults with her startled him, since he had never discussed them with any other person, not even Richmond. He sighed. Well, now she knows I am shy as well as resentful! His gaze drifted to the window, and although there was not a cloudy view of Hunsford, he wondered if she was looking out the window towards him. When he wondered if he had caused her any worry, he felt a twinge in his neck until he remembered he had ended the conversation with a compliment to her, 'You are perfectly right. You have employed your time much better. No one admitted to the privilege of hearing you, can think anything wanting. We, neither of us, perform to strangers.'

Darcy strolled around the room for several minutes before stopping at the window. Well, I definitely declared my intentions tonight! She can have no doubt as to my desires now. He forgot all thoughts of the uncle from Cheapside as he sipped his brandy and planned how he would spend his remaining time with her.

***

Darcy climbed up the front steps and waited while the young servant opened the door. She led him to the parlor where he expected to find the ladies of the house embroidering, reading, or writing letters. When he entered the room, his heart pounded. He observed only Elizabeth, standing to greet him in an otherwise empty room.

He apologized for his intrusion, letting her know that he had understood all the ladies to be at home.

After the usual civilities were exchanged, they sat down. He had just settled in the chair when his body stiffened at her question of why the Netherfield party had left so quickly and followed Bingley to town.

"I can only speak for myself. I had business matters that needed my attention." He relaxed when she changed the subject to Bingley's sisters' well being.

For several minutes, he was content to gaze at her. She held her shoulders straight and placed her hands delicately in her lap. Poise. She is overflowing with poise. His gaze traveled down the length of her body and back upwards. She does have a light and pleasing figure and her... Darcy looked away to conceal his face when he felt his cheeks burning after his gaze had wandered to the spot where the neckline and skin met. Today he confessed that he was disappointed to see a strip of lace added to her dress.

"I think I have understood that Mr. Bingley has not much idea of ever returning to Netherfield again,"Elizabeth asked.

Darcy squirmed in his seat. "I have never heard him say so; but it is probable that he may spend little of his time there in future." He saw her startle, and offered an explanation. "He has friends, and he is at a time of life when friends and engagements are continually increasing."

He paid no attention to tight-lipped smile; instead, he studied how straight she held her head and how she pushed her shoulders back and leaned away from him. She must be fighting her desire to draw close to me.

"If he means to be but little at Netherfield, it would be better for the neighborhood that he should give up the place entirely, for then we might possibly get a settled family there." She looked down at her hands, which were resting in her lap. "But perhaps Mr. Bingley did not take the house so much for the convenience of Meryton as for his own, and we must expect him to keep or quit it on the same principle."

Darcy shrugged. "I should not be surprised if he were to give it up, as soon as any eligible purchase offers."

Even though Elizabeth made no answer, he enjoyed the play of emotions crossing her face. Her expression went from taut and harsh to a softer more relaxed one. He examined her eyes, seeking the playfulness that appeared when she spoke to other men. He saw an unreadable blankness in them. Yes, she is excellent at controlling her emotions.

Remembering her suggestion to practice his social niceties, he searched the room for a subject to discuss. "This seems a very comfortable house. Lady Catherine, I believe, did a great deal to it when Mr. Collins first came to Hunsford."

He watched her lips move in a gentle motion as she continued. However, he was surprised when she responded to his suggestion that Mrs. Collins had settled within so easy a distance from her own family and friends.

"An easy distance do you call it? It is nearly fifty miles."

"And what is fifty miles of good road? Little more than half a day's journey. Yes, I call it a very easy distance." She must agree that she need not be settled near Longbourn.

He leaned back and waited for her volley. When she expressed her opinion of how close one should live to one's family, his heart pounded furiously. "*You* cannot have a right to such strong local attachment. *You* cannot have been always at Longbourn."

Elizabeth looked surprised and a bit offended.

He drew back in his chair, picked up a newspaper from the table and glanced at it. "Are you pleased with Kent?"

A short dialogue on the subject of the country ensued, on either side calm and concise—and soon put an end to by the entrance of Charlotte, just returned from her walk. Mr. Darcy related the mistake, which had occasioned his intruding on Miss Bennet, and after sitting a few minutes longer without saying much to anybody, went away.

***

Over the next week, Darcy regularly called upon the ladies at the parsonage. He was amazed at Elizabeth's composure. She is the most proper lady of my acquaintance. No silly flirting for her. She needs no wiles to capture my heart. Fearing others would notice their attraction to each other, and not wishing to place Miss Elizabeth in any awkward situation, he kept his visits short.

When his cousin accompanied him, he used Richmond to stay longer, contented to sit and watch her smile, laugh, and talk, all the while catching sight of her sly glances towards him. His heart pounded so loudly he had to concentrate hard to quell it. He had no doubt she understood his darkened stares were to help control his feelings in front of others. She would raise that brow and smile slightly, tight-lipped. Ah. That is her look she reserves for me alone. She is clever, perhaps the most astute lady in all of England. I do not have to explain my meanings to her.

Several times, he caught Mrs. Collins staring at him. I must be careful. She is suspicious. She may have acted foolishly in marrying such a man as the parson, but she is no fool. I will protect Elizabeth. Darcy turned slowly and gazed at the young lady smiling sweetly to Richmond. My Elizabeth. No one shall know, my dearest, until you want it known.

***

During the days that followed, Darcy was at his happiest when he came upon her rambling about the estate.

She was so clever to share the location for her favorite walks. He sought her out every day the weather permitted a walk. When they accidentally discovered each other, he would offer his arm and escort her back to the parsonage. Staring at her hand, he was tempted to take it and place small kisses upon her fingers, whereupon his mouth would dry up each time he visualized touching her skin with his lips. The sound of his heart beating thundered in his ears.

At night, he berated himself for his inability to string a complete sentence together when in her presence. He was pleased Elizabeth spoke little, and did not demand he engage in frivolous chit-chat. She knows me better than I know myself. But, she did say I must practice. I need practice. With his nightly brandy in one hand and his other held behind his back, Darcy stood in front of the window and practiced talking aloud on various subjects.

"Miss Bennet, I hope you find Rosings' grounds pleasant, or do you prefer something more natural?"

"Miss Bennet, were you trained in Greek studies? Who is your favorite philosopher?"

"Miss Bennet, am I correct that you are an admirer of walks in the countryside? Do you study the animals or the greenery?"

"Miss Bennet, does it not appear to you that Mr. and Mrs. Collins are well suited for one another?"

"Miss Bennet, you look lovely today. The green in your gown highlights the green specks sparkling in your eyes. The lavender scent fills my nostrils with joy. The softness of your skin causes my heart to beat furiously." Bah! What drivel! I cannot say such things to a woman.

By their third encounter, he had finally found his voice. At first, he did not say the words he had practiced, but rambled on several subjects. He was surprised at her questioning look when he spoke of Rosings, and how she would be staying there too whenever they came into Kent. Surely, she does not expect us to stay at Hunsford!

Satisfied he had given her leave to fantasize about their future together; he returned to Rosings and roamed around the house. He evaluated each room as to its suitability for a proposal, and quickly decided upon the balcony off the drawing room as the perfect spot. Pushing away thoughts of a different balcony and a different man holding Elizabeth's hand, he rushed to scrutinize the space. First, he looked forward to the breathing in the lavender fragrance, which would permeate the air. He first noticed it climbing the stairs to the assembly hall in Meryton. From the beginning, he thought, we were destined for each other.

"Now, how do I get her out here and all alone?" Darcy leaned against the railing, probing his mind to find a ploy until he spied an unusual unusual among the oaks. Ah ha! I will ask her to help me identify that one. He stared at the tree with its perfect blossoming heart-shaped leaves. Yes, it is unusual enough that it would not seem odd. I did not know its name, and yet it is not that uncommon she would be at a loss. She might say it is a lime tree, of which I could tease her with its Latin name, Tilia. Then, I will tell her I wish to speak seriously. Yes, that is how I will approach her.

The next day, Darcy dressed with care, choosing his blackest jackets and the whitest shirts. He looked himself over in the reflecting glass, first turning sideways, and then looking over his shoulder to view himself from every angle. The gold flecks in his blue waistcoat sparkled to match the gold specks in her eyes. Finally, running his fingers through his dark curly hair, he laughed. "Blake with his blond hair and fair looks did not win this race."

Breathing deeply three times, he calmed his nerves and left to join the others in the drawing room; but when he reached the top of the stairs, he overheard Mr. Collins apologize that Miss Bennet was not well and would not be attending.

Darcy grabbed the handrail and squeezed until his hands ached. Pleased that no one had noticed him, he quietly retreated to his bedchambers, where he marched up and down the rug, mumbling as he went.

After a quarter of an hour, he came to an abrupt halt and a wide smile stretched across his face. "She is clever, I understand it now. She is giving me the chance to come to her without fear of others being present. I must see her tonight. I must."

Darcy promptly left his room, dashed down the steps, and found himself advancing in his long strides along the path towards the Hunsford parsonage.

"I will propose tonight, and tomorrow she will be introduced as my future bride. Nothing will stop me now."

Chapter Seventeen

"I ardently admire and love you."

Darcy's words rang out proudly, his hands open at his side, and his shoulders relaxed. His heart pounded with such great force that he feared the sound boomed across the room. When she did not respond, he shifted his weight from one foot to the other and only calmed when he supposed that she wanted him to continue!

He moved closer to her, his gaze scanning her body while half-ignoring her backward retreat to the window. She stood tall with her back against the windowsill, her hands grasped in a tight hold in front of her. *She is waiting. What must I say now? Perhaps if I explain how hard this was for me to choose her, my admission will demonstrate my deep and abiding love for her.*

"I have long admired you. Ever since we first met, I witnessed your grace in spite of your family's ill-mannered behavior." He noticed how she flinched. *Yes, she is as embarrassed by them as I am. I must show her how I have overcome my disgust, but I must try to be kind as I speak the truth.*

"Miss Bennet, although your family is inferior to any whom I would wish as a connection, I decided to overlook any degradation the joining of our families would bring." He lowered his voice and relaxed his expression. "Even though many of my acquaintances may not consider you acceptable as the Mistress of Pemberley, I must respond to my desire, which grows stronger with each day. I cannot deny my feelings for you despite my beliefs, my duty, and my obligations. In seeking you out, I am disregarding what I know I should do; nonetheless, I will accept the consequences. And while the Bennets may never be permitted to attend my family's social gatherings, you, as my wife, will be by my side. I promise you that I will demand they accept you, treat you with respect that would be due Mrs. Darcy, and not dishonor you in any way in my presence."

Her eyelids narrowed and hands tightened during his speech. She must be impatient for the offer, he thought, and moving forward. The hint of a smile slipped out. "It is with great hope, therefore, that I humbly ask you to accept my offer of marriage." Standing within inches in front of her, he lowered his chin and spread his arms to welcome her into his embrace. He readied his lips for the kiss he had so long sought and moved another step closer.

Elizabeth held up her open palm and stopped him from leaning down.

He retreated to the fireplace and leaned against the mantle. She must be desirous of explaining how she longed for my offer and how she hid her love. I spoke my mind, now it is her turn. I will give her the opportunity to show her love. He nodded for her to speak.

"In such cases as this, it is, I believe, the established mode to express a sense of obligation for the sentiments avowed, however unequally they may be returned. It is natural that obligation should be felt, and if I could feel gratitude, I would now thank you. But I cannot—I have never desired your good opinion, and you have certainly bestowed it most unwillingly. I am sorry to have occasioned pain to any one. It has been most unconsciously done, however, and I hope will be of short duration. The feelings which, you tell me, have long prevented the acknowledgment of your regard, can have little difficulty in overcoming it after this explanation."

What? What did she say? He grabbed the mantle while his mind processed her words. Did she reject me? Me? But she loves me. Why would she deny me? Is she playing a game? I heard many women first say no before they accept. I did not think she was such a woman. While comprehension of the truth of her words inhabited his thoughts, he had difficulty swallowing. He studied her. Her hands had fallen to her sides; her shoulders thrown back, and her own chin was raised defiantly. This is no game. She meant it. She will not accept my offer. Who is she to reject me? A country nobody.

His cheeks burned. He felt the humiliation of the rejection, but a tone of anger crept in his voice. "And this is all the reply which I am to have the honor of expecting! I might, perhaps, wish to be informed why, with so little endeavor at civility, I am thus rejected."

When she did not recoil at his request, he lifted his head, and with the coldest and his most haughty attitude said, "But it is of small importance." Yes, a wounded animal must not show weakness if he wishes to survive.

In response, her words flew from her mouth in a ferocious, but controlled voice and a tone he had never heard used to address him before. She spoke of his separating Bingley and her beloved sister, quickly moving on with her next accusation to his unfair treatment of Wickham, and then finally, and to his astonishment, his alleged manipulation of Blake.

"Did you detach your friend, Lord Blake, from me as well? Did you persuade him to leave Netherfield Park and never to contact me again?" Elizabeth tilted her head but did not lower her cold stare or lessen the anger directed at him. "Are you the conductor of every one's life?"

He experienced a stabbing pain in his heart and responded with a, "No, of course not," but her quick reaction caused him to stop dead in his tracks.

"And if that is not enough, you showed your complete and total disregard for my family long before you spoke today in such an ungentleman-like manner. You have already proven yourself as an unfeeling person when you asked if my father had a book on gas lighting.

Why does she find gas lighting offensive? As he attempted to recall the exact event, she unleashed the rest of her accusations.

Elizabeth grabbed the back of the chair. "You showed your true character that day. I do not know how you found out our fortune was lost over an investment in gas lighting, but I thought your comment insensitive and cruel, mocking me and my father in that way."

Unable to control the surprised reaction he knowingly revealed by his eyes, mouth, and stance, he answered in an unrestrained agitated tone. "Your father? He may have acted foolishly, but I bear no ill feelings toward him. Mr. Gardiner convinced him to invest, so he should be the one to blame! Your uncle is the dishonest one."

"Why do you call my uncle dishonest? What gives you the right to slander such a good man?" Elizabeth squeezed the the chair tighter until her knuckles turned white.

"He hides his deceitfulness by blaming his problems on Mr. Cuffage."

Elizabeth's eyes widened. "Mr. Cuffage? You, sir, are woefully mistaken. That evil man caused my father to lose his investment in the Gas Light Company. Not my Uncle Gardiner."

"Miss Bennet, you are not familiar with the business world, and have not been privileged with the right information. Believe me, it pains me to be the one to tell you the truth. I nearly made a disastrous decision, had I listened to your other uncle, Mr. Phillips. He, too, tried to deceive me by placing Mr. Cuffage in a bad light."

Elizabeth announced, "You, sir, are just too proud to admit you are wrong." She raised her chin, stood tall as was possible and said, "You are vain, in addition to being proud. You believe your knowledge superior to everyone else's, even gentlemen who have lived twice your life. Well, one day you will find out how truly inferior your assumptions are."

"You have said quite enough, madam. I perfectly comprehend your feelings, and have now only to be ashamed of what my own have been. Forgive me for having taken up so much of your time, and accept my best wishes for your health and happiness."

She remained motionless by the window as he wished her a happy life and disappeared out of the room.

He bounded up the steps of Rosings, and did not slow until he had locked himself in his bedchambers. He rang for his man and told him to pack. They would leave in the morning, and when the man turned to leave, Darcy asked him to refill the brandy carafe. He began to pace the floor while he recalled the whole conversation. He directed his comments towards the window, other times to an invisible Elizabeth standing in the room.

"You did not seem ill when I arrived. I should have known then that something was wrong. I was polite about your health, but you were not welcoming. I did not comprehend your curt reply, 'I am well, Sir.' You spit the words from your mouth, I see it now."

His long legs carried him from the door to the window and back again as he tried to calm himself. His directed his words to an invisible audience seated around the room.

"The whole time I was pacing and trying to select the best words with which to propose, she just sat there glowering at me with laughing eyes, and she certainly did not offer me any help. 'In vain I have struggled. It will not do. My feelings will not be repressed. You must allow me to tell you how ardently I admire and love you.' Yes she must have been well entertained by me, and is no doubt laughing tonight."

He plopped into the chair. "She stared at me, her face red, her eyes black. I do not know why I thought that was encouragement to continue. Why did I assume she was not a woman that needed flowery words?" He jumped up and returned to marching across the room.

"I spoke the truth. She is inferior! There can be no argument with that. Her family? It would be a degradation. Did I not tell her how I conquered those feelings because my attachment was strong? Did she not know how difficult this decision was for me?"

He did not pay attention to the thud of his boots stomping on the rug. He wrongly assumed the rich carpet muffled his movement, or that his cousin, Richmond, could not hear him swearing through the door.

"Damn her. Damn me." He glared at his reflection in the window. The only image he could make out was of himself—no Elizabeth, no conjured up audience. "I did my best to use kind and gentle words when I explained to her my sacrifice. She seemed affable at first, but then her face turned to stone. Her eyes, those beautiful, expressive eyes tuned black, and I swear she singed me with her gaze."

Standing up to his full height, he glowered at his reflection. "Well, I did try to be kind, and besides, I did ask for her hand in marriage. Did I not tell her how anxious I was? Who is she to refuse me?"

He spun around and trudged over to the table holding the brandy decanter, and poured to the brim of his goblet. He saluted the invisible guests.

"Never once did I expect the words that flew out of her mouth when she said, 'In such cases as this, it is, I believe, the established mode to express a sense of obligation for the sentiments avowed, however unequally they may be returned.' She understood she was hurtful; the color in her cheeks was bright red. She knew, but she said it anyway. If I did not have the mantle-piece to keep me upright, I would have collapsed that second. I struggled, and she sat in her seat and did nothing to lighten my burden. Why did I go on? Why did I not leave then, and never look back?"

He slumped in his chair, both arms lying dead along the sides and his legs gone limp. He remained unresponsive for several moments while the images of Richmond, Kent, Rawlings, Blake, Bingley, and even Jane Bennet departed, they were not swayed.

"I will write her a letter. I will defend myself to her alone. Surely, she will go on one of her walks tomorrow as if nothing important happened today. She admitted she is not ill. I will hand it to her then. I shall defend myself against her accusations, but I will not degrade myself any further. And I shall make no more offers about my ardent love—not in writing, nor when I face her."

Darcy moved to the desk, retrieved his pens and stationary, and then began to write. He was not sorry for the first words he consigned to the smooth paper. He read them twice and sneered. "She needs to read these words to understand my feelings today."

> Be not alarmed, Madam, on receiving this letter, by the apprehension of its containing any repetition of those sentiments, or renewal of those offers, which were last night so disgusting to you. I write without any intention of paining you, or humbling myself, by dwelling on wishes, which, for the

happiness of both, cannot be too soon forgotten; and the effort which the formation and the perusal of this letter must occasion should have been spared, had not my character required it to be written and read. You must, therefore, pardon the freedom with which I demand your attention; your feelings, I know, will bestow it unwillingly, but I demand it of your justice.

Darcy leaned back in his chair and tried to recreate in his mind the exact scene. He spoke to his quill as if it was he and she was him. 'Had not my own feelings decided against you, had they been indifferent, or had they even been favorable, do you think that any consideration would tempt me to accept the man, who has been the means of ruining, perhaps for ever, the happiness of a most beloved sister?'.

I must apologize. He dipped his quill in the ink well, took a breath, and began to write the words swirling in his head.

If, in the explanation relates feelings which may be offensive to yours, I can only say that I am sorry

He reread it several times and was content. He dipped the quill in the ink again, to give his view.

I had not been long in Hertfordshire, before I saw, in common with others, that Bingley preferred your eldest sister to any other young woman in the country.

He sorted out the images spinning in his mind. Bingley had defended Miss Bennet after the assembly dance. He called her an angel. During their entire stay, Bingley fastened himself to Miss Bennet's side, regardless of the situation. He even carried her scarf and many times, it stuck out of his coat pocket. He knew his friend was more serious than he had been with any flirtation in the past. Sir William validated his fears with the admission of the neighborhood assumptions to the impending marriage between the two.

Yes, he thought as he drummed his fingers on the desk. It was the Netherfield ball when he realized the extent of Bingley's attachment He recalled every occurrence when Bingley and Miss Bennet were together, and could not discern her particular preference for him. "Was I wrong? Elizabeh would know her sister's feelings. And if she believes differently, then…"

Darcy dipped his quill in the inkwell and proceeded to write.

If you have not been mistaken here, I must have been in an error. Your superior knowledge of your sister must make the latter probable.—If it be so, if I have been misled by such error, to inflict pain on her, your resentment has not been unreasonable. But I shall not scruple to assert that the serenity of your sister's countenance and air was such as might have given the most acute observer a conviction that, however amiable her temper, her heart was not likely to be easily touched.—

Leaning back in the chair, Darcy shook his head. "I acted as a true friend to Bingley. I will not allow another friend to fall prey to a schemer, whether it would be the woman, such as Rawlings' wife, or a mercenary mother, like Mrs. Bennet. I will defend myself in this matter." He returned to putting words on the paper.

That I was desirous of believing her indifferent is certain,—but I will venture to say that my investigations and decisions are not usually influenced by my hopes or fears.—I did not believe her to be indifferent because I wished it;—I believed it on impartial conviction, as truly as I wished it in reason.—

"Was I vain to write this?" He reread the words. "No. Elizabeth, you do not know everything, and your sister is not as independent as you. Your mother may have been pushing the connection, and she is not as strong as you, and could not refuse."

Darcy shuddered, sighed, and then returned to his letter, writing words he knew would cause Elizabeth pain. Although he did praise her and her sister,he meticulously explained her family's improper behaviors, He assumed her youngest sisters would be compromised by any sweet talking scoundrel. His head shot up like a wilted flower in a rainstorm.

Darcy rose from his seat and moved to the window. He pulled back the drapes and peered out into the blackness. He recalled that day in Ramsgate when he discovered George Wickham attempt to elope with his sister. "I must warn Elizabeth. She must not remain defenseless from his charm even if...I must reveal my own sister's impropriety. Georgiana will understand."

He returned to the desk and began his next defense—Wickham and his relationship to the Darcy family. He explained about their childhood and their growing independence from one another. He wrote in detail about the living and the payment made to Wickham.

Pausing to take a large drink from his refilled glass, he attempted to select the best words to describe his sister's behavior. He knew Elizabeth was honorable, and would never reveal the truth, so he began the lengthy confession that he had never shared with anyon except Richmond, of course. Darcy stopped, stood, and finished his brandy.

"You bastard." Darcy stomped around the room for a quarter of an hour, not caring if the carpet did not muffle the sounds of his boots. He glowered at the door to the hallway. "It was you, Richmond. I am positive you told Elizabeth about my detaching Bingley. You did this to me. Why? Humph. I will charge you with your betrayal and demand to hear why!."

After draining the last of the brandy into his glass, a calmer Darcy returned to his writing. He finished the explanation about how his sister had only a year ago attempted to elope with Wickham, whose purpose was not love but revenge. He pieced together the words without emotion, otherwise he would have used inappropriate language—those vulgar words that presented themselves whenever the thought of that cur surfaced. He finished quickly, and did not bother to reread the painful words written on the page.

"Three more of her accusations left to defend. I shall address Blake next." Before he wrote the first word, he rang for his man and handed him the empty decanter. While he waited, he stood at the window, gazing at the darkness. The vision of the little children reappeared, but this time a fair-haired man was holding their hands. The servants were calling him "Your Grace."

He thought about what he should say about Blake. 'Did you detach your friend, Lord Blake, from me as well? Did you persuade him to leave Netherfield Park and never to contact me again? Are you the conductor of every friend's life?'

"Conductor? Humph. She does not know how much effort I expended keeping out of his way. I could have..."

With a smile on his face, he mended his quill before setting it to the letter. Darcy had assumed months ago that Mrs. Bennet was the one who had deceived Blake. He remembered clearly the moment she had opened the balcony door, and which part of the conversation she overheard. She had left, believing Blake was destitute, or at least penniless, and never learned his friend had resources of his own. Perhaps, he should have told Blake about Mrs. Bennet's eavesdropping, but he reasoned that if Elizabeth's mother discouraged the union, it would only be for mercenary reasons. He reasoned that concealing the truth to her was different than keeping Miss Bennet's visit secret from Bingley. He had no qualms this time. .He dipped his quill in the ink and carefully wrote the next words.

> I was neither a party to, nor the reason for, any sudden disinterest between my friend, Lord Blake, and you. Nevertheless, I am aware he went to Longbourn the day after

the ball only to discover by your own mother's words that you had left that morning for London because—and I wil try to quote my friend accurately—you wished to avoid him. He informed me there was no longer any reason to stay. I do not know what actions he took once we arrived in town.

Sighing, Darcy pressed his lips together, mended his quill, dipped it in the ink, and controlled the slight tremble in his hand. He would address the charge of mockery.

Your accusation of my total disregard of your family based on a request for a book on Gas Lighting was woefully misplaced. While I cannot go into detail without betraying confidences, I will admit, I was at that time pursuing new investments. Gas lighting was a particular interest of mine. Having seen Mr. Bennet's excellent library, and having had several judicious conversations about progress with him, I merely suspected he might be in possession of such material. I now understand your abruptness at leaving that day when I requested you to ask your father for such a book. Please understand, I meant no offense at that request.

He held his head in his hand knowing the next accusation would be the hardest for her to hear. He must be truthful if he wanted his name cleared, and there was nothing left except his good name. He understood no person wanted to admit their family member is dishonorable; even he would not want to discover this about his own relatives. He recollected their conversation dealing with the matter. They were standing close; she with her back to the window, and he, just inches away. and now even hours later, he still felt the heat of her glare when he remembered her words.

"Mr. Darcy, why do you call my uncle dishonest? What gives you the right to slander such a good man?"

"He hides his deceitfulness by blaming them on Mr. Cuffage." He tried speaking the truth without a hint of the disgust he felt.

"Mr. Cuffage. You, sir, are the one woefully mistaken. That evil man caused my father to lose his investment in the Gas Light Company—not my uncle Gardiner." Her gaze bore into his with a defiance he had only been a party to once, years before—Wickham accusing him of lying about the living. However, Wickham's defiance was a ploy, while Elizabeth's attitude was misguided.

Darcy sat at his writing table, tapping his fingers on the desktop. He stared at the blank section on the page where he would have to provide his position. When he lifted his quill, her final assault upon his person echoed in his mind.

Elizabeth's eyes had turned dark, and with her shoulders straight, sputtered the most unforgiveable accusation when she said:By calling my uncle dishonest you, sir, are no gentleman!"

He remembered exactly how she glared menacingly at him. He had never witnessed such hatred from anyone, with the exception of Wickham. With him, he did not give a damn, but her feelings mattered. He wrote,

> Nevertheless, I am saddened to report it was your uncle, not Mr. Cuffage, who caused the problem with the investment. If you have not been mistaken here, I must have been in error, but unlike your superior knowledge of your sister's feelings, I do not believe my understanding is false. I am sorry to inflict pain on you, and I understand your resentment of what appeared to be a callous request, but I merely believed your father has not shared the whole story, choosing instead to shield you from the odious truth.

There, he said it, and in writing. Refusing to reread the letter, he finished it with, "God bless you," and signed his name,

> Fitzwilliam Darcy.

He did not sleep that night, preferring to gaze out the window where he could see the Hunsford church steeple. He had spent many evenings searching for a just the smallest glimpse of her among the trees. Every so often, he would look at the sealed letter on the desk, and then close his eyes tightly in an attempt to shut out the image of her face, and her hands.

His valet prepared him for the day before daylight. Ignoring his man's slight raise of the brow at his untouched bed, he hurried with his dressing, picked up the letter, and left the room.

He found a strategic location to stand and wait for her, while the sun rose behind him. He waited for hours while he replayed every word, every look, every nuance from the day before. She would not try to avoid her preferred path. And so it was, when he spied her peeking into the park at the entrance gate, and she was on the point of continuing her walk, he moved her way.He stepped forward, calling her name, and then watched with sadness as her shoulders first slumped, then regained their proud position as she turned and faced him.

He caught up to her, held out the letter, and felt relief when she graciously took it from his hand. "I have been walking in the grove sometime in the hope of meeting you. Will you do me the honor of reading that letter?" His voice betrayed his desire to be unemotional, and his haughtiness rang in his ears.

With a slight bow and not another word spoken, he turned again, and never looked back.

Chapter Eighteen

D arcy was the first to enter the carriage, and glowered at Richmond who was finishing his goodbyes to his aunt and cousin. Damn him and his bloody charm. His gaze never left his cousin until he gave the signal to go. They began their journey in silence. Darcy retrieved The Vine and The Oak from his collection of poems and ignored his cousin while he read the poem again. He had put it aside many weeks ago unfinished, today he wished to discover what happened to the vine and, more importantly, the oak. He had identified Elizabeth as the vine and he the oak.

> A vine from noblest lineage sprung
> And with the choicest clusters hung,
> In purple rob'd, reclining lay,
> And catch'd the noontide's fervid ray;
> The num'rous plants that deck the field
> Did all the palm of beauty yield;
> Pronounc'd her fairest of their train
> And hail'd her empress of the plain.
> A neighb'ring oak whose spiry height
> In low-hung clouds was hid from sight,
> Who dar'd a thousand howling storms;
> Conscious of worth, sublimely stood,
> The pride and glory of the wood.

He caressed the paper with his fingers while looking out the window, hoping for one last glimpse of Elizabeth, unsuccessfully. He sighed deeply and moved on to the next verse.

> He saw her all defenseless lay
> To each invading beast a prey,
> And wish'd to clasp her in his arms
> And bear her far away from harms.
> 'Twas love -- 'twas tenderness -- 'twas all
> That men the tender passion call.

Wickham! He is a beast a prey. I pray she is no longer defenseless when it comes to that scoundrel. And yes, 'twas love I felt, and feel even still. He continued his reading.

> He urg'd his suit but urg'd in vain,
> The vine regardless of his pain
> Still flirted with each flippant green
> With seeing pleas'd, & being seen;
> And as the syren Flattery sang
> Would o'er the strains ecstatic hang;
> Enjoy'd the minutes as they rose
> Nor fears her bosom discompose.

No longer wishing to continue, Darcy folded the poem and placed it in his coat pocket. I urged my suit in vain. In vain, I struggled. In vain, I lost. She prefers the damn flowery words and blasted charm of lesser men.

He focused his attention on his cousin who was silently glaring at him with dark and brooding expressions.

Darcy shrugged, opened a book, and for the first half of the trip, he and Richmond sat thusly—one attempting to read while the other seethed. Even though he had not read a single word, he kept his head down and his hands steady.

Richmond chuckled.

Darcy lifted his head. "What is it? What exactly are you smiling and chuckling about?"

"Well, you."

"How wonderful how I give you such pleasure." He sneered, no longer caring about decorum. She had said he was not a gentleman, so be it.

"I did not say you give me pleasure at all. You have rarely done that."

"What? You say the most outlandish things. Explain yourself."

Richmond smirked. "Very well, since you have asked so pleasantly. You do as you wish and leave it up to me to follow. I understand how it works. In the army, the general barks the commands and I, the colonel, carry them out. In this society, you are the general and I am nothing greater than a private."

"Humph. I have never treated you in such a way."

"Humph! Not true, cousin. Not true. Why, this trip alone, you ignored my needs. Even a general worries about his lowliest soldiers."

"I suppose you will elaborate. You do like to talk and ooze charm while doing so."

"Ha! I normally do not share my opinions with you, preferring instead to keep my favored place in your house, but since you have issued this invitation in such a delightful tone, I will take the opportunity to shed sunlight on your cold and dark world."

Darcy settled back in his seat, curious.

"I know full well when I am finishied talking Darcy House and Pemberley will be lost to me forever. Promise me though that you will not throw me out until we reach the London's outskirts"

"You exaggerate so." Darcy rolled his eyes, and when his cousin sat silently, he added, "But if I must, I promise."

"I had made plans to spend several weeks in London before I had to return to my battalion. They were important weeks for me. You see, I will be leaving for the Continent shortly."

Darcy gasped.

"See! You had not given that possibility a single moment's thought. Well, I wished to spend time in those parts of town where you do not go. I wanted to drink, eat, gamble, laugh, and yes," Richmond glared across the seat at his cousin and continued, "whore around."

Darcy scoffed.

"I wanted to have my enjoyment in the arms of a few luscious London wenches. Do not act so supercilious." Richmond laughed. "What? Are you surprised that I know such a large word? Of course, only you are capable of intelligent thought and five syllable words."

"Do not stop," Darcy demanded. "If you have more to say, then say it."

"You never consider me when you change plans. Do not look at me so; it has always been this way. You do as you please, and my lot in life is to follow behind without saying a word. Salute is what we call it in the army. Well, I shall salute you no more." Richmond leaned back in his seat and turned his head away.

Darcy lowered his head. "I am sorry. I did not think you had plans. You did not share your news about leaving for the Continent. Why did you not?"

"You never seemed interested in my life—only yours and Georgiana's. "Still, I try my best to always look out for her, and you, cousin."

"Humph! Look out for me? Did the Army instruct you in how to utter fabrications with such ease?"

Richmond's brows shot upwards at his cousin's venomous tone. "When have I not looked after you?"

"When? When you revealed a recent confidence between us to someone. You deliberately spoke ill of me, but presented it in a humorous manner, of that I am sure. You hide behind your humor. I can well imagine your disloyal words."

"What are you referring to? I would never betray a member of my own family."

"You spoke to Miss Elizabeth about my saving Mr. Bingley."

Richmond nodded. "I assumed it was him. I spoke to her about your triumph, to show your true... worthiness." He spit the last word out.

"But did you know it was her sister that he was infatuated with? Ah, yes. From the coloring of your complexion, I can see you did suspect it. Why, then, did you reveal a confidence?"

"You spoke of no secrecy." Richmond brushed his sleeve with his hand. "When Bingley's name came up in conversation, I merely expounded on your superior abilities to oversee everyone's lives."

"You deliberately tried to show me in a poor light, and succeeded in causing me no small amount of harm."

"I own no remorse for your causing you harm. Stepping down from the pedestal would serve you better.

"Why?"

"Oh, let me explain. Your chin is raised so high, that coupled with your height, you cannot help but present a picture of a man peering down at everyone. Unfortunately, this is exactly how you view others. When surrounded by men you admire, you relax your shoulders, lower your whole head, and smile when you speak. But for the rest of the world, you are different. You present a... what do they call it? Yes, a noble mien, and that his how you maintain your sense of superiority. Furthermore, if anyone not of your close acquaintance utters a single word your way, or someone says something you do not find worthy, you merely *humph*."

"Humph."

"Even now you cannot help yourself." Richmond chuckled. "I always believed it was because all the Fitzwilliams say the damn word out of habit, but you use the word for intimidation."

"Humph!" Darcy uttered the word with emphasis.

"Your chin is higher now than when the conversation started. You prove my point. I am beneath you. Your father did not think so, or else he would not have made me Georgiana's co-guardian. Yet, my word has no sway with you. Today, I am not at all fond of you."

"Unless you explain why you acted as you did, then I am not fond of you today either."

"I merely wanted to be in town, and you selfishly kept me from it. It was not a betrayal so much as a weapon in my arsenal. I must use what I possess in order to gain what I want. And I longed for London, and you kept delaying our return because of her. Thus, I believed only she could make you wish to leave."

"You knew?"

Richmond smirked. "Yes. I imagine Aunt Catherine suspects as well. Anne recognized your desire whenever you looked at the pretty young lady from Hertforshire; we even joked about it. But as I said, I merely wanted to leave, and the only way was through Miss Elizabeth.

"You were successful; she rejected my proposal. She will not marry me."

Richmond sat upright. "You offered marriage? Marriage to her? She is a nobody. She has no fortune and no family connections important enough for you. I am shocked you actually proposed marriage. I... "

"What did you think I would offer?"

"I thought you were looking for a mistress. I never once thought you sought marriage. How was I supposed to know? You never share your thoughts with anyone. Well, she has charms, I agree, but she does not possess the status to become Mistress of Pemberley. Surely you must see that."

"With my wealth, I can offer wherever I choose."

"Sometimes you shock even me. I like Miss Bennet, and she was another reason I shared the information. I did not wish to see her put in an anxious situation. I... thought if she was angry, she would be able to thwart your overtures, if you approached her in that way." Richmond shook his head and creased his brow. "But with you choosing someone so below you, does this mean you would approve Mr. Kent marrying Georgiana?"

"What do you know of Kent?" Darcy said brusquely.

"Perhaps I should keep silent and not—"

"Speak your mind! What is it that concerns you? What do you believe has happened?"

"You should learn not to interrupt! It is most ungentleman-like and proves my point of how you believe you are superior to others. You are selective as to who you interrupt."

"Blast it. I must know! And do not drag this out, Richmond. I warn you. Today is not a day to test my temperament."

"Oh, well, perhaps I should just remain silent and deal with Kent myself. I share the guardianship, and I do not have to ask your permission any more than you ever ask mine. As I said, your father made me an equal in that regard."

"I am in no mood for your silly games."

"Humph." Richmond turned to gaze out the window. He sighed at the unchanging, mundane landscape. "You friend has been showing interest in Georgiana. He is a tradesman's son; the family will never approve. My father will take every action to thwart any attempts he might make to obtain her hand. Kent needs to be stopped, for his sake as well as hers."

"Oh, is that it? I had planned to speak with him upon my return." Darcy settled back in his seat, relaxing his body. "What exactly happened to cause such an alarm? At first, I suspected he had made an offer by your earlier remark, but now I am puzzled."

"I have witnessed several situations where Georgiana has defended him. However, one event in particular bothers me the most."

"Go on."

"One day, as I was escorting her and my sister on a walk in Hyde Park, your friend had deliberately hid along her normal path. He was laying in wait for her. With all my training, I easily spied him long before we came to his hiding spot. I, of course, never left Georgiana's side. She allowed only Mr. Kent's virtues to be discussed. I caught him winking at her, and she returned it with a conspiratorial-like smile. Victoria can attest to all I related. She had noticed him hiding too. Neither of us seemed surprised when he appeared."

"You do not need to involve yourself. I will speak to Kent immediately upon my return." Darcy waved his hand.

Richmond attempted to hide his own smile, still Darcy knew his cousin was pleased to return to the role of the good guardian while he took care of the problems. Nothing more was discussed until the carriage stopped at Richmond's home. A few polite words were shared and then Darcy headed off.

He entered his London townhouse with the intent of spending an hour or two considering all the accusations addressed to him. But before he could escape to his bedchambers, Geoffries impeded his progress. He expounded upon Mr. Kent's frequent visits with Georgiana, their constant walks, and that she had persuaded Mr. Kent to go shopping on several occasions. Lady Victoria and Mr. Kent's sister accompanied them. He handed over the list of Georgiana's mail.

Darcy became alarmed when he read Miss Sarah Kent's name repeatedly, both for incoming and outgoing letters. "Geoffries, when was the last time Miss Kent visited?"

"Today, sir. In fact, she is in the music room with Miss Darcy."

"Now?" Darcy rose from his chair.

"Yes, sir."

He penned a message for immediate dispatch to Kent's home, requesting him to come as soon as possible.

Darcy's long legs carried him down the hallway, up the stairs, and toward the music room with such swiftness, the servants backed up against the walls to give him room to pass. He burst into the music room. "Georgiana! I am home."

His sister's fingers froze on the keys of the last note played.

Miss Kent leaned over and whispered to the motionless young girl. Slowly they rose to greet him.

Georgiana's hand shook when she introduced her brother. "Miss Kent has been so kind to visit with me while you have been at Rosings."

Darcy bowed slightly in response to Miss Kent's slight curtsey. She lifted her head, and he was able to discern the likeness to her brother; both had dark hair and an olive complexion. They shared the same features—high cheekbones, prominent nose, and deep-set brown eyes. Her emerald green silk dress was fashionable and suited her. She stood upright with her shoulders back and her chin high, a look of defiance. Yes, she is Kent's sister in every way.

"I am pleased to make your acquaintance, Miss Kent. I hope I did not disturb anything important."

"Not at all. Georgiana was playing a new piece." Sarah Kent said. "It is one she wishes to play for my brother."

"I would not wish to keep her from practicing, but I did have a desire to speak with her... about my trip." Darcy remained standing until the two girls said their good-byes and Miss Kent left.

Georgiana turned around, and with a newly discovered resolve, asked sharply, "Why did you speak so brusquely with my friend."

"Why did you not tell me you had met Miss Kent?"

"Must I receive your permission?"

"Yes!" Darcy glowered. "You are too young to choose the right associations. Miss Kent is..."

"She is a lovely lady. She is most kind and has wonderful stories. Why can I not choose my own friends?"

"Because sister, I will never again take my role as guardian as lightly as I did last year. All social activities must first be approved by me!"

"You treat me as a child!"

"You are a child, and I am responsible for you. I cannot, and will not, let you fall into another schemer's trap."

"She is not a schemer! I am not the same foolish girl. I will speak to Richmond."

"Do not think you can hide behind his uniform. He will be more adamant than I am. We spoke about your growing attraction with Mr. Kent, and we have agreed to put an end to it. You kept your acquaintance with his sister a secret, and that is reason enough for me to end your friendship with her."

"You speak of my attraction to Kent? Humph. You do not know what you speak. I knew you did not trust me! I... I... I hate you." Georgiana sobbed and ran from the room.

***

Darcy raised his head and glowered at Kent when he rushed into the study. "I demand to know what your intentions are towards Miss Darcy."

Kent took a step backwards. "I will not answer you when you speak to me in such a manner. I am not Bingley, who you have reduced to a cowering, simpering fool." He took a few steps forward. "I am not afraid of you."

"You will leave my sister alone. I will never permit any courtship between you two."

"Why would I want her?"

"You are a social climber, a sycophant. I will not let you latch on to my world through her."

"Latch onto your world? Bah. You may keep it. I have grown to despise everything about your world. The upper class is comprised of lazy, rich men who prefer to squander their days in meaningless activities. If we were to sit around all day drinking, gambling, and in seductions with women of ill-repute, this country would cease to exist." Kent took another step closer. "We are the ones creating its wealth these days. We will be the ones creating the future. We will look down upon the likes of you."

Before Darcy could react, Kent moved another step closer and shouted, "You are a self centered cur. You are arrogant beyond reason. You are not an aristocrat, such a Blake, and you are not as wealthy as I will be in two years. You have no cause to treat me as one would treat dirt beneath their fingernails, solely because I prefer not to be a gentleman farmer!"

Darcy opened his mouth to speak.

"No, I shall interrupt you this time. You do not get a chance to speak until I have finished my thought." When Darcy nodded, Kent continued. "You think everyone is after your money or your good name. Well, keep it. I would not have it if you forced it upon me. You will scare away every man that seeks Georgiana's favor. She is doomed to a spinster's life unless, of course, you write a contract with an idiot with a title and his own money. You do not care for your sister."

"Do not speak to me about my sister."

"I will speak to you any way I want to. I am one man you cannot control and manipulate to your desires."

"I do not manipulate, Kent.

"Bah! You are a fool, as Rawlings once charged if you truly believe that. You manipulate everyone that crosses your path."

"For example?"

"Blake."

"Blake? How the hell did I manipulate him?"

"You never told him the truth about Mrs. Bennet." Kent tapped his own chest. "Yes, I know all about the balcony scene. I was there, off to the side. I had gone out for fresh air, after a long evening in hot, sticky clothes. Blake and Miss Elizabeth soon appeared, and before I could say anything, they spoke in terms I should have not have heard. I could not embarrass them by showing myself then." He stepped closer. "So, you see, I know what you did."

"And what, pray, was that?"

"You never told Blake about Mrs. Bennet only hearing a part of his situation, the part where you accused him of being penniless. In fact I believe you mentioned his financial situation only after you noticed Mrs. Bennet standing at the door. I noticed the glint in your eye and the smirk upon your face when she appeared. That is when you decided to use her to help keep her daughter away from him. Had Blake known who was listening behind him, he might have acted differently the next day."

"How do you know how he acted? You were in already in London."

"There are many things shared outside of your ears. I will not tell you how I know, but be aware that I know all about it. You never set him straight. I assumed that it was because you wanted her for yourself. Jealousy does make for unsound judgments. You managed the entire mess."

Darcy opened his mouth to speak until Kent raised his open palm.

"Again, I will not let you interrupt me." Kent paused until Darcy gave him the signal to continue. "I doubt you even know that you interrupt others. Humph! Did you know you utter that sound whenever you are not pleased with the conversation? Nevertheless, I digress. Shall we discuss Bingley now? Shall I explain how you manipulate him?" He waited until Darcy nodded. "You call him your dearest friend, and yet you ruined forever his chance for happiness."

Darcy pressed his lips tightly together.

"You talked him out of his plans to marry Miss Bennet. She loved him; that I know. I tried to talk sense into him, but, unfortunately, only your judgment was valuable to him. Rawlings tried too. I have no idea if Blake and Bingley ever commiserated with each other. Two men, destroyed by you. Well, Rawlings was only fortunate that his wife died, otherwise he would still be living in hell because of your selfish actions."

"You heard something about Margaret Stevens and me?"

"It is a gossipy place, London. Everyone talked about it. You are so vain you do not think anyone can be smarter than you are. Miss Bingley heard what happened, and when you did not return her attentions, it was not long before London knew. She has been busy since we left Netherfield. I tried to convince her it would not be wise to meddle with a Darcy, but she is, as they say, a woman scorned. All the particulars are hazy, but it is understood you allowed another supposed good friend to live with your mistake."

"This time you have gone too far, Kent. You are only correct in that you do not know the whole story."

"Perhaps, but I know enough to realize why Rawlings was included in the alliance. He had nothing to bring. I am not a fool."

"Humph."

Kent shook his head in a slow motion until Darcy realized he had uttered his familiar grunt.

"I suspect you treat your cousin, Colonel Fitzwilliam, as an underling as well. Did he have to wait until you were ready to return? Georgiana mentioned he had made plans with her. Did you even bother to tell him you were delaying your trip? When you extended your stay, you did not send word to me."

Darcy sucked in a quick breath.

"Oh! You forgot our plans to go north? Or did you deem the trip as unimportant? You still think my kind and I are beneath you, so much so, you cared not what my Aunt had prepared for you. The Kent family is not up to your status; we are not your kind. Yes, Darcy, my kind. When you attended the Lunar Society Meeting at Bingley's, did you show any kindness to my sister?"

"I was not introduced to her."

"I arrived late and assumed you had been introduced. Bingley would have done so if you had asked. But you never asked for any introductions to any lady attending. See? We are not worth your trouble. Well, I am rich, and on my thirtieth birthday, I will be extremely wealthy; so rich, in fact, there has already been talk of knighthood. And if all goes as planned, I will be *Sir* to you, and then you would be required to walk behind... me!"

"Then you will be a member of that horrible upper class you said you so despise. Even as a knighted man, I would not permit your marriage to my sister."

"Poor Miss Darcy. She has no chance."

"Not with you, Kent. I will never allow it."

"See, you have jumped to a conclusion that has never existed. You once accused Miss Elizabeth of willfully misunderstanding everyone, but you must own to that particular trait. She may do so as well, but not out of malice, only inexperience. You assumed, just because I was friendly to your sister, I wanted her fortune."

"I learned about your pending wealth at Bingley's dinner. Money has nothing to do with my decisions for my sister. But what is your agenda? You have one, and I have believed it for a long time now."

"You want to know the truth?" Kent waited.

Darcy nodded.

"First, it is true I attached myself on to you as closely as a leech would affix itself to a dying man. Bingley and I were friends long before we attended Cambridge together. Once there, I did manipulate events for the sole purpose of ingratiating myself with you. Yes, I do have an agenda, and I am also skilled at manipulation; but it is not about you, your fortune, your name, or even your sister."

Hearing Darcy scoff, Kent pointed to the chairs, inviting him to sit.

Darcy sat down, crossed his arms, and waited.

"I have been in love with Lady Victoria ever since the day I saw her visiting you at Cambridge."

"Victoria?" Darcy dropped his jaw and uncrossed his arms.

"Yes. Everything I have done, I have done to win her. Fortunately for me, I had moved into the house before you and Rawlings had invited Blake to join us. He would never have allowed me to live there. Another reason I despise him. He never went long without holding his superiority over me. You and Rawlings were much the same."

"He is superior, Kent. He is a Marquess and one day he will be a Duke. But if his attitude disturbed you, why did you stay?"

"I would not have had I not seen Lady Victoria. But by then, all I wanted was to find a way to be meet her and be near her. You do not know how difficult it was for me when she never returned to Cambridge. I kept waiting."

"Her brother had graduated. So all this time you stayed just to catch a glimpse of her?"

"Yes. But I decided I would have to wait until I could gain an introduction from you at a ball or party in town. I believed my association with you would be the simplest path to gaining her hand. Surprisingly, it was not you, but your sister who helped me meet her. Miss Darcy is adept at spotting angst in another person. She called me on it right away."

Darcy wondered if she had revealed her past with him, but he feared asking.

"Your sister is a sensitive soul, and one day I will challenge you to treat her in a more deserving fashion. I have grown fond of her, as an older brother or cousin would. She is a sweet child."

"Yes she is."

"Your sister delivered a rose to Lady Victoria for me once, and I admit this is not exactly honorable, but I sent Lady Victoria letters through my sister. Sarah sent them to Miss Darcy, who in turn snuck them to your cousin. And before you bark at me, yes; I did secretly introduce my sister. They have become friends. It is obvious that you would never let her associate with a tradesman's daughter. Remember, you did not bother to speak to my sister at the Lunar Society dinner. I am surprised you spoke to any of the attendees."

"I admire the people that attended that dinner. And I would not keep her from friendship with your sister as long as I am confident the purpose is not for deceitful reasons. I have no problem associating or socializing with the Kent family."

"Not true; you cut me one evening. You cannot imagine how I felt when you, Miss Darcy and Lady Victoria left for the theater when we first returned from Netherfield. You left me behind without so much as a by-your-leave. From that moment, I despised everything about your *kind*. You take what you want and then ignore us."

Darcy leaned forward and pointed his finger at Kent. "To willfully misunderstand is another trait we share. You have done the same."

"How so?

"That night my uncle requested I take Lady Victoria to the theater, and demanded none of my friends attend with us. I suspect he was trying to protect her from Blake, but I agreed. So, you see, you are also culpable of misunderstanding the situation, and are guilty of assuming the worst.

Kent shrugged. "You could have told me. I would have understood. I would have helped you keep those two separated."

"You did not give me the benefit of doubt."

"And you could have given me the benefit of the doubt. There never was anything beyond friendship with Miss Georgiana. I tell the truth. She is a child, Darcy. I seek a woman."

Darcy puzzled over a thought. "So your antagonism to Blake was—"

"Because of the cruel way he treated Lady Victoria. How I hated him. How I hate him still. I have tried to put it all aside, but I cannot. I do not know if you are aware that he has moved on to another lady, a Miss Godwin. They would make a good match. She has standing and money. I do not believe she has a heart either."

"About Blake. You are not aware of the whole story with Victoria. He is worthy of your respect. I cannot divulge a confidence, but I ask that you trust me in this regard. I know you find that hard to do today; I implore you to try."

"To use your word... humph!"

Darcy opened his mouth, shut it, and then opened it again. "Kent, my uncle will never allow a connection to his daughter with a tradesman's son. Whatever you thought my beliefs were, they are multiplied tenfold with him."

"It does not matter; she is of age. He will come around, I suspect, if my plan works. I doubt he would choose to disown her, once my place in society has been gained."

"I warn you, he is not easily swayed. I have never succeeded on any subject." Darcy twisted his signet ring around his finger as he contemplated a new concern. "Will you be leaving the alliance?"

"Of course not. Regardless of any disagreement subsisting between us, I always honor my signed contracts. And, I will proceed with my plan for knighthood. The alliance will speed it up; two years is a long time to wait to start the process." Kent laughed as Darcy smiled. "We are much alike, I think. We own many of the same faults."

"Oh?"

"We are stubborn men who expect everyone to accept us without reason."

Darcy tapped the arms of the chair and then pointed his finger at himself. "This stubborn man needs to be alone for a while. By that, I mean days, not minutes. I need to consider everything everyone has said."

"Everyone?"

"Yes. You, my cousin Richmond, and Miss Elizabeth Bennet."

Kent's eyebrows rose in surprise.

"She was at Rosings. I am surprised you did not possess that little piece of information. You seemed to be aware of everything else. I admit it; she is what held my interest. I had the chance to be with her with no Blake to get in the way."

"Oh. No wonder you forgot about me. I understand better. Still..."

"Yes, it was unforgivable of me not to send word about the delay."

"Unforgivable is a strong word. Perhaps rude is a better one. You forgive rudeness all the time. I, too, understand the power unrequited desire for a young lady has on a man."

"Thank you. But it is you that forgives my rudeness. I cannot recall a single instance where you were ever rude to me."

"I assume she spoke forcibly?"

Darcy nodded. "Yes, and with great gusto and verbosity."

"Ah. Well, I will leave you then to sort it all out. Nevertheless, remember all that I said. I warn you that if you do not change your ways, then life will become as you see it. No one will ever want to connect themselves to you for any reason other than money or name. Do not let it be so."

Kent left for the front door. Darcy followed behind and directed Geoffries to stop monitoring Georgiana, but when he headed to his study, he overheard Kent at the front door greeting the one man he did not wish to see.

Chapter Nineteen

"Blake." Kent straightened his hat and smoothed his jacket while descending the steps at Darcy House. "You rode the Andalusian. As I have said before, he is a mighty fine piece of horseflesh, and I will admit I am jealous."

"My invitation still stands. I insist you play on my golf course this summer." Blake patted the horse's neck, and with a twinkle in his eye added, "I can teach you how to perform certain strokes better, and the two of us can challenge Bingley and Rawlings. Darcy is just horrid at putting, and I would not handicap Bingley that way."

"Perhaps we could spot Bingley a few extra strokes to compensate for having Darcy as his partner. Ten strokes would be my guess."

"More like twenty! What brings you to Darcy House? Is he in?"

"Yes, but he is in as foul a mood as I have ever seen."

"His visit to his aunt's did not go well?"

Kent shrugged. How should I tell him? Damn. Why did I not just let him find out for himself? I am an idiot. Damn.

"What is wrong? Is something amiss with the alliance? Does he need my uncle to take action?"

"No, nothing of the sort. While I was not told our conversation was confidential, I believe it is a private matter between us."

"An argument, I assume." Blake leaned down and in a half-whisper asked, "Does he suspect your interest in his little sister?"

"You, too? Good God, why does everyone think I could be interested in a little girl?"

"Oh. I beg your pardon. I noticed your particular attention to her lately, and I am truly sorry for my pompous manner. I misspoke, and I do apologize."

"Do not worry so. Darcy suspected I took an interest in her too. He truly does overreact sometimes. I suspect it was because he returned home in a horrible mood." Suddenly worried that he was deliberately trying to create a problem, Kent put his hand over his mouth. Blast, can I not keep my own mouth shut?

Blake dismounted in one fluid motion. "You must tell me what is wrong!"

Kent looked down at his boots. "Miss Elizabeth was at his aunt's parsonage with Miss Charlotte Lucas, well, Mrs. Collins now."

"Which one is Mrs. Collins?" Blake asked sharply.

"Miss Lucas. He had an awful row with her."

"With Mrs. Collins?"

"No! Miss Bennet."

"Miss Elizabeth Bennet?"

"Yes, of course!" Did I not just say she was visiting Mrs. Collins? "Apparently she was forceful in her words."

"Miss Elizabeth or Mrs. Collins?"

"Miss Elizabeth!" Kent shook his head in disbelief. Can he not keep up with the conversation?

Catching his breath, Blake glanced at the door and then back to Kent. "Would you be so kind to excuse me? I need to speak to Darcy."

"Wait, Blake. I was not privileged to know what transpired, but I caution you to leave him alone. I spoke harshly to him earlier. I attacked his character and, I believe, so did she."

Blake spun around and glared at Kent. "Was he unforgivably rude to her? I must know. Surely you are aware of my preference for her."

"I believe it was more that she hurt him."

"He must have done something for her to act in such a manner. Excuse me."

Kent worried while Blake bounded up the front stairs and banged on the door. What have I done? Oh, God.

***

"May I help you, sir?" the doorman asked the distinguished gentleman standing in front of him.

"I would like to see Mr. Gardiner." Rawlings handed his card to the man, who bowed, and offered the foyer as a place to wait. Rawlings did a quick survey of the room and was surprised by the understated elegance of the room. He had assumed those that had recently improved their fortunes would opt for a gaudy display of their new wealth.

In less than five minutes, a tall, broad shouldered man with gray specks in his hair approached in a hurried manner. "Mr. Rawlings, welcome to my home. This is a great honor."

Rawlings bowed and followed Mr. Gardiner to his study. Once there, Gardiner poured drinks and then politely inquired about his trip.

"I hurried my return to England once I discovered a troubling matter. This passage went well. No British escort this time!" Rawlings remembered that night with a smile. "I hope you received my letters."

"I did indeed, sir. How did you find my old friend, John Astor?"

"He is well. He is an energetic man; I grew tired just hearing about his trips to the west. He possesses a grand vision of the future and he will be enormously successful. Although he is a bit brusque at times; I found I liked him."

"I fear his tendency to be hardnosed will win out in the end. He never could tolerate anyone who rested on his laurels. He did send me a message about your proposition, but I suspect his wife took charge of it." Gardiner laughed. "He was always focused on business concepts, never the details."

"I can attest that has not changed." Rawlings hemmed. "I promised him I would meet with you straight away. You see..." He looked down at his hands, cleared his throat, and explained, "We were fooled into believing you were..."

"Dishonest? Astor did write about it to me."

"Good. Then perhaps you know John Cuffage? He is the owner of the New World Cigar and Wine shop on Bond Street. Astor thinks the man is identifying himself under a false name."

"I have been there, and Astor is correct; Cuffage is not his name. I suppose I never knew his real name, because I recently learned he had called himself John Rogers. Astor knew him by that name while I only dealt with him as a Cuffage.."

"Astor suggested that is his name too. I have yet to visit my friend, Mr. Darcy. I must leave soon. I sent him a message to warn him of the duplicity. I fear there is a connection between Cuffage and Darcy's steward, Mr. Rogers, since he was the one that recommended we collaborate with Cuffage. But I needed to speak to you first, and I promised Astor to come directly here from the ship." Rawlings was reaching for something in his coat pocket when he caught sight of Mr. Gardiner busy at his desk, rummaging through the drawers.

Finally finding what he wanted, Gardiner handed Rawlings several letters. "Perhaps he would accept these from you."

Taking the letters, and upon recognizing them, Rawlings jumped up, nearly spilling his drink. "Bloody hell. What is going on?" He stopped abruptly, turned to Gardiner and in a lower voice apologized.

Gardiner stood. "No need. I felt much like you when I was turned from his house."

"What? No, do not tell me more. I will take my leave and speak to Darcy immediately. Something is amiss here." Rawlings gulped his drink, bowed, and added, "I would still find it an honor to do business with you." Before Mr. Gardiner could answer, Rawlings pulled a document from his pocket. "Here is the outline of our final plans with Astor. You, of course, will be a full partner, although I am somewhat doubtful you will want to connect yourself to Mr. Darcy."

"Ah. Do not worry. We all make mistakes when we are young. I am not at the old, wise stage yet, but every day I approach it quicker than I like. Go speak to Mr. Darcy and clear up this matter. My door is open to you anytime… and to him, too. This man, whatever his name is, almost ruined me as well."

When Gardiner escorted Rawlings to the door, he slapped him on the back. "I also look forward to hearing about the competition. I believe I paid for it several times."

"Who was your favorite?"

"Why, Mr. Kent, of course!"

Rawlings bowed his head. "I shall endeavor to see your losses covered by the profits we shall realize in the future."

"Hear, hear!"

With that, Rawlings climbed aboard his carriage and left for Darcy House.

***

"I demand to know how she fares." Blake glared at Darcy. "Were you ill-mannered to her in any way?"

"To quote another gentleman, it is none of your concern. Stay out of it."

"I will not!" Blake rose to his full height. "Did you insult her? Or harm her?"

"Of course not! She is perfectly fine, and I assure you she is in full command of her voice."

"What happened? Blake paced around the room. "Did she ask about me?"

"I am surprised you are interested. Have you not transferred your feelings to Miss Godwin?"

"Miss Godwin? Transfer my feelings?"

"Atterton's ball! You entertained yourself, and you two slipped out of sight as we left." Darcy sighed. "Another balcony? Another lady to woo and leave behind? Do you court every pretty woman you meet? Do you always end up on a balcony?"

"Why do you constantly think ill of me? Can you not give me the benefit of any doubt? Can you not believe in my character or look upon me with respect? I may not have your wealth, but I am an honorable man. I remember the night well. Miss Godwin claimed her dance from a dinner conversation we had at Lord Harrowby's. She then escorted me to the back room, where I met with my uncle and a few other Tories. I do not know where she went afterwards; nor did I care. She merely did Lord Harrowby bidding."

"I beg your pardon."

"Now will you tell me? Did Eli… Miss Bennet speak about me at all? I must know!"

Darcy studied his friend's concerned expression not know how to begin, so instead of rambling he pointed to the chairs. When he took his seat, he tried to compose his words. He suspected that the moment he revealed the truth to him, Blake would react furiously. Sighing, he sat down and began his answer.

"Yes, she did ask about you. It was in politeness."

Blake gulped his drink, and leaned forward in his seat. "I need to know how she feels about me. Did she indicate in any little way that my company was wanted? Were there any hints as to her leaving Longbourn so suddenly? I know she would not have specifically spoken about that day, but please, tell me everything she said."

"No, she merely asked if you were doing well. Blake, think; this all may be for the best. The Bennets have no money, and what connections they have are not honorable. Her family would never be accepted by your father, and he would treat her meanly."

"Phew! I care not what he thinks. I would protect her. She said nothing more?" Gazing at nothing in particular, Blake tapped the arm of the chair and, after a moment, he cleared his throat. "Kent mentioned you two argued. What did you argue over? Did you make an idiotic reference to her dishonest uncle in Cheapside?"

"No, we argued after I asked her to…" Darcy hesitated and then added, "It was in response to a personal question. She strongly objected to my request. I did not expect her reaction, and the words flew out of our mouths. She was vehemently opposed."

"Vehemently opposed. What did you ask of her?" Blake stared at him. When Darcy rubbed his forehead and mumbled that he had wanted her to be his, Blake leaned forward and yelled, "Did you… did you ask her to become your...?" Blake furrowed his brow. "You disgust me. I hope she spit in your eye. What kind of man are you? She is a gentleman's daughter—"

Darcy jumped up. "Calm down. I offered marriage. I offered marriage! Why does everyone think ill of me?"

"Marriage? Dare I turn around in your presence and give you an opportunity to stab my back with a real knife? It could not hurt any worse than this, I assure you. And I called you my friend! I wanted to be like you! "

Darcy retreated to the window. His shoulders slumped, his head hung low.

Blake noticed the change in Darcy's countenance. "Ha! She turned you down."

"Most decidedly."

Blake's smile widened. "So perhaps there is still a chance for me then? Perhaps I . . ."

Darcy gulped the remnants in his glass and turned to face Blake. "I know she does not want me. She..."

"What?"

"She did say she wished the whole lot of us from Netherfield Park would rot in..."

"Hell?"

Darcy nodded. "She did not say that but she is not pleased with any of us and indicated so."

"Damn. She hates us all! I cannot stay here. I must think." Blake set down his drink to leave, but before he could depart, he heard someone's loud footsteps approaching the study.

"Darcy!" Rawlings yelled as he made his way down the hallway, Kent followed behind after noticing the anger on Rawlings' face while he bounded up the steps two at a time, without speaking to anyone, and burst into the house.

"Rawlings! You have returned early. My God, is there a problem?" Darcy raced toward his friend.

"I need to speak to you now," Rawlings said when he stormed in the room and slammed the door shut without realizing Kent and Geoffries were close behind him. Blake slid into a chair out of Rawlings' line of vision.

Rawlings poked his finger in his friend's chest. "What the bloody hell is going on? Why did you treat Mr. Gardiner the way you did?"

Darcy pushed Rawlings' hand away. "Sit down and calm yourself. Can I get you a glass of wine, or something stronger perhaps?"

"No! What you can do is tell me why you treated Mr. Gardiner in the inexcusable way that you did?"

"We spoke about Mr. Gardiner before, Rawlings. Nothing has changed." Darcy raised his tall frame up as tall as he was able. "I am no mood for dramatic hysterics today."

"I cannot oblige you. I will speak in any manner I wish today. I will not sit down! I sent you a warning from America, and you should have been on your knees begging for Mr. Gardiner's help."

Feeling the heat from Rawlings' glare, Darcy rose stepped towards his friend. "You sent only one letter." He poked his finger on Rawlings chest. "One damn letter! Why did you not write more often? I should be the one who is angry, since I had no idea of what was happening over there. You were inexcusably rude."

Rawlings knocked Darcy's hand away and sputtered, "Inexcusable?" He shook his head. "Rudeness is thine name. For your information, I did write a second letter, and it was one of great warning, since it explained the real Mr. Cuffage and the real Mr. Gardiner." Rawlings began to stomp around the room, each step pounded louder, his face burning and his hands repeatedly opening and closing into fists. "Why did you not take heed of my warning? Why did you bar Mr. Gardiner from your home? He had letters from me for you."

Darcy stopped Rawlings forward motion by grabbing his arm. "Did you not hear me? I did not receive a second letter. See for yourself!" Darcy moved swiftly to the desk and started rummaging through his old mail.

Darcy quickly flipped through letter after letter, shaking his head, but when he waved his hand over the whole stack, it hit upon the old journal, which fell forward revealing the letter in question. His face drained of all color. He tore it open and read the contents quickly. "Oh my God. Damn." He looked up with the letter shaking in his hand. "I swear, I did not know it was here. See how poorly the address was written. It would have been brought to my attention immediately otherwise. Everyone was instructed to watch for a letter from you. And to be misplaced on my own desk! " called for his man, who entered instantly. Kent followed behind.

"Geoffries, when did this letter arrive?

He examined the letter. "A few days before you left for Rosings, sir. The messenger said he had just recently determined it was yours after holding it for a long period. Mr. Rogers studied it and then suggested I place it here with the other mail not considered urgent. We doubted it was even your letter."

"Has Mr. Gardiner called here?"

"Yes, sir. You advised me to send him away in such a manner that he would never call again. I followed your orders exactly."

"Did he have letters?"

Geoffries nodded. "I attempted to inform you, but you did not wish to hear about them, sir. You were strict about him leaving with his letters. I believe he did just that."

Darcy waved his man away and as he was leaving, he noticed Kent standing in the doorway. Darcy was about to gesture him in when he caught sight of his secretary hurrying away. "Kent, bring Mr. Rogers here. Make haste!"

Kent left to pursue a now fast moving man.

Darcy dropped into his chair. "I wish I had read this before. It would have saved me many problems."

"I am not finished with you. Today, I will be the speaker and you will be the listener. You will not interrupt."

Blake remained still, hardly breathing, and not saying a word. He snuggled into the chair, trying to make himself invisible.

"You are the most self-centered cur I have ever known." Rawlings raised his hand to stop an opened mouth Darcy from speaking. "I said you will not interrupt today."

"No one, not even Blake, is such a gut-griping skainsmate." Rawlings looked his way and sent an apology to the man mentioned. Blake tipped his head, and encouraged Rawlings to continue.

"Darcy, all you ever worry about is *you*. How does everyone treat *you*? Everyone wants something from *you*. Are you following what I say? I am sure *you* are not!"

Rawlings paced up and down the room with his hands clasped together behind his back. He cleared his throat. "I shall start with Hertfordshire, where I first discovered your new-found nature. I did not like what I saw. Were you aware of that? No, you assume everyone admires you. No one in Hertfordshire admired you. They did not even like you."

Darcy lowered his head; his strength sapped and his heart heavy. First, Elizabeth, followed by Richmond, Kent, Blake, and now even Rawlings. He could not move. He remained motionless and did not attempt to defend himself as Rawlings continued.

"I remember so vividly your attitude at the Assembly Hall dance. It was pompous, to say the least. You had said something callously about

Miss Elizabeth Bennet, and with her sitting so close by too, and yet you were unaware she could hear you. That, my friend, is the epitome of arrogance—one does not need worry if a cruel remark is overheard. She heard you, and even from across the room, I knew instantly your comment was unkind from her expression. She was quick to recover."

Darcy jolted his head up. "What? You are making this up."

"I speak the truth. Afterwards, I watched her laugh at you with her friend. Kent saw it as well." Why do you think so meanly of those beneath you? Do not speak, for I will give you specifics to prove my point."

Standing before his distressed friend, he tapped each finger as he proceeded to identify every instance of his condescending manner, from his hidden true anxiety about the tradesmen taking power away from the aristocracy and current ruling class to his separation of Bingley from Miss Bennet. He reminded Darcy of his haughty attitude towards even those in London society who did not come up to his level. Rawlings spoke for a half hour without stopping for breath. Once finished, he sat down and waited for a reaction.

Darcy had only one question. "Is there anything at all about me that you find worthy?"

Rawlings sighed. "Most everything is worthy, my friend. You are the best of men in essentials, except somewhere you lost sight of the value of others. You are kind, as evident by your assistance to Bingley on managing his estate. You spent your free time helping him with the tenants and their problems, instead of concerning yourself with the leisurely pursuits available to us."

"How do you know this?"

"Logan, of course, but I have witnessed your other excellent qualities. You spend more funds on charitable institutions than anyone of my acquaintance does. You do not allow anything to harm your own tenants' lives. Your mining operations are the safest in the country, perhaps the world. You found work for displaced spinners in Derbyshire when machinery took hold in the textile industry and destroyed the cottage industry there. I also am aware that you forced the mills to pay well. These traits belie your prideful belief in yourself."

Darcy dropped his head.

Rawlings leaned forward and tapped Darcy on the shoulder. "I shall always call you friend. If I were in needed help, you are the only living person that would respond without question and do so secretly. Other gentlemen, having received your benevolence, cannot keep their mouths closed after downing a few drinks. I heard many stories of your generosity during those years I idled my time away in clubs and taverns."

"But still, it is not enough, according to you and according to everyone." His words faded at the end.

"I am your friend. But without my fortune, would you have treated me with the same consideration? Would I have been someone that received nary a word from you other than the occasional humph? Yes, I have been blunt, but subtlety did not work whenever I attempted to warn you about your own failings. Not too long ago, you said that once your opinion is lost, it is lost forever. Now prove yourself wrong, and demonstrate your ability to revise your opinions on those you deem beneath you!"

Darcy rose from his chair, watching as his friends glanced at each other. During their university days, there had been a tendency to form separate alliances among the five friends. Sometimes he was with the majority, and occasionally he stood alone to champion a radical stance. Today, he stood alone.

"Darcy?" Rawlings asked quietly.

"I will not respond today. I need to think on all that you say and, as much as I am able, I will be fair. But at this moment, we need to discover the truth about Cuffage." Darcy directed everyone's attention to Kent and Geoffries standing in the doorway and holding Mr. Rogers firmly between them.

"Bring him in and shut the door. Geoffries, lock it on your way out."

While Darcy paced, Rawlings, Blake and Kent kept their gaze on Mr. Rogers, who had begun to fret for his safety.

"Mr. Rogers tell us who Mr. Cuffage is? And I warn you to tell the truth. I will have you arrested today and brought up on charges of fraud otherwise."

Rogers swallowed hard and looked at his feet. He raised only his eyes when he spoke. "You are correct, Mr. Cuffage is not whom you think. He is my father, John Roberts. My real name is James Roberts."

"What did you stand to gain? I took you into my confidence."

"His business on Bond Street is a front. He works, as I do, for someone rich and powerful. In fact, our employer is a distant relative."

"What does this man want? I do not understand at all."

"He wants to defeat your alliance. He knows all, and has put into motion many actions to stop you."

"Who is he? I demand you tell us now!"

Mr. Rogers sneered at Darcy. "Lord Harold Roberts Winthrop."

Darcy gasped and dropped in his chair, his mouth agape. "Oh God."

Blake asked, "The Falcon? Why are you so upset?"

Slumping in the chair, Darcy frowned. "He is my grandmother's brother."

Kent shuddered. "Why would he do this?"

"I do not know, but we will soon find out." Darcy pointed to Mr. Rogers. "You are going with us to The Peregrine House. We will not leave until the Falcon answers all our questions."

Chapter Twenty

Harold Rogers Winthrop rifled through the papers on his desk while waiting for his guests to arrive, when his butler came into the room, bringing with him the silver tray holding the visitors' cards.

"Sir, four men have arrived unannounced and they insist on meeting with you immediately. Young Mr. Rogers is among them, but, I daresay, not of his own free will." The butler handed him their cards.

Winthrop's brows shot up when read the names, and then, with a shrug of the shoulders, agreed to meet with them. "How ironic the truth will be revealed on the second Saturday of the month. Escort the young men to the drawing room and send Mr. Rogers here." Winthrop sat at his well-worn desk, and then unlocked the bottom drawer to retrieve a sack of coins. He placed the overstuffed bag on the desktop before the door to his study opened.

"Rogers, it is so good to see you again."

"My lord." Rogers bowed and seated himself.

"I have your payment. Oh, I have secured a new position for you, although I must finalize the arrangements."

"Oh. With a new estate owner?"

"No. He is young man, one of the new industrialists. He will be a force in his own right." The old man released a *humph*. "I need to create a buffer against him. He has the intelligence and the funds to destroy us if he is not outwitted early. We must find a way to stop these new industrialists as they call themselves these days." The Falcon chuckled. "Mr. Kent's supremacy will be jeopardy too!"

"I informed Mr. Darcy about my father, and that we work for you. Apparently, Mr. Rawlings was able to discover the truth while in America."

"It is of no consequence. They will discover everything today. I will deal with young Darcy and his friends in a few minutes. Did you pack your things?"

"No. They brought me directly here."

"I will advise him that I released you to do so. Be quick about it, and do not take anything not yours."

"Not even the papers in the locked cabinet?"

"Well, perhaps a few documents might make for interesting reading. You did keep a key for yourself?"

Rogers nodded, and pulled the key chain from around his neck. "I have used it many times. I worried it might tip our hand."

"Tell your father this play has ended. I am sending him on to America. He needs to undo any contract they may have made with Astor. I will provide him with the funds necessary and a letter revoking Astor's trade rights with China and the East Indies if he does not break the connection. He owes me."

Rogers took his leave and left promptly for Darcy House.

The Falcon entered the drawing room to find the four men huddled together, whispering to one another.

"Darcy. We need to talk. But first, I request Mr. Kent leave."

"No, sir. He is my partner... and my friend." Darcy glanced at Kent, who in turn nodded his head.

"So be it. I shall not deny your wish to degrade yourself in such a manner. I suspect you have questions for me?"

"Why are you trying to destroy our alliance?"

Winthrop smiled. "You have no need for such a partnering. In fact, the time has come for you to know everything. Follow me. Yes, all of you... even you, Mr. Kent. You need to understand the real world you live in."

Darcy muttered. "It will be easier, I am sure, than learning the truth about oneself."

Rawlings chuckled and patted him on the back. "Everyone faces their true reflection in the mirror, or in your case, the window pane. It is never what one expects, but one cannot become whole without it."

"You faced yours?"

Rawlings nodded. "Yes, indeed. Most certainly. I faced all my failings in tavern while nearly unconscious."

"I might wish to add a few suggestions." Darcy gave his friend a smirk.

"As you wish. I have learned to listen, observe, forgive, and accept."

Winthrop looked back towards Rawlings, "How is my dear sweet cousin, Mary?"

"You are related to him, too?" Darcy asked.

"Apparently. She is my mother's Aunt. Shall I call you cousin now? How did we not know?"

"Good gracious, Rawlings. Anyone looking at you two could see the resemblance." Blake said. "Of course, we always thought there was a mischievous couple among your ancestors."

Winthrop led the men up the stairs. Rawlings turned to Darcy, "Can we not take money from our profits and give to an inventor to find a better way to elevate us to the next floor?"

"Mm. A lift of sort! Not possible." Darcy chuckled. "Besides, with the way you eat those sweet treats, you need the exercise, *cousin*!"

"Humph." Winthrop turned to glare at Rawlings as he continued towards the ballroom.

"A dance. He will show us the world through a dance." Rawlings chuckled, leaned in and whispered, "Why, Darcy, he steals my technique, does he not? Did I not do a good job showing the Hertfordshire society to you?"

"I doubt he is planning on educating me on the value of those without the most impeccable status or connections."

When they entered the ballroom, the young men gasped. Sitting in chairs spread about the room were twenty or so men of distinction.

"Oh my," Lord Blake exclaimed loudly. He identified his uncle, Lord Attwood, rising from his chair. Although they had not spoken for years he was surprised to see a member of his family connected in any manner with the Falcon.

"Lord Cheswick!" Darcy said when he spotted his uncle, and then he noticed his cousin, the Viscount, sitting nearby. Rawlings grabbed Darcy's shoulder when he, too, found his family members; Lord Wolverly and his brother jumped up.

"What is this, no ladies? How can we dance without them?" Rawlings said, tersely.

The Fitzwilliam family, the Wolverly pack and the Lords Dembry, Atterton, and Altook stared at them. There were other distinguished gentlemen present that they had met, albeit briefly, over the years, most members of the circle with whom Blake traveled. Peppered beside the old men were their first-born sons, creating a mixture of the old and the new —the past and the future. Blake's mouth fell open when Lord Liverpool tipped his head towards him.

The man introduced as Miss Long's father clearly shocked Rawlings. He began to think about all his dealings with the young lady. She had asked many probing questions on the ship, and then again, while they spent time together in Boston before she left for New York. Sighing,

Rawlings recalled Winthrop was the name of her family in New York. Instantaneously, he understood she had been a spy And her purpose in befriending him and Logan was to locate Astor first. Neither he nor Logan had fallen for her violet eyes, pretty smile, or pert talk; but now he worried about Lowell. Was he a distant member of this secret guild? After a second to think, he dismissed his thought, and felt secure in the Bostonian's friendship.

Kent watched his friends' shock reactions. He was the least surprised, since for years the Falcon had been interested in their business. Somehow, he had not heard Darcy was related to the man that had nearly collapsed the Kent family's business ten years earlier. "My friends," he whispered. "I assume we are staring at the power behind the Honorable East India Company.

Darcy shot a look at Kent. "The East India Company? Did you know about these men before?"

"I was only aware Winthrop kept records on our business. I apologize. I believed he was only interested in my activities. He has been trying to destroy the Kent family for years. But I am surprised you did not know about this, since you are his relation."

"No. Not a word." Darcy turned face his great uncle.

Winthrop nodded. "True, but had your father lived, he would have brought you into this inner circle years ago. He was a member, Darcy, and he would have replaced me as leader had he not died."

Darcy turned to his other friends. "Blake? Rawlings? Were you aware of…"—Darcy waved his hand over the attendees —"this?" Both men shook their heads.

"Come, come, young men. Let us get down to business." The Falcon motioned for them to sit in a row of chairs facing the well-dressed army of men.

"An inquisition, sir?"

"No, Mr. Rawlings. This is a lesson on the ways of the world. Now, we know all about your alliance, but once I have explained the purpose of our meeting here, you will realize it is unnecessary. Surely you do not believe you are the first men to join together to obtain power and wealth?" The Falcon laughed when he spied the flush rising on Darcy's face.

The young men shifted from foot to foot waiting for Winthrop to finish his laugh.

"Sit!"

They remained standing.

"Humph. There is only one true coalition when it comes to business, and it is here in this room. Every second Saturday, we meet to solve the problems of the world. Moreover, Mr. Kent, you are only partially right. We are major stockholders in the *John Company* as we call it, but we do not control the East India Company itself. I must warn you, however; we do wield great power in their decisions. We have had to bail out the government several times, and our wishes are usually met without question or argument."

Winthrop pointed his head towards his other guests. "This group you see before you is much more than just that one trading company. Sit and I shall explain."

Darcy took his seats, crossed his arms, and leaned back into his chair. The other men followed.

"Sir John Banks was my grandmother's grandfather and he founded this particular business alliance in 1622. Ironically, he began his syndicate by arranging contracts with the navy. He supplied saltpetre; you are selling the modified Baker rifles. You see, Darcy, you own much of his character."

"Oh?"

"Yes, He was known to say: 'Keep your accounts punctual, be honest to all men, be careful of your company, converse not with ill company for evils do follow thereon.' Now you need to take notice of his warnings. Be careful of your company."

"He was a businessman. Perhaps he was speaking of the likes of you!" Darcy glared.

"True, Sir John Banks was first and foremost the leader of business. His group dabbled in many areas from trade to transportation to financing explorers and building churches. His company's profits grew at an alarming pace. He established a duplicate East India trading company, but Sir John had been too successful that Queen Elizabeth's original company had no choice but to integrate his into theirs. So you must find it amusing, my young Darcy that history is repeating itself."

"I do not understand." Darcy glared at his great uncle, and tightened his arms.

"We are here to offer you a merger. You will join us, and we will pursue your ideas. You, my boy, shall take your place as leader of this group. You have the skills, knowledge, and all the natural abilities to do just that. We have picked you."

"But I have signed agreements with these men, and I shall not back away. Remember, be honest to all men; are those not Sir John's words?"

"Well, Blake and Rawlings are invited to join. We will see that Bingley and Kent receive compensation. We can be honest in that regard."

"Receive compensation?" Kent jumped up.

Winthrop glared until Kent returned to his seat. "You cannot expect to join this group. Why, we are all members of the aristocracy, or have strong familial bonds with peers of the realm."

"John Banks was nothing but a businessman, and he was not born with his title," Kent added.

"True, but that was a long time in the past. Do not forget, his little company merged into the larger one, and the stockholders took over. Nevertheless, he was a brilliant thinker, and that is why they made him Governor of the East India Company after the merger. And Darcy is much like him."

"Stop, Darcy." Bingley's cry diverted everyone's attention to the doorway as he burst in, followed by his Uncle Watt and Mr. Murdoch. "We need to talk somewhere privately. I have learned much on my trip north. I hurried back as quickly as I could. The letter I sent you barely touched on the problems."

"I could not make out anything you wrote. Too many blots, Bingley! How did you know we were here?"

"Geoffries. For a moment, I thought I might have to beat it out of him."

Darcy chuckled at that vision. Geoffries was a tall, well-built man, and although he was older than his friend, he could not reconcile in his mind any way that Bingley would have won.

"You have information for us?" Rawlings asked.

"Can we talk privately in another room?" Darcy asked Winthrop.

"There is nothing he can say to you we will not discover. So speak up, Mr. Bingley. Perhaps we can clear up any misunderstandings and avoid apologies later."

Bingley eyed Darcy, who shrugged and indicated that he should reveal his information. "They do seem to know everything."

"Here is the situation. These men plan to take over our alliance, bringing only you, Blake and Rawlings into theirs and paying off Kent and me."

"Yes. That is what Winthrop told us before you came in."

"But do you know they purposely deceived Mr. Bennet at the cost of his daughters' dowries? These are not honorable men, Darcy."

"Mr. Bennet? How?"

Mr. Murdoch spoke for Bingley. "I started the Gas Light Company, and had avoided entering into contract with them." He tilted his head towards the gentlemen assembled.

"Humph." Winthrop muttered.

Undeterred, Murdock continued. "When I received financial backing from Mr. Bennet and a few other gentlemen, they took action. They forced me to delay my progress by intimidating my suppliers, and somehow held up the legislation in Parliament for my patent. I will not bore you with the intricacies, just know, that they coerced me to give up the deal. I did not understand the sole purpose for doing so was to removal my investors from the project, including Mr. Bennet, as one benefactor. Now that I have discovered Mr. Cuffage arranged for a loan through an anonymous banker—The Falcon. Once they delayed the project, Cuffage demanded the loan be paid. They," Murdoch waved his hand across the room and said, "they relieved them of their money, it angers me; I am saddened, and wish to make amends."

"But why? Why would they do that?"

Bingley spoke up. "They will not allow the enormous profits from such a venture to flow to anyone but themselves. Mr. Murdoch was not willing to bend to their will. He stayed loyal to Mr. Bennet and the other investors until all appeared lost."

Winthrop and his coalition appeared unconcerned at the allegation. Darcy opened his mouth to speak, but everyone had turned their heads towards the door again, for yet another disturbance.

Kent's Uncle Daniel barged in, dragging a member of the Lunar Society. "Bingley, we found Mr. Gaston."

"He works for these men, and has been setting about to ruin our modified Baker rifle sales. Tell them the truth." Bingley grabbed his arm and shook it hard. "I am ashamed to have introduced you to Darcy."

Blake glowered at Lord Liverpool. "I cannot believe this. Why did you bother to get the sale approved if the goal was to destroy it?"

"The British Army still needs the firearms, but we, and not your alliance, will take the profits," Liverpool answered matter-of-factly. "We would not be able to obtain the same deal as you did, so when Samuel Gaston agreed to help us, we devised this deceit."

Samuel Gaston moved closer to Darcy. "I am to take over the rifle distribution. You will not see any profit once I take control of the guns."

"You did rush away from Bingley's dinner party. Did you run here?" Kent asked.

Gaston nodded.

"Blake," Lord Liverpool said, "why do you think I was so quick to agree to the purchase? I am not that easily swayed, young man. I was laying in wait for the offer. Bingley's butler sent us your plan and we sent for him."

Gaston looked down at his shoes. "I had no choice. They threatened to destroy my business. They have been behind my flintlocks sales for the slave trade for years."

Kent faced Blake, Rawlings, and Darcy. "The time has come. You must decide to unite with them or stand with me and Bingley. However, before you do, let me explain the consequences succinctly. I will never do business with them, and I speak for any member of the Kent family."

Winthrop placed himself between Kent and Darcy. "Nephew, before you answer him, are you aware he has entered into contracts with many tradesmen, and that the agreements only identify him as the purchaser? Mr. Kent is not as honest as you think."

Blake, Rawlings, and Darcy gawked at Kent.

"Yes, Winthrop speaks the truth, but before you react stupidly, let me show you one of the agreements." Kent pulled out a document and passed it to his friends.

"I am the one who signed the contracts with all our trading partners, except for the East Indies and, more specifically, China. Read carefully; mine is the only name on the document, not the alliance. I am not hiding anything from you; I placed many more contracts exactly like this one signed in this manner to these in the locked cabinet in your library. They are there now and if you had looked, you would have come across them. They are the property of the alliance, but if you join this gang of thieves, I will take them back."

Darcy nodded. "Why the secrecy?"

"Since these men in this room do not pay their invoices timely, they were willing to sign with me, knowing my word is gold. True, they are unaware of your existence, but if they did, I doubt they would have agreed to the contracts."

"But I am not *them*," Darcy pointed his gaze to the other men. "I have my own reputation for being honest and fair."

"Yes, but the Falcon has badgered them through his underlings, and demanded they not do business with you. Many who would not sign mentioned their fear as the only reason for not signing. Thanks to those blasted competitions, they knew we had been together at Netherfield. The newspaper accounts identified us as being friends and they guessed the rest."

"Gerald." Lord Wolverly approached his son.

Rawlings stood. "Why did you not tell me about this group?"

"Only first-born sons are allowed, and secrecy is maintained. Winthrop is the spokesperson and its face. Many people assume the P on his gate stands for Peregrine. It stands for the præsidentum, as he is our chosen leader. I often suggested we bring in younger sons who show promise, and I repeatedly sought your admittance. And now I rejoice; you are allowed."

"I am a partner with these men." Rawlings glanced at Kent and then Bingley. "I gave my word."

"Do not turn down this opportunity. We... we can work together, son." Lord Wolverly placed his hand on his son's shoulder. "I wish it. I have dreamed of this day."

Rawlings shook his head slowly, but his shoulders slumped and shook his head.

"Gerald, what are you doing? You belong here," Lord Wolverly demanded. "Join us. Make me proud. It is your duty. You have obligations to the house of Wolverly. And... I desire you to work by my side. We can accomplish much together." Rawlings' father lowered his voice and put his hand on his son's shoulder, his voice cracking when he added, "Please, son. Do this for me, do this for us. Do this so I will feel secure in your future. I want you by my side. I have longed for it, son. No more *what ifs*."

Rawlings froze reveling in the touch. He felt a sense of deep connection to his father, who had aged considerably even since he last saw his father on the *Lively*. In this moment, he finally admitted all his life he had wished to be the son who received this attention. He did not care if he was the heir, but he loved his father deeply and had spent a lifetime yearning for his affection, this closeness, and bond his father was offering him today. He and his father locked glares as Rawlings searched for the truth. His hands trembled.

Bingley quietly moved and stood with Kent. "Count me in with you, but I admit I was never out. We have all that is necessary for building the future. Darcy will join us, I am positive."

Winthrop approached Darcy. "Do not be a fool. I will find a way to shut down your little alliance. Only we have the power to ensure success. Look at the men in this room, and take note that we have brought the next generation into the fold. Join us, and I will personally educate you on the running such an organization, as your father would have done, had he lived. There is a lot more you do not know."

Darcy looked at all the men in Winthrop's group. "But why not include the next generation of tradesmen? They bring more than shop keeping. They are the builders, inventors, and manufacturers. Must you limit membership? Cannot the likes of Kent and Bingley join and enhance the group? I do not see the problem with including them."

"Humph." The Falcon placed his hand upon his nephew's shoulder. "Do not be a fool, boy. They are a greedy, dishonorable lot. Even Mr. Kent had signed contracts to him and not to your alliance. You must rid yourself of these interlopers."

Kent glowered at the Falcon. "I am not an interloper, Lord Winthrop. I am a power. It would behoove Darcy to join with me if he wishes to see his fortunes rise. We upstarts are the future." The men standing with Kent nodded agreement.

"And if I do not join with you?" Blake asked, yet searching the faces of the assembled men. "I do not see my father in this room. He never joined you, did he?"

"We denied him access to the group soon after your mother passed on. I took his place," Blake's Uncle Attwood said as he approached. "My boy, the time has come for you to take your place. You shall be powerful in your own right. Come join with us. We will make certain your future is secure. Do you not understand? Your father refused to join us. He in fact tried to buck us. He spit in our eye. But then we used Cuffage to teach him exactly where the power in England is and it is here!"

"When did my father do this?"

"Yes ago, Blake. You were a toddler. He had to be taught that tradesmen were not to be trusted."

"I see it all now. No wonder he hates tradesmen. He never found out who stole his fortune, did he?"

"We have kept it safe for you. Join us and we will restore everything. Your father always had a tendency to gamble and when he is caught up in his latest wager he talks. He cannot maintain secrecy. In fact, if he knew he would sell the information to the highest bidder just to place another bet. Blake, we will return his losses to you if you join us. You will be free to do as you please without regard to your father's wishes. Do not turn your back on this opportunity."

"And Lord Harrowby? He is not here."

Attwood shrugged. "Your other uncle is too idealistic for our coalition, and is only worried about politics. When he was the Vice-President of the Board of Trade for the government, he was foolish; he would not assist any of us. If you shun our offer to stand with the tradesmen, you will be relegated to your little estate. Not even Harrowby can offer you as much riches as we do. The right people will not accept you. We will see to that." Lord Attwood glanced towards Kent and Bingley. "They will only bring you misfortune."

Lord Cheswick approached his nephew. "That is true for you too, Darcy. I stand with Attwood here, and of course, with Uncle Winthrop. You will lose all connections with those of great status and rank if you do not also disassociate yourself. There will not be a seat at my table at any Cheswick house. Come, join your cousin and myself, and become the leader of the next generation of Peregrines."

Winthrop cleared his voice. "You must make a decision now."

"Wait! First hear me out before you choose." Bingley's Uncle Watt approached Darcy, Rawlings, and Blake. "The men of knowledge, the inventors, and other members of the Lunar Society will support your new alliance. I have their assurances." Watt smiled at Darcy. "You opened the door for two tradesmen's sons, and we shall stand with you." Watt turned to speak to the other men. "We will bring all our new inventions and those of our acquaintances only to this young fledgling group."

Kent's Uncle Daniel announced his backing in the import and export business. Then, in a possible lapse of judgment, he glared at Winthrop, and cried out, "One day you will ask to merge with us."

Winthrop rose to his full height. "I would rather rot in debtors' prison than unite with the likes of you. You will be the one shackled, not me."

"I stand with the young men." A booming voice filled the room.

Everyone turned to see two men in the doorway.

"Astor!" Rawlings cried out as he swiftly moved to shake his hand. "Mr. Gardiner, please join us." He glanced at Darcy. "Astor came over on the ship with me. He was worried for his friend, Mr. Gardiner." Rawlings tipped his head towards the well-dressed gentleman standing beside Astor.

Astor acknowledged the handshake, prompting murmurs in the room. "The time has arrived for tearing down aristocratic barriers. I do not mind the separation of wealth from the poor, but this arbitrary partitioning of men based on birth must end. While still prevalent in New York, I assure you it is swiftly dying, and reform must take hold here as well if you wish not to lose every good man to America."

Mr. Gardiner nodded agreement with Astor.

Winthrop remained rigid with his arms crossed. "Astor, we control your permission to trade with China. We will retract your license if you support these men."

"Ah. I am far too wealthy, and have great status in my home country. I am an American now, and plan to help her rise above England and France and the rest of the European continent. No one tells me where to stand. Trade with China is not my first priority," Astor said.

Winthrop scoffed. "Bah! You were a poor man worth a mere four thousand but with our help, your wealth increased to five hundred thousand pounds. Was it not us, this group you face today, who secured your wealth? Did you not use our ships at little cost, or rather Mr. Kent's uncle's ships? Was it not all due to trade with China?"

"My Uncle Milton works for you?" When Winthrop nodded, Kent scowled. "I will speak to him later."

Winthrop glowered at Astor. "Do you not owe us allegiance? Did we not assist you in obtaining licenses with the East India Company?" Winthrop glanced towards Darcy, although he continued to question Astor. "Did you not obtain wealth through the sale of opium?"

"Not true. I used a Chinaman named Wingchong to build my fortune. During the embargo, I obtained permission from President Jefferson to return him to China. He took along forty thousand dollars worth of my merchandise while he sailed by the port authority in my ship, the Beaver. It was the only ship in America sailing to China. I netted over two hundred thousand in profit. I am too rich to owe anyone now."

"Humph. That was only a few years ago, but before that time your early wealth came from smuggling drugs to China." Winthrop glowered. "Admit the truth to Darcy."

"You admit to him how your fortune comes from opium. Did I not do your bidding, and were you not handsomely paid? And have you explained to these young men how your profits also came from the slave trade; be it guns or human beings?"

"Enough, Astor!" Winthrop shook his finger at the German-American. "You must decide whom you wish to deal with in the future. You cannot deal with both of us."

Astor moved to stand alongside Gardiner, Kent, Bingley, and the inventors—Watt, Murdoch and Samuel Gaston. "I have decided to maintain my partnership with this young men's alliance. Mr. Gardiner will continue as my representative in London, since I understand he is to be a full partner. Mr. Kent seems capable to take the reins if Mr. Darcy accepts your offer."

The Falcon scoffed. "Humph! Astor! Choosing a tradesman over us? We do not need you."

Blake turned to Darcy, "Another tradesman? How many more will be included as partners? Should I hang a sign? Lord Blake, Marquess and tradesman?"

Astor thundered in a voice heard in the farthest reaches of the room. "Let me make myself clear—only those whom I approve will be allowed to dock in my pacific trading post. No global strategy will work without Astoria."

"Now is the time, boy; decide you must" Lord Cheswick glanced at his nephew and when he spied Darcy glancing at Kent added, "That man does not care for you. He would tear you apart if given a chance and show no mercy when he did. In truth, do you even know what Kent thinks of you? Well, do you? Has he ever shared his opinion of men of our rank and status? He hates our kind and that includes you. Family is all you have in life and we are family. He is not."

"Yes." Winthrop said with authority as he stood next to Lord Cheswick. "Do you want to unite with the man who concealed you as a partner in the contracts, or even with a man willing to deal in opium to bring him wealth in his new country? As leader," Winthrop swept the room with a wave of his hand and then continued, "You will have a say in how we conduct business in the future. Consider all that is offered to you."

Winthrop stepped towards Darcy, fidgeting with his ring. "As leader, you dictate what is traded. Consider all that has been offered to you. Take the ring of the Peregrine." The Falcon removed the gold signet ring from his finger. "Be the Falcon, Darcy. Be the leader." He held it towards his nephew.

Lords Wolverly and Attwood joined Winthrop and Cheswick to form a single line across from the three young men. "You must now decide your future."

Rawlings, Blake, and Darcy glanced back and forth between the two groups; family on one side and friends on the other; aristocracy to the left and tradesmen and inventors to the right.

With his sense of foreboding returning, Kent stood anxiously while he wondered if all five partners would ever again raise their glasses in their alliance toast. This time there was more than an Andalusian stallion at stake.

A silence fell over the room while the three men decided.

Chapter Twenty-one

Lord Winthrop's ballroom had grown so silent that everyone could hear three young men's heavy breathing.

"Well, I for one know I am not abandoning the alliance, Kent," Rawlings said, the first man to make up his mind. "I established trade partners for the East Indies and China locations through my Bostonian connections." He moved alongside Kent and then glared at Blake and Darcy. "Are you planning to walk out on us?" Rawlings cast his gaze upon the older men. "I will never join them."

His father approached him, this time Lord Wolverly had replaced his pleading expression with one of anger. "Gerald, what are you doing? You belong here. I demand you cease this foolishness." Lord Wolverly took his son's arm. "Do not fall into their clutches. Join us. Make me proud. It is your duty. You have obligations to the house of Wolverly."

Rawlings jerked his arm away from his father's clutch. "Sorry, Father, but I made my decision the night of my Celebration Ball. I detest everything about your life. I have seen a new world, one that cares not one speck about the order of one's birth. Merit is all that is required." He remained alongside Kent. "I shall remain with this alliance." He shook his head, and in a half-whisper, said, "Damn. My own arrogance may have cost the alliance a great deal. I am sorry, Kent. I wish I could retract the words I spoke to Darcy today."

"My comments were no easier for him," Kent said. And Darcy's cousin unleashed his anger this morning!

"All of us? Oh my God. What have we done? Well, I am sorry, but it does not change my decision. I am with you, regardless of what Darcy decides."

Kent grabbed Rawlings' shoulder as Darcy cleared his throat to speak. The room stilled.

Darcy glanced at his friends for a split second before facing Lord Winthrop. "I also have no problem making my decision. It is an easy one for me. I stand with Kent, Bingley, and Rawlings. They are my partners and… I gave my word. I want no part of your group, sir. In fact, the more of the truth I hear, the more disgusted I become." He was quick to stand next to Kent, who clasped his shoulder.

While Rawlings uttered a sigh of relief, Kent laughed. "No need to mull this decision over and over? Seriously, my friend, I respect you more today than any other time in my life. The Kent family will support us in every way. I promise you their backing. But you are going against your family, Darcy. Are your positive this is the right choice?"

"Without any doubt."

Winthrop did not seem upset. "So, Darcy, you chose to lead a small band of nobodies instead of taking charge and leading the real power of England. I tried to interest you in this many times. You never listened to me; you treated me as a dithering old fool. Well, you are no longer a member of the Winthrop family. So it shall be. Now I will not just destroy your alliance, I shall decimate it."

"We do not fear you," Darcy called out as the other men alongside him mumbled in agreement.

The room suddenly stilled again as all heads turned to the last man to decide. Blake studied both groups: the larger, more successful, and powerful one, filled with men of his own ilk, and the smaller group made up of four men that he had come to know and admire, but supported only by men of lower standing. He had lived with his friends during Cambridge, and stayed at Netherfield when no one of any significant standing in the *Ton* had sought him out. Suddenly at the remembrance of words spoken earlier, a painful stab gripped his heart. He gasped for air before glowering at Lord Winthrop.

"You stole from the most wonderful woman of my acquaintance. She did not deserve such treatment. She is an innocent, and now her future has been damaged, and I will never forgive this group for that. And for that reason alone, I will never join you."

Darcy moved to stand beside his friend to give him encouragement when Blake blocked his approach.

"No, Darcy. You are not without blood on your hands either."

Darcy stopped.

Blake scoffed. "You have repeatedly questioned my honor. I am an honorable man, but you never truly accepted that about me. You believed I was capable of toying with a lady, in fact, ladies. You believed the worst possible things about me; things which had no basis in truth. You never gave me the benefit of the doubt, even after I revealed my family history. You are guilty of that same willful misunderstanding that you accused another of owning. You chose to think ill of me based only on rumor and gossip."

Darcy took a step closer, but Blake stopped him with a raised open hand while he took several deep breaths. "I know I gave you no easy path to the partnership, with my feelings towards trade, but my arguments were heartfelt and fair." He pointed to Bingley and Kent with the tilt of his head. "They are inferior in rank and status to me: a marquess and heir to a dukedom. It is not that I think a connection with Kent and Bingley would be a degradation, but they are not my peers. I was born to privilege, and I have an obligation to that privilege. Did you expect me to rejoice in the inferiority of these connections?"

Blake began to draw closer to Darcy. He stood toe to toe with his him. "My confession to you of my concerns which prevented my forming any serious connection with the tradesmen was honest and candid. I am not ashamed how seriously I considered the association before deciding to connect myself with such men. Obtaining the additional share helped me accept my partnership, without it I would have been lowered in status."

"Blake—"

"Say no more. This afternoon at Darcy House, you said quite enough, and you showed how insufficient our friendship was to keep you from pursuing someone that I admitted to loving. I will never forgive you for that."

Blake studied Darcy and the other members of his alliance before turning and fixing his glare upon Lord Winthrop and his assembly of gentlemen. With a scowl on his face, he announced, "A plague on both your houses." He left without looking back.

***

"Good gracious!" Charlotte's sister uttered, after a few minutes silence as she and Elizabeth sat in the carriage leading them towards London. After a six-week visit, their time at Hunsford had ended. The final week had been the most difficult for Elizabeth. Every word spoken and written down in his letter given to her swirled around in her head. She found no escape from him. She could see him waiting by the tree when she walked or standing by the pianoforte when they attended to Lady Catherine. In every vision, he held a letter towards her. Why did I take it? Why did I read it? My would still possess my old beliefs.

Maria Lucas prattled on about the visit, this being her first journey away from Meryton. "It seems but a day or two since we first came!—and yet how many things have happened!"

"A great many indeed." Elizabeth turned her head to gaze out the window.

"We have dined nine times at Rosings, besides drinking tea there twice!—How much I shall have to tell!"

Elizabeth whispered so low no one would hear. "And how much I shall have to conceal."

The next four hours afforded Elizabeth the opportunity to consider all that passed. Inside the book she held closed in her lap lay the most astonishing letter she had ever received. Her fingers twitched. She wanted to read the words again, even though she spent the nights memorizing every word written and then comparing his words to every meeting between them.

He is in London. Elizabeth shook her head demanding that she not care where he is. Settling back into the seat, she opened the book without thinking. His letter fell to the floor, and swiftly she leaned down to retrieve it before Charlotte's sister noticed the bold penmanship he used to write her name.

Clutching the letter safely in her chest, she leaned back, and then as inconspicuously as she could, returned the letter to the book.

His words rang in her ears—I ardently admire and love you. "Phew!"

"Lizzy?"

I beg your pardon, Maria. I… I… was remembering Lady Catherine's remark about the Bennet girls being out at the same time. Perhaps I should return to my book." When Lizzy opened the book, the verse Blake had recited at dinner flashed on the page.

> 'Tis liberty alone that gives the flower
> Of fleeting life its lustre and perfume,
> And we are weeds without it.

Lizzy recalled Lord Blake discussing the merits of Cowper and the hidden messages found within the words. Strange, he gave me a book of poems expressing veiled political thoughts. I had expected something that was of less sense and of more sensibility.

She flipped the pages back to the beginning of the book.

> 'Tis morning; and the sun, with ruddy orb
> Ascending, fires th' horizon: while the clouds,
> That crowd away before the driving wind,
> More ardent as the disk emerges more,

Ardent? Elizabeth wished she could cover her ears as his words bellowed within her head. *I ardently admire and love you.*

Unable to shush the voice in her head, Lizzy slammed the book closed and returned it to her lap; however, the letter's edge poked out, teasing her with an appeal for another reading. This week she did little else but read it. She sent a message to her young companion she no longer welcomed any more chit-chat. The quiet in the carriage gave her an opportunity to revisit their conversation; no, their debate; no, their venomous argument.

Who is this man who has no shame for separating Jane and Mr. Bingley? He rejoiced, yes, rejoiced in the effort. Colonel Fitzwilliam called it his triumph? She pressed her lips together to hold captive her disgust. I doubt he is rejoicing today at his brilliant offer of... Lizzy sighed. Marriage to me? In love with me all this time? Why I am merely tolerable!

The clicking noise made by the horse hooves filled the carriage. Maria had nodded off with a small smile on her face. Elizabeth's mouth had turned downward when she recalled more of his words.

Your family is inferior! She scrunched up her face. Inferior? What did he say? 'Inferior to any with which I would be expected to seek a connection.' She sighed again. He spoke the truth; even I did not expect him to lower himself to my level. I am not of his circle.

She recalled an offer within his proposal when he said, 'I would accept the consequences by seeking you out.' Yes, she agreed that Lady Catherine deBough would be seriously displeased. Lizzy chuckled at her vision of the older lady ranting. I suppose that would explain why my family would not be included in Fitzwilliam family gatherings, but I do not know if those family gatherings were the only ones he meant. But if he were allowed to attend, my father would be amused with their condescending nature; why else would he want to come?"

She could not control the shudder and her embarrassment with every remembrance whenever Mr. Darcy was in her family's company. Why can they not all be as gracious as Jane? When she recalled her sister's calm, unemotional expression, she fidgeted in her seat. The beating of her heart raced. Why did Mr. Darcy think Jane did not have feelings for Mr. Bingley? Insufferable man! Just as quickly, Charlotte's voice whispered to her, *She should show more affection than she feels.*

Understanding that to be true, she attempted to rationalize her sister's mask of indifference even though she knew Jane felt greatly for Mr. Bingley, until Charlotte's other suggestion caused her to bolt upright.

'There are a few of us who have heart enough to be really in love without encouragement.'

She tapped her forehead with her handkerchief. Apparently, Mr. Bingley does not have heart enough, sadly; however, it appears that Mr. Darcy does. I never encouraged him.

Suddenly her mind focused on another man. How big is Lord Blake's heart? Lizzy whispered, "Mama!" She shook her head. Why would she tell such a falsehood? She wanted the connection! I do not believe this is true.

I long to be curled up in the chair in Papa's library, reading…She gently shook her head. Oh my. I was wrong to accuse Mr. Darcy of mockery over the gas lighting book request.

Lizzy attempted to nap a little before reaching London. The proposal whirled in her mind as she argued, debated, and even chided the condescending attitude of the man expecting a positive response. Silently, she felt her own remorse for the tone and demeanor for every word she had spoken; that is until she heard him say in a defiant timbre in his voice, '*Your Uncle Gardiner is the dishonest one!*' She stiffened at his words. I will tell Uncle tonight about his accusation, and I will not conceal how I despise Mr. Darcy for speaking so. He will know what to do to correct this falsehood. This cannot stand.

She remained distressed even after she arrived in London and greeted her uncle. Her stay would be brief and she worried if she would be able to speak to him. Later that night she snuck into the kitchen and caught him devouring a late night treat. She shared a full accounting of the accusation about his dishonesty alleged by Mr. Darcy. She did not mention that she made the accusation during his proposal.

"Are you going to hate me too?" Mr. Gardiner cut a piece of cake, placed it on a plate, and handed it to her. He noted her unusually incensed tone when she spoke. "Lizzy?"

"Why would I hate you? I have no reason to find fault with you. I cannot tolerate Mr. Darcy. You did nothing to cause alarm."

"What I did was worse."

"I do not believe you. No one could have behaved worse than he did." When her uncle shook his head, she whispered, "You do not agree?"

"No, I do not. You are angry that he thought ill of me and said so aloud. I do not know exactly who gave him this accounting of me, but I do know Mr. Cuffage. He is deceitful and cunning. He can convince anyone of his goodness, as I discovered much to my own chagrin."

"But you did not know his evil ways."

"Did Mr. Darcy? You have spoken forcibly against the young man, wrongly, in my opinion. Mr. Darcy remained loyal to a man someone in his confidence had recommended. Should your anger be directed more towards the man who gave the recommendation?"

"That person should not go unpunished, but then neither should Mr. Darcy be free to repeat what he does not personally know to be true."

"So then you agree what I did was worse."

"No! What did you do that was dishonest?"

"Not dishonest, Elizabeth. I was careless with another man's money. Your father trusted me, and I recommended and encouraged him to invest his daughters' money. I convinced him that Mr. Cuffage was worthy; I never properly checked him out. Only after it was too late did I discover the real Mr. Cuffage. Do you not understand?"

Elizabeth shook her head. "Mr. Darcy acted worse. He spoke dishonabley about you, an honorable man. And when I informed him of the truth, he refused to listen."

"Do not forget Mr. Darcy has many friends dependent upon his decisions. They trusted him, and he could not take any chances. If it had been me, I would not have listened to you either, preferring to accept the word of men who are paid to know these things."

"Oh, but..." She lowered her head. "My word should have held sufficient weight. He was... still, I do not understand."

"Since Mr. Darcy had been informed that I had a bad reputation, he rightfully chose not to put his friends in jeopardy. When you are the one in charge, you cannot afford careless mistakes. Now should he have investigated me? Who is to say he did not. I will tell you a secret revealed only to the partners, but I must tell you in order for you to understand. Mr. Cuffage's son was Mr. Darcy's secretary—the two men used different names purposely to deceive the world at large, and Mr. Darcy in particular."

"Oh my! Is this the man that spoke ill of you?"

"I do not know, but I do suspect it was him."

Lizzy sat for a full minute biting her lower lip while she contemplated what her uncle revealed. The two of them finished their sweet treat in silence until Mr. Gardiner patted his niece's hand.

"I am not angry, Lizzy. Neither should you be."

Sighing, Lizzy gazed at her uncle. "When you explain it in that light, I will acknowledge there is merit to his opinions. Even though, he should not have called you dishonest."

"Now, my child. Mr. Darcy's only failing was once he made up his mind, it was made up forever. You have said even he recognizes that as a failing of his. I think he has had to rethink that trait, do you not agree? Elizabeth, he was merely loyal to his friends. In fact, he seems to be one of the most loyal men I have ever met."

"Perhaps in business."

"One more argument—"

"Yes."

"Mr. Darcy has invited me to be a full partner in his alliance. Would he do that if he were not sincerely sorry for his disrespect?

"A partner?"

"Oh, yes. A full partner. I am to be treated as an equal. It will be a rich association, too. I cannot believe my great fortune to be so closely connected to the Kent family and to *The Heir* himself!"

While finishing their cake, Mr. Gardiner revealed how the young men had formed an alliance while staying at Netherfield Park. He described the other alliance, the one that had been in place for hundreds of years. But he caught Lizzy's interest when he explained that three of the men were forced to choose between the two groups. Mr. Darcy and Mr. Rawlings turned away from their families and stood by the men of trade and science. Lord Blake chose neither group and at the same time broke all connections with Mr. Darcy.

Elizabeth kept her gaze down on her plate when her uncle discussed Lord Blake's decision. She felt the flush rising on her cheeks, and did not regain her composure until he patted her hand. She looked up at him. "I am astonished. I am happy for you. Still, my father's—"

"Mr. Murdoch, owner of the Gas Light Company, will be joining us for dinner tonight. He has worked out a plan to secure your father's funds."

"He should!"

"My dear, Lizzy. You must not be so harsh. Mr. Darcy's alliance has offered to assist Mr. Murdoch in the advancement of his gas lighting endeavors. Can you not guess now who actually was behind the scheme to recover your dowry?

"Mr. Darcy?"

"Yes. He felt a sense of obligation."

Elizabeth scoffed. "Why. This did not happen because of him."

"But Mr. Cuffage and his son worked for Mr. Darcy's great uncle, Lord Winthrop, who was the mastermind behind the whole plot."

"Oh my! Did Mr. Darcy know?"

"No, and not only did he not know about this, his great uncle pursued every avenue to destroy his alliance. It seems he wanted him to work for his venture; one with only the highest ranking of men as partners; a group I would never be allowed to join."

"His own relative deceiving him! I must think for a while. This is just too much for me to digest."

Do not take too long. Miss Darcy has invited you, Jane, and my wife to tea tomorrow."

"No!"

"I will be leaving for Birmingham tomorrow, along with the other partners of this new alliance. Our ladies will spend time together while we are gone, and that includes you! I demand it. I believe Mr. Darcy asked specifically that you be included. He mentioned how much he desired that you meet his sister."

***

While Mrs. Gardiner, Jane, and Elizabeth climbed the front steps of Darcy House, Elizabeth took in its grace and beauty. The limestone and terra cotta brick building seemed immense compared to other houses on the square, but not in any showy ornate way. The doorman appeared and acted exactly as she assumed any a servant a gentleman of great wealth would. But when she stepped inside, she could barely control her admiration. The spacious lobby was lofty and handsome, with furniture neither gaudy nor uselessly fine. She decided she preferred this man's interpretation of elegance.

Miss Darcy approached the ladies, proper introductions and civilities were made. While they climbed the stairs to the great room, Elizabeth studied the young girl, and five minutes had not passed before she realized the girl was shy and not haughty. Another lie told by Mr. Wickham. She gasped when she realized what could have happened to such a sweet young girl, and felt anger towards the man she previously had admired. Wickham was not gentleman-like at all!

"Elizabeth, are you well? You look pale." Jane took her sister's hand in hers.

"I am well... I have a sudden headache. I merely need to rest a moment."

Mrs. Annesley tapped Georgiana's arm, and she, in turn, stepped closer to Elizabeth. "Let me show you to a room close to where we will be. It has a comfortable chair and a warm fire. I will send for wine." She led Elizabeth to a small room. "Would you like your aunt or sister to stay with you?"

"Thank you, but no. I will be fine. I just need a few moments of quietness."

She stepped into the room and took in its beauty. The furnishings were bright and the walls painted in a pale yellow. The furniture's blue and yellow silk upholstery gleamed in the sunlight. The tables held beautiful crafted sculptured pieces and small items made of crystal. A timepiece ticked away on the mantle, also crystal. A fire had been lit, not too high but enough to give the room a cozy feeling. Books lined a small bookcase, and on the desk lay the most unusual writing instrument she had ever seen.

Fascinated, she moved to the desk and placed the object in her fingers as if she was going to write a letter.

Miss Darcy joined her. "That is a steel dip pen. They are new. Have you ever used one before?"

"No. This surely must save mending."

"Yes, my brother insisted all our quills be replaced with these pens. Mr. Kent brought them back from one of his journeys north to Birmingham." Georgiana retrieved paper from the drawer and opened the ink well. "Try it. It is wonderful."

Elizabeth dipped the pen slowly before writing her name on the paper. "It is smooth. I like it very much."

"My brother suggested that the inventor find a way to add the ink in a container right on the pen. No dipping, he says! I laughed and teased him about being lazy! What is so hard about dipping your pen?" The two girls laughed, but Elizabeth studied the pen for such an opportunity.

Georgiana led Elizabeth to a comfortable looking chair, just as a servant entered carrying a glass of wine on her tray.

With her guest seated and sipping her wine, Georgina moved to the door. "I must return to my other guests, but I will come back shortly. Or you may join us when you are rested." Georgiana pointed to the connecting door with her head.

When Elizabeth attempted to rise, the young mistress motioned for her to remain seated. "My brother will be distressed if you were not cared for in his home. He is the best of brothers. He had this room done up just for me after I remarked how much I enjoyed the morning sun in here. He suggested pale yellow as the color. He said it reminded him of a dance, and that it has become his favorite hue. He comes here often to sit and think. He closes his eyes and a smile appears."

"He is certainly a good brother." Elizabeth felt the heat rising on her neck and cheeks.

"And this is always the way with him," she paused as she tried to conceal the smile from forming when she spotted the blush on her guest's face. "Whatever he can do to give me pleasure, he does in a moment. There is nothing he would not do for me or anyone he admires, and I love him for that."

"And I am sure he loves you. I never had a brother, only four sisters. I am quite jealous of you now."

"I would have liked a sister."

"Be careful in your wishes. Some sisters are silly girls and are always taking your things." Smiling, Elizabeth took another sip and leaned back, snuggling in the cushion. "I will be better after a short rest. I will join you soon."

"Do not hesitate to ask for anything you wish."

Georgiana left, but neglected to close the door to the hallway behind her. Within minutes, two young maids appeared in the hallway, their voices carrying into the room.

"You are fortunate Mr. Darcy did not dismiss you when that letter was lost. He was as angry as I have ever seen."

"I did fear it. I can't think of what may have happened to me if I was dismissed. Why didn't he?"

Elizabeth, intrigued by the question, moved closer to the door.

"He is the best master in all the land, that is why. There are hundreds of girls wanting to work here? He takes care of every one of us."

"He does pay the best wages."

"He does more than fill your purse. He will take care of you if you are in trouble."

"Bah. Rich men don't care about the likes of us."

"Look what he did for the maid before you, and tell me he is not the best of masters."

"She was let go because she was with child. I heard 'em say he made her leave, and her husband just recently dead. That proves he isn't any different than other masters."

"Do not be a silly goose. Mr. Darcy sent her to live in Pemberley. He found her a home where she and her baby will be cared for, and paid her wages even though she could not work."

"Maybe he likes the girl more than you know? Perhaps the child is his."

Elizabeth covered her mouth to conceal her gast.

"Hush! Do not speak about the master that way. He is a gentleman. He treats all the girls as a gentleman aught too. Go work for Lord Atterton. He fits the type of master you are talking about. Not our Mr. Darcy. The poor girl was with child when she came to work here after her husband's carriage accident. She did not know she had a baby coming."

"Oh. "I suppose then we should be more worried if he marries."

"Gad! I cannot bear to think of it. What if he marries one of those haughty society ladies? They are always trying to be friends with Miss Darcy just to be near him. I do not know who is good enough for him."

"The master hasn't smiled once since he came back from Kent."

"Well, he did smile at Miss Kent. She is a sweet one. He could marry her."

"Ah, yes! A sweet girl she is, and nice to everyone. I like her, and she comes here often with her brother. Miss Kent is handsome too. She would look good on the master's arm. She has come for tea today, but our master is gone away—"

"Girls! Stop talking and get back to work or I will have you scrubbing pans for a week." Mrs. Geoffries voice boomed as she stood with her arms crossed, the corners of her mouth turned down.

Elizabeth looked away and leaned against the wall. Miss Kent? Mr. Darcy? She had not time to imagine Mr. Darcy with another lady when she heard a knock at the door. She rushed back to her chair and settled down when the housekeeper peeked in the room. She waved her in.

"Miss Bennet. I came to ensure that you are not ill." Mrs. Geoffries drew near Elizabeth.

"I was just returning to the others, I only needed a moment to rest. I am better now."

"Mr. Darcy left word to take special care of you. I will not let you leave this room until I am satisfied." She touched her forehead to determine if there was a fever.

"No, no. I am well." Elizabeth moved her hand to smooth her gown when she remembered she still held the metal-tipped pen. She moved to the desk to return the pen to its place, she spied a cameo of a young man in a frame with a striking resemblance of Mr. Darcy. She picked it up.

"That is Mr. Darcy. And do not you think him a handsome gentleman, Ma'am?" Mrs. Geoffries handed the cameo to Elizabeth

"Yes, very handsome." Her fingers traced the face's outline.

With a twinkle in her eye, Mrs. Geoffries stared at Elizabeth Bennet. "I am sure *I* know none so handsome." She placed the cameo of her master back in place and glanced sideways at the young lady's suddenly reddened cheeks. "I am lucky in having such a master. If I was to go through the world, I could not meet with a better. But I have always observed that they who are good-natured when children are good-natured when they grow up; and he was always the sweetest-tempered, most generous-hearted, boy in the world."

Elizabeth almost stared at her. Can this be Mr. Darcy?

"He is the best master who ever lived. Not like the wild young men now-a-days, who think of nothing but themselves." Mrs. Geoffries tuned to face Elizabeth. "There is not one of his servants, but what will give him a good name. Some people call him proud; but I am sure I never saw anything of it. To my fancy, it is only because he does not rattle away like other young men."

Elizabeth nodded her head slowly dawdling a moment while she memorized the silhouette.

Mrs. Geoffries smiled before moving to the door. "Would you like to join the others now?"

"Yes, please."

Mrs. Geoffries led her into the music room, where Jane sat conversing with Mrs. Annesley and Mrs. Gardiner. Georgiana and Miss Sarah Kent were sitting at the pianoforte.

She is beautiful, Elizabeth's chest tightened as she admired a handsome woman sitting beside the young hostess. Miss Kent lifted her head, whispered to Miss Darcy, and then rose from the bench. Darcy's sister also jumped up, knocking the sheet music to the floor.

Elizabeth ran to help retrieve the music, and the three women bumped heads when they reached for all the wayward sheets. They stood, exchanged civilities, and then laughed together when the one remaining sheet slipped from the piano.

***

That night, Jane slid under the covers with her sister. "Miss Darcy is a sweet girl. I think Mr. Bingley will be happy with her."

"Bah! She has no interest in him. Did you hear her mention his name once?"

"That would have been impolite. I am resigned. Miss Kent is so interesting; I like her. Perhaps, Miss Bingley has a rival." Jane chuckled.

"Miss Kent is not a rival because Miss Bingley is not even being considered. Mr. Darcy has…"

"What is it Lizzy? You have been withdrawn ever since you returned from Hunsford. What happened? Did Mr. Collins say anything impolite? He can be a little foolish at times."

"No. In fact, he was kind. In his own way, he tried to put me at ease before I met Lady Catherine. Mr. Darcy said things that left me perplexed, upset, and a little angry. I am astonished beyond words."

"You must tell me now. Did he say you are even less than tolerable? Did he refuse to dance with you again?"

"Stop! What he said has caused me never to want to go home. Ever!"

Jane bolted upright. "Why. What happened?"

"Mother. She is the problem."

"What did she do? Did she write a letter telling Mr. Darcy he is a horrible man? She detests him, you know."

"Worse. She lied to Lord Blake."

"When?"

Lizzy got up and retrieved her handkerchief with the broken chess pieces in it. "Remember when I told you how Lord Blake did not wait for me."

"Yes, but you said little else."

"I thought he had abandoned me, but I learned he came to the house looking for me when I did not meet him that day."

"I never thought he was a man without honor. But, why did you not see him? I do not understand."

"You were visiting with the Lucases. Mama forced me to stay in my room to contemplate marriage to Mr. Collins, and then she lied to Lord Blake when he called on me. She told him I had gone to London to avoid him. Mama lied."

Jane jumped up and held her sister in her arms. They stood together for many minutes, the tick of the clock and the crackle of the fire filled the room. "You may cry on my shoulder, Lizzy, if it will help."

"No. I do not need to cry. I am angry and... embarrassed."

Jane straightened a wayward curl on Lizzy's neck. "How did Mr. Darcy come to tell you this?"

"I accused him of separating Lord Blake from me. Since he believed we were beneath him, I supposed he felt I was not worthy for his friend. But that does not make any sense when you consider he asked..." Lizzy placed her hand on her mouth.

"Why would you speak of Lord Blake to Mr. Darcy? How did this come about?"

"Oh, dear, sweet sister! I cannot talk of this now. So many things are not the way I believed. I am confused. People I trusted are not trustworthy and someone I found despicable is perhaps the most honorable of men. I must never again be so quick to judge, or to think I am extraordinarily wise. I must think before I speak."

"Oh." Jane turned away, her shoulders slumped.

Lizzy hugged her sister. "Mr. Darcy proposed."

"Proposed! I can scarcely believe it. But you refused?"

"Yes. You do not blame me, however, for refusing him?"

"Blame you! Oh, no. Is it because you still have hope for Lord Blake?"

"I refused Mr. Darcy based on my feelings towards him. Give me a little time to overcome my anger, my hurt, and even my astonishment before I speak further. I must consider everything before I come to any conclusions. We return to Longbourn soon, and I must decide what to say to Mother, if I bother to say anything at all. What is done is done, and I cannot change the fact that Lord Blake and I will never see each other again.

"Did you tell Mr. Darcy that you had not gone to London? Perhaps he will convey that to his friend."

"No. I only asked him why he separated Blake from me. His letter explained what Mama said. Now it is too late for Lord Blake to hear the truth. He and Mr. Darcy have dropped their association with each other. Truthfully, I doubt if Mr. Darcy would have wanted to say anything since he, himself, proposed to me. And after speaking to Uncle and spending a day at Darcy House, I am no longer clear in my mind who…"

"Did you say Mr. Darcy wrote you a letter?"

"Yes." Lizzy forced a yawn. "I am tired and my head aches. Please, no more questions. I wish to go to bed. I will explain more once we are in our own bedchambers in Longbourn." The two girls jumped into bed; Jane blew out the candle, and with their backs to one another, and even though they did not fool each other, they pretended to sleep.

Chapter Twenty-two

During the week that followed, Darcy spent his available time on the business of the alliance. His priorities required a different focus. They needed to move quickly to shore up the contracts and protect the business.

Once the dust had settled and everyone believed they were on good footing to forestall the Falcon with many more contracts in hand and other deals struck, Darcy had time to pursue earlier commitments.

Bingley had returned north with his Uncle Watt and Samuel Gaston to monitor the progress on the manufacture and distribution of the modified Baker Rifle. Gaston had the organization to reap further profits. And since Lord Liverpool would not deny the army the use of these guns, the Falcon did not force the cancellation of the order. Darcy and the other partners left for a tour of the Boulton Soho Manufactory as he had promised Kent.

The entire week spent in Birmingham had been enlightening; Darcy discovered the depth of the prestige held by the tradesmen for the Kent family; and that the strength of their business was staggering. Between the Kents and the Boultons, he doubted any other family could have acquired such a hold on the production, manufacturing and trading of such a variety of products. But the treatment of their workers is what caused Darcy to truly admire them. Much like the respectful and caring manner in which he dealt with his tenants, the Kents and Boultons treated their own employees.

The trip was a diversion from his day of self-discovery, but only to a point. Darcy caught himself wondering about Elizabeth's visit to his home. Before he had left, Georgiana had asked to invite Gardiner's wife and nieces for tea. He agreed and suggested she include Miss Kent in the group, which made his sister hug him tightly and whisper how sorry she was for her recent outburst. He had left strict instructions with his staff to provide anything the ladies desired, and in particular to respond immediately to Miss Elizabeth Bennet's wishes. He directed not even the simplest of requests go ignored. All week, he fretted about the tea.

When he returned to London, he bounded up the stairs in search for his sister. He needed to discover if Elizabeth had come. His heart filled with joy while Georgiana expressed her own admiration of her. Not only was Elizabeth beautiful, her interpretation of the sonnet she played on the pianoforte was much more expressive than her own. She told her brother how kind she had been to Miss Kent and how she had treated all the servants with great respect. Darcy ached with every word; he asked if she commented on his home. Did she admire the artwork, the statues, or the furnishings? He begged for every little scrap of information until it pained him to hear the words that she was here and he was not; still, he would not stop Georgiana from speaking about her. When his sister mentioned how much she liked the new pen, he had one sent for each member of the Gardiner family, nieces included.

Mrs. Geoffries had been quick in revealing every detail of their time together. Ill? Was it because of me that caused her to seek a room to compose herself? He imagined her holding his cameo and felt a sense of relief that she had even touched it. That night He took the cameo to his bedchambers and spent an hour gazing upon it. Did she find my face handsome? Mrs. Geoffries said she had admired my image. He touched it where he had imagined where her fingers had stroked.

The moment had arrived. He must make a full assessment of his life; a harsh honest look that could not be delayed any longer. He had made a muddle of everything and he needed to determine what caused everyone's animosity towards him. Perhaps if he could figure it out, then he would not continue to cause such ill feeling. He vowed to take his time and not allow business or pleasure to divert him. He must mull this situation over. Yes, his friends were correct. He needed to mull this over and over again. He accepted this as his nature. He would not hurry to understand what the others saw in him.

First, he worried how Georgiana would react to his shutting himself up, so he informed her he had to resolve a problem. He did not wish to cause worry or concern to her or the servants, but he must be alone.

Georgiana offered him a slight smile and squeezed his arm. "I understand, dear brother. I will see that you are not disturbed."

Safely behind locked doors, alone with his pen and papers and brandy and tea, he began the search for the truth. In the beginning, he denied everything everyone said. He was not at fault, they were. He listed ever accusation and glared at it before he prepared his arguments. His routine did not change. He spent his days locked in his study and his nights locked in his bedchamber. The servants delivered his meals to his room on trays although he returned them with barely a morsel removed.

Every day he saw *them*. He could make out their irate faces and hear their harsh words. When they made their accusations, he wrote down what they had said, trying to be exact. After a few days, his writing in anger subsided, replaced by a round of spelling out his arguments and reasons for what he did. He made a list and studied it, made changes, crossed out entries, and finally balled it up and threw it in the fire. He would start a new list and repeated the pattern. This behavior lasted for several days. He could not find justification for his actions for every charge and the ones he did sounded hollow when he read them aloud. He grew quieter than was usual for him. He had the reflecting mirror removed from his bedchamber when he had discovered he could not stand to see the person whose image appeared.

Locked in the study early one evening, he consumed more brandy than what was wise and nodded off into a deep sleep in his comfortable chair. Within seconds, he found himself transported to a strange room at the end of which stood a long bench where a man dressed in black, wearing a gray wig, sat with a gavel in his hands. Darcy strained to identify the man, but could not. The face was blurred except for a pair of sparkling blue eyes.

The judge banged his gavel on the bench. The room hushed as a bailiff stood in front of the bench and bellowed, "Hear ye, Hear ye. Order in the Court. The Trial of Mr. Fitzwilliam Darcy is about to begin."

Feeling himself slumping, Darcy grabbed onto the handrail in front of him. He now knew he was in the Assizes Court, the highest trial court in the nation, and was standing in the box assigned to the accused. He had been stripped of any sign of his wealth and prestige. The room was full of every known acquaintance, and unfortunately, he could not detect a single smile on any of their faces. His eyes widened and his jaw dropped when the man read the charges.

"The Grand Jury has formally indicted said person for crimes against his fellow man. Five citizens have charged him with arrogance, willful misunderstanding, conceit, slander, knife attack, vanity, and pride. How do you plead?"

Darcy opened his mouth to speak, when Rawlings appeared from nowhere, leaned in, and whispered, "Say not guilty. Do not admit your guilt; otherwise, they will lead you outside, shackle you to your offenses, and leave you all alone for the rest of your life. Defendants must prove their innocence against the prosecutors' evidence as required by law."

"Who are the prosecutors?"

Rawlings sighed. "Those hurt by your actions and deeds. Victims are always the prosecutors."

"Am I entitled to a lawyer?"

"You may hire one if your wish. Shall I notify... Mr. Phillips from Meryton? He knows you well!"

Darcy violently shook his head. "No, Rawlings. I interrupted him when he attempted to warn me, and I fear he would relish a guilty verdict. Could you do it?"

"No, I cannot." Rawlings prodded Darcy with his finger. "Enough. Say not guilty and let the trial commence. You must offer a defense and accept the consequences if you wish to be free. The judge is waiting; everyone is waiting."

With a slight crack in his voice, Darcy looked up to the judge and said, "Not Guilty."

The crowd murmured, and he could hear sniggering among the twelve members of the petty jury sitting to his left. Darcy felt a stabbing-like pain in his chest when he made out their faces—men he had met at Meryton, with Sir William Lucas as the foreman.

"Colonel Richmond Fitzwilliam, please rise and give witness to your charge," the bailiff announced.

Darcy rose to his full height and watched his cousin move toward the witness stand. Richmond had not glanced his way until situated behind the wooden podium.

"My cousin is an arrogant bastard and—"

"I am not!" Darcy yelled.

The judge banged the gavel down. "Do not interrupt, or I shall end this trial with a guilty verdict. You will be given an opportunity to question the witness, but at the appropriate time. Continue, Colonel, but do not use vulgar words."

The colonel nodded, and sent a charming smile, causing the judge's blue eyes to sparkled brighter. "My cousin gave not a single moment's thought to delaying my return to London. I had made plans that were important to me. He assumed, arrogantly, he did not need to consult with me before changing the departure date. I was not worth the trouble."

When the judge motioned for Darcy to begin his questioning, he again struggled to make out the face with the vaguely familiar blue eyes, but could not. The gray wig that the judge wore covered too much. He turned his attention to his cousin, and caught sight of the smirk upon his face. He recalled his cousin's words from the carriage ride home. *You do as you wish and leave it up to me to follow.*

"Richmond, you did not have to stay with me! I did not force you to do so! You could have left at any time."

"By post?"

"I would have provided you with my carriage if you had asked. You did not ask."

"True. But then you never were interested in my life and not knowing about my plans proves my suspicions."

"Humph." Darcy caught the word in his throat and drew the back of his hand across his mouth. *I will rid myself of this word from my very being!*

"Mr. Darcy?" The judge banged the gavel. "Do you have any more questions?"

"No further questions." Darcy glowered at his cousin while he stepped down, walking away with a decided limp. *Was he injured on the continent? Ah, Richmond you are worthy of my attention. Why did I not know about your orders? Why did I not ask him questions about his life?* He felt an ache when he realized his cousin no longer wore his uniform. *What will he do now? He cannot survive on a half-pay pension.*

The bailiff rose. "Mr. Stephen Kent, please rise and offer your testimony."

Kent entered the witness stand. "I charge him with willful misunderstanding and arrogance. Mr. Darcy did deliberately, and without cause, falsely accused me of courting his sister. He also treated the Kent family rudely by not acknowledging their worthiness. He ignored my sister and imposed upon my aunt by not notifying her of a delay in his visit. With conceit in his heart, he looked upon me and all the Kents and Boultons as underlings."

The room grew quiet.

"Mr. Darcy! Mr. Darcy, you may cross-examine him now." The judge banged the gavel again. "Mr. Darcy!"

Darcy hung his head and sighed loudly before he answered. "Kent. I cannot believe how fairly I treated you, and yet you believe this of me. Did I not let you partner with me?"

"To use your word, humph."

Darcy leaned over the railing. "You do not get off so easily. Why did you even bother to collaborate with me? Oh yes, you were using me to get to Victoria. You pretended to be a man wooing my sister."

"Perhaps, but would you have offered assistance? Speaking of sisters, when you attended the Lunar Society Meeting at Bingley's did you show any kindness to my sister?"

Darcy glared at Kent. "I did not know she was there. Did you introduce me? No. You did not. But..." Darcy ran his fingers through his hair, his thoughts flying. *But, why did I not suggest introductions to all the guests? Why? Did I ignore everyone but the men of science? I cannot believe I treated the ladies in such a manner.*

"But what?"

"No further questions." Darcy hung his head and stared at the floor as his partner stepped down. Lost in his thoughts, he missed the announcement of the next man that had now found his way into the witness stand.

"My friend suffers from an overabundance of conceit." Rawlings settled back into the witness chair, turned his head away from the judge and towards Darcy. "All you ever worry about is you. How does everyone treat you? Everyone wants something from you. Well, *you* owe us an apology, my friend."

Darcy lifted head to address the friend who was gazing directly at him but without any anger. "Rawlings, you are mistaken. I worry about everyone, not the other way around. The truth is that no one ever thinks of me, nor do they care about any of my burdens. They just see me as a bag of coins. They do..." When Rawlings sent him a questioning look, Darcy thought, *Or do they? Am I really only worried about me? My God, it is true. I answered him with a defense of myself. Me!*

After a moment of silence while Darcy contemplated his actions with other people, the faceless judge banged the gavel. "Mr. Darcy?"

Darcy shook his head and then let his chin drop down. "No further questions."

The bailiff spoke. "The Most Honorable Robert Henry Schofield, Marquess of Blake. State your case, Lord Blake."

When he replaced Rawlings in the witness stand, Darcy let his shoulders drop and his hands dangle by his side. He could not imagine mounting any defense against this man. He knew the accusations would be truthful. He knew he was guilty.

Blake cleared his throat and in a calm voice said, "He lied. He lied to me, and then stabbed me in—"

"When did I lie?" Darcy yelled. He recalled every instance where he had spoken to Blake since they met up at Netherfield and could not find a single spoken lie.

The judge's gavel hit the bench so hard not a single soul misheard the sound. "Do not interrupt, Mr. Darcy. This is your last warning!"

Darcy nodded.

Blake glared at Darcy. "He told us Miss Elizabeth Bennet had hardly a good feature in her face, more than one failure in her form, and her manners were not those of the fashionable world. And when asked if he thought she was a beauty, his exact words were '*She* a beauty! I should as soon call her mother a wit!' You see, he lied from the beginning. And then he stabbed me in the back."

"Explain the circumstances, Lord Blake," The judge said. "I heard of no physical injury."

"Perhaps not physically, but he pushed that hard, cold blade between by shoulder blades by his actions. He attempted on several occasions to dissuade me from pursing Miss Elizabeth Bennet. He interrupted—"

The entire room chuckled.

"He interrupted my proposal. He did so deliberately and used that moment to separate her from me. And I recently discovered," Lord Blake leaned forward and pointed his finger at the man in the accuser box, "you then sought her out and proposed. The woman you said was barely tolerable. You lied."

"Mr. Darcy? You may cross examine Lord Blake now."

The spectators and jury stilled. Darcy hung his head low, his shoulders slumped. His breathing filled the silence, but when he attempted to speak, no words came out. He could not deny the truth. He had lied to him. He lied to all of his friends. He lied to himself. He loved her from the instant he saw her, and he manipulated things to keep Blake from winning her. Finally, he shook his head and the Marquess left the stand. Just when he thought nothing more hurtful was left to charge against him, he heard her name announced. He slumped in the accused box, falling against the rail. His legs were limp; he could not force himself to stand.

"Miss Elizabeth Bennet."

Darcy's heart beat furiously, his palms felt damp. The sweat rolled down his back. He pulled at his cravat, coughing repeatedly. A solid gray fog enveloped the room, shielding him from her accusatory gaze.

"He was ungentleman-like in the words he used."

The judge sputtered, "Did he use vulgar words?"

"No." Elizabeth sent the judge a sweet smile. "He could have behaved in a more gentleman-like manner, but he chose to describe the Bennets in the most unflattering terms. I cannot forget what he said, although some of it was truthful. No true gentleman would ever say such things. He thinks his beliefs were natural and just."

Darcy felt the insides of his throat tighten. What poppycock! What I said was not natural and just. The stabbing pain returned striking harder with each recollection of the words he had used: degradation, inferiority, scruples, rejoice in my success, contempt and ridicule, so evident a design of offending and insulting me."

"Mr. Darcy?"

"Yes, your honor, I have defense for her accusation, but I am fully aware she has more to say; let her continue."

"I have no other charge."

The grey fog lifted as Darcy stared at her holding a cameo of him. She read my letter! She read my letter. He felt a sense of relief that she had accepted what he had written.

"Mr. Darcy?" The judge spoke louder this time. "Mr. Darcy!"

"I am guilty, your honor, of all charges. Guilty. Do with me as you wish. Give me the sentence I deserve. I cannot bear any more truth." Darcy hung his head and covered his face until the judge called for his attention. When he looked up at the judge he choked on his own breath as he now could clearly see the judge's face. It was not the face of a man, but the face of an angel. Jane Bennet? Oh my God. After what I did to separate Bingley from her, I shall surely be strapped to my offenses for the rest of my lonely life. The stabbing pain changed into a dull dead feeling encompassing his entire body.

She smiled at him with the most comforting smile he had ever received. "The verdict is guilty by your own admission. You sentence is hereby, to make amends to each person, Mr. Darcy. And change your ways. I believe you have the strength of character to do so."

When she banged the gavel down Darcy woke up and found himself safely back in his study. Accepting that he owned every accusation, he thought about each person and the steps he would need to take. This week had been his worse, yet at the end of it, he felt peace, almost a return to the days before his father had died.

"Richmond, please return to England unharmed, so I may apologize properly." Darcy whispered, and then he thought about Georgiana's letter from his cousin. Only one had arrived, but enough to indicate the danger he faced daily. I must make amends. I must find a way. I will begin with a letter. Damn. It seems I am always writing letters to explain myself! I have no other method with him so far away. He pulled out his stationary, pen and ink. He was quick, since he did not use any four or five syllable words other than the two that he needed to say: apologize was one. He admitted he was as Richmond had said, supercilious. But that was not the only apology he rendered in the message. He wrote a heartfelt letter, the words flowed about how he planned to treat their relationship in the future, and ended by thanking him for his honesty.

Darcy stretched his body and then thought about his treatment of another man. "Kent, I cannot believe I would treat such a great man as you are as unimportant. How could I tell you that? How could I have said that you were not important? But, I did believe that. Without you, there could not be an alliance. You, it seems, are more important than I am." He considered ways to show his friendship to this man. "I will host a dinner party and invite all of Kent's family. I will show even greater respect than I did on the trip to Birmingham. I will speak at great length to his sister. And I will play a prank on her and it will not be spiders in the bed! Kent, you are not clever in that way, but I can invent devious pranks. Did not Richmond discover that side of me? Ah, Kent, we can have such fun, and I will ensure you get your revenge on her." Darcy laughed aloud for the first time in many days. He dashed off a message for delivery early the next morning to Kent and. He would not delay or postpone this dinner for any reason.

He realized Bingley and Blake presented the toughest obstacles to righting his wrongs. He would speak to Rawlings, and seek his advice and show him he has addressed the issues he raised. He would call upon his friend at his home that next day. With his plans made, he retired for the night, and slept peaceably for the first time in a long time.

***

Darcy sighed when he approached Rawlings' townhouse, realizing it was the first time he had entered it. Whenever he had wished to speak with his friend, he had always summoned him. Why Rawlings came, he could not fathom. With a heavy heart, Darcy presented his card to the butler.

"Come in." Rawlings said after hurrying to door. "Welcome. I am pleased you have called upon me. Let us go into the study. It is quiet and private there. I have missed our talks."

Darcy sensed the calm surround him the moment he stepped into the study, although nothing was in its proper place in the room. Rawlings' desk was larger than his own, although he could at least see the top of his desk. Here, piles of papers were stacked in a haphazard fashion with a coffee cup and a teacup resting on different ones. Several newspapers were strewn about, and Darcy made out that they were several days old.

Still, warm colors filled the room: greens and blues with a smattering of gold. He caressed the dark leather on the sofa, which matched the two chairs. Gold studs outlined the furniture, and he found the material warm to the touch. He sent Rawlings a questioning look.

"Spain. My mother's grandfather was Spanish. I loved his leather furniture. Perhaps we both are of Spanish descent."

Darcy spied the cabinet along the far wall, where many bottles of Oban whiskey were displayed. "You have not touched your prize?"

"I cannot drink it. Would you care for it? You are welcome to every bottle, but for one. I need it to remind me of what could have been. An Andalusian!"

"The symbol of strength and power. Ironic! Do you not agree with how things have changed?"

"How so?"

"Remember the rowing race between the aristocrat, the gentleman, and the tradesman, fighting for this symbol of strength and power as the prize."

"But Blake won, and the aristocrats are still in power. Where is the irony?"

"The world is changing, and I fear we have reached the point where the change is permanent. Our alliance is the example." Darcy chuckled as Rawlings' curious expression continued. "When we started, there were three members from aristocratic families, with only two tradesmen's sons as partners. Blake won the horse, suggesting that the power still rested with the aristocrats. Today, we have three tradesman partners, and only you and me, neither one of us a titled member of the nobility. We reside on the outskirts of that rank as a nephew of an earl and the second son of one. So you see, the balance of power has changed, and I believe so has the world, permanently."

"Interesting. I could add further evidence by describing life in America. But what brings you here? Surely it was not to educate me on the symbolic nature of progress." He opened the cabinet, placing a bottle of Oban and a bottle of French brandy on a tray as well as two glasses, and then he found his way to his favorite chair. He nodded to the empty chair, a silent invitation for Darcy to stay.

"I am in need of a friend. You recently said you are my friend."

"Always, and apparently your cousin as well! So, what exactly is it you need to disclose to me? Is it about that day, the eleventh day of April? Come, come, Darcy. You shut yourself up in your home for nigh on a week now. What else would you do except mull over and over what was said and done to you. Or is this about your alliance?"

"*Our* alliance. And as always, you know me well. My conduct, my manners, and my expressions during the whole of it are inexpressibly painful to me now."

When Rawlings attempted to respond, Darcy held up his hand. "Today I will be the speaker, and you will listen. I promise not to interrupt you in the future." Both men shared a forced laugh.

"Painful recollections have intruded into my daily thoughts which cannot, which ought not, be repelled. I have been a selfish being all my life, in practice, though not in principle. As a child, I was taught what was right, but I was not taught to correct my temper. I was given good principles, but left to follow them in pride and conceit. Unfortunately, as an only son, I was spoiled by my parents, who, though good themselves; and my father in particular was all that was benevolent and amiable, allowed, encouraged, almost taught me to be selfish and overbearing. I learned to care for none beyond my own family circle; to think meanly of all the rest of the world; to wish, at least, to think meanly of their sense and worth compared with my own. Such I was, from eight to eight and twenty."

Darcy sipped his scotch. Rawlings remained attentive; he did not speak or drink, giving his friend time to compose his words.

"What do I not owe you! You, Kent, Richmond, Blake and, most of all, Miss Elizabeth. I was taught a lesson, hard indeed at first, but most advantageous. I was properly humbled. Before then, I had no doubt of my reception by anyone. You all showed me how insufficient were my pretensions."

"Darcy, I told you once, we all have to accept ourselves for what we have been, what we are today, and what we will become. It is a rite of passage which a good man cannot avoid."

"But I need to show everyone, by every civility in my power, that I am not so mean as to resent the past. I hope to obtain forgiveness, to lessen everyone's ill opinion, and I need to let each of you see I have attended to all your reproofs. I never experienced such shame as I have this past fortnight. I cannot stand the sight of my own reflection."

"What? No more standing at the windows glaring at the glass panes?" Rawlings chuckled.

"Perhaps one day I will return to standing there, but not right now. I keep all the drapes shut." Darcy leaned back in his chair, cognizant of the warmth of the leather. "I have taken steps to right the wrongs with my cousin, Richmond, and with Kent. I am here to apologize for my behavior to you."

Darcy placed his glass on the table. He stood before Rawlings and with his head hung low said, "I do apologize. For Miss Margaret Stevens, for not standing by your side the four years you were married, for being such an arrogant boor and not treating you as a equal, as you are, but as a underling. I am truly sorry."

Rawlings placed his glass down, rose and held out his hand. "In America, men shake hands as a form of acceptance. Shake mine, Darcy. I will accept your apology if you accept my hand in apology for pretending to be you and forcing Margaret to marry me. It was wrong of me to do so."

The two men shook hands, their clasps firm.

Rawlings spoke up as they returned to the chairs. "I am sorry I spoke so bluntly when I could have been kinder."

"What did you say of me, that I did not deserve? No, do not answer. I see I cannot win this argument. I need advice."

"Oh. Do I need to find us a ball?"

Darcy chuckled. "No, I have learned that lesson. For the remainder of my days, I will never again expect others to look at me as something to be gained. I will treat them as I treat those I admire and respect until such time they have earned my disregard. I promise you that. But your advice is needed when it comes to making amends with Bingley and Blake."

Rawlings refilled his glass with brandy. "Excuse me." Rawlings left the room, spoke to his servant, and then returned, shutting the door behind him. "We will not be disturbed for any reason. I will do my best to help you, but I am not always the cleverest of men."

"You write the cleverest of letters." Darcy smiled, thinking about the first letter from America. He gulped his drink. While Rawlings refilled his friend's glass, Darcy looked out into the distance.

"I ruined everything when it comes to the Bennets. You do not know I accused Mr. Bennet of lying about Mr. Gardiner, whom I called a dishonorable man. No, I called him dishonest, a crook."

"Gardiner understands. He collaborated with Cuffage, or is it Rogers or Roberts? I get confused on the names. Do not dismiss how Gardiner collaborated with him before we did and he was nearly ruined himself. He does not hold your earlier opinion against you."

"But he is not the one I... He is a better man than I am. In truth, I am an arrogant bastard. I must overcome this. I must."

"You mentioned Bingley and Blake?"

"Yes, I did, and I do seek your help. Both Bingley and Blake are still heartbroken over the two eldest Bennets. It was my mess. Much happened that you do not know. Had I been forthright in my assumptions about Mrs. Bennet, I have no doubt Blake would have returned to Longbourn and demanded to see Miss Elizabeth. I never lied, but I never revealed the truth. Until now, I used that as my justification for being correct in my actions, but I cannot do so any longer."

"I doubt he would have believed you. His pride was hurt. He owns the same arrogance you criticized yourself with having. No, you should not have spoken up. It was just an opinion—nothing more, unless you know for a fact that Miss Elizabeth had not been sent to London as a precaution." When Darcy shook his head, Rawlings continued, "Blake is his own man, and must make his own decisions. In the same circumstance, would you have not been more forceful in finding her?"

Darcy shrugged. "I do not know. I cannot fault Blake." He leaned over and stared at his boots.

Rawlings coughed. "And now, what is it about Bingley?"

"I have come to learn that Miss Bennet did care for him. I was wrong in my judgment, which should not be surprising!"

"How exactly did you learn this? Did Mr. Gardiner share a confidence?"

"No. Miss Elizabeth Bennet informed me that my separation of her sister from Bingley is what facilitated her rejection of my offer of marriage."

Rawlings sat upright. His brows lifted up high. "You proposed to Miss Elizabeth? Blake accused you of pursuing her, but a marriage proposal? I had no idea. Does he know?"

"Yes, that fateful April day I had just finished informing him during *his* moment to educate me about my shortcomings when you came bursting in the room. I had been selfish in speaking so to him. I should never have caused him further pain. But he did seem to cheer up when he realized I was declined."

Rawlings stood and patted Darcy's shoulder. "Did you not know how she felt? We all knew of her dislike of you."

Darcy shook his head. "Phew, as I said, I am an arrogant bastard. I believed she was wishing, expecting my addresses. I was a fool. I never expected any lady to dismiss me, and she did so with great passion. I still shudder when I recall her words."

"Did she indicate a preference for Blake? If so, then you must tell him about your supposition."

"No. She never spoke about Blake, except once for general politeness and once when accusing me... I do not know how she feels about him; quite angry, I suspect. I should have spoken up when he informed me what happened upon our return to London from Netherfield Park. But..."

"You loved her even then."

"Yes. I did not want to admit it, but I did not want him to have her either. I pretended to be her protector, when what I really wanted was for her to be mine. I concealed this from him. I was wrong to act the way I did. I would never have gone on the balcony that night if... if I had admitted my own feelings. He would have asked her, and she would be his wife by now. I should tell him about Mrs. Bennet."

"If you are wrong about her feelings, then it will be cruel. But when did you speak to Miss Elizabeth and offer marriage?"

"When I visited my aunt in Kent, she was there."

"Oh? Did you pursue her with great abandonment?"

"I thought I needed to do little. She never even realized I was courting her. I thought I was showing her the most honorable attention. The day before I returned to London, I proposed. I am such a damned fool."

"Yes. But so are all men when it comes to women. Is that when you learned about Miss Bennet's true regard for Bingley?"

"Yes. Should I tell him? And before you answer, I have another confession to make."

"Let me refill my glass before you begin." He refilled his own, and when his friend held his empty glass forward, he questioned him with his gaze.

Darcy sighed. "I have drunk an excessive amount recently. I understand your habit much better now."

Rawlings laughed. "It does not help. Now, your confession?"

"Miss Jane Bennet came to visit Bingley's sister in January. Miss Bingley concealed her visit from her brother, and I assisted her in that. You see, I am not only arrogant, but a dishonorable, deceitful man. I am not gentleman-like at all."

"Do not be too hard on yourself."

Darcy whispered, "That hurts me the most deeply."

"What?"

"I am not gentleman-like. Elizabeth accused me twice, so I know it was not just something she said in anger or haste. She truly believes it."

"When did she say it?"

"When I proposed."

"You proposed in an ungentleman-like manner? A most unique method, I must say. Do you agree it was done in such a way?"

"Most definitely. I am an arrogant bastard."

"I think you have established that point. I disagree, but then you still need to discover the truth about who you really are. So what did she say? You cannot leave me in the dark."

"The words ring in my ears, every night, and any moment I am not focused on business."

"And?" Rawlings leaned back and put the glass to his lips.

"Well, the first instance she used the term was when I called her uncle dishonest."

Rawlings choked on the brandy he had just swallowed. "During a proposal? You said that? I cannot believe it."

"It is true. I did say that and more. I used many horrid words to describe her family. I even said they would not be included in any family social events. I told her I would deprive her of her own mother and silly sisters. I told her many would think she was unworthy to be Mrs. Darcy. I never told her I believed her to the best woman of my acquaintance to hold the name. I am an arrogant bastard."

"Not the best negotiation tactics, my friend. In fact, it was rather stupid. I assume there were no sharp objects in the room."

"I know I am an idiot, and I am glad she did not seek out the fireplace poker!"

"And the second time she said you were ungentleman-like was...?" Rawlings leaned forward.

"Oh, she had no problem unleashing her loathing on me. Her exact words were, 'You are mistaken, Mr. Darcy, if you suppose that the mode of your declaration affected me in any other way, than as it spared me the concern which I might have felt in refusing you, had you behaved in a more gentleman-like manner.' And..."

"And?"

"Yes, it is her words that burn in my ears. I cannot make them go away." He recited them from memory careful to imitate the venomous tone in her speech:

'From the very beginning, from the first moment I may almost say, of my acquaintance with you, your manners, impressing me with the fullest belief of your arrogance, your conceit, and your selfish disdain of the feelings of others, were such as to form that ground-work of disapprobation, on which succeeding events have built so immoveable a dislike. I had not known you a month before I felt that you were the last man in the world whom I could ever be prevailed on to marry.'

"Ah, the callous remark you made at the Assembly Hall dance." Rawlings lowered his voice and in the gentlest of tones asked, "Do you really love this woman? Or do you just want to bed her? You are too honorable to do so with a gentleman's daughter without marriage." Rawlings tapped Darcy's shoulder and continued only when he looked up. "Your proposal does not seem to have come from a man who truly loves a woman. I suspect she also did not believe you felt this way. She was just another object for the rich man of Derbyshire to own. Therefore, she could not overlook the way you proposed to her. Only you know the real truth."

"I love her with every inch of my body, my mind, my soul. The world looks gray without her, even on the brightest of days. Food is tasteless; music is dull. My whole body craves her smile, or just the tiniest of touches. My arms are empty even when they are full of objects. I am surrounded by a dark cloud and nothing gives me pleasure." Darcy dropped his head, and sighed loudly. "I take her image into my bed every night, and never once do I do more than hold her tightly in my arms. I treasure her that much."

"To quote you, *Humph*. You promised to be truthful and honest, my friend."

"Yes, well, perhaps I am not so chaste in my dreams, and the condition of my bed each morning indicates otherwise, but I do hold her for a long time first. I speak to her in… in… flowery words."

The two men sat quietly, sipping their drinks. They stared at the unlit fireplace.

After a long silent pause, Rawlings cleared his throat. "About Bingley, do nothing. Unless you determine Miss Bennet's present desires, you cannot further burden your friend. If she has transferred her affections elsewhere, he may never recover from your confession. He had happiness in his hands and he let it slip away. Telling him without knowing would be a selfish act with the sole purpose to make you feel better. Now, if Miss Bennet continues to have a desire for him, then our association with Mr. Gardiner will help reveal it. Then, and only then, you must confess to him. Bingley will hate you for a moment, until he realizes he has won the lady of his heart. He will be joyous, and will not care that you did this."

"Yes, I see your point. I will wait as you suggest. But my heart remains heavy."

"Your expression indicates you have another question."

"Is it wrong for me to wish Elizabeth would never marry another man?"

"Is it wrong for me to be happy my wife died? Yes, but we are men."

Darcy nodded.

Chapter Twenty-three

Regardless of our burdens, life uncaringly continues to propel us along the heavily travelled road, down which no one can see what awaits them. A protective shadow cast over the path cloaks our lives much like an oak tree provides cooling shade in a sweltering summer, thus giving us the opportunity to continue even when our strength is sapped. Curves in the highway make us laugh and smile with joy while other turns literally break our hearts due to lost love or the death of a loved one. Then there are the potholes that jolt us into speechlessness. Perhaps the carriage carrying us forward is rundown from the wear and tear of the journey, and is not as speedy as when it was new, but still, the road lies ahead, pulling us forward with windy whispers of hope for better days to come.

And so it was, after weeks of reflection, Mr. Fitzwilliam Darcy ventured forward as a different man, a little wiser and a lot kinder, cautiously listening to the soft voice suggesting better days and a brighter future just around the bend.

With Mr. Gardiner as a full partner, Astor lived up to his agreement, and assisted the young men on matters that they were not prepared to handle. Bingley and his family of inventors provided great support, and transferred their endeavors away from the Falcon. The Lowell family in Boston provided the connection needed for trading with the East Indies, including China, and Rawlings repeatedly remarked on the irony that the Falcon created the relationship by having the ship diverted from New York to Boston. Kent and his family solidified their importance to the group. They built the ships, handled the trade of goods, and assisted in every business request.

As news spread throughout the gossipy ballrooms as well as the lowly taverns of London, everyone lined up on one sides. Almost every Tory supported Lord Winthrop's coalition, the Peregrine, while many Whigs preferred the young men's alliance. Arguments abounded between the rich and the poor, those with established wealth and those recently rich.

The servants supported whomever their master supported, but the tradesmen lined up behind Darcy and Kent—even those that had once turned away from them. They ensured timely payment of invoices, even if Darcy or Kent had to pay them from their own pockets. Together, these two co-leaders proved capable of overcoming most every obstacle Winthrop placed before them. The Corn Laws presented the biggest problem, and using this most devastating weapon, the Falcon's directed Lord Liverpool to push through more legislation aimed at hurting the manufacturing and trade market. Darcy had much to learn about the difficulties faced by tradesmen at the hands of the aristocracy and the impact of laws passed.

The young men worked hard and the fledgling alliance was able, within two months, to stand on its own and become the driving force behind the new world of machinery, and with it gained an advantage on the rapidly emerging industrial world.

Blake never returned to the alliance nor did he join the Falcon's group. An honorable man, he did complete the work he had started with Darcy's alliance, but had his solicitor act for him. After moving to his own small estate in the country, and away from his father's house, Blake spent most of his London time with his political Uncle Harrowby. He was conflicted by the Tory's new emphasis on passing more Corn Laws, because the effort went beyond protecting the aristocracy and large estate owners to deliberately attempting to decimate the Darcy's alliance. Nevertheless, as a Tory and an aristocrat, Blake chose not to ask his Uncle Harrowby, a political force in the House of Lords, to intercede on this issue. Blake ignored every one of his father's invitations and demands.

***

Business filled Darcy's days, continuing along in a routine manner, but he did attempt to change his personal affairs with his acquaintances. His first endeavor was to correct the authoritative relationship he maintained over his sister.

"Yes, brother. Did you send for me?" Georgiana moved to her normal chair in front of his desk.

Darcy rose from behind his desk and used his open hand to point to the more comfortable chairs in front of the fireplace. He felt a sting when he caught sight of Georgiana's shocked reaction. They took their seats, and Darcy leaned forward, his arms resting on his thighs to support his upper body. "You look lovely this morning."

"Thank you." Georgiana held her breath as fear filled her eyes.

"I have decided to treat you as my sister, and one fully grown, and not as my child. I promise you, I will no longer be arbitrary in my decisions. Firstly, I will offer you the opportunity to express your thoughts. Secondly, I will completely explain the reason for any prohibition or denial of your wants. Thirdly, I will allow you to respond, without interruption. We will work out any problems together."

Georgiana relaxed, but only allowed her posture to slacken by the smallest of margins. "I am pleased, but... " She waited for her brother to inject his thoughts, and when he remained quiet, she continued, "I am surprised by your change. I do not understand what you expect from me."

"To be the beautiful, sweet, and loving sister you are. I will be depending upon you to be my hostess with larger groups of guests, but first I need to know if I ask too much. I will never again demand you perform, unless you have indicated your willingness to do so."

"Brother, I have overcome so much, and you were correct, the little dinner parties with your friends have made it easier for me. I am sure I can succeed, but occasionally I may need help."

"Please, do not shy away from asking me to help with anything. We can do this together."

Sitting quietly for a few moments, the siblings contemplated the tasks before them. Georgiana, twisted her handkerchief and asked in a soft voice, "Did you wish to scold me?

"Not at all. Why would think I would?"

"For my assistance to Mr. Kent. I have been waiting for you to do so."

Oh, Georgiana! I beg your pardon for not easing your anxiety on this. I am proud of you. I only wish I had been the man you wanted me to be and not the one in which you felt the need to conceal your activities from."

"Does this mean had I been interested in Mr. Kent you would not object? Bear in mind, I am not interested, but I need to understand who you consider a worthy man for me."

"Any man that is kind, good, and honorable. I no longer care if his status is high or low. I do not seek titles or wealth as a pre-condition. I want you to be happy, and that means I will accept anyone that you wish to marry, as long as..."

Georgiana caught her breath.

"He is not seeking merely your fortune or our name. We," he pointed to her and then himself, "must be vigilant, but we can do so together. I promise."

She smiled and relaxed her entire body until gasping at her lack of good posture. She attempted to straighten up when he shook head. "In this room, when we are alone, you do not need to sit so rigidly. We are brother and sister, you know!"

Georgiana sprung to her feet and gave her brother a hug and a kiss upon his cheek. She studied him for a lingering moment.

Darcy presented a half-smile. "Did you know Kent remarked once that you could spot angst in a person?"

"And I suppose you want to know if I see yours? Your eyes have lost the light that flickered in them, they seem dull." Georgiana whispered.

"Do not fear me! Yes, it is true. I am saddened; in fact, my heart has been wrenched from my body and by my own hand. Well, that is how I feel, and I know you are curious. I also know you will understand, because now I finally comprehend your melancholy last summer." His voice caught in his throat, and when he did release the words, it cracked. "I am so sorry for my boorish behavior."

Georgiana waited for a moment then touched his cheek. "Miss Elizabeth Bennet declined your offer of marriage."

Darcy nodded. "See, you know without my saying a word. Yes, she did; she was right to do so. I do not deserve her." He lowered his head until his chin touched his chest.

"But you do. You are the best brother."

Darcy straightened upright and inhaled deeply. "But not the best man. I realize that I have much to change. I must attend to my selfish and conceited traits if I wish to become the type of man she would approve of. Even though I have no hope of..."

Georgiana grabbed her brothers' hand when he gasped. "Do not give up."

"My dear, sweet sister, I have no hope for a future with her. I have no one but my own self to blame." Darcy's last words cracked.

She placed several light kisses upon his hand. "There is always hope."

Darcy caught his breath in his throat, blinked several times, and then gazed into his sister's kind face. "An unknown powerful force is demanding I change for her. Everything I do is aimed towards her approval. I want her to see me as a gentleman worthy of her acquaintance. I know it cannot be more, still it is what drives me to change."

Georgiana wiped away the mist in his eyes and squeezed his hand tighter. He rose, pulling her up with him, and hugged her tightly. "Help me, dear, sweet Georgiana. Help me become the man she would want to know. Teach me how a woman worthy thinks and feels."

With tears falling down her cheeks, Georgiana hugged him tightly. "I will."

***

Two months had passed since the eleventh day of April, the day that everyone referred to as the Eligo, the Latin word meaning *to choose*. Kent had suggested it would be appropriate as the trademark for the group, and every man agreed, since each had to decide which group to ally with on that fateful day.

Darcy held a dinner each month for all the partners, and had invited the remaining members of the Lunar Society—Watt, Murdoch, Keir, and Gaston—to conduct their meetings at his house on those nights. They had agreed with alacrity. He also invited men of means, those whom might sponsor or invest in their endeavors. The inventors brought their newest accomplishments to demonstrate, which proved the best entertainment, until Georgiana performed for them on her pianoforte. Her playing tamed the wildest of the men.

Only Blake and Bingley were missing. Blake had chosen a different path, living out his own eligo; Bingley remained up north. He did not return to London, even with his Uncle Watt for the dinner meetings. Instead, he kept himself busy with the rifle orders. Watt had spoken to Darcy about his nephew's lack of interest in anything other than business. Darcy suggested they meet at Pemberley in late August for that month's dinner meeting, and promised Watt that he would insist upon Bingley's attendance. The two men concocted a plan to draw Bingley out of his self-imposed exile. Darcy was most disturbed when Mr. Gardiner remained mute when he inquired about the Bennet daughters. He did not press the issue, believing protectiveness was the reason behind Gardiner's silence.

During the dinners, Darcy had made a point of not only meeting everyone, including the ladies, but discovering more about each person. He asked many questions, and charmed the ladies with his new ease of conversation. He practiced with every opportunity to speak kindly and with respect, regardless of the social or financial status of the guest. He allowed his wit to compete with Rawlings, which surprised only those who had not been a close friend to the earlier man, before he had become the current Master of Pemberley.

Georgiana enjoyed the dinners, and looked forward to each one. She blossomed into an excellent hostess, although her shyness and uncertainness still had its grips in her being. She invited Victoria to every occasion, but since the day of the Eligo, Lord Cheswick had barred her from Darcy House. Miss Sarah Kent, on the other hand, accepted every invitation. She kept her gaze turned to one man, and when he chose to include her in conversation, her heart would pump furiously, which unhappily was not as often as she liked, nor was she pleased he did not speak on anything aimed at romance. It was all pleasant and surprisingly witty, but not the words a young lady wished to hear when conversing with the most dashing of men.

So it was, on the fourteenth day of June, 1812, the dining room of Darcy House was filled to capacity. A harmony of voices flourished, as the astonished servants served the meal. Women spoke their mind, but unlike Bingley's party, a pre-determined seating arrangement was followed. Darcy worked with Georgiana to decide the best grouping of attendees, in order to make sure everyone was included in conversation.

They had just begun the meal, when Geoffries handed his master an urgent message. Darcy was quick to open it, and carefully read the note. He held his hand up to quiet the others sitting around the table. Looking at his guests, Darcy smiled. "Blake has sent word. As of today, the government has lifted the trade restrictions with America. There will be no war."

"Hooray for Blake. Cheers!" Everyone held their drinks high.

Blake had worked tirelessly on getting the restriction lifted. His Uncle Harrowby had used every political favor. The uncle and nephew had grown close over the previous months; Harrowby had educated him on Parliament, politics in general, and the Tories in particular.

Blake had an agreement with Darcy that once the government lifted the restriction of trade, he would no longer have any part of the alliance. However, during this period, he learned his heart was not in the world of business; he did not care for it all. In the end, connecting with the tradesmen's sons did not bother him the most; it was the dull and boring details of the everyday activities. He also discovered he no longer cared to win approval from the members of the *Ton*. He did make one important discovery—politics were different. He believed he could make a difference; an honorable difference, as his Uncle Harrowby had taught him. He had found his calling in life, for which he would eventually thank Darcy. Had it not been for the alliance, he would never have given this life a chance, nor re-established a relationship with his uncle.

The conversation during dinner celebrated the trading possibilities now that the embargo was no longer a problem. Rawlings thought about Lowell and his Boston friends. He recognized that New England had had difficulties with the restrictions, having seen a few signs of it when he visited. Ships lay wasted in the harbors. Families were losing their financial security. Lowell, however, would profit from a continuation of any embargo. Business problems in one area opened up success in another. Since Rawlings had purchased stock in Lowell's cotton mill, he made money regardless.

Kent was pleased with the progress and his family's acceptance and role in the alliance. His Uncle Daniel had a fortune riding on averting war. Kent had warned him to diversify, but to no avail. His uncle was a determined man. Darcy, too, had tried to dissuade him, but also to no avail. Privately, the two friends had made a plan to protect him. Today, however, Daniel Kent rejoiced in the news. He crowed about the decisions he made.

In July, the alliance made a second trip to the Soho Manufactory, and remaining true to his word, Darcy led Kent in playing many pranks on Sarah. Kent had shared Darcy's carriage on the way to Birmingham in order for them to devise the most devilish of pranks.

"She hates her food peppered, but I do not see how we can do it."

"Yes we can, Kent. You just need to see the whole picture. We will butter the underside of her spoon and then press it into pepper. She will not see it before she takes her first bite of dessert!" Darcy laughed.

Kent guffawed when she took her first taste of cobbler. Darcy kept his countenance until Kent glanced at Darcy and then burst out, "Vengeance is mine, dear sister. I have the master of pranks to assist me so you are warned."

Happily, the next day she retaliated by placing a spider under in his coffee cup , causing the war of pranks to escalate until three days later Mrs. Boulton put an end to it. They came to a truce over dinner one evening with a handshake between Darcy and Miss Kent, who in turn made Rawlings shake hands too. He had been secretly assisting and helping her to win. Rawlings smiled widely when Darcy's expression revealed his shock when his friend announced, "Remember, I was the one who taught you!"

The week at the Soho Manufactory ended, the tradesmen were proud of their *Heir* and satisfied to be associated with Mr. Darcy, a gentleman whom treated them like equals.

Farther up north, Bingley remained the quietest of the men, no silliness in his life. He and his family toiled on with their responsibilities in the alliance. There was no end to their creativity. Their activity caused the first failure of Winthrop's coalition. Surprisingly, the Falcon's group, without the support of many tradesmen, needed the lifting of the trade embargo with America. In fact, without it, they continued to spiral downwards while Darcy's alliance continued to succeed.

An early August dinner party at Darcy House ended well, after much of the discussion focused on the war declared by America on the 16th day of June, two days after Parliament had lifted the trade embargo. Darcy had repeatedly complained to Keir about the necessity for his telegraph to cross the oceans. He had previously joked about the cost of the slow delivery of Rawlings' letter, but now lives were at stake. Had America received word of Parliament's action, then the war would not have happened.

On a lighter note, everyone enjoyed the experiments conducted after dinner, except that everyone missed Mr. Gardiner and his easygoing manner. He, his wife, and Miss Elizabeth had left for a trip to the Lake Country. The partners, including Gardiner, planned to meet up at Pemberley in four days time, on August 6, to rethink what the war would mean to their alliance. Darcy invited not only the partners, but also many members of Kent and Bingley's families to his country home as well.

When the dinner guests finally departed for their homes, Rawlings stayed. He had an important message to convey.

"She has had a change of heart."

"Who?" Darcy asked.

"Miss Elizabeth Bennet."

Darcy sat upright. He held his breath until his friend continued.

"I have it on good authority, Gardiner that is, Miss Elizabeth is no longer angry with a certain young man."

"Is it Blake or me?"

"Gardiner would not say. I believe he is a little cautious, especially when it comes to his nieces. I suspect he is trying to discover if the young man is still interested."

"Have you told Blake?"

"No! I am hoping it is you she has had a change of heart over."

"But if it is Blake…"

"I hope not. You have changed into the kind of man that deserves her. Blake is still the same man, still proud, and a little arrogant. I will tell you another secret."

Darcy jerked his head up.

"She will be in Lambton the day after tomorrow. They will be staying at the Red Rooster Inn. Logan has set up horses for you along the way. If you leave now, you will be able to see her before the entire alliance descends upon Pemberley. Go to her, tonight."

Darcy shook his head.

Rawlings stood and grasped his friend's shoulder. "Go. Find her. Find out if you are the man she wants. You will arrive several days ahead us. Do not let this opportunity pass. Oh, and tell her about you being a selfish being all your life, and all those other things you told me months ago. Women like to hear men grovel. I promise you, the passionate reward is worth it. And do not say anything that would make her ashamed of who she is or where she comes from. Tell her how your life is gray, and nothing tastes good and music is dull, and all that boring talk. You remember, it is what you told me. Now say it all to her!"

Darcy nodded slowly.

Rawlings took his leave, careful to hide behind a nearby bush, where he was able to watch any inhabitants of Darcy House leave. He did not have to wait long. Darcy was out of the door and upon his horse in less than a quarter hour, and he was dressed for a long. Rawlings hummed a tune as he made his way home.

"Excuse me, sir. No one is permitted to enter tonight."

"It is imperative I speak to your master. It is urgent, and cannot wait."

"Very well."

"What are you doing here and at this time of night?" Blake asked. The muscles in his neck were taut.

Dressed in his traveling clothes, Darcy held his hat in his hand. "I have come to confess, and to offer you hope."

Chapter Twenty-four

Blake led the way to the sitting room he used to greet acquaintances, a room designed to discourage visitors from overstaying their welcome. His friends, he took to his library where the surfeit of books surprised anyone entering the room. The library contained comfortable chairs and sofas, filled beverage decanters, and a fire blazing at all times during the cool weather, or filled with flowers during the spring and summer. The room he led Darcy to contained the hardest of chairs, the smallest of fires, and the gloomiest of colors. He motioned for his former friend to sit.

Once in the room, Blake turned towards Darcy, who had sat down in the most uncomfortable of chairs. "What do you want? Another favor? Another scheme? Another chance to betray me?"

Darcy held his head steady, but did not raise his chin high. "No. I… came on a different matter, and one of importance to you. I… have news about someone, although not all the details were provided."

"I assume you mean *her*?" Blake chose the chair the greatest distance away from his former friend.

"Yes."

"Well, what is it? My time is valuable. Do not keep me waiting. I believe you mentioned a confession? What else have you have done?"

"I concealed the whole truth. On the balcony at Netherfield Park I… I…" Darcy hung his head, no longer able to say the words he needed to say.

"Speak up. I am in no mood for you drag this out or to mull this over. Say what you came to say and be done with it. Then be on your way."

Darcy raised his head and caught sight of Blake's glare. "On the balcony that night, when I spoke of your dire financial condition, I did so only after Mrs. Bennet had opened the door to the balcony. I believed she was—"

"Wait! You mean to tell me Mrs. Bennet overheard you accuse me of being penniless? Is that what you are trying to say?"

Darcy shook his head. "Yes, but... in fact it is worse than that. I *deliberately* made the comment when she appeared. I believed she was mercenary in all respects, and I thought you were going to offer something other than marriage. So, yes, I did consider her useful in protecting Miss Elizabeth."

Blake shrugged. "But what of it? I admitted to my own personal wealth, which does not compare to yours, but is sufficient. And I do have a title, unlike you. Mrs. Bennet would prefer her daughter to be duchess than a mere wealthy Mrs."

"She left the moment after I spoke. She never heard the whole truth."

Blake jumped up, pulled Darcy to his feet, and shook him. "You cur! Why did you not tell me this before? I would have threatened to destroy Longbourn if Mrs. Bennet did not give me the information about her whereabouts. I would have been more forceful. My God. She may have told Elizabeth."

"Blake—"

"No wonder she ran from me. My God."

"Blake! Think man! You do not know if she had actually gone to town. Remember Mrs. Bennet is the one who told you she had. She may have been trying to protect her daughter from a life of poverty, and kept her away from meeting you through a lie."

"Yes. You did a wonderful job depicting me as the worst kind of peer. Damn. I remember now. You even suggested I might have to live off the Bennets. You..." Blake's fist landed on Darcy's chin, knocking him to the floor.

"I do not know what Mrs. Bennet did, but I..."

Blake pulled Darcy to his feet. "All this time!" Blake's fist landed on his chin again.

"Get up you cur. Get up so I can knock you down again."

Darcy rose to his feet but before Blake could level him with his right fist he yelled, "Please, call me a scoundrel, call me a cur, but cease from crying out 'all this time' with every punch. I am sorry. There is no excuse for what I have done. But hold up before you hit me again. I have more to tell you, something that may offer you hope."

"What is it? I will not strike you again until you have spoken; besides, there is no satisfaction in beating a man who will not fight back."

"I do not fight back, because I have earned every blow. I have news of Miss Elizabeth and her feelings towards a gentleman."

Blake froze.

"Tonight, I learned she has had a change of heart with a gentleman. But I admit I do not know who he is."

"How do you know this?"

"Mr. Gardiner has been most secretive about his nieces, but just recently he shared the news with Rawlings."

"Why tell me? Go ask her. Find out before you get my hopes up."

Darcy shook his head. "No! It is not that simple. How do I make you understand?" He wiped the blood from his lip with his handkerchief. "She needs to speak to you before she makes any decision, and especially one which may fall in my favor. She needs to be told the truth. I cannot consider a future with her if deep down she regrets you. Would you want her if she had regrets about me? You would not, and neither do I. I want her to be happy, whether with you or me. I love her, but I do not want only duty and obligation. I could never bear being married to her, and all the while she is wishing it was you... at her side."

"So? What am I supposed to do? Why should I help alleviate your fears?"

"How can I not give you the opportunity to win her? Blake! Do you want the chance or not? I cannot tell you which of us she prefers, but are you not desirous of finding out? Do you want her to accept me when you may have won her heart?"

Blake took a seat. "Tell me everything you know."

Darcy explained his deceptive role as her protector, described the desire he had for her, his proposal, her manner of refusal, his letter he wrote to her, what Gardiner had said about his niece, and finally the arrangements Rawlings had made. He offered to provide a letter for Logan demanding that he make the horses available to Blake. Although his former friend listened politely, Darcy sensed the bond of friendship they once shared was lost forever. Blake's cold demeanor left no doubt of his feelings.

Darcy touched Blake's shoulder, "Go to her. Tell her you feelings; tell her the truth. I promise to do the same when I arrive in two days after you. She should know everything before she commits herself to any man."

***

Rawlings moved down the stairs to enter his carriage for the two-day trip to Pemberley. He had not stopped smiling since helping Darcy two days ago. The footman had just reached to open the door when he heard a whistle.

"Rawlings, wait!"

Shocked, Rawlings turned to face the man he had assumed was almost to Pemberley by this time. "Darcy, why are you here? You look horrible. What happened?"

"I have much to tell. Shall we ride together?" Darcy pointed to the carriage with his head.

Rawlings nodded and the two men climbed inside.

"I am at a loss. I admit I waited that night to see if you would leave. Did you change your mind?"

"No. I visited with Blake."

Rawlings jerked back into his cushion. "Blake? Why?"

"Because it is as much his right to find out as it is mine. I have done enough damage."

"What happened? Is Blake on his way?"

"No."

"I must hear all. I know I am a gossipy old dowager, but I will not let you leave this carriage until you give me the whole story."

"I expected, and received, a right punch to my jaw. Blake has an unquestionably strong punch." Darcy wiggled his jaw. "In fact, he pummeled me quite rightly. Did I tell you I punched him months ago?"

"No!"

"You had left for America. Blake arrived on my doorstep, drunk I might add, and I landed a right fist on his chin as hard as I could. He did not deserve it, and that is another of my sins I will forever regret."

"We all have sins, Darcy. You digress. What happened with Blake this time?"

"Blake allowed me to enter his home. Of course, I piqued his interest when I admitted I had something to confess."

Sighing, Rawlings shook his head.

"I told him the truth. All of it: Mrs. Bennet on the balcony, Kent on the balcony."

"Wait! Kent was on the balcony?"

"Yes. He heard it all and watched Mrs. Bennet's reaction. He knew! Yes. He knew what I had done. I am surprised he continued to connect himself to me."

"Bah! Kent has his own agenda. So, that is when you received the blows—after you confessed your great sin of being a jealous man."

"Needless to say, yes. Blake kept saying 'All this time. All this time.' He repeated it over and over with every punch until I had to yell at him to shut up."

"No!"

"Well, politely."

"Go on. Do not stop now."

I told him of my feelings for Miss Elizabeth, and how I believed my dealings were deliberate, without acknowledging even to myself the real reason behind my actions. I wanted him to fail, because I wanted her. I caught Blake off-guard when I admitted attempting to warn her about him at Netherfield Park, but she refused to listen."

"He was surprised? I was not. You were most entertaining!"

"I could have used a bit more enlightenment."

"I shall not hold back in the future. Was there anything else you told him?"

"I explained that it was not until one night while visiting my Aunt in Kent I finally decided to seek her out. Before then, I never once pursued her. After my thrashing, I mentioned the word *hope*. I carefully told him what you said. Once I explained how Mr. Gardiner indicated Miss Elizabeth has had a change of mind over a particular young man, his entire countenance changed, his face brightened. You must understand how important hope is to a man."

Rawlings leaned forward and with the gentleness of voice said, "You may have raised his hopes when there is no hope she will chose him."

"Every man needs hope, Rawlings. Everyman. Well, I gave him the plans on where to meet Logan. I warned him several times though, Gardiner did not name the young man, and for all I know, it could be Mr. Goulding."

Rawlings opened his mouth to speak when Darcy's body suddenly stiffened. "Good God!"

"What?"

"Wickham. I had not thought of Wickham. That scoundrel is still loose in the world. Oh my God. She had befriended that rake."

"Settle down. Do not worry so. Mr. Gardiner indicated he was a young man who had stayed at Netherfield Park.

Breathing easier, Darcy stared out the window. "I should have warned her father at least about Wickham. He was always sniffing around Longbourn."

"I tried to warn Mr. Bennet, but unfortunately my attempt came immediately after the waltz. He was not in a mood to listen, and to be honest, he believed Wickham over you."

"I could have explained Wickham's behavior to him in a way you could not. But I never felt his daughters were in danger since they have no fortune. Damn. That predicament is due to my family. I accused Mr. Gardiner as dishonest. I am the biggest simpleton in all of England. Mr. Bennet and Mr. Gardiner are saints compared to my relatives. My own father had been a member. What a fool I have been."

"Stop this pity blabber! You have changed completely."

"Oh?"

"Look at you. After these few months, you are completely different when it comes to the men that cross your path. Although you were not unpardonably rude before, now you treat even the lowest of persons with the type of respect you used to show only those whom you admired. I have heard you speak to the tradesmen as equals, and even begin conversations with them. You do not hesitate to invite a variety of guests to your home. In fact, I have had the most entertaining meals at Darcy House lately. These men of knowledge are an interesting group. My opinion of them has changed a great deal, too. I have witnessed the amends you made in your own character. Do not think ill of yourself."

Darcy shrugged. "I admit I am anxious about Blake obtaining Elizabeth's acceptance and I let those thoughts prevail. I will try not to wallow around in the pool of pity, well, at least not in the deep end!"

Rawlings laughed.

"I will continue to try to improve. I need practice. Did I ever tell you that she once accused me of not taking the time to practice? That was not true. I practiced at everything I thought was worthwhile, but never did I expect speaking to those people as a worthy endeavor."

"Enough self-indulgence. Now what did Blake do with all this new information?"

"He gave orders to pack his trunks. He is coming to Pemberley, and we will face her together. I must tell her the truth about what I saw. I offered Blake even more hope after I admitted doing something that may be the reason for her change of heart of him." Sighing, Darcy stared out the window at the passing scenery.

Rawlings waited patiently, but had to cough to get his friend's attention; he raised his brows in a pleading motion. "Are you going to keep me in suspense the whole journey?"

With a solemn expression, Darcy leaned towards his friend and said, "Please do not think ill of her, but I wrote Miss Elizabeth a letter after her refusal to my marriage offer. I placed it in her hand before I left my aunt's home in Kent."

Rawlings brows shot up.

"I included the truth about her mother's appearance on the balcony that night and what she had told Blake the next day. He was not to blame. I suspect this is the reason for the change of heart. From my own hand, Elizabeth learned about Blake seeking her out the day after the ball at Longbourn.

"Oh, and what did he say to that?"

"His usual response to something shocking, he repeatedly said, ' *Oh my* '." Both men chuckled. "But Blake relaxed afterwards. He smiled for a while, and I can only imagine he was picturing her reading the letter. He actually patted me on the back as he said I was a friend, even when I was stabbing him in the back. I suppose I did him a great favor by revealing the truth to Miss Elizabeth. But… I did not think of Blake at the time, only the need to defend myself against her accusations. I was not a friend."

"What now?"

"We are both prepared to meet with her and discuss everything. Blake refused to go on ahead. He believes there is as much chance she prefers me. I would be so honored if she did. And it would work to your advantage too."

"How so?"

"Well, I would send you word when Miss Lydia visits Pemberley."

"You have changed."

"I believe she is too young and silly for you, but I no longer wish to substitute my opinion for yours. If she pleases you, then I will stand by you. Perhaps, we can find out if she is still at Longbourn."

"Yes, perhaps."

"I also had Georgiana invite Lady Victoria. Her father relented and let her come at my aunt's insistence. They grew tired of her tears and tantrums, I suspect. Kent will be surprised. This is their chance to discover how they feel about each other. Georgiana and Lady Victoria are there now. I hope Blake's attendance does not give Victoria concern. Good God. Now I must think of how to handle this."

"Calm yourself. If Victoria has transferred her affections to Kent, it will not matter. If not, then Kent needs to know the strength of her feelings towards another man. So truthfully, this may be for the best. Is that not what you are pursing for yourself? A lady with no regrets? You are not responsible for every person's life. We are grown men and women, and must handle our situations to suit our own selves."

Darcy chuckled.

"What?"

"*She* accused me of trying to be the conductor of every friend's life. As you see, she was correct!"

The two men continued to converse about their visit in Hertfordshire. Darcy indicated he was looking forward to seeing Bingley again, and this time he would not hesitate to confess his sins to him either; but first he needed to learn if Miss Bennet had transferred her affections elsewhere. He solicited Rawlings' help, since Mr. Gardiner seemed to speak more openly with him. Talk turned to business issues, and the impact the war with America was having on their shipping business. Rawlings had sent word to the Lowell family that a shipment would be delayed until a resolution between the two countries occurred.

Silence permeated the carriage while they continued on their journey to Pemberley, until they reached the inn Darcy had arranged for the night's stay. Kent had reached the destination first, and Blake was the last to arrive. Bingley would arrive at Pemberley directly from his uncle's home north of Derbyshire.

Choosing to avoid Darcy, Blake spent the evening debating the reformation of parliament with Kent, who no longer professed the Tory line. Kent was now a full-fledged member of the Whigs, much to the happiness of his uncles. The two men spoke in friendly, respectful tones, although the words became a little heated at times. With Blake and Kent occupied, Darcy retired early for the night and, surrounded by the political talk, Rawlings soon followed Darcy's lead.

*** *** ***

Mr. Gardiner had planned to stay in Lambton until the rest of the partners arrived so that his wife could easily visit with her former friends, but once Darcy offered his home, which was a mere five miles from Lambton, Gardiner believed it would not be polite to refuse now that he was a full partner. He only hesitated because his niece was traveling with them. Elizabeth had expressed her uneasiness, although she had never mentioned Darcy's proposal to either her uncle or aunt. But in the end, Georgiana's insistence won out, and that was how Miss Elizabeth Bennet came to stay at Pemberley only two days after arriving in Lambton.

Georgiana, Miss Kent, and Lady Victoria had spent a few days together while waiting for the men to arrive. The ladies had grown fond of each other when they secretly were sending letters between Kent and Victoria. Although she was apprehensive about spending time with Kent, Victoria had expressed her appreciation for the chance to get to know him.

Hoping to catch a particular man's gaze and turn his head towards her ever since that first day he smiled at her at Darcy House, Sarah Kent anxiously waited as well. She could not erase the image of his tall frame sauntering through the manufactory door, displaying his laughing eyes as he inspected the products her uncle manufactured. She had studied him as earnestly as he studied the intricate details of whichever object he chose from the display case. He had dimples of which he seemed to be unaware. His air spoke of nonchalance, and he was natural, unlike the stilted manner of her brother and other young tradesmen trying to impress the world. And yet, his broad shoulders rarely slumped, and he appeared ordinary in the way he held his hand behind his back For the first time, she was without control over her yearnings, and, regardless of the unlikelihood he would ever entertain her as a possible match, each day brought her closer to another opportunity to win his favor. She feared the difference in their status was too great. He never looked upon her as anything more than as his partner's sister. She feared his heart belonged to another.

Pleased with her guests, Georgiana hoped that the visiting women would remain close friends in the future. While the Gardiners visited during the day, Elizabeth usually remained at Pemberley with the other ladies. She had only added to the liveliness.

Darcy had sent word Lord Blake would be joining them, and had asked his sister to let the Victoria, the Gardiners, and Elizabeth know.

However, when the men arrived, the Gardiners and Elizabeth were out visiting. Mr. Gardiner suspected Elizabeth had desired an occupation away on this day. She had become quieter and more circumspect on their return back to Pemberley. When they arrived, they learned everyone had gathered in the drawing room, and the servants led them there immediately.

Lord Blake and Darcy stilled when Elizabeth walked through the doorway. Lord Blake had been speaking to Miss Kent with Lady Victoria listening nearby. Kent stood slightly apart, his gaze remained fixed on Lady Victoria. Rawlings was jesting about nothing and to no one in particular. Darcy and Georgiana were sharing a quiet conversation. She had touched his hand several times when Elizabeth entered, and then squeezed tightly when he inhaled sharply. She gave him a small smile.

Bingley sat alone in the chair, subconsciously tapping his fingers on the arm. From the instant he had arrived at Pemberley and learned Miss Elizabeth was also a guest, he contemplated a way to learn about her sister. He practiced his question repeatedly, *Are all your sisters at home?* He felt satisfied that she would tell him if Miss Bennet had married. It had been nearly eight months since he had last seen her, and he would not let this opportunity pass without discovering if his angel had accepted another.

Blake and Darcy approached the Gardiners and Elizabeth quickly.

"Miss Bennet." The two men bowed, and before even she completed her curtsey, Darcy whispered, "I invited Lord Blake to join us, because I believe you and he need to discuss a matter you mentioned a few months ago."

"Miss Bennet, please. I would be honored if you allow me to speak to you. Perhaps not this moment, as you have just arrived, but we could meet tonight after dinner?"

"It is unlikely my uncle would allow a private discussion. Perhaps my aunt should attend as well?" Elizabeth glanced at her uncle and aunt.

"Yes, of course." The two men nodded.

Mr. Gardiner reluctantly agreed once his wife signaled her acceptance.

For a few minutes, the conversation centered on the men's trip to Pemberley and the mutual acquaintances Darcy and Mrs. Gardiner shared. Soon Elizabeth parted, making her way to her bedchambers to prepare for dinner. As if a servant had rung a bell, everyone separated to their own chambers, with the exception of Darcy. He led Gardiner to his study, where they shared a brandy before conversing for a brief period.

When dinner began, everyone sensed the tension in the room by the strained voices and forced laughter. Elizabeth remained quiet, striving to be composed, and without daring to lift up her head. She sat flanked by her uncle and Mr. Rawlings, her aunt placed directly across from her. Neither Blake nor Darcy sat near her, which resulted in their silence. Elizabeth had ventured only one glance at Darcy. He had maintained his serious mien much in the same manner as he had been in Hertfordshire. He felt his heart ache when she glanced at Blake but he too held a serious demeanor, unusual for the charming and friendly man. Neither man smiled, and instead of eating, they pushed the food around the plate. Miss Kent, sitting to the left of Darcy, remarked upon something humorous, which resulted in his chuckle and a lowly spoken comment in return.

"Miss Bennet, have you traveled in this area before?"

"No, Mr. Rawlings. This is my first trip this far north. I find the countryside astonishing, and so unlike Hertfordshire."

"Were you able to visit the Lakes?"

Elizabeth shook her head before releasing a long sigh. She glanced at Darcy first and then Blake while she gulped her wine.

Rawlings leaned in a whispered, "All will be well, Miss Bennet. They are both honorable men, and only seek *your* happiness, wherever it resides." He presented her with a smile and reached for his glass.

Bingley talked less than he had in Meryton. He sipped his drink, and when Elizabeth caught him looking at her, she assumed he was trying to trace a resemblance. He leaned towards her, and in a tone of real regret said, "It was a long time since I had the pleasure of seeing you. It is above eight months. We have not met since the 26th of November, when we were all dancing together at Netherfield." Elizabeth gave him a smile at his memory. He took a deep breath and then asked her whether all her sisters were at Longbourn, with such a look and manner, which gave them meaning, she immediately gave him the answer "All my sisters are Longbourn, except one. My youngest sister is in Brighton."

Rawlings coughed. "Brighton? Do you have family there?"

"No. She is the guest of Colonel Forster's wife. The militia has left Meryton, and is spending the summer at Brighton."

"All the militia? Does that include Mr. Wickham?" Rawlings's fingers tightened around the stem.

Georgiana gasped. Darcy attempted to rise from his chair, but was not as quick as Elizabeth who had knocked over her glass. She patted the wet spot with her napkin and asked for forgiveness of Georgiana, diverting her attention away from the conversation. "Miss Darcy, I fear this means I must play the song you wanted to hear tonight as my punishment." Georgiana laughed at Elizabeth's jest, and offered to turn the pages for her.

Darcy leaned back in his chair, and kept his gaze on Elizabeth, admiring her and the manner in which she diffused the situation. He felt his heart leap and before this moment, he had never believed the poets when they described it. But it did leap and even flip flop. Elizabeth was a woman without competition. Why had he not seen the truth? He no longer cared if she had name, connections, fortune, or skill. Her family was a part of her, now he understood. If he loved her, then he would not despise anything about her and that included an inattentive father, a ridiculous mother, or the most silliest girls of all England. If he could not overlook their faults, then he did not deserve her, he was not worthy. His own family disgraced him, but she never uttered a negative opinion about his officious aunt, Lady Catherine deBough. She did not use this disgraceful family connection as a reason to decline his offer. What an obnoxious fool he had been.

When the conversations began to return to their normal flow, Elizabeth whispered to Rawlings, "Sir, Mr. Wickham has gone there, yes, but I believe it would be best to speak of this at another time."

"You are wise, Miss Elizabeth. I meant no offense to anyone." He pointed his gaze at Georgiana. "You handled her situation with magnificent grace. Thank you."

Soon, the time had arrived for the separation of the sexes. However, in an unusually short time, the men joined them. Elizabeth and Georgiana stood at the pianoforte searching through the sheet music. Miss Kent and Lady Victoria had continued the game of backgammon begun the night before. Victoria was winning, much to the surprise of Sarah since not even her brother had defeated her since she had turned twenty. Mrs. Gardiner and Mrs. Annesley were deep in conversation; they discovered they had several mutual friends in London.

Elizabeth was true to her word to Georgiana, playing and singing to everyone's appreciation. Blake and Darcy rose at the end of it, along with Mrs. Gardiner, and excused themselves as they escorted Elizabeth to the library. The remaining guests had a little inkling of what was about to transpire, but no one dared to broach the subject openly.

"Thank you for agreeing, Miss Elizabeth." Darcy's words caught in his throat. "Mr. Blake would like a word. I will be over there looking for a book."

"On gas lighting, sir?" Elizabeth raised her brow, and with a chuckle added in a half-whisper, "I hope you find it this time."

He twisted his ring in circles while he watched Blake lead her to the chair closest to the fire. Darcy led Mrs. Gardiner over to the bookshelves where no words reached his ears.

***

Blake looked directly into her eyes. "Miss Elizabeth. I must apologize, but I do not know where to begin."

"No. I am the one who should begin. I must ask for forgiveness for the actions of my mother. I know you will not understand, but she was trying to keep me from harm."

"I do understand. But I must apologize. Darcy admitted how your mother heard him speak of the rumors my finances on that balcony that night. She did not hear of my independent wealth from my mother, or my own estate and townhouse in London. She only heard the rumors of financial ruin; she left after Darcy had spoken."

Elizabeth sat still as she calculated this new piece of information.

"I should have sought you out. I should have heard the words from your own lips, not rely solely on your mother's reply. I was a fool. I believed her, when in my heart I knew it to be different."

"It is true; I did not conceal my interest. I have wondered what you must have thought of me after my mother told you I had gone to London."

"I admit, I was not charitable towards you at first. The thought swirling in my head was how I had planned to defy my father and follow my heart. He would not have been pleased. He wanted someone with fortune and connections. I knew he would unleash his anger on me, but his wishes were not mine. When I heard you had gone away to avoid me, I was angry."

"The crushed knight."

"Yes, and now I can only regret leaving it behind. But Miss Elizabeth, my anger was only in the beginning. I felt abandoned, and then I began to blame myself. I searched my mind, trying to pinpoint what I had done. I had expected a different response."

"Why did you not search for me?"

"I did not know where you went. Your mother did not say. But once I discovered your uncle's home, I did spy on it. I had followed Miss Bennet there one day. She was leaving Mr. Bingley's house when I arrived. I had hoped—"

Elizabeth leaned forward and tapped Blake's arm. "You knew my sister visited with Miss Bingley? Did you mention this to her brother? Did he know? Please, this is most important."

Blake shrugged. "I assumed he did. He was home when I returned that day. I do not recall any conversation about your sister visiting.

"Oh." Elizabeth sighed. "Did you say you watched for me outside my uncle's house?"

Blake nodded. "For days I waited, but without any indication you were visiting, I assumed you had gone to another relative."

"Why did you not come in? My aunt and uncle knew where I was."

"I have never been introduced to your relatives in London. I felt uncomfortable with an uninvited visit when your mother had said you wished to avoid me."

"But my sister was there. You are acquainted with her. Did you not speak to her? She would have known where I was."

Blake shook his head. "No. I believed you did not wish to see me. My only hope was if I could catch you on a walk. We could have talked. I wished to spare you any embarrassment in front of your family."

"What is it you wish to have said, because I am at a loss to understand what you wished to say to me that could not have been said in my uncle's home?"

"I wanted to know why you ran away to London. You mother said you wanted to avoid me."

"I did not run away. I was in Longbourn the day you came."

Blake grabbed the arms of the chair so tightly his knuckles turned white. "Darcy suggested as much; however, I believed your mother." His tone grew harsh when he added, "She will never be invited to my home, please understand I can never forgive her deceit."

"Oh? Why would she visit?"

"I get ahead of myself. Please forgive me."

Elizabeth nodded her head. "You said you got ahead of yourself? What else do you want to say?"

"The day after the ball, I wanted to ask you to be my wife. Even now, I still want you to marry me. I have never been able to forget you, your eyes, your scent, your hands, and your elegant manner. Tonight, I offer you marriage. Please accept. I cannot offer you wealth as others can, but I do have an estate and fortune of my own. I am not penniless and can take great care of you. I will inherit the dukedom, and there is no one else I wish to be my duchess. I have loved you since our first dance at the assembly hall, and I will love you when we can dance no more. I am sorry. I have not been as eloquent as I had wished, as I have practiced."

Elizabeth placed her hands in her lap and sat as straight as possible. "As your wife, Lord Blake, what would be expected of me?"

He smiled. "Other than filling my life with happiness? I assume the normal expectations. Providing an heir is important. And you would be required to manage the home." Blake's smile stretched across his face. He patted her hand. "I have no doubt you could handle any problem which might surface."

"Problem? Do you speak of dealing with matters such as a young maid with child? I am aware of a situation of that nature happening elsewhere. What do you think would be the best action to take?

"Why, dismissal. Do you not agree?"

"She is without family and would have nowhere to go."

'Miss Elizabeth, a servant's life is of little concern of yours. If you find it difficult to dismiss a maid for that, or any reason, I have an excellent housekeeper who could handle everything. I would not want you to be distressed by the intricate decisions of running a household, especially those of unseemly matters." Blake leaned forward and patted her hand again. "I would do anything to shield you from a difficult situation. I only want happiness in your life. I would never allow you to come to harm or be made uncomfortable in any way."

***

Darcy's quick glance caught Miss Elizabeth with her brow raised, and if not for the slightest smile, her expression was of a serious manner. He suddenly felt the grayness of the room take hold in his heart. The conversation appeared to turning more intimate between the two, with Blake patting her hand. Darcy slid into the chair and thought about his life. So many mistakes. I could not compete with Blake. I came too late. Not aware of how long he sat in contemplation, Darcy had not noticed the quietness surrounding him until Elizabeth caught his attention by coughing.

"Miss Elizabeth." Darcy jumped up and quickly searched the room. "Where is Lord Blake?"

"He has retired for the evening. I have stayed behind to speak to you."

"Please, be seated." Darcy pointed to the chair. When he could not find Mrs. Gardiner, Elizabeth advised him her aunt had mentioned a chill and removed herself to sit in the chair closer to the fire. He took his seat, but his hands trembled as he clasped them together.

"Mr. Darcy, I want to thank you for allowing Lord Blake the opportunity to explain what happened that day. I..."

Darcy did not move. He rubbed his hands and held his breath.

"I never understood why he left without taking his leave, and had it not been for your letter, I do not know how I..."

When she looked down at the floor, he caressed her hand. "Say no more. Please. I am pleased for you that the misunderstanding has been resolved." With the softest of voices he asked, "Is there anything you wish to ask me? I will tell you anything you want to know, and I will speak honestly."

"I have one concern, Mr. Darcy. If you would be so kind to explain to me why you allowed my mother's head to be filled with rumors about Lord Blake. Did you really believe them, or did you have another purpose for such a breach of conduct? I do not understand your purpose, because at that time, you had not shown any interested in me."

"I am ashamed to admit the truth. I had convinced myself that my friend was not going to offer marriage, just a..." Darcy looked down at his boots and then added quietly, "a flirtation. I did not wish to see you put in an awkward situation. But I lied to myself and deep down I knew it." Darcy looked down at his hands as he willed them to hold still. When he lifted his head, he caught sight of her surprise. "I wanted to believe it to be that way, because I did not want him to have you. I wanted you even then. I loved you."

"Even though you did not seek me out?"

"I struggled against connecting myself, and for no excuse other than prejudice and false pride."

Elizabeth whispered, "In vain I have struggled." When he cringed, she touched his arm. "I remember you did tell me. But I did not realize you felt this way even then. What set you off in the first place? When did it begin?"

"I cannot fix on the hour, or the spot, or the look, or the words, which laid the foundation. It is too long ago. I was in the middle before I knew that I *had* begun. By then Lord Blake had revealed his preference for you. I felt much like a drowning man, and I searched for a rope or raft, but all I could do was pretend to be your protector. I fabricated in my mind, that he would not offer you marriage, so I tried to warn you, nay, to keep you from him. I invented a reason to come between you and him." Darcy's last words caught in his throat. "I manipulated the conversation on the balcony with your mother listening." Darcy breathed deeply several times. "I beg your forgiveness for such an officious act."

The only sounds heard in the room were the breathing of the two.

"Mr. Darcy, why were you so silent when I arrived today. I had hoped you would engage in a little conversation.

"Because you were grave and silent, and gave me no encouragement."

"But I was embarrassed and confused."

"And so was I."

"You might have talked to me more at dinner."

"A man who had felt less, might."

"A very reasonable response." Elizabeth chuckled. They sat quietly as she composed her next question.

"Now be sincere; did you admire me for my impertinence"

"For the liveliness of your mind, I did."

"I recall the veracity of the words I spoke in ... I assure you that I have long been most heartily ashamed of my manner for the rejection of your offer."

"No, Miss Elizabeth. I have been a selfish creature all my life and did not see the error of my ways until you opened my eyes in Kent. The lesson was hard, but one I had to address."

"Is that why you invited Lord Blake?"

"Once I faced the truth about what I had done, I could not allow the misunderstanding between you and Blake to continue. I seek only your happiness regardless of how it may hurt my own desires. You must not live a life of regret, duty, or obligation." He whispered her name.

"Thank you, Mr. Darcy." Elizabeth raised her head. She offered what he thought was a weak smile.

He watched her chest rise and fall with her breath. Her neckline was at an appropriate height. "I will escort you back to the others." He offered his arm when she did not speak again. They walked silently to the music room where music from Georgiana's pianoforte filled the air. Darcy found a chair apart from the others and spent the evening trying to swallow the lump in his throat as he recalled every word she said.

***

The sun had barely risen when Darcy entered the dining room. Elizabeth sat at the table in front of a now empty plate, and was the lone diner for breakfast, spreading a fruit jam on her toast. "Good Morning."

"Good Morning, Mr. Darcy."

"I expected to see Blake."

"He finished breakfast early and has taken a morning ride." Elizabeth watched while Darcy filled his plate with eggs, ham, and toast. He chose to sit in the chair across from her.

"Mr. Darcy, I want to thank you again for the opportunity to speak to Lord Blake. But I also would like to have a word with you in the garden if—"

Rawlings rushed into the room. "Darcy, a carriage is approaching and it sounds like it is in a hurry!"

At once, Darcy pushed the plate of food away, rose, and moved to the window. "It looks like… yes, I am sure of it …Oh God."

Chapter Twenty-five

"Who is it?" Rawlings asked.

Darcy strained to make out the family crest on the swift moving carriage. "It is Lord Charnwood."

"Lord Charnwood?"

"I beg your pardon. He is Lord Blake's father. Please, Miss Elizabeth, remain here." Darcy signaled to Rawlings to locate Blake while he left to greet the Duke.

He reached the front door as Lord Charnwood stepped out of the carriage. He was of average height with a slim build, and a hint of his fair hair was still evident, although gray locks covered his head. His blue eyes might have been sky blue, had it not been for the anger turning them jet black. His clothes were disheveled but not unduly for a man who had charged forward all night. His boots, however, were dull and scuffed, and one might assume they were merely his favorite pair. When he leaned down to brush his trousers, Darcy spotted the tip of a flask bulging out of his coat. He approached Blake's father, then bowed respectfully. His gaze drifted towards the stable, but retuned to the Duke when he did not see Blake anywhere.

"Where is *she?*" Lord Charnwood said, in a tone that defied challenge.

"She?"

"Miss Bennet. Miss Elizabeth Bennet. "

"Your Grace, I have sent someone to locate your son. He is riding this morning. Perhaps you would like to wait for him in the drawing room."

"He is here? I should have assumed as much. Well, I am not a man to be kept waiting. Young man, I asked and I demand an answer now, where is *she?*"

"Lord Charnwood, I am Miss Bennet." Elizabeth moved swiftly, but not hurriedly.

Darcy motioned for her to stand beside him, and then pointed to the house with his hand. "Lord Charnwood, please, this way. Let us go inside, and I shall order refreshments. You must be tired after the journey." When the man did not move, Darcy glared at him. "If you prefer, you can wait for your son in my study."

Lord Charnwood glared at Elizabeth. "I must have a few words with you. Is there somewhere we can talk... privately?"

Darcy moved between the duke and Elizabeth. "Sir. I cannot allow Miss Bennet to go. Now, if you would be so kind to follow me inside, Blake should be here shortly. You should speak to him first." Darcy turned to Elizabeth. "Your uncle, I believe, is in the library."

"Mr. Darcy, I would like to speak to His Grace."

The Duke held his arm to her. "Very well, young lady, and since Mr. Darcy will not secure us a private space inside, I suggest we take a walk to the garden."

She nodded as she took his arm. Darcy would not be deterred and followed closely behind.

Charnwood looked back with his blackest glare. "Mr. Darcy, this conversation does not concern you."

Darcy threw his shoulders back, raised his chin. "All conversations in my home concern me, sir, when a guest of mine is imposed upon in such an unexpected manner." Darcy rose to his full height, which was at least four inches taller than the Duke's. "I will remain by *her* side."

"As you wish." The duke shrugged. "But I will have my say."

"He is superbly skilled as a protector, your Grace." Elizabeth glanced over her shoulder and presented Darcy with a raised brow and a slightly upturned mouth.

Darcy nodded, unsure if she offered him a compliment or a tease.

They proceeded in silence along the gravel walk leading to the garden. Elizabeth made no effort at conversation with the man who was now giving off the appearance of a more than usually insolent and disagreeable guest. As soon as they arrived, Lord Charnwood and Elizabeth separated.

"You can be at no loss, Miss Bennet, to understand the reason of my request to speak to you. Your own heart, your own conscience, must tell you why I come."

Darcy grew concerned. He recalled Blake's story on how his father had treated Lady Beatrice. He glanced at Elizabeth and while she did not seem intimidated. She viewed him with a curious expression.

"Indeed, you are mistaken, sir. I have not been at all able to account for the honor."

"Miss Bennet, you ought to know, that I am not to be trifled with. But however insincere you may choose to be, you shall not find *me* so.

My character has ever been celebrated for its sincerity and frankness, and in a cause of such moment as this, I shall certainly not depart from it."

Elizabeth did not move and choose to remain silent. Darcy moved closer to her but never diverted his gaze away from the duke while he stomped around them.

"A report of a most alarming nature reached me many days ago. I was told that you, Miss Elizabeth Bennet, would, in all likelihood, be soon united to my son, my own son, the heir to a dukedom, Lord Blake. Though I know it must be a scandalous falsehood, though I would not injure him so much as to suppose the truth of it possible, I instantly resolved on setting off for this place, that I might make my sentiments known to you. I have had to expend innumerable effort to locate you. I have come here directly from Hertfordshire."

"If you believed it impossible to be true, I wonder you took the trouble of coming so far. What could Your Grace propose by it?" Elizabeth felt the heat rising in her face.

Darcy moved a step closer until he could feel her arm touching his. He moved only to keep his body slightly in between the two.

Charnwood glare at Elizabeth. "At once to insist upon having such a report universally contradicted."

"Your coming will be rather a confirmation of it; if, indeed, such a report is in existence."

The Duke huffed. "If? Do you then pretend to be ignorant of it? Has it not been industriously circulated by yourselves? Do you not know that such a report is spread these past few months?"

"I never heard that it was." She tapped Darcy's arm when he had opened his mouth to respond. She caught his attention, shook her head and then bestowed a smile upon him, one that he vaguely remembered seeing from somewhere.

"Miss Bennet! And can you likewise declare that there is no foundation for it?"

"I do not pretend to possess equal frankness with Your Grace. You may ask questions which I shall not choose to answer."

"This is not to be borne. Miss Bennet, I insist on being satisfied. Has he, has my son, made you an offer of marriage?" Lord Charnwood moved closer to her.

Darcy stepped in front of Elizabeth and glowered down at the duke until satisfied his message was received. He watched as Blake's father move backwards.

Elizabeth's right brow rose. "Your Grace has declared it to be impossible."

"It ought to be so; it must be so, while he retains the use of his reason. You have no fortune and no connections. But your arts and allurements may, in a moment of infatuation, have made him forget what he owes to himself and to all his family. You may have drawn him in."

"If I have, I shall be the last person to confess it."

"Your Grace! You have gone too far," Darcy bellowed. "I insist you refrain from making such slanderous attacks. Come Miss Bennet. We will find your uncle." He held out his arm.

Elizabeth shook her head. "Mr. Darcy, please allow us to finish. His Grace's words are of no importance to me."

A red-faced Lord Charnwood sputtered. "Miss Bennet, do you know who I am? I have not been accustomed to such language as this. I am his nearest relation, and am entitled to know all his concerns."

"But you are not entitled to know mine; nor will such behavior as this, ever induce me to be explicit."

"Let me be rightly understood. This match, to which you have the presumption to aspire, can never take place. No, never. You are not worthy of the title of duchess, nor is the connection available. My son is engaged to another. Now what do you have to say?"

"Only this; that if he is so, you can have no reason to suppose he made an offer to me. I suspect the choice was yours and not his."

"The arrangement has just been settled. The family has signed the papers as have I. She is of noble blood, and I will demand he carry out his duty and obligations, which fall upon his shoulders as my heir."

"By your own admission, Lord Blake is neither by honor nor inclination confined to this person, why can he not make another choice? And if I or another lady is his choice, why should anyone not accept him?"

"Because honor, decorum, prudence, nay, interest, forbid it. Yes, Miss Bennet, interest; for if I do not approve, then you should not expect to be noticed by his family or friends, if you willfully act against the inclinations of all. You will be censured, slighted, and despised, by every one connected with him. Your alliance will be a disgrace; your name will never even be mentioned by any of us."

"These are heavy misfortunes," replied Elizabeth. "But any wife of Lord Blake must have such extraordinary sources of happiness necessarily attached to her situation that she could, upon the whole, have no cause to repine."

"Obstinate, headstrong girl! I am ashamed of you! Do you know your station in life? You are to understand, Miss Bennet, that I came here with the determined resolution of carrying my purpose; nor will I be dissuaded from it. I have not been used to submit to any person's whims. I have not been in the habit of brooking disappointment."

"Your Grace!" Darcy shouted, moving towards the man until he took two steps backwards.

Lizzy touched Darcy's arm again. She glanced around and noticed Georgiana, Kent, and Lady Victoria had arrived in the garden. "That will make Your Grace's situation at present more pitiable; but it will have no effect on me ."

"Miss Bennet, hear what I have to say. I will not be interrupted."

Darcy laughed, catching them off guard.

Lord Charnwood held up his hand. "Hear me in silence. My son is destined for someone who can provide a splendid fortune and name. I have completed the negotiations with…"

Darcy and Elizabeth waited.

"Why, with your uncle, Mr. Darcy. I have made arrangements for my son to marry Lady Victoria Fitzwilliam."

Elizabeth and Darcy's mouths dropped open And heard the others gasping. Kent moved quickly to stand beside Victoria, who had a stunned expression on her face. She covered her mouth as she stared at the Duke.

Lord Charnwood stepped around Darcy and glared at Elizabeth. "So, you see, the upstart pretensions of a young woman without family, connections, or fortune such as yourself will not win the day. If you were sensible of your own good, you would not wish to quit the sphere in which you have been brought up. My son is a peer, and you are but a lowly daughter of a poor country gentleman. And who is your mother? Who are your uncles and aunts? Do not imagine me ignorant of their condition."

"Whatever my connections may be, if your son does not object to them, they can be nothing to *you*."

"Tell me once for all, are you engaged to him?"

When he heard Darcy quick intake of breath, Rawlings appeared and grabbed his shoulded as he whispered, "Steady yourself, my friend."

Though Elizabeth would not, for the mere purpose of obliging Lord Charnwood, have answered this question, she could not but say, after a moment's deliberation, "I am not."

The duke seemed pleased. "And will you promise me, never to enter into such an engagement?"

"Father! What are you doing here?" Blake sped towards Elizabeth. He stood between her and his father. "Darcy, would you be so kind to escort Miss Bennet into the house. Miss Bennet, Lady Victoria, Miss Darcy, Kent, Rawlings, please, I would like to speak to my father alone."

Elizabeth nodded and took Darcy's arm, and the others followed behind. When Elizabeth glanced up at him, Darcy noticed the sparkle in her eye. The duke had not intimidated her. A smile spread across his face; her matching smile lifted his spirits. They searched each other's faces for a full minute, ignoring the father and son arguing. They were barely in the house when they heard loud shouts from the garden.

The duke sent a parting glare to his son and shouted so loud everyone heard, "We are not finished, Robert. You will do as I say." He stormed towards the driveway. Blake stood, unable to move, while he watched his father disappear around the corner.

At the door, a hurrying Mrs. Reynolds nearly bumped into the couple, holding several messages in her hand. "Sir, these urgent letters have arrived for Miss Bennet.

Elizabeth accepted the letters and studied the envelopes. "These are from my sister, Jane. I…"

"We are close to the library. Would you like to go there and read them?"

"Yes. Thank you. I have been wondering why I had not received any news from her. She wrote the address very ill."

While he led her to the library, the others left for the music room as Georgiana suggested. Darcy closed the door, giving Elizabeth privacy. He waited patiently outside, and when Blake arrived, they heard sobs coming from within. They burst in the library and rushed to her side.

"Would you like to sit down? Please! You are not well." Darcy said.

Blake rushed ahead and held the back of a chair near the window. "Please, Miss Bennet. Rest here."

"No. I am well." Still she plopped into the chair while she tore open the other letter. Blake and Darcy moved their chairs closer to her.

Her sobs grew louder as she sped through the next letter. Darcy gently took hold of her hand. "Good God! What is the matter?" When her tears rolled down her cheeks, he gave her hand a slight squeeze. "Shall we find your Aunt and Uncle? Let me help you, Miss Elizabeth." He stopped himself from pulling her to his chest. Every inch of his body ached to hold her, comfort her, and offer her solace; it was a Herculean effort not to do so.He rang for a servant. "Find Mr. and Mrs. Gardiner immediately, and bring them here. Make haste."

Elizabeth lifted her teary eyes at Darcy when he handed her his handkerchief. "Yes, I must speak to Mr. Gardiner this moment, on business that cannot be delayed; I have not a second to lose." She rose to leave.

Blake leaned in.. "What can I do? Just say the word and it shall be done. Anything."

It was impossible for Darcy or Blake to leave her side. She appeared sorrowfully despondent.

Blake turned to Darcy. "What happened? What did my father say to her to upset her so?"

"It was not your father causing her distress." After using his gaze to direct Blake's attention to the letters in Elizabeth's lap, Darcy refocused his attention on the sobbing woman. "Let me call your maid. Is there nothing you could take, to give you present relief?—A glass of wine; shall I get you one? You are very ill."

Elizabeth shook her head and attempting to recover herself, said, "No, I thank you; there is nothing the matter with me. I am quite well. I am only distressed by dreadful news which I have just received from Longbourn."

She burst into tears as she alluded to it, and for a few minutes she could not speak another word. Darcy and Blake watched in wretched suspense and in compassionate silence. At length, she spoke again. "I have just had a letter from Jane, with such dreadful news. It cannot be concealed from any one. My youngest sister has left all her friends, has eloped, and has thrown herself into the power of... of Mr. Wickham. They are gone off together from Brighton. You know him too well to doubt the rest. She has no money, no connections, nothing that can tempt him to—she is lost for ever."

Darcy's attention was fixed in astonishment on the trembling woman before him. While Elizabeth continued to cry and dab her eyes with his handkerchief, he threw the back of his hand across his mouth and squeezed his other hand into a fist. He fought the urge to wrap his arms around her, lift her chin, and kiss her tears. He heard nothing but her words and her cries.

Blake leaned back into his chair, "Oh my." He pulled back and returned his hands to his sides. He jumped up and and stepped backwards, rubbing his forehead and then shook the thoughts away, his focus returning to the flustered woman, sobbing and wiping her tears with a wet and crimpled handkerchief. He looked down at his hand and realized that she had accepted Darcy's. His handkerchief was still in his own hand, dry and crisp.

When she spoke again, she used an agitated tone. "When I consider, that I might have prevented it—I, who knew what he was. Had I but explained a part of it only, some part of what I learned to my own family! Had his character been known, this could not have happened. But it is all too late now."

Darcy's body stiffened. "I am grieved, indeed, grieved, shocked. But is it certain, absolutely certain?"

"Oh yes! They left Brighton together on Sunday night, and were traced almost to London, but not beyond; they are certainly not gone to Scotland."

Blake moved his chair closer. "And what has been done, what has been attempted, to recover her?"

Elizabeth looked up at Blake with a dazed expression. "My father is gone to London, and Jane has written to beg my uncle's immediate assistance, and we shall be off, I hope, in half an hour."

"Yes, of course. We will not keep you here, but if there is anything at all that I... we can do..." Blake leaned forward in his chair and took her hand. "anything at all."

Nodding politely to Blake, she pulled her hand back and then turned back to Darcy. "But nothing can be done; I know that nothing can be done. How is such a man to be worked on? How are they even to be discovered? I have not the smallest hope. It is every way horrible!"

Darcy shook his head, thinking how it was his fault as well. Why did he not speak to Mr. Bennet?

"When my eyes were opened to his real character.—Oh! had I known what I ought, what I dared, to do! But I knew not—I was afraid of doing too much. Wretched, wretched, mistake!"

Darcy made no answer. He seemed scarcely to hear her. He walked up and down the room in earnest meditation, his brow furrowed, and his air gloomy. "Mrs. Younge, she will know where they are. I will her and make her give Wickham to me. Who can I trust to find Mrs. Younge? She must reside in the seedy section of London. He continued to create a plan for locating Georgiana's prior governess. His mind was reliving everything that happened one year earlier. He recalled a letter Mrs. Younge had sent him asking for monies due to her. It had an address. Yes, he would hurry back to London, find the letter, and seek her.

Blake glanced at the doorway. "Where is your uncle? Where is your aunt?"

Elizabeth turned away from Blake and towards Darcy; she quickly observed his demeanor and instantly understood it. Her power was sinking; everything must sink under such a proof of family weakness, such an assurance of the deepest disgrace. She should neither wonder nor condemn, but the belief of Mr. Darcy's self-conquest brought nothing consolatory to her bosom, afforded no reduction of her distress. It was, on the contrary, exactly calculated to make her understand her own wishes; and never had she so honestly felt that she could have loved him, as now, when all love must be vain.

Elizabeth's depth of feelings for Darcy was not lost on Blake. He rose from his chair, mumbling something about finding her relatives, and left the room.

Elizabeth wiped her tears. Lydia—the humiliation, the misery, she was bringing on them all—soon swallowed up every private care; and covering her face with his handkerchief, she was soon lost to everything else until she heard her aunt and uncle calling her name from the doorway.

Darcy, who, in a manner, which though it spoke compassion, spoke with restraint, said, "I am afraid you have long desired my absence, nor have I anything to plead in excuse of my stay, but real, though unavailing, concern. Would to heaven that anything could be either said or done on my part, that might offer consolation to such distress!—But I will not torment you with vain wishes, which may seem purposely to ask for your thanks."

"We will help her now, Darcy," Mr. Gardiner said as he and his wife moved closer to their niece.

Darcy again expressed his sorrow for her distress, wished it a happier conclusion than there was at present reason to hope, and, with only one serious parting look, went away.

As he quitted the room, Elizabeth felt how improbable it was that they should ever see each other again on such terms of cordiality. She threw a retrospective glance over the whole of their acquaintance, so full of contradictions and varieties, and sighed at the perverseness of those feelings, which would now have promoted its continuance, and would formerly have rejoiced in its termination.

In the hallway, Darcy directed the nearest servant to find Kent, whom he believed was in the music room with Victoria, Miss Kent, and Georgiana. The footman left to carry out his orders.

Within moments, Kent entered the study just as Darcy was handing several letters to his steward. "Darcy, did you wish to see me?"

"I need your advice."

"Mine? You usually seek out Rawlings."

"This involves him, and, besides, you have great insight, as I have learned."

Darcy paced back and forth in front of the window after Kent took his seat. When he finally stopped walking, he sighed. "What I have to say must be kept confidential, although I was not asked for secrecy."

After Kent nodded, Darcy released a long sigh before delving into the situation with Miss Lydia.

"Oh my God. You are correct. Rawlings will not be pleased. This scandal will not help any of us. Mr. Gardiner is our partner, and the Peregrine will have a good laugh at our attaching ourselves to this family. Tradesmen! I can hear them now. This cannot help us, Darcy."

"That is not my biggest concern. Our success will generate its own respect. Now, I need your advice. I plan on leaving for London and locating the scoundrel. I am the only one with any chance of finding him. I know all his old haunts and his old friends. I will start there."

"And the advice?"

"What do I tell Rawlings? And Bingley, should he be kept in the dark? I want to act in their best wishes, it is just I am not the best one to know what that is."

"And you think I do? Why do you ask me?"

"Your heart is the only one not tied to the Bennet family."

"Oh. Yes, I see."

Darcy poured him a cup of tea to match the one he fixed for himself. He asked for Kent's opinion.

"You have no choice. If this had happened to Lady Victoria, I would never forgive you for not telling me. You must bring Rawlings into this. He must be told regardless of how hurtful it will be."

"He has been hurt before. Oh, why, did that silly girl not see the true value in Rawlings? He would have cared for her like no other and would have slowly lowered her willful ways to where she would still have fun, but within reasonable limits. He would have been the best of men for her. I cannot tell him."

"You must. He would never forgive you."

"I know, I was merely dreading it." Darcy chuckled. "On the way to Pemberley, I even told him I would bring Miss Lydia here one day."

"Much like you brought Lady Victoria here for me?" When Darcy nodded, Kent sighed. "We are grown men and should be able to handle our own love affairs."

"You did not mention Blake. Should he not be told?"

"He is aware of the situation."

"You realize he cannot overlook his status. One day he will inherit his father's title. I do not believe he can ignore the damage first as done by Lord Charnwood's gambling, and now to overcome how this scandal would impact his name."

"And Miss Elizabeth must be shielded from the viciousness of the *Ton*. They will never accept her once this is known. The moment the word leaks out, the duke will begin spreading the gossip."

Kent shrugged. "I doubt she cares. She laughs at them."

"But her children would be hurt."

"By whom? This scandal will long be forgotten."

"His family will not overlook it."

"His family? Or yours, Darcy? Are we really talking about him?"

"No. You are correct. I lapsed back into my old self."

"A lifetime of prejudice is hard to overcome."

"That it is, but what you say is true. Blake has plans for his future and scandal will hurt him."

"Yes, I agree. But only he can make the decision. Did he and Miss Elizabeth come to an agreement last night?"

Darcy sighed. "So you know about last night?"

"I have great insight, as you said." Kent chuckled, but Darcy remained serious.

"Miss Elizabeth indicated they are not engaged, but I do not know if it is because she has not given her answer, or if Blake has not yet proposed."

"Oh. And, Bingley?" Kent sighed. "He is a different problem. The scandal does not affect him as much, and I know he would be willing to lie in front of a stampeding carriage to help Miss Bennet. But he should not do so if she does not return his feelings. Miss Bennet would undergo a sense of obligation, and he does not want her that way. He desires only her love, not her body."

"Ah, Bingley." Darcy's pace picked up.

Kent refilled his cup and handed it to him. "Miss Bennet's feelings are the key. Still in this case, I would tell him. He is able to handle things."

"I would first like to find out how she feels. Has Mr. Goulding won her affections? Mr. Gardiner was vague about his attentions to her at dinner last night. After this scandal, would he continue to pursue her? I just do not know. Perhaps Mrs. Gardiner could reveal it to me if I explain it in the right context. Wait. I am sure they have already left for London."

"I believe they have."

Darcy stopped pacing. "Damn!"

"What?"

"I have known since Easter that Miss Bennet favored him above others. I also concealed her visit to his townhouse to visit his sister this past winter."

"Oh? Why have you waited to tell him?"

"Bingley would be heartbroken a second time if she has since transferred her affections to another. Mr. Gardiner has not been forthcoming regardless of my attempts to learn the truth. I have waited to speak directly to Miss Elizabeth. She is the only one who will know the truth. If Miss Bennet still favors him, I will admit everything. If not, then I cannot hurt him just to satisfy my guilt. I cannot."

"I see." Kent sipped his drink. "He is a dilemma. But once the others know would it be possible to keep it from him?"

"No. I suppose not. If it was just him, I would wait."

"But now?"

"I will tell him." Darcy sighed. "I will tell all of them everything."

Kent patted Darcy on the back. "It will be well, my friend. It will be well."

Darcy first checked to determine if the Gardiners had left, and when he discovered they had, he then sent for Bingley, Rawlings, and Blake. He secured their promise for secrecy for what he would reveal must remain confidential. While he spoke and unfolded the situation with Elizabeth's youngest sister and Wickham, he studied their reactions. Bingley's jaw dropped, and he raised his brows to full height, a blank expression remained on Blake's face, but the third man's pupils turned black.

"Wickham. Wickham." Rawlings bellowed. "Blast that man. I tried to warn Mr. Bennet. He rebuffed everything I said. Why did you not warn him, Darcy?"

"What I am about to repeat is to go no further. Do I have your promise?" They agreed.

He recited from memory the words he had written to Miss Elizabeth. He explained his sister's intended elopement and the revenge Wickham sought. He also told them he never once suspected the rake would be interested in the Bennets once he had heard about their lack of dowries. He admitted his mistake. Darcy slumped into a chair. Kent poured all the men a drink.

Darcy continued. "I plan on leaving at first light. I will send word to a few well placed individuals to be on the lookout for Wickham and a few of his associates. I must return to London. I must locate an address for one particular associate." He stood. "If you wish to help, meet me in the morning. I will explain everything to my sister now, and then I am retiring for the rest of the day."

Blake remained silent, excused himself, and left for his chambers. Rawlings departed as well, his steps slow and plodding as he mumbled curses. Bingley remained, sitting quietly as he tapped the arm of the chair. "I will pack my things immediately. I will be heading out to Netherfield Park at first light."

"Do you recognize the significance in this elopement?" Darcy asked. "I have no doubt he will not marry her, which will reflect poorly on her sisters."

"Yes, of course, but I have no care along those lines. I am positive that today, Miss Bennet is burdened with her family, and with Miss Elizabeth away, there is no one to help her. Mr. Bennet would be in London and Mrs. Bennet would be hard to handle. And yes, I understand that with no funds, as Caroline rejoiced repeatedly about Miss Bennet's status, and now hampered with a scandalous sister; no one would be willing to take on the Bennet family. Miss Bennet would be relegated to spinsterhood or someone's companion or governess. I know that she never loved me, but I loved her. I must help her during this time. Perhaps if the neighborhood witnesses my friendship, the Bennets will not be shunned. I must do this for Miss Bennet's chances to marry in the future, otherwise no man would be willing to connect himself to her."

Darcy pointed to the chair, inviting Bingley to sit. "I need to reveal a deception on my part, but at the same time I am concerned that your hopes may be raised.

"Every man needs hope, Darcy."

He felt a shiver down his spine when he heard those words. "You are correct. I... I learned from Miss Elizabeth months ago that Miss Bennet did favor you. I had been wrong in my assumption."

"She did!" Bingley jumped up excited and then glowered at his friend. "Why did you not send me word? I do not understand. All these months you left me wondering!"

"I have more to admit. Miss Bennet called on your sister in town in January. We concealed her visit from you. We believed her family to be desperate."

"After you knew she cared for me?"

"No. She was in London in January."

"I understand why Caroline would do such a thing, but you—I do not understand at all." Bingley leaned back in his chair. His surprise was great at first, and then he squinted as he contemplated what he heard. "But why would Miss Elizabeth tell you?"

"Because she rejected my proposal of marriage and said separating you from her sister was one of the reasons for her refusal. She told me Miss Bennet happiness depended upon you, and that I was the one who ruined any chance you two had, leaving you both in misery of the acutest kind.

"You offered marriage? To Miss Elizabeth?" Bingley asked. "I thought you said the Bennets were beneath us! No, I cannot believe she loved me. My God. If she loved me, what must she think of me? I never returned. Why did I listen to you? All this time!"

"Miss Bennet is a beautiful woman that would please any man. I planned to tell you if Miss Elizabeth said her sister's feelings had remained unchanged. I did not wish to raise your hope if she had transferred her affections. I planned to confess, not to alleviate my guilt, but to give you a chance. But only if she still loved you. Now, however, with this situation, I could not ask her since they have left for Longbourn. I do apologize, Bingley. My interference was absurd and impertinent."

Darcy watched the range of emotions cross Bingley's face. From his own recent experiences, he recognized the angry glower and furrowed brow that turned into quizzical expression and finally to the down turned mouth of depression.

Bingley sighed and lowered his head. "She must despise me. She thinks I did not care for her and abandoned her for London society. How she must have suffered.

"I am sorry to give you such pain," Darcy said quietly.

"Me? My pain is of no consequence. Hers is all that is important." Bingley dropped his head in his hand. "In her eyes, I acted like a flirt, a cad. What she must have endured at my absence."

"She does need support. You said so yourself. She may still love you, Bingley. You said every man needs hope. Do you not wish to discover the truth?"

After contemplating the possibility for several minutes, Bingley lifted his head, and with a grin said, "Yes, I do. Today you have given me something I have not had for eight months. Yes, I will go. I will help her, and I will discover for myself if she still cares. There, I am resolved."

"No, you cannot. Not yet."

"Why?"

"If you went to her now she would surely accept you. You must consider what her life has become. Everyone in Meryton has learned of this scandal by this time. The Bennets will be shunned."

But that is the reason to go. I cannot bear to think of her that way."

"But you cannot force her hand either. First, we must right the situation. I am the one responsible and I must repair the mistake. I believe it is possible. Do not go to her until then. And we must never reveal how we interred and especially if we successfully gave them back their good standing. Never, Bingley. Do not make it impossible for her to say no if she does not love you. Is that not what you fought all this time?"

"I cannot bear to think of her in distress. I cannot."

"If you love her you must. You must, my friend. When you go to her, she must be able to choose you freely and she cannot do so if she must answer while a scandal surrounds her. Let her choice be true. She will never question her decision. When you see her again make sure she is not ashamed of her situation."

"I see you point, except I am not you and Miss Bennet is not her sister. Jane is a truthful and honest person and she needs me. I will go to her. I will not allow you or anything else to keep me from her this time. I will not let one more day of unhappiness rule her life."

Darcy opened his mouth but closed it again when he felt his friends black glare falling on him.

"I once claimed I was a man of action and you laughed at me, all of my friends did so. No more shall I allow anyone to think so little of me. I will rely upon my own opinion. These past six months with Uncle Watt has proven that I am a worthy man. I admit I have a much to learn before I am truly independent, but today will mark my change. I am going to Netherfield Park. I will offer my dear, sweet Jane my help. I will admit my failure in not trusting myself, trusting her. I will propose, but I will not accept an answer until this scandal is resolved. In doing so, she will have hope while we wait. Darcy, I am resolved."

Darcy moved to his friend and squeezed his shoulder. "You are the most worthy of men, Bingley."

Bingley slipped off to his bedchambers with a smile on his face and a lighter step to his walk.

***

The next morning found Darcy standing at the door, looking up at the stairs. Bingley was at his side prepared to leave for Netherfield. Kent was not present; he had agreed to remain at Pemberley since many other guests would be arriving over the next several days. He and his sister would assist Georgiana in her hostess duties. The Lunar Society Meeting would be held as scheduled.

Darcy waited for several minutes more before turning to leave.

"They have their reasons, my friend." Bingley said. "Do not think less of them."

"Yes, they do each have their own reasons, and I understand how Miss Lydia's actions have affected them. Rawlings is hurt and Blake believes, as a member of nobility, he cannot overcome this scandal. I do not hold it against either man, but I must do something. I am the only one that knows the rake well enough to save the silly girl. I had only hoped to offer her a different…"

"Choice? No, Darcy." Rawlings called out. "Do not offer me up. I will find the right woman for me. I have done as you do—I mulled this over and over. Sometime in the early morning, I arrived at a conclusion. I was using the delightfully pert Miss Lydia as more of a stab at the members of the *Ton*. It would have been wonderful to thrust a silly girl their way. But that was selfish. I was selfish. I never thought about her."

"Why are you here?"

"I will help, but I will not be the solution. Agreed?"

"Agreed. But we must leave now."

When the two opened the door to the front steps, they gasped in surprise. Blake stood next to Hercules, saddled and ready to go.

"You slept in this morning. I have been ready for hours."

"Miss Elizabeth will be worthy of her title. I will fix this for you, Blake, and then you may wed."

"Do not be so downbeat, Darcy. I suspect Elizabeth had made her decision. She had asked I meet her in the garden before she received the letter. I suspect she was going to decline my proposal. Elizabeth loves you. I saw it in the way she sought you out when she spoke of her problems. She watched your every move, and they sparkled whenever she caught hold of yours. When she looked at me it was, well, rather dull and boring. You have won her heart and mind. In fact, I believe she loved you all along. She reacted passionately to you as a woman would. With me, she was a young girl reacting to pretty words. So you see, she has chosen you!"

"Then why are coming with me?"

"I will help drive away the scandal because I love her. I do not wish to she her hurt or cry ever again. But understand this, Darcy, we are not now friends."

A lump formed in both men's throats. They bowed to each other before Blake mounted his Andalusian.

"So, Darcy, what part of town will you drag me to this time? Can you not find better friends?"

Darcy entered his carriage and the men left for London. Once seated, he retrieved the poem, *The Vine and the Oak,* he had started many times, but had not finished. This morning he searched for an answer.

> But now the boding clouds arise
> And scowling darkness veils the skies;
> Harsh thunders roar -- red lightnings gleam,
> And rushing torrents close the scene.

He braced himself while the carriage sped down the road. "I will right this wrong, my dearest, loveliest Elizabeth."

Epilogue

It did not take long for Darcy to find Wickham and arrange the marriage. Afterwards, Bingley sent word about his engagement. Darcy needed nothing else to convince him of Elizabeth's true feelings. Blake's acknowledgement had been enough. He moved quickly this time propelled by the whispery winds of hope and courted the woman he loved, had loved, and would love until the end of his days.

***

"Finally, we are alone!" Darcy nuzzled Elizabeth's neck while he pulled the blanket tighter around them. The carriage lurched forward. "Mrs. Darcy, my beautiful bride, are you comfortable? We have many miles to travel."

"Four and twenty miles of good road, sir. I call it a very easy distance." Elizabeth raised her brow, and her smirk did not widen until Darcy laughed.

"Indeed. Less than half a day's journey. Oh, Elizabeth. I was such a fool in Kent. Why did you change your mind about me? I never believed you would ever accept my attentions."

"I assure you, ever since I read your letter; I have long been most heartily ashamed of what I said."

"Did it... did it soon make you think better of me? Did you, on reading it, give any credit to its contents?"

"Yes, it was the beginning of removing all my prejudices."

Darcy clasped her hand and drew it to his mouth. He placed several gentle kisses on it, before gazing into her eyes, unable to conceal the sadness he felt. "I knew that what I wrote must give you pain, but it was necessary. I hope you have destroyed the letter. There were several parts, especially the one about Mr. Gardiner, which I should dread you having the power of reading again. I can remember several expressions which might justly make you hate me."

"The letter shall certainly be burned, if you believe it essential to the preservation of my regard; but, though we have both reason to think my opinions not entirely unalterable, they are not, I hope, quite so easily changed as that implies."

He pulled her hand to his chest, pressing it against his pounding heartbeat. He willed her touch to still his heart. "When I wrote that letter, I believed myself perfectly calm and cool, but I am since convinced that it was written in a dreadful bitterness of spirit."

She caressed his cheek with the gentlest of touches. "The letter, perhaps, began in bitterness, but it did not end so. The adieu was charity itself. But think no more of the letter. The feelings of the person who wrote, and the person who received it, are now so widely different from what they were then, that every unpleasant circumstance attending it ought to be forgotten. You must learn some of my philosophy. Think only of the past as its remembrance gives you pleasure."

"I cannot give you credit for any philosophy of the kind. Your retrospections must be so totally void of reproach, which the contentment arising from them is not of philosophy, but of innocence. But with me, it is not so. Painful recollections will intrude which cannot, which ought not, to be repelled."

Elizabeth sighed. "My manners must have been in fault, but not intentionally, I assure you. I never meant to deceive you, but my spirits might often lead me wrong. How you must have hated me after that evening?"

"Hate you! I was angry perhaps at first, but my anger soon began to take a proper direction. And even now, I catch a glimpse of a pair of sparkling blue eyes—"

Elizabeth pulled away. "Blue eyes! Mine are brown!"

"Not yours, my dear wife, but your sister Jane's. And yours are brown with flecks of gold and green that either sparkle in happiness or flicker in anger. I have been the recipient of both reactions." He softly massaged her temples with his fingers and when she closed her eyelids, he placed a soft kiss on each one. "Your eyes are always in my mind. I know every fleck, every nuance, every sparkle, and every tear."

"I am pleased you know mine so well, but why would you think of Jane's?"

"Let me tell you a story about a trial of a most arrogant man." Darcy described his catharsis and detailed not only the dream he called *Acceptance* but all the actions he took to improve himself.

When he finished, Elizabeth leaned in, kissed his cheek, and gently rubbed the small scar on his chin. "He was wrong to hit you. I had wondered that day if he had done this to you. His hand was bruised. He should not have done this."

He shook his head. "I deserved it. I kept him from making you his wife." Darcy hung his head. "I am the worst of all the prideful men."

Elizabeth placed her soft lips on the nick on his chin. "I love you. Indeed, you have no improper pride. You are perfectly amiable. You do not know how good you really are; pray do not pain me by speaking of yourself in such terms."

Darcy pulled her close, wrapping his arm around her shoulders. He kissed her head. "Elizabeth, I cannot believe you are here with me. Me! I do not deserve you, my dearest, loveliest owner of my heart." He felt her shiver when he tasted her neck with his lips and then nibbled her ear. Finally, he whispered, "You have made me the happiest of men. I love you with all of my body, my soul, my very being." His lips met hers and as the kiss deepened, he felt her pressing herself into him. Pulling back slightly, he whispered, "But why did you choose me? I believed your heart belonged to him."

"Lord Blake is a good sort of man. He is charming and has a pleasant way with words. But…" She turned her head away and watched the snow falling in tiny flakes outside the window. Elizabeth pulled the blanked tighter when she heard the wind howl.

Darcy gently turned her chin towards him until their gazes locked. He pleaded with her to continue.

"But, there was something lacking. It is hard to explain, but he is everything proper and he was always most pleasant. I think I enjoyed his attentions. It was most flattering a marquess pursued me. I liked him very much, and at one time, I even thought about what life would be like as a duchess. But then he left, and yet I only felt anger at my mother; I did not cry for him."

Darcy whispered in her ear. "My dearest, that may explain why you did not choose him, but why did you choose me?"

"Oh, my choice was easily made once…"

When she did not continue, Darcy pulled her face closer to his until their lips met again. "Do not tell me it was because of your youngest sister. I never wished you to feel obligated—"

"No! I fear to tell you the truth." She gazed at him and recognized his fear. She caressed his cheek with her fingers until he caught hold of her hand and brought it to his lips.

"Please, do not fear me."

"After reading your letter and after Uncle Gardiner's suggestion as to who was behind the return of our dowries—"

Darcy straightened up. "I beg your pardon for interrupting, but your uncle should not have discussed this. And my dearest wife, I was not the only one working to right the wrong done to your father. Blake pressured his uncle, Lord Harrowby, to issue the Parliamentary patent under the new gas light company name. Without his help, it could not have been so easily fixed. I do not deserve the credit."

"You are an honorable man, William, to champion Lord Blake in this way. What you say may be true, but you are the one that helped Mr. Murdoch begin again, and that was just as important."

Darcy sighed. "I do not believe you have told me yet why you choose me. Do not be anxious about telling me the truth, Elizabeth."

"By the time I attended tea with your sister, my eyes had been opened to your true nature, and I had begun to look upon you in a different light. I discovered exactly how foolish all my opinions had been when, by accident, I overheard several things your servants said you had done."

Darcy jerked his head up. "What! Mrs. Geoffries must be made aware of this. Servants should not gossip, and I will not tolerate it."

"William. This is why I did not wish to tell you. Everyone shares stories."

Darcy caressed her cheek, skimming his fingers up and down along her jawline. "Do not fret. This breach was to my advantage. I will do nothing more than to remind Mrs. Geoffries gossiping is not allowed." His fingers stopped, and he leaned closer until their faces were close enough for their foreheads to converge. He inhaled the lavender scent enveloping the space between them. "Now what did they say? You have left me curious."

"They spoke of your generosity to a maid when you found her a place for her confinement. At that moment, I knew I had misjudged you in every way. Yes, my love, you showed much of your true character when you included my uncle in your business. Your efforts to reclaim our dowries, assisting Lydia, and even by your confession to Bingley helped change my opinion, but it was the maid's plight that turned me completely to your favor." She nestled back into the velvety seat cushion and then laughed. She bolted upright.

"What?"

"I remember a tray of treats sent to Jane's room when I rudely left you sitting alone at breakfast at Netherfield one morning. I just now realized you sent them. See, my love. How can I not love a man who sends me sweet treats after being ill-treated by my own prejudice? I did misunderstand you and did so willingly. I was just as you said."

He smiled; a twinkle appeared. "Is it my vanity or pride you love more?" His lips met hers before she could answer. "I am vain. I want you to think of me as handsome, witty, and charming, damn charming."

"I have always thought you were handsome. I recently discovered the witty and as to charming...you are the most beguiling of men." She snuggled next to him, and when she patted his jacket, she heard the crinkle of paper. "What is this?"

He pulled out two papers. When he opened the first sheet, she gasped when she recognized her signature.

"The pen! Oh, I cherish the metal tip, and to think you sent it to me so soon after I abused you so abominably to your face." She lowered her head. "I felt ashamed."

"Do not. I deserved every word, every glare, everything."

"We will not quarrel for the greater share of blame annexed to that event. The conduct of neither, if strictly examined, will be irreproachable; but since then, we have both, I hope, improved in civility."

"Such as this?" Darcy kissed her hand. "Or this?" He leaned in and kissed her neck. "Or is this the definition of civility?" He placed his lips upon hers, pressing them against her mouth, tasting her lips. If he could have fused her body to his, he would be a contented man.

Breaking the kiss, Elizabeth gazed at him. "You are the best of men, and when considering your fundamental character, you own no faults. Especially your... civility!"

When she held her mouth for another kiss, he placed his lips upon hers, gently at first. As she leaned in and her lips parted, he tapped her tongue with his. She pulled back, but could not break the kiss as his hand holding her head tightened its grip and his kiss deepened. And when her lips parted again, he slipped his tongue inside causing her body to arch. He drew her closer when she responded in a way he had only experienced in his dreams. One arm held her close, as the other explored her neck, and then her shoulder before slowly moving down her body until he seized her waist, crushing her against him, as they continued to discover each other with their lips, their tongues, their hands. After a few moments, he pulled back and straightened his cravat.

"You are a most civil person, William. Most civil!" She dabbed her forehead with a handkerchief, *his* handkerchief, the one she carried with her every day since that fateful day in the Pemberley library.

"Wait, my love. You said they mentioned several things. See, I am vain. Now, no more civility until you reveal all, Mrs. Darcy! You must tell me, or else I would, um, withhold my special brand of politeness for a month." He spied her flushed cheeks through her exaggerated petulant expression, causing his smile to stretch across his face.

She raised her chin. "But perhaps a little civility might cause me to recall what exactly they said."

Darcy did not waste any time, leaned down, and almost met her lips with his. He held his position for a second before pulling back. "I never knew being so courteous could be so delicious, but my dear, sweet Elizabeth, you must tell me first."

With a smirk on her face, Elizabeth leaned back into the cushion, feeling the softness of the material with her hand until she felt a finger nudging her in her side. "Very well. Miss Kent."

Darcy lifted his brows. "Miss Kent? What did they say I did with her?"

"You smiled at her." She turned to face Darcy. "You never smiled at me, and yet you smiled at her. She is very beautiful."

"My dear wife, I was practicing. You did admonish me to practice! Now let me practice being civil again."

She acquiesced, and they spent the next several minutes involved in all types of their personal mode of good manners. Until, that was, when Darcy laughed. "You were jealous."

"Yes. I admit it. I did not like hearing that you were smiling at another lady; and then to meet this beautiful woman. Oh, William. I felt a pain deep in my heart. And that is also how I later knew I did not feel the same way about Lord Blake."

"Oh? I do not understand."

"Men never do!" Elizabeth laughed but when Darcy silently pleaded with her she continued, "When I entered the drawing room at Pemberley and spotted Miss Kent I was so relieved when she was talking to Lord Blake and not..." She whispered, "you. I looked around immediately, searching the room in fear and I was comforted to find you standing by your sister."

Darcy pulled her into his lap and kissed her while his hands roamed her back, and when the carriage jolted, he grabbed her tightly pulling her in close. After a moment, he traced her neckline with his finger. "I look forward to tonight when I can see the whole of your... sliver. I do not believe you know how much I wanted to do this." He lowered his head and ran his tongue along the edge of her dress before stopping to place small kisses upon her spot above the nipple on breast. "Many nights I could not remove the image of your," Darcy stared at her chest, "sliver from my thoughts. I wanted to pummel anyone talking to you and letting their gaze drift downward."

"Oh goodness. Mother was right!" Elizabeth laughed. "Promise you will not tell her. Promise me."

"If you wish, but Francine will always have a special place in my life. She saved you for me."

"Francine?"

"Your mother has made me her particular friend." A red-faced Darcy lowered his gaze.

Elizabeth had released a long contented smile when she caught sight of the present sitting on the unused seat. Sitting up quickly, her gaze repeatedly darted from the gift to him until he presented her with a dimpled smile so wide it caused small winkles to appear around his temples.

"Yes. A present for my beautiful, lovely bride. Now is a good time to open it." She reached for the gift; he folded and returned her signature to his pocket and opened up the second sheet of paper.

She tore the ribbon off and pulled opened the box. "Ah! I have never seen anything similar or so beautiful." She held the necklace in her hand and caressed the small golden pendant that took the shape of an oak tree. She studied the jewels upon the trunk. "Grapes? Is that a vine entwined around the tree?"

"Yes, my sweet; you are the vine and I am the oak tree. Let me read you this poem, and you will see how it foretold of our acquaintance." She snuggled into his chest as he covered her with the blanked and embraced her with his free arm. He began, *"The Vine and the Oak, a Fable* by Major Henry Livingston, Jr. and ended with:

And felt & gave sensations new.
Enrich'd & graced by the sweet prise
He lifts her tendrils to the skies;
Whilst she, protected and carest,
Sinks in his arms completely blest.

***

Pemberley
July 1815

Is everything ready? When do our guests arrive?" Darcy smiled at his beautiful Elizabeth.

"You are worse than a chicken trying to lay a double egg."

"What?"

"Hopping from one foot to the other. Rawlings is in the billiard room. Go occupy yourself with that Twenty Points game you men play all the time."

Darcy kissed the back of his wife's neck and put his arms around her. "It is now Fifty Points. I had to find a way for Rawlings to be competitive. I let him go twice for each one of mine."

"Well, at least I can putt." Rawlings entered the room.

Darcy swung around. "I was coming to the billiard room to show you how to sink a ball in the corner pocket. Besides, I have a new strategy with my golf game."

"Oh."

"I plan to lie on the ground and, using a large pole, putt the golf ball in the hole as I would a billiard ball. Who says I must stand up straight?"

"Well, I have a suggestion, why do you not stand on the billiard table and try putting the balls in the hole using a club instead of a cue stick. I might actually beat you then. But you could always show me what I am doing wrong with the cue stick, and then I would reveal your problem with golf. It is a simple fix, my friend."

Lizzy huffed. "Games. Is it always games with men? Wait, is that the Bingleys' carriage arriving?"

They arrived at the window just in time to spot Bingley's carriage coming down the drive. "I am sure Jane is pleased not to be confined again this year."

"Well, I think she has a surprise for you." Darcy laughed.

"They already have two darling boys. It has not been three years since they were married."

"Bingley wants a girl."

They made their way to the front to greet them when the carriage came to a stop. Caroline was the first one out of the door. "Good afternoon, everyone. It is a glorious day."

"Congratulations on your engagement," Elizabeth said.

"Lord Atterton sends his regrets. He has business in town." Caroline curtsied to the waiting group. Everyone knew Atterton would not be coming. He occupied himself with the latest actress to arrive on Drury Lane. Caroline did not seem to care, so neither did anyone else. Bingley was pleased to have his sister finally settled somewhere, and she had her dream. Lord Atterton was an earl and she would be a countess. Nothing satisfied Caroline more than to be a higher ranking member of society than Mrs. Darcy.

Elizabeth hugged her sister the moment Jane's foot touched the ground.

"Again?"

Jane blushed, nodding but when she caught sight of her sister's downturned mouth, she lifted Elizabeth's chin. "Your day will come, Lizzy."

"Well, congratulations, Jane! We are waiting for the Kents. Everyone else has arrived."

Quickly the Gardiners, Mr. Bennet, Richmond, Georgiana, and Miss Sarah Kent joined the group. With Kent and his wife arriving later that day, all the partners of the alliance would be assembled. The Eligo had proven to be the stronger of the two rivals. The war with America was the only obstacle. Astoria's trading post had been sold to the British North West Company before Great Britain seized and took control of it in 1813. Britain's Hudson Bay Company ruled the traders, settlers, and Indians and was the last successful initiative of the Peregrine. This would cause difficulties in the future for the young men, but not insurmountable

Everyone met again in the drawing room later that afternoon. Kent and his lovely wife had arrived, along with his children, twins, a son with a serious nature and a daughter full of liveliness. Miss Avery Anne Godwin and he had made a strange love match. She, a dyed-in-the-wool Tory, as Blake had discovered years earlier, and he, an emerging leader for the Whigs. After the banns had been announced, Blake had sent Kent a message:

> For god sakes, man, hide your Baker Rifle before you so
> much as mention a Whig position.

Kent and Miss Godwin were not that far apart, in terms of class. She was similar to Darcy, in that no one in her immediate family held a title. She did have an earl or two among her ancestors, but none that they visited regularly. Kent had begun to take the lead over many young up and coming Whigs. His passion won him victories and brought in new supporters. However, the truth behind why his speeches were so pervasive was the due to the arguments he and his wife shared every night before they compromised long enough to, well, compromise one another. Avery Anne was fiery; Kent was calm. She called him treasonous; he called her short-sighted. She attempted to change his mind with words and then with seduction. He, a smart man, allowed the seduction before rejecting her ideals. They were a love match in every way.

The Gardiners grew wealthier as the years passed. As a member of Darcy's family, a wider group of people accepted him. He became much sought after as the country progressed forward into the industrial world. Mr. Bennet visited more often than the Gardiners. Darcy had an apartment made up for him that included his own private library. No one dared barge in on him there. His life turned more often to books, since his wife had passed away. "Trifling colds will not kill anyone," she had unfortunately said one time too many, for in the end, one did just that. His other two daughters had also now married, one to a parson and the other to a clerk. Mr. Bennet had turned down Darcy's invitation to move to Pemberley many times, but once his last daughter left Longbourn, he finally agreed. He would return in a month after turning over Longbourn to Mr. Collins. On this trip, he discovered his heart was in Derbyshire.

Georgiana had her debut at the age of nineteen. She had grown into a handsome woman, tall and with a gentle ease, which few young men could resist. Regardless of the social event, the guests begged her to play. Her own sonata was the most requested. She had finished it and played it for her brother for his wedding, and entitled it, *Superare Gli Ostacoli a Felicità: Overcoming, Obstacles to Happiness.* Selecting an Italian name revealed just which of the handsome young men she favored. Marzio was the first-born son of an Italian Count, and spoke passionately, with his hands flailing about his face, hands that played the violin to his own enthralled audiences. Half his words were in Italian and the rest in English, which resulted in interesting stories. He was warm and loving and welcomed at Pemberley. Georgiana was in no hurry to marry.

Richmond had returned from the continent unharmed, but disillusioned with war. He resigned his commission. At his request, his cousin had purchased stock in the Eligo alliance and in Francis Lowell's textile mill in Boston with funds Darcy's father had set aide for his him. Richmond's wealth increased every day. He had moved to Pemberley when his own father turned him away for defending Darcy and refusing to shun him. He carried Darcy's letter with him every day to remind him not to overlook men of all kinds. Richmond adapted to business quickly, and became an important asset to the alliance. His battlefield experience worked well when they needed to stand up to the Falcon's Peregrine. Richmond had chosen well.

The Peregrine had selected Richmond's brother, Brandon, to lead after the Falcon died, one year earlier. Brandon did not have the Darcy's abilities or even Kent's and the old alliance began to slow fading away.

Elizabeth and Darcy proved to be the happiest of couples, although the absence of any children brought them a certain level of angst. He had wanted to fill the halls with the sounds of tiny voices and laughter, but found solace in merely loving his wife. Elizabeth was not as content; she had not produced an heir. Once they had married, she had charmed most of the women and all of the men, and the talk about Lydia's scandal died away in London. His friends, including Blake, had struck down any viscous rumors or tittle-tattle circulating around the town after the engagement was announced.

Darcy's wealth also grew, but what was more important, so did the friends he made. He discovered a plethora of people born under difficult situations who had risen to the top of their field. He realized Kent was right. One day these brave men would succeed in ruling the world, perhaps not in England, but surely in America where success and money were gods. Had it not been for his friends, he might have missed participating in the greatest developments at the time: steamboats, railroads, industry, and banking. Before the confrontation, he had deemed all these areas beneath him. And through he had connected himself with one of the most influential men of the nineteenth century—Kent.

Blake, on the other hand, stayed the course of old. His Uncle Harrowby led him into the Tory party and upon Lord Charnwood's death in 1815, took his father's place in the House of Lords. He argued rationally and judiciously for the continuation of aristocratic rule and championed all areas supporting that principle. Britain had won the war against Napoleon largely because of her economic resources, but upon his admission to the House of Lords, he discovered the huge debt and shaky economy of the country. He and Lord Harrowby championed additional Corn Laws, this time dictating the price of grain. Manufacturers raised the wages and soon the lower classes found it difficult to survive. Turmoil ensued. The Peregrine alliance made a final stab at maintaining its dominance; however, without the support of those people they tried to keep down, they did not succeed.

The British government was one of the most class-biased governments holding onto power. The aristocracy lived in fear of revolution. But, rather than acting to deal with the problems that created discontent, members of the most reactionary elements of the Tory Party headed by Lord Liverpool, turned to repression.

Blake was tenacious and considered every cause to be a competition. Most of his arguments were opposite that of Kent, but the two men did remain friends. They played golf several times together after Blake took possession of his father's estate. Blake, who never accepted any invitations to Pemberley or Darcy House, spent his time absorbed in studying legislation and parliamentary procedures.

"Your Grace." The servant bowed and then replaced yesterday's flowers with today's fresh picked lavender.

"Blake!"

Blake barely looked up. "Yes, what is it?"

His wife abruptly stopped beside her husband, placed her hands on her hips and glowered down at him. "Now, my dear husband."

"Victoria. Good afternoon. I was trying to keep up with the latest Whig maneuvers. They are a persistent group. How did your little hawk do today?"

She huffed. "I insist you allow another politician do this work. And my hawk is a merlin. He did very well. I am thankful my great uncle taught me how to be a success in that sport."

"The Falcon may have done many appalling things, but he was the champion of falconry. He taught you well!"

"He trained me on many things, a few have been successful and..." Victoria whispered, "others have not resulted in as much success, yet." Sighing, she patted his shoulder while her focus stayed on the vase. "Why do you insist on lavender flowers? I know they are your favorite ones, but dear, must you keep your study full of them? Do you not grow tired of the scent?"

Blake moved to the table with the flowers, and leaning down, inhaled the sweet fragrance. "I shall never tire of it."

"Well, then I will have lavender water made from them and wear it every day.

Blake turned around sharply, stood behind his wife, wrapped his arms around her waist, and placed a small kiss on her neck. "Do not do so. I... I... prefer your own perfume on you, my dear. It is exotic, and I think only of you when I am around it. I love the scent from—"

"As you wish, Blake." Victoria pulled away and stepped towards the door.

Blake hurriedly stuffed the unfinished document in its folder and his metal-tipped pen in its box. "My dear, wait for me.. I believe our little Robert will be waking up soon. I want to teach him how to ride."

"He is only one year and six months old."

Blake scoffed. "It is never too early to learn to ride. Oh, and chess. I want to teach him, same for our little girl." He held his arm out, and when his wife placed her hand on it, he patted it gently. "And let us hope she is as beautiful as you."

Victoria rubbed her stomach. "A girl? We shall see, we shall see."

The two walked arm in arm together in the house, chatting about their unborn child. They discussed names—Olivia after his mother and sister; Marie after hers, but they agreed on Victoria as her middle name.

***

Darcy waved goodbye to the Gardiners and Mr. Bennet when they departed for London. The younger guests remained—Rawlings, Richmond, Miss Kent, Georgiana, and the Kents. They planned a picnic for the afternoon, near the pond to the east under the oak trees. Someone, years before, had carved a grape vine in the largest tree trunk. Every so often another cluster of grapes appeared. Many times Georgiana sought an answer, and every time she was left to assume it was a private matter between her brother and Elizabeth. She often wore her oak tree pendant.

Rawlings had stayed a fortnight with his friend. He no longer associated with either his father or brother, preferring to make his own way in life. He never returned to the Four Horse Club. He spent his time knee deep in business and discovered he liked it more than he was willing to admit. His search for a wife had proven unsuccessful. He had decided he wanted what Darcy, Bingley, and Kent had found—a true love match. However, he had come to realize he was unlikely to find such a woman among the *Ton* and was at a loss to where to look.

Darcy and Rawlings sat together while the others feasted on the picnic. Their friendship had grown even closer over the years. Rawlings remained the only person that could, or would, challenge Darcy when he lapsed into the haughty or arrogant fellow, which was rare these days. Darcy would challenge Rawlings to drink less and spend time on charitable projects. Both men thrived on the possibilities of the future.

And so it was, they were deep in yet another discussion over the trend towards building railways when Logan appeared. By the disheveled look of him, he had run to find his master. He handed Rawlings an express post, which he tore open immediately.

My dearest Mr. Rawlings,

The war is over. There is no one to hold my hand when the lightning strikes and the thunder booms. My Aunt Marie is so sad, nothing I can do can make her laugh. You made her smile when you visited, and she has waited for your return. When do you come? Soon? My father misses your stories.

Your little Countess (There is still a king of England!)
now fully grown,

Miss Lucinda Lowell

Rawlings jumped up. "Logan, pack our trunks. We leave immediately for America. We have no time to waste!"

Darcy stood next to his concerned friend. "What is it? What is wrong? Let me help you."

"Logan and I will set sail at the earliest opportunity. Rawlings handed him the letter, which he read aloud.

Kent moved to sit beside his sister, and in a half-whisper said, "Sarah, I believe the time has come for you to secure your place in the Kent family business. I suggest an appraisal of our textile holdings in Boston might be a perfect place to start."

Sarah's eyes grew wide. Although her gaze had stayed on Rawlings the entire time they were near each other, she did glance at her brother. She smiled and kissed him on the cheek. "Yes, I agree. Thank you, brother."

Kent leaned his head towards Elizabeth. "But first, before you leave for America, I want you to speak to Lizzy."

"Why?"

"Please ask her... Well, you must ask her to help lower the neckline on your gowns. You need to show a tiny glimpse of heaven if you wish to attract a certain someone's attention. And giggle. And don't forget to bat your lashes."

"Why?"

"Rawlings is our treasure, and I do not wish for any colonial strumpet to lay claim to him." Kent laughed.

Darcy, overhearing the siblings strategizing, decided to take the cue. "Richmond!" He waved his hand to summon him over.

Richmond jumped up and approached his cousin although he stumbled over his own foot. He had kept his gaze on the beautiful Sarah Kent.

"Do you feel a need for new scenery? I have need for a man to look into our holdings at the Lowell mill now that the war is over."

Richmond smiled widely. "Yes, Darcy. I see your point. I agree, Rawlings might not be the best man for the job. In fact, I think I should leave immediately and secure my... our property."

Darcy placed his hand on his cousin's shoulder. "Yes, indeed, but remember the property is not an object, cousin. She is a beautiful woman to be loved and cherished."

Richmond hurried until he caught up with Sarah Kent. He offered, in his most charming manner, to escort her.

Elizabeth tapped Darcy's shoulder. "You, sir, are a matchmaker!" She whispered in his ear, "I wonder which man Sarah will end up with?"

He placed his arm around his wife's waist and pulled her close. He leaned in and whispered in her ear, "That, my dear, is a story for another time. Now what is this thing Kent called the *glimpse of heaven?*"

Made in the USA
Lexington, KY
24 June 2010